Psychobyte

Cat Connor

I0650615

For information regarding permission email the publisher at 9mmPressNZ@gmail.com, subject line: Permission.

Original Editor: Jayne Southern (Rebel ePublishers)
Formatting: 9mm Press, New Zealand
Publisher: 9mm Press, New Zealand
Original Publication date: 2016
Country of first publication: United States of America
Current country of publication: New Zealand.

ISBN: D2D paperback:978-1-0670072-4-9
ISBN ePub: 978-1-3700548-9-3
ISBN Print:978-1-9440770-6-8

"A man is a method, a progressive arrangement, a selecting principle,
gathering his like unto him wherever he goes."
—Ralph Waldo Emerson

Chapter One

Some nights.

Flinging open my door, I climbed out. Reaching through to the backseat I hauled out my backpack. Hoisting the bag over my right shoulder and pocketing my keys I walked across the grass toward the dark-haired woman sporting a long ponytail and a Fairfax PD vest.

"SSA Ellie Conway, FBI," I said, extending my hand.

"Detective Troy Fallon, Fairfax PD," she replied, giving my hand a firm shake.

"Did you make the call for FBI assistance?"

She nodded. "That was me."

"Who made the initial nine-one-one call?"

"A co-worker of the deceased, Emilio Herrera."

The name rolled around in my head for a moment. Familiar. Good or bad? I gave it a second. Good. Emilio Herrera worked for us. For the FBI. Images slithered into place until they hit the right combination and put Herrera in context. Administrative Services Division. Human Resources. Now I knew why the early call to Delta: if the victim was a co-worker of Herrera's then the crime was committed against a federal employee.

I sighed without intending to. "Give me a minute, Troy. I need to make a call." Phone in my hand, I walked a few feet away and called Sandra at the office.

"How can I help, O Mighty Leader of Delta?" Sandra replied with her usual zest.

"I'm on scene at a murder of a federal employee. I need you to contact HR. Get two employee records released to Delta. Emilio Herrera and ... one sec." I moved the phone away from my mouth and called out to Troy. "Victim's name?"

"Jane Daughtry."

Not a name I recognized but that didn't mean much. I smiled a thank you and carried on talking to Sandra. "Jane Daughtry is the victim. Also, Kurt, Lee, and Sam?"

"Lee and Sam are helping Delta B with an arrest. Kurt is in a meeting with the Chief."

Just me for now. Okay. That's fine.

"Okay."

"You need backup?"

"No. Got police on scene. I'm good."

"I'll have those files waiting for you." The familiar sound of Sandra's fingers tapping on her keyboard at breakneck speed punctuated her words.

"Thanks."

I hung up, pocketed my phone and rejoined Troy.

"Everything okay?"

I nodded. "Is Mr. Herrera here?"

"Yes. Talking to one of my officers." She turned and tipped her head to a marked car on the opposite curb. "We kept him here until you arrived."

Kept him here? I doubt he would've left. He's FBI. He knows the drill.

"Give me a minute, I need a quick word with Mr. Herrera."

I strode toward the marked car. Emilio clambered from the car and met me halfway.

"Agent Conway." Relief cocooned his words. "Thank God, you're here."

"You all right?" I asked, noting his pallor. "They treating you okay?"

"Yes."

"Hang here. I'll go see what's what then we'll talk."

His hand grabbed mine. I extracted my hand from his grip. Before I could move away, he grabbed my hand again. This time, I added a reassuring smile and gave his hand a small squeeze.

"I need to do my job." I withdrew my hand. Emilio rocked from foot to foot, wringing his hands, tears welling. I opted to hear him out. The victim wasn't going anywhere. "Tell me what you can about this morning."

"We carpool." He wiped a hand across his watery eyes. "She's always waiting out front when I arrive ..."

"She?"

"Jane," he said, his voice breaking. "Jane Daughtry."

"Tell me what happened when you arrived."

He sniffed, took a handkerchief from his pocket and blew his nose. "I arrived at seven. Parked there." He pointed to his car by the curb. "Jane wasn't out front. I went and knocked on the door. There was no answer." He blew his nose again.

"Take your time," I said. "There was no answer?"

"No answer. I went back to the car. I thought she was, you know, indisposed, and would be out any minute."

4

"Of course."

"Ten minutes later, she was still not out. I called her cell phone. She didn't answer and it went to voicemail. I tried her landline. Nothing. A few minutes later I texted her. She didn't reply. I got out of the car and walked around to the side of the house." He pointed. "And that's when I saw the open windows and the crushed flowers in the bed below."

"Did you see anyone when you arrived?"

"No."

"Open window, crushed flowers. Then what?"

"I listened and heard water running. I called out. No answer. I rang nine-one-one."

"Thank you, Emilio."

"If I'd called sooner—"

"That's not helpful thinking. Go and sit in the car. I'll be back." I patted Emilio on the shoulder. "We'll find out what happened."

Detective Fallon waited for me at the entrance to the apartment. There was something about her that made me uneasy. Something I couldn't quite put my finger on. I let that thought settle. The cop at the door handed us disposable booties.

"Let's do this thing, Detective."

"Troy, please, Agent Conway."

I nodded. "Troy it is, as long as you call me Ellie and not Agent Conway."

She appeared friendlier than before. Maybe it was initial nerves I'd picked up on.

"Come on through. I'll think you'll find this worthy of your time," Troy said. Her mouth set in a grim line. She led the way past several officers. At the bathroom door, I stopped and patted my pockets. Damn. No gloves. I usually carried small black nitrile gloves. I swung my pack off my shoulder and checked the front pocket where my spare gloves lived. Growling internally, I remembered intending to replace the gloves but the box in my office had disappeared.

"Troy, do you have nitrile or latex gloves on you?"

"Sure." Troy dipped her hand into her jacket pocket and handed me a pair of latex gloves.

"Did Mr. Herrera come into the apartment at all?"

"No. He waited outside for uniforms to arrive."

Good.

"This is the cleanest murder scene I've attended. Our victim ..." she swung open the door and pointed to the shower, "... is in there." Troy waited by the door while I entered the room.

Yep, it was clean.

At first glance, the victim's body appeared awkward, crumpled yet leaning against the shower wall. It looked as though she wanted to curl up but prevented somehow or unable to. Strands of her long wet blonde hair stuck to her blanched cheek. My eyes skirted the slashes and stab wounds on her body, not yet ready to take in the extent of the injuries.

"Jane Daughtry," I said, "we're not meeting under the nicest of circumstances."

"Did you need something?" Troy poked her head around the door.

"Nope." I bent down to Jane. "We'll talk soon. I just need to have a look at your bathroom first."

A fresh towel hung on a rail within reach of the shower. A clothes hamper stood in the corner. I lifted the lid. Empty. A faint scent intrigued me. I bent down to the hamper and sniffed: musky, wet dirt. I dropped the lid. The cabinet under the sink contained four drawers and one cupboard. The drawers contained all manner of expected things; hair brushes, hair dryer, styling tools, tissues, body lotions. In the cupboard were cleaning products, cloths, and a roll of paper towels. On the wall beside the sink was a shelf with folded towels, stacked in three groups of two. Lime green, bright blue, lime green. I turned and looked at the towel she'd chosen to use.

Dark blue. Perhaps the stacked towels were for show?

A vase containing bright blue and lime green skinny branches sat on the vanity countertop.

Arty.

Behind the large mirror above the sink was another cabinet, containing prescription medications, over-the-counter medications, hair products, and makeup. One of the pill bottles sat with the label obscured, yet all the others faced out. I lifted it out for closer inspection. Sleeping tablets. A new prescription dated three days prior. I opened the lid, expecting a month's worth of tablets minus maybe three pills. Tipping the contents into my gloved hand, I counted ten pills.

Ten.

"Troy?" I called.

She appeared next to me. "Problem?"

"Did you look in the medicine cabinet?"

She nodded. "Glanced more than looked. Very orderly cabinet."

Yes. Except for one bottle facing the wrong way.

"Have you considered suicide?"

Troy's face clouded. "Suicide?"

I showed her the pill bottle and the contents of my hand, then tipped the pills back in the container and placed it carefully on the shelf, the way I'd found it.

"Something to think about," I replied. "I'll be right back."

I left her in the bathroom and did a quick tour of the rest of the house. Nothing out of place anywhere. Open windows in the living room, dining room, and the main bedroom. I checked the bedside table for something that might explain her state of mind.

A notebook. I flipped through it and cold tendrils wound through my soul. A darkness in Jane emerged from the poetry on the pages. I held the book by the spine and shook it. A folded piece of paper floated to the ground.

I bent down to retrieve it and saw another book under the bed. I took both and sat down on the edge of the meticulously made bed. First the piece of paper. I opened it to find a sentence: Don't leave me.

Comparing that sentence with the handwritten poems,

even I could tell they were by the same person. Jane had also written her name inside the front cover of the notebook. I turned my attention to the book from under the bed. Familiar oranges on the cover set off a carillon of bells and whistles. Warning. Warning. I turned it over in my hand. Whispers in the Water.

Ever since my brother, Aidan, found a publisher for it, unbeknownst to Mac and me, I'd been haunted by that book. I opened it and saw Mac's handwriting: Dear Jane, keep writing. All the best, Mac Connelly.

He'd dated it. I stared at the date and tried to remember what we were doing that day. Was it an official book signing? Did it matter? Probably not.

I turned it over in my hands a few times. A much-read book. Some pages were marked. I let the book fall open at the first of the marked pages. Stolen. A shiver ran through me. I hated that poem. Hated what it became at the hands of a killer. Finding my poetry at another potential crime scene did not sit well with my last coffee.

Troy's voice rang out. "Agent Conway? Ellie?"

"Master bedroom," I called back.

Footsteps approached. Troy walked through the doorway. "Find something?"

"Yes, I did." I cleared my head by reminding myself it was not about me. "She wrote some dark poetry." I didn't say she'd been reading it as well.

"Could this be suicide?"

Did I really think so, even though I'd asked the same question? No, but we'd have to explore it like everything else.

"You wouldn't have called me in if you thought this was suicide," I replied. "What did you see that made you call me?"

"Stab wounds and no blood."

"Weapon?"

"No knife in the bathroom ... unless it's under the body. We haven't moved her."

I stood up. Something about the scene unnerved me. Judgment call time.

"I'll call our crime techs. You'll get copies of the reports but I want our people involved."

She didn't argue. I made the call to the techs and our medical examiner. Then I called Delta.

"Let's go back to Jane and see what she has to say," I said, ushering Troy from the room. I left the book on the bed. The techs would get it along with everything else. Something was very wrong in the apartment.

The cleanliness of the bathroom bothered me. Nothing out of place. Not even a stray hair from a hair brush. I knelt by the shower, close to her head and whispered, "What happened, Jane? What do you need to tell me?"

Her cloudy eyes stared at something. I wriggled around until my head was as close to hers as possible without contaminating the crime scene. Her fixed gaze pointed to the side of the vanity unit. A tiny triangle, out of place, poked out from behind it. Scrambling to my feet, I lurched toward the vanity. Looked like a small piece of paper. I pulled a packet containing sterile disposable forceps from my bag and tore it open. Carefully, I grasped the eighth of an inch of visible white paper and extracted it.

"How did you see that?" Troy asked.

"Jane told me," I replied, dropping the paper into my hand. I handed Troy the forceps and inspected the paper. It was no bigger than a piece from a memo cube, white, and folded in quarters.

"What is it?" Troy ignored the comment I made about the dead woman telling me where it was.

Wise lady.

"Paper," It contained four words. "'Don't take it personally.'"

"Pardon?"

"That's what it says, 'Don't take it personally.'" I showed her the note.

"Wonder what it means?"

"Nothing good," I replied. "Good things are not usually hidden in a crime scene."

I held the note carefully by one corner and took an evidence bag out of my pack. Troy took it and opened it up, allowing me to drop the note into it.

I wrote the date, time, and Jane Daughtry's name on the chain of custody form printed on the evidence bag then added a description of the evidence and signed my name. I dropped it into my bag. My gut told me this would be our case so I'd generate a case number back at the office.

Turning to Jane Daughtry's body, I started by counting

and inspecting stab wounds. Most of them appeared shallow. The deep, life-ending gashes were down her wrists.

Did someone want this to look like suicide? All the wounds could've been made by the victim. None were in difficult to reach places. But why would someone repeatedly stab themselves? Where was the blood? Who took all the sleeping pills?

"There isn't one drop of blood anywhere ... why?" I said.

"When uniforms arrived the shower was running hot. The showerhead is removable and high-powered. There are water drops high up on the walls."

"Disregarding the suicide idea for the moment, someone cleaned up."

Which didn't rule out suicide; family members have been known to clean up after suicides. If you intended to murder someone, killing them in a shower was a good option. It confined the mess and made it easier to clean up.

"So we have a clean killer?"

Be nice if all killers were so considerate.

What was missing? Smell. If the killer cleaned, he did so with water not with bleach or any other cleaning product. I breathed in through my nose. No residual chemical smells. I took a closer look at the cleaning products I'd seen in the cabinet under the sink and pulled out two spray bottles and a cream cleanser. All were hypoallergenic non-scented cleaning products. One of the sprays was for glass, the other a general bathroom cleaner.

"This stuff might have been used on the surfaces," I said, checking each bottle just in case there was a residual smell. Sometimes non-scented wasn't.

Replacing the bottles, I noticed a roll of paper towels behind the stack of cleaning cloths. I opened the swing-top trash can next to the vanity. Scrunched paper towels.

"So the Unsub hosed down the shower and the body, then wiped over all the external surfaces with paper towels and cleaning product?" Troy said, writing in her notebook.

"Maybe. Or Jane cleaned the bathroom earlier."

It's never straightforward. People complicate things.

I bent down to Jane and said, "I'll find out what happened here." And smelled a warm scent rising from her skin. A fleeting ethereal image filled my mind, of Jane stepping into the shower, reaching for shower gel from the caddy on the wall. My eyes swung to the caddy. No shower gel.

So where was it?

When I looked up, Troy was watching me.

"Do you always talk to the dead?"

"Yes. She's the only one who knows what really happened here, apart from the killer and Jane won't lie."

"I suppose," Troy said.

"There's no shower gel or soap in the shower," I said. Breathing in the same scent again. It reminded me of something, a perfume I'd smelled before.

Troy wrote in her notebook. "That's odd. But you found hypoallergenic cleaning products so maybe she's allergic to soaps and so forth."

I didn't really want to say I saw her reach for the shower gel before she died.

"Or, the killer took it," I said.

"A trophy?"

"Possibly."

"What are your thoughts?"

"I think our Unsub is just getting started." The note created a special kind of disturbance in the force. One that told me we would see more notes and more death. "There's something familiar about this scene. I'll get back to you."

Bits and pieces of the crime scene and Jane's home swirled in my mind. What happened to the missing sleeping pills? How many sex offenders lived in the area? Was there a sexual aspect to the killing? Where was the shower gel she'd used? And I knew without a shadow of a doubt that the Unsub had left some kind of evidence in the house, we just had to find it. Every contact leaves a trace. There is no exception to that rule.

A female voice I didn't recognize spoke from deep within my head, telling me to start with the prescription bottle. I checked the bathroom cabinet again. That bottle was the only one from that particular doctor and the only one facing the wrong way. Using my phone, I photographed the label.

Chapter Two

That's all.

"Where are you?"

I closed my eyes for a moment and rested against the car, gathering strength from Mitch's voice to tell him I would be late home. Things I'd discovered back at the office didn't bode well for a speedy case resolution. The earlier feeling that the Unsub was just getting started wouldn't go away.

"El, where are you?" Mitch said again.

"Ox Road, Fairfax. I'll probably be late home tonight. Sorry."

Mitch didn't even sigh. "How late?"

"Dunno?" I tried to cover my disappointment and knew I was unsuccessful. "I'll be there as soon as I can."

"Ellie, you all right?"

"Uh huh. I just want to be home with you." I did my best to let a smile fill my voice. "I'll see you when I see you."

"How come I can't get an image of you right now?"

Because for now, I don't want you to?

"This is not a nice case. Best you don't see it to start with."

That was weak. Since when do we investigate nice cases?

"You sure that's the reason?" His voice lightened. "You all right, not getting cold feet?"

I laughed. "My feet are quite warm." I wriggled my toes inside my boots.

Yep. Warm. No cold feet here.

"Smart ass. As long as you're okay." His smile bounced. "Miss you."

"I am okay. Hey, my place or yours tonight?"

"Yours."

"Good."

"Be safe. Three things."

I smiled. "Three things." The three things made my smile widen. Love. Want. Need.

Mitch hung up. I felt bad; it was easier when I mentally took him with me. But not this afternoon. I didn't want him seeing what I saw or knowing what I know, yet. I still felt mean for shutting him out.

Complicated? You betcha.

I pocketed my phone and stared at the semi-detached houses in front of me. I knew from the aerial photographs I'd seen of the subdivision that there were sixteen houses in total. All the houses were outwardly identical and all backed onto a large grassed common area. This was crisscrossed by paths and contained raised flower beds, trees, and park benches.

Pleasant. Probably a really nice place to live. If you liked neighbors close by.

Crime scene tape fluttered in the warm breeze. Police cars with lights still rolling lined the curb in front of my car.

A black Chevy Suburban pulled in behind mine. Sam, Lee, and Kurt piled out and approached.

"What have we got?" Kurt said.

"A murder," I replied, standing up straight. "I want you to view this scene. I need your eyes."

"My eyes are at your disposal," Kurt said with a small smile.

Sam tipped his chin at me. "Where do you want us, Chicky Babe?"

"Do a door-to-door for me, Sam, I'm not buying that no one in this subdivision saw anything."

"You got it," Lee replied. He and Sam walked toward the home on the left of the crime scene tape.

"Shall we?" Kurt motioned me to join him as he walked up the path.

Yes, let's. I can hardly wait to get back in there.

The police officer guarding the door handed us disposable booties and latex gloves. I led the way to the body.

Kurt took a few longer strides until he leveled with me. "Talk,"

"Jane Daughtry, twenty-six-years-old, works for us."

"Really?"

"Yeah, she works for human resources, a civilian."

"Okay. What else?"

"Another FBI employee made the nine-one-one call," I said. "Apart from that tidbit of information, it looks like the Unsub gained entry through an open window in the living room."

I stopped at the open bathroom door. From the hallway, I could see part of her body slumped in the shower.

"I counted seventeen stab wounds, no blood. The shower was running when the first officer arrived on the scene."

Kurt stepped into the room. Moments later he came out and beckoned to me. "What haven't you told me?"

So much.

"Wish you'd brought me coffee," I replied with a small smile. "What I know is not going to make this easier or make you happy."

"Figured that," he said. "Just tell me."

"Jane was a poet. She wrote dark poetry. She had a signed copy of my book – signed by Mac."

Kurt's eyes met mine. "You okay?"

"Yes." Gathering facts, leaving emotions to flounder in the dark where they belonged. "I found a loose piece of paper in her notebook. It said 'Don't leave me.' She pointed me to a small piece of paper hidden behind the vanity." I waved a finger to where I'd found the memo. "And that said 'Don't take it personally.' The handwriting didn't match hers from the notebook." Facts made it easier. "She had a new prescription for a month's worth of sleeping pills three days ago, not her usual doctor by the look of the label. There are ten pills left." After a slight pause, I plowed on. "I saw her reach for shower gel – there's no shower gel here."

Kurt's eyes never left mine. "You saw her?"

"Yes."

"All right." He thought for a few moments. "Who did

she think was going to leave her?"

"No idea. There was no reference to a name anywhere."

"Who wrote the words 'Don't take it personally' and hid it?"

"No clue. My money is on the Unsub."

"What happened to the pills?"

"I kinda hope she took them and never knew what happened to her, but somehow I doubt it."

"I'll check out the doctor and the pharmacy, if you like?"

"Please."

"Missing shower gel is interesting – unusual trophy?" Kurt commented.

"Maybe he liked the smell of it," I let the words wander in my head. It was something to do with the smell but I couldn't prove it, yet. "Opinion?"

"She probably bled out."

I figured that.

"Anything else?"

"No defensive wounds. I doubt we'll get anything from under her nails but we'll try." Kurt's mouth set in a grim line. "She may well have had sleeping pills in her system but no one would swallow seventeen tablets willingly, unless it was suicide."

"This isn't a suicide, Kurt."

"How far away are the crime scene techs?"

"Maybe another ten minutes, depending on traffic." I'd called them twice that morning and twice in the early afternoon. In a perfect world, techs would be available as soon as I picked up the phone. In a perfect world, we wouldn't need crime scene techs.

He nodded. "There were a lot of stab wounds on the woman's body but they appear tentative, the wounds on her wrists, however, were meant to kill."

"Her name is Jane," I said softly. "Jane Daughtry."

"What's going on here?" Kurt tapped my head with his index finger.

"There was a similar case in Winchester two months ago."

"How similar?"

"Very. Access gained through an open window, sleeping pills unaccounted for, and the victim stabbed multiple times and found in the shower, water running." I sighed. "No defensive wounds, a similar pattern to the stab wounds and the fatal wounds were downward slashes to the wrist."

"That's interesting."

"Yes, I thought so. It was deemed a suicide by the coroner."

"How did you find it?"

Fair question. Suicides weren't usually loaded onto the violent crime database, ViCAP. It's one of the first places I look when a murder or violent assault feels like I've seen or heard something similar before.

"There was a discussion about it on a LEO forum. The local cop wasn't convinced it was suicide but no one was listening." I'd listened but couldn't offer much in the way of help at the time.

Kurt waited. It's like he knows me.

"I gave him a call and told him what I found this after-noon. He's sending the case file."

"Was there a note at that scene?"

I nodded. "It was considered to be a suicide note. The investigating officer read it to me over the phone." I flipped my notebook open and handed it to Kurt. "Two separate lines."

He read aloud, "'Everything that came before. Lies fragmented on the floor.'" And looked at me. "What does that sound like to you?"

"Part of a poem ..."

"Not loving this, Conway."

"Me neither." I pulled out my phone and called Sean O'Hare. "Hey, it's me. I need scene guards."

"Give me the address and the invoice goes to Delta A?"

"Yes, thanks." I rattled off the address and hung up.

Sam and Lee met us at the front door.

"You're not going to like this, Chicky," Lee said. "We didn't get much. No cars reported that didn't belong over the last week. Except a neighbor told me this was Jane's week to be collected for work. Last week she left earlier and drove her own car. This week, she was picked up by a man in a red Ford Taurus. The neighbor recognized the car, alternate weeks it picks her up for work. No one saw anyone hanging around."

"Emilio Herrera drives a red Ford Taurus," I replied. "That fits with what he told me about them carpooling."

Sam turned a page in his notebook. "Jane was out a lot, according to neighbors. Not noisy. Nice girl with nice friends. She broke up with her boyfriend a few weeks ago."

That was worth looking into.

"Name?"

"Matthew Collins."

"Let's find him," I said. My phone rang. I glanced at the screen before answering the call. "Sandra?"

"Do you want to speak with Jane Daughtry's parents? Troy called, said she'd informed the parents of Jane's death and they'd like to talk to you."

"Yes. Can you arrange that?"

"Will do."

"Set it up. I'm on my way back now."

Chapter Three

Whataya want from me.

Dusk eased over the city as I sat at my desk reading the case file from the Winchester suicide. I leaned back in my chair, crossing my ankles and resting the heel of my left boot on the edge of my desk.

Everything I read told me Winchester was linked. I compared the photo of that note to a photo of the note I found in Jane's bathroom: close enough that I would say they were written by the same person. The Questioned Document lab would be able to tell us for sure.

Why kill one woman in Winchester then the next in Fairfax? That's quite a wide geographical gap.

I placed the photos of the victims next to each other on the screen. Similar in appearance: blonde, slim, fine features, blue eyes. Planting my feet on the floor, I scrolled through the case file, trying to find what the Winchester woman did for a living.

"Violet Cramer worked for ..." I said to myself as I searched the file, "... the National Park Service. She was a park ranger."

A link beyond a similar appearance and a government job wasn't showing. Time to hit social media and see what that turned up. Fifteen minutes later, I knew both women had Facebook, Twitter, and Instagram accounts. Neither was on the other's friend list but they did have two friends in common on Facebook and followed about two hundred of the same people on Twitter. I puffed air into my cheeks and let it out slowly. Truth be known, I probably followed about a hundred of the same people on Twitter. Still, I needed to double-check any overlap.

Time-consuming.

I hauled myself out from behind my desk, left my cell behind, and wandered out into the bullpen in search of coffee.

Lee and Sam were working, both on phones. I'd asked them to track down Jane Daughtry's boyfriend. Kurt was nowhere to be seen.

Sandra waved at me from her desk. "Can I help?"

"When you spoke to HR, did they have anything that could relate to Jane's death?"

Sandra pulled up files and scanned over the contents on her screen. "Her team leader said she'll be very much missed."

"You think she's still in?"

"Doubt it."

"I'm going to take a look at Jane's desk. I won't be long."

I hurried over to HR. Peering through the glass main doors, there was no one at the reception desk. Dim lighting bathed the area with a yellowish tinge. I swiped my card to open the door. Nothing.

Damn.

I called Caine.

"Hey, it's me, I'm on HR's floor. There's no one around. I need to look at Jane Daughtry's desk."

"You want me to authorize that?"

"Please."

"Logging you on the floor now with SAC approval. You got five minutes."

"Thanks." I swiped my card again. The light flashed green. I pushed the door open. No sounds of life came from the offices along the hallway.

Scooting around the reception desk I searched for an office plan. I found it stuck to the interior of the Fire Warden's cupboard. Daughtry was in office seventy-four. Herrera was across the hall in seventy-five. Time ticked on. I hurried. Opening the door to Daughtry's office revealed a tidy work environment. I pulled her top desk drawer. Locked. Nothing but pens and stationery in the second drawer. No personal things. Her wastepaper basket revealed nothing.

I looked at the walls. She'd hung her degree and a diploma, both framed. It was time to go. I zapped my card to leave. The heavy glass door closed behind me as I hurried back to our floor.

"Anything?" Sandra said, looking up as I walked toward her.

"Nothing stands out. Might stretch my legs and head for the Firehook. You wanna come with?"

She nodded. "Good idea. Jane's parents won't be in for a minimum of an hour."

It would be at least two hours before I'd be on my way home, all going well.

I ducked into my office, pulled on a jacket, shoved my

cell into my jeans pocket, fished my wallet from my bag and stuck it in my jacket pocket. All set.

Sandra and I walked down the corridor to the stairs. Running down, we hit the door into the foyer at the same time. Our laughter echoed around the cavernous room. The agent at the desk glanced up, smiled and went back to monitoring the screens in front of him.

"It's going to be a long night, isn't it?" Sandra said.

"I think so."

"You all set for the wedding?"

"As much as we can be."

"Did you write your own vows?"

"Yes, we did. That's a lot harder than it seems."

Sandra smiled. "Two weeks. Exciting."

"Two weeks."

One big family dinner before the big day and I was glad it wasn't tonight. When was it? Three days until the dinner and the last minute prep is sorted. Then I could relax. A small laugh escaped. Yeah, right. I could relax once we were on the plane leaving the country for our honeymoon.

Sandra nudged me. "Are you going to take his name?"

"Yes." The speed with which this fell from my lips surprised me. I didn't take Mac's name but I'm taking Mitch's. Funny how life changes.

Sandra bought coffee; I went with hot chocolate and walked quietly back through the darkening streets. Nice to feel safe in D.C. again. It can take a while to get that sense of security back after things explode around you, but it was back. This was my city and life wouldn't leave it in ruins.

*

Thirty minutes shot by in the blink of an eye. Mostly sucked up by social media, scouring each woman's overlapping followers to see if there was any real connection. I'd broken the two hundred into groups of fifty. Sandra knocked on my door just as I'd finished the first fifty and found nothing significant.

"Yes?" I said as Sandra poked her head around the door.

"Mr. and Mrs. Daughtry are here."

"Thanks. Show them in."

I stood up, wiped my hands down my thighs and met them in the middle of the room. Handshakes all round. They were a nice looking couple in their mid-fifties.

"Please, have a seat," I said, holding my hand out to the couch in the corner.

"How can we help you find out what happened to our daughter?" Mr. Daughtry said, taking his wife's hand.

"Tell me about Jane. What was she like as a child?"

He frowned for a second then smiled and nodded. "Happy. She was a happy kid. Liked to sing a lot."

Mrs. Daughtry laughed at a memory. "She was always singing. We thought she'd be a singer but as she grew older, she developed a love for numbers."

"And that led her to the FBI?"

"Yes," Mr. Daughtry replied.

"She didn't want to be an agent?"

"No."

"Did she carry on singing?"

Mrs. Daughtry said, "Yes, at family events. She wanted to audition for American Idol a few years ago but never did."

"Do you know why not?"

"She was still in college when she thought about auditioning. I think her workload was quite high. Her degree was important to her."

"Boyfriends?"

"She didn't talk much about boys," Mrs. Daughtry said. "Except for Matthew. She adored him."

"Do you know why they broke up?"

"She never said much about the breakup."

"Have you spoken to Matthew?" Mr. Daughtry wanted to know. "We never met him, but she talked about him all the time before they broke up."

"I haven't spoken to him yet. But I will ... he's next on the list." I considered how to ask about him without causing the parents concern. Lightly. Tread gently. "I'm hoping that between you two and Matthew, I can get a clear picture of the woman Jane. Also an idea of anyone I should be aware of in her life."

"Matthew would probably know more than us," Mrs. Daughtry said. "He would know her friends. I don't think Jane was in touch with many of her old high school friends. She was the only one of her friends to attend George Mason University."

I wrote George Mason in my notebook. "Are you staying in The District tonight or heading back to Maryland?"

Mr. Daughtry said, "We're going home. We have arrangements to make for ... Jane."

An hour later I was no closer to finding anything from her parents that struck me as a jumping point for the investigation, apart from the ex-boyfriend and that she went to George Mason in Virginia. But I did know she was a much-loved daughter. I gave the parents my business card and escorted them out.

Chapter Four

Into the night.

My phone rang at seven in the morning. Welcome to Tuesday. A warm arm snaked around me and pulled me back under the covers. I listened to the caller tell me there was a new crime scene, possibly linked to yesterday's.

"Send the address to my cell, I'll be there soon," I said and hung up. I dropped the phone over the side of the bed and curled into Mitch. "I have to go."

"Soon," he said, kissing my neck as his fingers caressed my thigh. Warmth trailed slowly upward across my hip and onto my stomach. For a split second, I saw our future: bright and happy. Everything I'd denied myself thus far in life.

"Hey," he said. My eyes opened as his thumb brushed moisture off my cheek. "What's wrong?"

I smiled and brushed away another rogue tear. "I just ..." My voice crumbled. I tried again. "I just never knew I could love anyone as much as I love you."

He leaned over, his warm lips touched mine. No words. His kiss grew firmer and deeper. I wrapped my arms around his neck. Safe. Loved. Protected.

***

Mitch placed a plate of scrambled eggs in front of me and a fork in my hand. Orange juice, coffee and eggs. Breakfast.

The radio announced traffic building up on the Belt-way. I pushed the eggs around my plate. Mitch talked about the day ahead of him. Meetings, contracts, tenders, and all the things he was working to get resolved before our wedding and honeymoon.

"You're quiet," he commented, refilling his coffee. "And slow. You're usually on your second cup by now." He replaced the pot and ate more eggs.

I pushed another forkful of eggs around my plate.

Mitch looked up from his breakfast. "Not into eggs to-day? I could make you some toast?"

"I'm not very hungry."

Everything stopped. I saw my words flashing neon pink, orange, and green, as they hung over the table. Mitch lowered his fork, letting it rest on the edge of his plate. I watched him thinking. The words slipped from the still air and splashed into my OJ and coffee.

He smiled.

Life began again.

"I'm not surprised. You're working too hard." His gentle tone tugged at my heart. "Eat a little?"

I forked scrambled eggs into my mouth and willed them down my throat. Counting in my head to distract myself and not touching the juice or coffee. That really would be pushing my luck. In less than twenty-four hours coffee had gone from being my drink of choice to a roast-ed bean concoction from the devil himself.

Mitch touched my hand. "What you said this morning – was the nicest thing you've ever said."

I grinned. "Yeah, I kinda got that from your, ah, reaction."

"And she's back ..." he said with a laugh.

"And she's gotta catch a killer." I stood up. Breakfast settled.

"Take care out there today," Mitch said, hugging me tight.

I wished I could stay wrapped in his embrace or take his hug with me. Tears threatened.

What on earth?

Chapter Five
Burning Bridges

Another bathroom and a new, yet familiar crime scene; neither of those things ideal. My mind skipped over the lifeless body of the latest victim. My eyes scanned the room. The great start to the day overshadowed by death. Stepping back to the doorway, I made a call.

"We've got another crime scene," I said as Kurt answered his phone.

"Same?"

"Yes."

"Send me the address and I'm on my way."

I texted the address to Sam, Lee and Kurt. Meanwhile, Serena Sorensen needed someone to talk to. Dropping my pack on the floor, I crouched down by her head.

"I'm sorry this how your life ended, Serena." She said nothing. "I'll need your help to find the person who did this."

Serena made no miraculous recovery to aid me in my quest. Her cloudy eyes stared at the shower wall and gave nothing away. I scrunched lower until our heads were level and looked around the room. A small piece of white poking out from the woven cane of the laundry hamper alerted me to a possible note. I stood up, with care. Not feeling a hundred percent I knew that standing up too fast wouldn't help. The thought of having to explain how I contaminated a crime scene was less than appealing.

From my pack, I took an evidence bag and pair of disposable forceps. With care, I extracted the piece of folded paper from the weave.

Same writing as on the previous note at the last crime scene. 'It wasn't easy.'

Bagging the note, I hoped that meant she fought back. A quick visual inspection of her arms didn't show defensive wounds but two fingernails were broken and jagged. No water on that hand. Chances are DNA might be under the broken fingernails. Using a larger paper evidence bag, I slipped it over her hand, securing it at the wrist with paper tape.

"Serena, I'm going to leave you for a little bit," I said. "Try not to dislodge that bag, yeah?"

It was probably a good thing she didn't respond.

A police officer waited by the front door of the apartment. "Ma'am?"

"Secure the scene, officer. No one but FBI goes inside the building."

"Yes, ma'am."

"I'll be back." I gave him a quick nod of encouragement and left him standing guard.

Waiting in my car for Delta, my phone rang. Mitch's photograph beamed at me from the screen.

"Hey," I said, catching sight of my reflection in the rearview mirror. Pale. I plastered a smile on my face hoping it would make a difference.

"Thought I'd see how it's going?"

"It's going. Just waiting on the team. Same Unsub

struck again."

"You okay?"

"Yep. Trying not to let this ruin my day."

"Certainly started well ..."

"Hold that thought ... it might end well too."

"I like the sound of that." Mitch's voice sounded a little husky all of a sudden. "Call me later?"

"Will do. Gotta go, M, I can see Kurt walking toward me."

"'Bye."

My door opened.

"Conway."

"Henderson."

Kurt smiled. "Good morning so far?"

"Crime scene, what do you think?"

"I think the answer is yes, someone has a sparkle in their eye."

"Yeah, yeah. Shall we?"

Kurt stepped aside, letting me alight from the vehicle, then gave the door a firm shove.

"This way," I said, leading the way into the house. "Let's do this."

I stood in the bathroom doorway of death number two or possibly three; I considered the Winchester death to be the first. I flipped open my notebook. "Serena Sorensen, twenty-seven, federal employee," I said.

"Again?"

"Yeah. Serena worked for Department of Treasury. She was in admin. The lock on the back door was forced."

Kurt inspected the scene while I waited by the door. "Did you cover her hand?"

"Yes. Hoping we can get some DNA from under some broken nails."

He nodded.

Soft deep voices alerted me to Lee and Sam in the hallway not far from me, waiting. "Grim" best described the collective mood. I watched Kurt as he crouched down by Serena's body. A few minutes later, he straightened up and joined me.

"Any poetry links with this one?"

"Not that I've found," I replied, pleased that the book hadn't surfaced twice. "I did find a square of paper, just like the previous crime scene."

"And it said?"

"'It wasn't easy.'"

"I see shower gel in this bathroom. She has several types. Do you think anything is missing?"

"Not that I can tell."

Kurt summarized, "So, we have two women, both federal employees, both killed in the shower possibly while showering. In both cases, the shower was left running. Violent attacks, multiple stab wounds. It looks like death by cxsanguination. Jane Daughtry's fatal wounds were to her wrists. Serena's fatal wound was to her inner thigh."

Sounded right to me. Except there were three deaths, counting Violet in Winchester.

"Sam, Lee, door to door, please. Utilize the cops out front. Someone had to have seen something," I said.

Lee and Sam left.

"Kurt, the woman, Violet, from Winchester was a federal employee. Park Ranger."

"Three federal employees then ..." Kurt said more to himself than to me. "That could be part of the MO." He paused and eyed Serena again. "Or is federal employee a signature thing for him, can he only get his rocks off by killing people in government jobs?"

Could be. That felt like a broad brush stroke. A signature tended to be things that weren't necessary for the murder but the killer needed for whatever reason.

"The stab wounds," I said. "A form of mutilation – we've viewed it twice now. Signature?"

"Yes."

"The notes, signature?"

"Yes."

"The missing sleeping tablets in the first case here and in Winchester, signature?"

"Any missing here?" Kurt replied.

"Not that I found."

"Then MO. This one may have fought back but that doesn't mean she wasn't partially incapacitated by some sort of drug."

"If he needs to subdue the women before mutilating and killing, couldn't that be signature?" I asked resting my shoulder against the doorframe. Playing devil's advocate was fun.

"Depends on why he needs to do that. If he doesn't have the strength to subdue the women, then it's probably MO and that might evolve as his experience or confidence grows. If he can't kill unless they're semi-conscious because it's some kind of ritualistic thing, then signature."

More to think about.

"They're all naked, all in a shower, all mutilated, all died from exsanguination, and every scene had a note on white memo paper," I said.

"Why is there a two-month window between Winchester and Fairfax?" Kurt asked. "Where was he?"

My eyebrows rose.

Kurt grinned and with a shake of his head he said, "Yes, I said he."

"Let's keep gender out of it for now. We can't afford to narrow our focus that much." I smiled. "As for where the Unsub was ... Jail? Hospital? Out of state working, or on vacation?"

We had something to work with. It wasn't much but it was something; someone left Winchester after Violet's murder and eventually arrived in Fairfax after a brief interlude somewhere undisclosed. I opted to start with jails. Or rather I opted to let Sandra start with jails. I am all about sharing the love.

My phone rang. The vibration rattled the bones in my hand as I pulled the phone from my pocket. The name on the screen made little sense. Mike Fisher. I showed Kurt before answering.

He grinned as an eyebrow rose. "Better find out what he wants."

I frowned at the screen and answered the call. "Mike, always a pleasure getting a call from you."

"Glad you feel that way. Lunch?"

Now that shouldn't be possible. He's supposed to be in Los Angeles, filming a new television series, not out here on the East Coast.

"You're in town?"

"This woman I know is getting married in two weeks. Thought I'd fly in early. Try to change her mind?"

"Sure you did. Lee know you're here?"

"Not yet. I'm still at the airport. If you can't make lunch, have you got time for a coffee this afternoon?"

Doubtful.

"I'll call if I can get away, no promises, though."

"You sound stressed. Take five minutes, it'll do you good," Mike said.

I chewed my lip and kept my knee-jerk response in check. "We've got a tough case. It's time sensitive."

"Dinner, you and me?" He paused for a microsecond. "There is spaghetti Bolognese in our future." I heard amusement ring in his voice.

Not in my future, buddy.

"You, me, Mitch, Lee and Tara," I counter-offered.

"Way too many people at that table ..."

"Smooth, Mike. How's the widower thing working out for you?"

"Wearing off."

"Sorry. Wish I could help."

Kurt attracted my attention and pointed to a man

standing in the shadow of a large tree on the curb. I peered out the window. Offenders sometimes like to watch the mayhem they cause.

"Well, that was five minutes. Gotta go, Mike." I hung up and followed Kurt. He went left. I went right. Neither of us looked at the man, doing our best to ignore him until we'd skirted around the area and could approach without him seeing us until we wanted him to.

About ten feet out, he turned toward me. Startled he broke into a run, in the opposite direction.

Damn!

Without warning, a bass rhythm pounded in my ears. I raced after him. He ducked to the left. My fingers caught the fabric of his shirt, tearing it as he pulled away. Lunging at him, I managed to grab an arm. He stumbled and tried to shake me off. I stuck a foot in front of him and pushed. Thud. He hit the grass verge. A hand shot around my ankle. I tripped, landing heavily on my left side, my lungs emptying in a rush. Unsuccessfully trying to inhale, I kicked the hand off my ankle. My boot connected with something hard. The guy yelped.

Must've been his head?

"FBI," I groaned, dragging my badge from my belt, twisting and shoving the badge in his face. He tried to scrabble away but couldn't. The bass came back; this time I heard words and recognized the song: Ace of Bass "I Saw the Sign." Not a song I wanted stuck in my head.

A shadow fell. I looked up at Kurt. Unimpressed by the man's behavior, Kurt cuffed him, sat him up, and then helped me to my feet.

The song played on, lyrics bounced across the road and up onto a car roof.

What did it mean? What sign?

"Conway?"

"Yep," I replied, still trying to catch my breath. "Winded."

"Take it easy for a minute." Kurt turned his attention to the male. "Name?"

"She kicked me!"

"Nice name," Kurt quipped. "She kicked me who?"

A smile edged across my lips. It wasn't like Kurt to play with people; that was more my thing.

"That's not my name," the guy said.

"She kicked me. That's not my name," Kurt repeated with a straight face. "Your parents must've hated you."

"I thought FBI had no sense of humor?" the guy complained. "Just my luck to meet a comedian."

"Yeah, you're lucky," I said. "Why are you outside this apartment?"

"My ex-girlfriend lives there."

I looked at Kurt. The guy seemed familiar.

Why?

Kurt took a step back. By the look on his face, I figured he thought so too.

The song came back, louder, more insistent. Serena was happy living without him. Whatever she saw made her leave him. I didn't need much more than that to determine he was bad news and his presence outside her home now wasn't without meaning.

"You are?" Kurt asked.

"Matt Collins."

Imagine? What were the odds of him being the same man I wanted to talk to about Jane Daughtry? Coincidence? I preferred to think of it as fate.

"You're coming with us, Matt," I said. "Helping us with our investigation."

"What happened in there?" He inclined his head to the crime scene tape and police lights near Serena's home.

"Nothing good," I replied. "Walk toward that black Suburban ahead of you."

If he was the same Matt who'd been dating Jane, he now had two dead ex-girlfriends. I'm not a fan of coincidences.

"I haven't done anything," he said, trying to shake Kurt's hand off his arm.

"Never met anyone who did," Kurt replied, opening the back door of his car. "Mind your head."

"I'll go back to the scene and make sure we have a forensic team on the way," I said.

I saw Sam and Lee approaching from across the street.

"Keep Lee with you, Conway. Sam can come with me," Kurt replied, closing the door firmly on the complaining passenger.

"Yo," Sam said, rounding the back of the Suburban. "Transporting?"

"Yes. Matt Collins," Kurt replied. "You're with me."

"All righty. Let's get Mr. Collins back to the office."

Sam peered through the tinted windows. "He don't look happy."

"Anyone ever look happy in the back of our cars?" I replied. "Apart from us, that is."

Sam shook his head. "Nope. It's disheartening how many people don't like us, Chicky Babe."

"Take it easy, you two. Lee and I will be along soon."

Kurt stepped next to Lee, facing away from me so I couldn't see or hear him when he spoke.

Intentional. Unnecessary. Over-protective crap.

With a wave, Kurt climbed into the driver's seat and Sam in the back with Collins.

Lee and I walked back to the house.

"You get hurt?" Lee asked.

Yep, definitely over-protective crap.

"I got winded that's all."

"Kurt said," he replied, lifting the tape that surrounded the area near the front door.

"Get anything from the neighbors?" I ducked under crime scene tape.

"Nothing unexpected. She was quiet, not a party girl. Worked a lot. No strange cars in the area that anyone noticed."

That wasn't helpful. There had to be something. Collins was definitely something but I had a feeling there was something else.

I stood in the bathroom doorway and closed my eyes. Lee standing behind me was comforting as only the presence of Delta A can be. A video played in my head. Serena had the starring role.

Swirling images encompassed the entire room, swallowing me until Serena and I were one. Using her eyes, I searched the room for signs of the Unsub. Nothing. Serena stepped into the shower and stood under the hot water. Her eyesight blurred, eyelids became heavy. She reached for the shower control and missed. The door opened. Her head turned toward the rush of air. Steam raced from the shower. For a moment, he was there.

Short dark hair. Dark eyes. Clean shaven. Olive complexion. Serena lashed out. Her eyes closed as she fell.

What was that? My mind jumped through a jumble of thoughts and none made sense. Logic said I couldn't have seen what I thought I saw, but it felt real.

Lee spoke. I jumped.

"Sorry," he said with a laugh. "You okay?"

I turned to face him while trying to settle the images and find words to tell him what I'd seen.

"Chicky? Ellie?"

I held up my hand to get him to wait.

Just wait.

Breathe.

Who did I see?

He was right there. His face. Who was he?

"I saw the Unsub," I said.

Lee's eyes darted around the room. "Ellie, it's just us here." His hand moved to his phone sticking out of his pocket.

"Don't. I saw him, Lee."

Too late. He called Kurt then passed me the phone.

"Something happen?" Kurt asked.

"Nothing major." A moment of uncertainty preceded my revelation but I said it anyway. "I saw the Unsub. I can draw him."

"How?"

There was no way to make this sound less insane.

"I used Serena's eyes before the drugs took hold properly. He was there. I. Saw. Him."

"Give me back to Lee," Kurt said.

I handed Lee the phone and waited, fully expecting him to be given instructions to take me to the nearest hospital. Lee hung up and put his away. I waited for the inevitable.

"Let's go. You've got a date with an identikit program."

Holding the sigh of relief in check was not easy.

Chapter Six
I Saw the Sign

Kurt was waiting in my office. I acknowledged him as I entered the room, hung up my jacket, set my holster and weapon on my desk then slid into my chair.

"You want to tell me what happened after I left?" Kurt placed his elbows on my desk. His face bore the strain of a man whose patience had worn thin.

Here we go.

I opened my laptop. As much as it'd be fun to push him over the edge some days, I didn't think today was that day. "I went back into the bathroom."

"And?"

"And ... I used Serena's eyes to show me the moments before she died."

"Just like that? Casually used a dead woman's eyes to show you her death?" Kurt moved closer. "Is that how it happened? Because ... this is new freakiness, Conway. Over and above your usual Christopher Chance visits or songs."

I sighed, my irritation hiking up a notch. "You think I like this? Do you? You think it doesn't freak me out when I see things I shouldn't possibly be able to see?" I touched the identikit icon on the screen to open the program then glared at Kurt over my screen. "Do you have any idea how much I did not want to say anything to Lee?"

Kurt watched me as inputted characteristics into the

46

program.

"What did he look like?"

"Greek. He looked Greek," I said, adding facial features.

"Nothing like Matthew Collins?"

Nothing olive about his skin: Collins was a whiter shade of pale. I steeled myself for a potential Procol Harum onslaught but no one skipped the light fandango or turned cartwheels anywhere. Just when I thought it was safe to continue, they paraded sixteen vestal virgins past me and I hoped like hell there weren't sixteen victims. Kurt cleared his throat. Procol Harum took their virgins to the coast and normality returned.

"Conway. You with me?"

"Yep."

"Is Collins anything like the Unsub you saw?"

"No. But he's not off the hook," I said, looking up for a minute. Going for broke was a good idea. Not. Yet I knew I was about to say something else that'd elicit a frown from Kurt. "When I was chasing Collins I heard a song. An Ace of Base song. 'I saw the Sign.'"

"Play it for me," Kurt asked.

"Sure. Bet it's on YouTube."

I opened a browser and located the song. It successfully removed all traces of "A Whiter Shade of Pale." "I saw the Sign" played while I carried on creating a likeness of the person I saw through the eyes of a dead woman. Yeah, that's normal. It felt like it was going to be the new normal. May as well get used to it.

The song finished.

"What'd you get from it?" Kurt said.

"That she'd left Collins, that he was trouble. Have you run him through the system?"

Kurt nodded. "Nothing there. He's clean."

That just meant no one had laid a complaint, not that he wasn't a violent ass. Why did I think violent? There was nothing to indicate he hit Serena or Jane. And he wasn't the man I saw in the bathroom.

"Do something for me?" Kurt nodded. "Talk to Jane's and Serena's co-workers ... ask if they ever saw bruises."

"Collins?"

"Yeah, something about him. Why was he outside the house today?"

"You can ask him yourself when you're finished up here. He's in interview room four waiting for you."

Great. Can't wait.

My screen showed a picture of the man in the bathroom. I tweaked his eyes a little then sat back and looked. It was him.

"Come here," I said to Kurt.

He joined me on my side of the desk. "That him?"

I nodded. "Look at all familiar?"

"No."

Didn't to me, either.

"I'll run him through facial recognition and see if we get any hits back from our databases. I'm also sending a copy to the officer who raised questions about Violet Cramer's suicide in Winchester."

I hoped he could tell me if it was someone he'd seen and maybe why the person left town.

"You going to add the image to a BOLO?" Kurt asked.

"Yeah … nah." I had no evidence that he was the guy.

Could I go public without a real witness? Yeah, maybe?

"Hold off on the BOLO, I'll have police go door-to-door in the vicinity of both crime scenes with that image. Maybe we can dig up someone who'll confirm he was in the area."

"Yeah, then we'll send out the BOLO."

I liked that plan. It'd make me seem less insane in the long run.

Chapter Seven
Rebel Yell.

I walked into the interview room and closed the door behind me. The man at the small table in the middle of the room looked up. There was something about him. I couldn't decide if it was violence I sensed, or something else.

"Matthew Collins," I said, sitting at the table across from him.

He said nothing.

"I'm Supervisory Special Agent Conway." I threw a half-assed smile at him. "See the game last night?"

"Yeah, as usual, the Wizards could've done better."

"Yeah, they could've."

"What's this about? I don't think it's about basketball," Collins said.

"Serena Sorensen."

"We broke up."

"So you said. Why was that? Who broke up with whom?"

He frowned. "How does that matter to you?"

"Humor me."

"I broke up with her," he said, running his hand through his hair.

"Why?"

He shrugged, rubbed his chin, and dropped his hands into his lap. "We weren't getting along," Collins said. His brow furrowed. "What happened at her house?"

"Thought you might be able to tell me ..."

His eyes darted up the wall behind me to the camera in the corner. "I don't know."

"Why were you there?"

"I was going home and saw the police cars," he replied, running his fingers through his hair again.

"Home from?"

"Work."

"What kind of job finishes before nine in the morning?"

"I finished at seven."

"I didn't ask when you finished. Try answering the question." I rephrased the question, making it easier for him to answer. "Where do you work?"

"I'm a paramedic, I work for the city."

His short answers were tiresome but he answered the question.

"Which house?"

"I'm with the four-forty."

I ran that over in my mind a few times. The four-forty wasn't far away. He didn't go straight home.

"You finished at seven and?"

He was silent for a few beats. Looked like he was trying to decide what to tell me.

"Went out for breakfast with a friend. I was on my way home when I saw the police cars."

"The friend have a name?" It was like pulling teeth. I suspected if I started pulling his teeth he'd be faster with his responses.

"Is that necessary?"

"You're a paramedic, you know it is."

His agitation spilled over.

Time to change tactics. Cue friendly non-threatening Ellie. "How long have you been a paramedic?"

"Three years."

"Like it? It's a tough job."

"It's rewarding, can be tough." He sighed. His shoulders relaxed. "Last night was tough."

Something told me to wait, let him talk.

"We got called to a baby," he said, running his hands through his hair. He looked up at me. "Sudden infant death."

"That's rough. Sorry." That must've been hellish. Dead baby, distraught parents, and no good outcome. "You can't save everyone," fell from my mouth before I could stop it. "Sorry, that was trite. I didn't—"

Shut up, Ellie. Just move on. "Is being a paramedic something you always wanted to be?"

"Yes."

"How old are you?"

"Thirty-two."

So he did something before becoming a medic.

"What'd you do before?"

"Army."

"Is that where you trained?"

He nodded.

"Wanna tell me why you tried to run?"

"Spooked."

An army medic spooked by a fed? Nope. Not buying that.

"Try again."

"I don't know. A moment of stupidity?"

"You're the one telling the story." I kept my expression neutral. No judgment here. "Who'd you have breakfast with?"

He hesitated.

"Come on, Collins. Don't make this hard."

We could all be somewhere else. Anywhere else.

"A colleague."

"Name?"

He sighed. "Sarah Ng."

"That wasn't so freaking tough was it?" I said, "And Sarah is?"

"... A colleague."

"There's more to it than that."

"That'd be nice but it's not looking good so far."

Neutral became second nature. "I see." I see. No, I didn't but I wanted too. "Do you have a photo of Sarah?" Bit random.

He frowned and lifted his phone from his shirt pocket.

"I think so," he said, scrolling through screens. Images flicked across his eyes. He stopped and handed me the phone. "She's the one on the right."

"Pretty," I replied. Pays to check. Blonde. She looked similar to Serena and Jane and Violet. Ng conjured Asian traits in my mind but there were none evident in Sarah.

"What color eyes does she have?" I asked, handing him back the phone.

"Blue-green," he replied. "Like the sea."

"Good luck with her, Collins," I said.

I continued our chat until I had plausible alibis for all three deaths. And all three alibis would be easy to check. He worked shifts and seemed quite social. When I brought up the subject of Serena again, he moved back in the chair and looked at me.

"Did you really break up with her?"

He shook his head. "No. She broke up with me."

"Why?"

"I couldn't keep it in my pants. She caught me with another woman."

A player rather than a violent dickhead.

"Who was the other woman?"

"Jane Daughtry."

You have got to be kidding me.

A sigh escaped. For all he was an idiot, I didn't dislike the guy but the cheating thing wasn't making it any easier for him.

"You've made quite a mess. Does Sarah know?"

He nodded. "I told her."

Ah, that would explain his reservations about any impending relationship.

It was good that he told her. It was time to tell him what happened that morning.

"Serena was murdered this morning." I watched him as he took my words on board.

"What?"

"Serena. She was killed."

"Jane and Serena ..."

"And you're linked to them both."

He shook his head; disbelief sailed across his face and leaked from his eyes. "That can't be ..." He rubbed his face with his hands.

"I'm going to keep in touch with you," I said. "From my point of view, you are involved in this case. I'm prepared to acknowledge that that could simply be bad luck."

I would like to think it was bad luck.

Nothing tingled to let me know something bad was happening. "Meanwhile, I need you to remain accessible."

"Of course." He moved forward. Frown lines furrowed his brow. "I swear I didn't kill anyone. What if this has something to do with me? What if Sarah—"

"I'm going to ask the PD to up patrols. Give me her address."

I spun my notebook toward him and passed him my pen.

"You don't know a woman called Violet Cramer do you?" I said as he passed the notebook back. I glanced at the address then at him. His frown deepened. He swallowed hard. Beads of perspiration gathered on his forehead. His shoulders heaved.

I jumped up and opened the door as he threw up all over the table.

Deep breath. Another deep breath.

Bile rose. I swallowed hard and used the wall outside the door for support. Retching continued from the interview room, the smell of vomit thick in the air. A horrible shaky feeling swamped me, sending the blood rushing from my face. Trying to control my breathing and focus on something nice took all my energy.

Just when I thought I was losing, a shadow fell over me. Lee's voice gave me something to focus on. "Chicky, hit the restroom. Get some water. I got this," he said, sticking his head around the open door. "Collins, I'll get you some water and someone will come clean that up. Sit tight."

I pushed myself off the wall and hurried to the nearest restroom. Splashing cold water on my face helped. I caught sight of myself in the mirror. No living person should ever be that pale.

Maybe I wasn't alive?

Chapter Eight

Welcome to my World.

"You okay?" Kurt wanted to know as he entered my office.

"Yep, never better," I replied, looking at him from over my screen. "You need something?"

"We could try the truth, how would that work for you?" He sat on the edge of my desk.

"About?"

"Whether you are feeling all right ... because, Conway, you're not usually spectral in appearance."

As I suspected, I'm dead.

"I'm good." I tried to dislodge the image of the interview room Kurt had stirred up. "I just ..." It wasn't happening. I switched gears and filled my mind with a flower-filled meadow and watched a dragonfly dart about.

"Not like you to have a sensitive stomach," Kurt replied. "I'll get you some water." He chuckled as he opened the small fridge in the corner of the room.

"It's not funny," I grumbled as my meadow vista gave way to the computer screen.

"Oh, but it is, Conway," Kurt replied, sitting a bottle of water next to my right hand. "It really is."

I swigged on the water and concentrated on the screen. Ignoring Kurt.

"I've got Fairfax Police Department set up to patrol

Sarah Ng's home during the night and tomorrow morning," I said.

My finger tapped the mouse button opening our email client. I scrolled through the latest forty emails. Nothing from Winchester about the sketch, yet. I'd hoped it'd set off a sudden flurry of information and we could stop more deaths.

Damn me and my Pollyanna ways.

I did a quick background check on Sarah Ng. Never been in any kind of trouble. She was twenty-five and a paramedic with the four-forty. Facebook tossed up family photos. Parents both Asian. I surmised she was adopted, like her older brother who appeared to be African-American. Digging around some more confirmed that she was adopted from a Russian orphanage at age three. Her brother was adopted from an orphanage in Louisiana as an infant.

But if the deaths had something to do with Collins and not just the type of woman the Unsub enjoyed killing, then the danger level for Sarah Ng had ramped up a few notches. Leaning back in my chair I thought about Sarah Ng and her ever-diminishing survival rate. It wasn't worth the risk.

My hand lifted the telephone handset from the cradle on my desk. "Hey, Sandra, connect me to Fairfax PD?"

"Sure, anyone in particular?"

Names rolled around in my head. Josh. "Is Joshua Konstrum back with Fairfax?"

"He is," she replied. "Connecting you in three ..."

The line noise changed from hollow to ringing. Moments later I heard Josh's voice. "It's Ellie Conway. I need a favor."

"Hi, Ellie." He paused. Fingers on a keyboard filled the airway between us. "They're calling your new case The Psycho Killer case."

"Apt description but I'd rather that wasn't made public. I need the PD to provide surveillance and possibly protection for a woman, tonight. There's already a request to have extra patrols in her neighborhood, this is additional."

"You got it. Send me the details. I'll put a team together."

That was easy.

Felt a little too easy. "Why so amenable, Josh? You're usually pretty good at helping but you didn't even ask about Murphy's bar this time."

"Serena Sorenson. A few of us knew her."

Bells rang in my head. Kurt waved from the doorway. "Do me another favor and get me a list of everyone who knew Serena?" I said as I motioned for Kurt to wait. "How'd you know her?"

"She's a local. Her sister is dating a paramedic and his brother is a cop."

The bells got louder. "Her sister is dating a paramedic ... who?"

"Cliff White, know him?"

"Nope. What house?"

"Four-forty."

The clanging continued. "I need that list."

"I'll get an email off to you A-SAP."

"Thanks, Josh."

I hung up. Kurt had taken up position in the chair by my desk again. He watched me as I emailed Josh all the details pertaining to Sarah Ng. I felt his unspoken words and looked at him. "Serena Sorenson was known to a few of the officers down in Fairfax PD."

I didn't have to say anymore because he knew we could be looking for a cop. A cop would know how to clean a crime scene but then, so would a paramedic.

"We'll be working late tonight then?"

"Yep. Josh is sending me a list." Four emails arrived in quick succession. One was the list from Josh. I opened it and scanned the names. "I have fifteen names in front of me. We'll divide up the list and get to it."

"You want Sam and Lee?"

"No." I glanced at the clock on the wall. Evening loomed. "I'd like them to go back to both crime scenes and try to get more information from neighbors. Some-one saw something."

"Okay. And Collins?"

"Make sure he's okay, ask him if he knows Cliff White, a paramedic from the four-forty, and see if there is any-thing he can tell us about Serena's sister."

"Her sister?"

"Yeah, she's dating Cliff White. That's Collins' station."

"Another link."

I nodded. If only I knew what the link meant.

Kurt pushed his chair back as he stood. "You drink that water. You've hardly touched it." He wagged a finger at me. "I'll be back."

Chapter Nine

Beneath your beautiful

At six in the morning, the phone lying on my desk lit up. I'd turned the ringer off during the night. It vibrated while the screen flashed ominously. I was pretty sure it wasn't good news.

I stretched my tired body, yawned, picked up the blinking vibrating phone, and swiped the screen. "Agent Conway."

"Agent Conway, it's Troy Fallon. Sorry to call so early but I thought you'd want to know how the night went."

My heart sank to my stomach. "Is Sarah Ng all right?"

"Yes."

I breathed a sigh of relief. Maybe we were on the right track. "Give me a sitrep for Sarah?"

"She had a quiet night. No visitors. Sarah was sighted four minutes ago as she left for work. We have a plain car following her and another continuing surveillance on her home."

"Keep everything in place for now. I'm not convinced she's safe."

Or that this is over. My gut still said our Unsub was just warming up.

"Sure," Troy said. "Did you hear what the PD are calling the Unsub?"

"I did," I said.

I don't like cute names for killers. It trivializes their

actions. A yawn escaped as another thought popped up. "Hey, we'll need to hold a media conference. I'll have my people set it up but would like you to join me on camera?"

"Let me know when and where," Troy replied.

"Will do, and thanks, Troy. I'll be in touch."

Hanging up, I scrabbled around in my top drawer until I found the business card from a journalist, Rosanne Lette, who'd been quite helpful to me once. I even liked her somewhat. Not easy: the media and I had a hate-hate relationship. I fired off an email to Rosanne letting her know there would be a media briefing later in the day and that she should contact Sandra for details.

I checked the rest of my inbox in case I'd missed something during the night. There were emails from Lee and Sam, they hadn't found anything of use from revisiting the neighbors. A vague memory lurked of sending them home about midnight.

Kurt left me several messages; mostly they were of the "go home" variety.

Yeah. Nah.

I didn't go home. I stayed and ran every name on the list from Fairfax PD against Facebook and Twitter accounts belonging to our victims.

Matthew Collins wasn't the only one who knew both victims. Five Fairfax police officers made it to my list of potential suspects, and Cliff White the paramedic from the four-forty.

I rang Mitch's cell.

"Missed you last night. How's it going?" Behind his words, I heard the shower.

"Can you wait for me?" I said, chewing my lip. "I need —"

"Absolutely. How long will you be?"

I glanced at the clock on the wall. "Twenty minutes." Mitch's place was closer than mine. I could be there in twenty with traffic.

"See you soon," Mitch replied.

I hung up, pocketed my phone, slid my holster back on my belt, and left my office. Sandra was just coming in as I opened the stairwell door.

"I'm going home for a little while," I said, holding the door for her.

"You've been here all night?" Sandra adjusted her handbag on her arm.

"Yes."

"I'll organize the troops when they come in."

"Thanks, Sandra. I'll be in touch. My phone is off for an hour or so. Kurt is urgent contact until I'm back on deck."

Taking time for me was a new thing. I started doing it during a particularly brutal case a few months ago, at Kurt and Mitch's insistence. Turns out I have less crazy in my head and apparently it's less scary for everyone else if I look after myself. Imagine that?

I needed a decent run. Running gave my mind thinking time. Swinging the stairwell door open I hit the stairs sprinting. Stairs were a poor substitute but it'd have to do. Felt like I wouldn't be going for a proper head-clearing run for a while.

Fifteen minutes later I pulled into Mitch's driveway; before I got to the front door, it swung open. Greeted by a half-dressed Mitch, I grinned. More often than not it was a shirtless, barefoot, belt open, jeans unbuttoned, sleep-tousled Mitch who met me at the door. Unbuttoned shirt with no pants was new.

"Nice start to the day. Pants optional?"

He laughed, pulled me close, and shoved the door till it clicked behind me. "Such a wiseass," he said, hugging me then taking a step back, his eyes traveled down my body. "Those are yesterday's clothes. Pull an all-nighter?"

"Got a bit busy."

A thought flashed into his eyes. I didn't want him to think; thoughts became questions. I didn't want questions.

"Everything all right?"

I smiled. "I need a shower and would like company."

"Guess that answers my question," Mitch said, smiling.

And just like that, I was off the hook. No squirming required.

I dropped my holster and phone on his bed, throwing my jacket over them. The sound of running water drowned out Mitch's voice.

"Did you say something?" I asked from the bathroom door.

"I said, come here," he replied, taking my hand. When I was close enough, his fingers unbuttoned my shirt and slid it over my shoulders and down my arms. Mitch's shirt followed. Clothing piled up on the floor. Mitch steadied me as I kicked my jeans away from my feet.

He smiled and stepped into the shower taking me with him. Hot water cascaded over me and down the drain, taking the night with it. Mitch slid an arm around my waist holding me close, his free hand against the wall. His muscles rippled as he moved against me.

Breathing. One hand on his shoulder, the other arm around his neck.

Blue eyes penetrating blue eyes.

Smiling. Water flowed down our bodies.

Sometime later I was trying to dress in clean clothes.

"That's not helpful," I said with a slight chuckle as Mitch undid the buttons I did up.

"I know," he replied, nuzzling my neck.

"Really, again?"

"Uh huh."

"You're going to be worn out before the honeymoon ..."

The losing battle continued for a minute; we both knew it was token resistance on my part.

"You complaining?"

"No," I said, giving up and wrapping my arms around his neck. "Not at all."

Chapter Ten

With or without you

My phone rang as I walked to the car. I pulled it from my pocket: Detective Troy Fallon. With a wave to Mitch, I slid behind the steering wheel and touched the speaker icon. "How can I help?" I said, turning the ignition key.

"There is a new crime scene."

"Ah, crap. Sarah?" My brain clicked in telling me Sarah had left for work, so unless she'd returned without her police surveillance, she was still safe.

"No. She is at work. In fact, she was one of the paramedics who arrived on scene about three minutes ago. The victim is twenty-six-year-old Terri Kane."

I breathed. Pleased it wasn't Sarah but fighting anger that someone else died on my watch. We were failing. Failure is never an option. I needed a direction.

"And there's no doubt it's the same Unsub?"

"I'm sure it is," she replied.

"Gimme the address, Troy, and then email the details of the latest victim. I'll head over to the scene. Wait for me."

She gave me a nearby address. "Sending those details via text now." She paused for a moment. "I'll be out front."

"I'll be there soon."

I hung up, punched the address into the GPS and waited as it plotted the shortest route. The robotic female voice droned out directions. Today I was happy to just follow them without trying to make her explode by taking different streets. One day I'd make the calm voice screech obscenities. I'm a woman on a mission.

The thought of missions warped in my mind. Before "Mission Impossible" became a thing, I switched gears and crawled inside an Ian Fleming novel which morphed into a movie. A smooth voice inside my head said, "Bond, James Bond." Daniel Craig made a great James Bond. There was little possibility of dislodging my smile before I arrived at my destination.

According to the voice of the GPS, my destination was on my right. Sure enough, police cars with their lights rolling and an ambulance were parked out front of a house. I pulled in behind a police car and flung open my door. My phone rang. A number I didn't recognize flashed insistently. "Special Agent Conway."

"Ellie, this is Martha Gerrard."

My brain whirred and my stomach sank as her introduction hit home. Martha, mother of retired NCIS Agent Noel Gerrard. This couldn't be good. "How can I help, Mrs. Gerrard?"

"You can call me Martha, dear. I was wondering if you'd heard from Noel recently." Her voice spiked and cracked, anxiety filtering through.

"Not for a long time, Martha. Is something wrong?" I shifted in my seat and drummed my fingers on the steering wheel in front of me as I thought about my last conversation with Noel. He'd wanted to know we were all right after the DC bombings.

"He's missing. I haven't heard from him in six weeks."

"Missing?"

"He always checks in with me. Every week. I've heard nothing for six weeks."

"I'll see what I can do. I'm sure it's nothing. Probably got caught up fishing … I'll be in touch."

"Thank you, dear."

"No problem."

I added Martha's number to my contact list. Not contacting his elderly mother for six weeks could spell trouble. He was close to his mom. I made a note on my phone to check up on Gerrard as soon as I had a moment then plastered on my game face and clambered out of the car.

Troy traipsed across the small front lawn to greet me. Beyond her, crime scene tape flapped in the warm breeze.

"You made good time," she said, shaking my hand.

"I wasn't far away," I replied, grabbing my pack from the back seat.

"The victim is twenty-six-year-old Terri Kane. She works for the DMV," Troy said, reading from her notebook while we walked to the house.

"State level government employee," I said, more to myself than Troy.

Troy handed me booties and gloves from two boxes by the front door. I pulled the booties on first, using the doorframe to balance. Once suitably attired, Troy led the way to the bathroom and the body of Terri Kane.

"Give me a minute?" I said to Troy and entered the

room alone. She waited, watching but silent, by the doorway.

Two steps in I knew it was the same Unsub. No doubt in my mind at all. Another clean crime scene. My eyes closed. I breathed slowly, taking in all the subtle scents and aromas. Four breaths later, I approached the slumped naked body in the shower.

"Terri, I'm Ellie Conway. I need you to help me find out who did this to you," I said, kneeling by her head. Her glazed eyes stared vacantly at the corner of the shower. "I need your help. Show me what happened."

It felt like I'd tilted, I tried to straighten up then realized it was the room. No, not the room: it was Terri. I was Terri. She was moving? I breathed. Standing up, I let Terri's incorporeal arm reach through me. Her hand grasped the shower control, turning the water to hot. I shivered as she stepped right through my body and into the stream of water, closing the curtain as she moved. My mind danced, trying to fathom what was happening as I was stood in a shower with a ghost and a dead body but not getting wet. A voice told me to go with it: maybe it was Terri's.

Who am I to argue with the recently deceased?

I looked at Terri. We were the same height, five foot nine.

Terri took shampoo from a caddy in the corner. She washed and then conditioned her hair. The shower filled with a light coconut scent. I'd noted it when I walked into the bathroom. It smelled like summer. Coconut body scrub followed. She rinsed off the scrub. A noise startled her. Her eyes blurred. She struggled to focus. The outer door opened. Someone launched themselves into the shower, wrapping Terri in the cold, wet curtain. She fought to get her face free. One glimpse was all I got before her eyes closed. Half a face. I thought it was the same man I'd seen before.

From the way he'd launched himself and how he'd wrapped her, I had the feeling he was tallish. Six foot maybe. No shorter than that. Terri's ethereal self folded back into her dead body. I blinked a few times and checked the shower caddy. Nothing I'd seen her use was missing.

What did I know?

She was drugged, it was the same male, and I had an approximate height.

I sank back down to the floor by her head. "Thank you, Terri. Thank you for showing me," I whispered. My eyes roamed the room looking for a telltale piece of folded white paper. Sure enough, I spotted it poking out from the laundry hamper. Retrieving it, I read, "'I broke when you looked at me.'"

Troy said, "Another note?"

I jumped. I'd forgotten she was there.

"Sorry," she said, curtailing the nervous giggle I heard in her voice before she spoke again, "What does it mean?"

I shook my head. "I don't know."

"Do you have evidence bags or shall I get some from my car?"

"My pack," I said, pointing to the pack by the door. "Main compartment. Please."

Troy unzipped the pack and held open an evidence bag, then dropped it with the note back into my pack. I resumed a thorough inspection. Clean, tidy, nothing out of place. No sleeping pills in the medicine cabinet. No prescriptions of any sort. She had some over-the-counter cold and flu medicines, pain killers and vitamins, but that was all.

There wasn't even a stray hair on the floor or basin. The garbage bin contained scrunched paper towels. The cabinet under the sink had a roll of paper towels and two different spray cleaners. Neither had much smell. More hypo-allergenic cleaning products.

Could that be a link?

It was time to go back to Terri and inspect the wounds on her body. Several stab wounds on her torso. I moved her long blonde hair and found the fatal wound to her throat. A stab, not a slash. That would've squirted blood up the walls. There wasn't as much as a stray drop on the white walls. I moved closer and sniffed. The coconut con-ditioner was still strong. I expected that the amount of water needed to shift a substantial quantity of blood would've diluted the coconut a lot more than it was.

Maybe. Something to ask about later.

I leaned in and gave one last inward breath through my nose. Coffee. She drank coffee.

I was done. With a nod to Troy, I hoisted my pack onto my shoulder and left the house.

Outside I called Kurt. "I'm at a new crime scene. Would very much like you all to join me."

"We're just tidying a few things up at the office," Kurt replied. "Address?"

I rattled off the address and hung up. While Troy and I waited, I sent some uniforms to canvass the neighborhood. Sometimes people responded better to a uniform than an FBI badge.

Go figure.

Chapter Eleven

Wherever you will go

I swallowed, took a breath, and once again led the way into the latest house of death.

"Crime scene four but I don't think it'll be the last," I said as I beckoned to Kurt down the hallway. I stopped near the bathroom door.

"You okay, Conway?" Kurt asked. "I've never seen the color drain from you like it just did."

Concentrate.

"Draining."

Blood. How much blood would've sprayed up the walls of the shower?

"Conway?"

"Let's do this first, then I have a question."

"I don't like how pale you are."

Ignoring Kurt, I flipped to work mode. "Terri Kane. Twenty-six. Works for DMV. That makes her a state level government employee and she's blonde with blue eyes."

Kurt nodded.

"Worked. Made," Kurt said as he entered the bathroom. "How'd the Unsub gain entry?"

"No signs of forced entry and no open windows. She might have let him in."

"That's new." Kurt turned to face me. "You thinking what I'm thinking?"

For a split second, I wondered if he knew how close I

was to hurling in a crime scene. That wasn't what he was thinking. "That she knew him or her? I've sent uniforms to canvass the neighborhood. Hopefully, someone will know if Terri had a boyfriend or girlfriend or frequent visitor."

"Girlfriend?"

"Stabbing just feels like a female crime."

Grasping at straws; it wasn't a woman I saw. It was possible that my view of women and knives was clouded by several incidents with knife-wielding fans of Michael Fisher. The amount of force used could easily mean the Unsub was male.

Options wide open. Could be anyone with opposable thumbs. I rolled back to my initial suicide thought. Yeah. Nah.

I saw a male.

"You didn't see a woman at the last crime scene, Conway."

"Didn't see one this time either."

Crap.

"This time? You saw the Unsub again?"

"Not completely. He covered her face she could only get a partial looksee but it looked like the same guy to me."

Kurt frowned, lines deepening in his forehead. "You scare me."

I scare myself.

I shrugged. "How much blood are we talking about?" I faced the shower and the clean white walls. "How much blood would've sprayed up these walls?"

"Give me a minute and I'll do the math."

"She's my height."

"That's helpful. Looks about your weight too." A few taps on the calculator on his phone and he had an answer. "Blood will only squirt as long as the heart can pump. The point of no return for Terri happened once she'd lost almost two liters."

"And that is what in pints?"

"Just over three and a half."

"That would've made a mess."

My phone rang. My boss, Special Agent in Charge Caine Grafton.

"Caine," I said and left the room, passing Sam and Lee.

"Where are you?" Caine said.

"Homicide crime scene investigation."

"We just got an anonymous tip. The tipster asked for the FBI agent in charge of the Ox Road murder."

"That'll be me. What now?"

"Another murder."

He'd broken his pattern. That wasn't good.

"Send the address to my phone." Gerrard's mom popped into my head. "While you're on the line. Have you heard from Noel Gerrard at all in the last few months?"

"No. He's a friend of Sean O'Hare. If you're trying to find him, Sean may know where to look."

I knew they knew each other. But friends? I didn't know that. I added another note to my phone to check with Sean.

I walked back to Lee and Sam. "Saddle up, we got another one."

Everyone's phones went at once. My screen said it was an incoming map reference from SA Sandra Sinclair. I guessed we all had the same thing. Kurt emerged from the bathroom.

"Again already?"

"Yeah, Caine rang. Sandra sent us directions."

Noise from the front door alerted me to an arrival. Two crime scene techs walked toward us.

I nodded at them, held up a hand to tell them to wait, and made a phone call. "Sean, Ellie here. I need more scene guards."

"How many and where?"

"Two. Sending address now."

"Okay. Done. Invoice Delta A, your name on it?"

"Yes."

Out of my budget, just like last time.

"You going to need more today?"

"I think so. Put another two on standby. I'll let you know in the next hour if I need them."

"Take care, Ellie."

"Hang on, have you heard from Noel Gerrard recently?"

"No." He paused for a tick. "Something I should know?"

"Not sure yet. If you do, tell him to call his mom."

"Will do."

The techs who had worked crime scenes for me before

were waiting. Carol Higgins and Jerome Sand.

"When you're done, hand over to the scene guards from O'Hare Security."

"Yes, ma'am," Carol said.

"The ME is going to be busy today." I glanced around. "Where is she?"

"On her way, ma'am."

"Good."

"Anything specific you want us to look for?"

"Point of entry." A sigh escaped. "Pay especial attention to the bedrooms, kitchen and bathroom. We need some prints. We really need some prints."

Carol nodded. "Anything else?"

"Yeah, she was drugged." There was no doubt in my mind. Her cloudy vision spoke to me of drugs. "I want to know how. She had coffee this morning. Don't know if it was take-out or she made it. Find out."

"Yes, ma'am."

"Maybe someone tampered with her morning coffee?"

"Something for us to look into, ma'am."

"We'll leave you to it." I walked away from her. Kurt, Sam, and Lee caught up with me. I shot Kurt a sideways glance. "Remember the Son of Shakespeare case?"

Kurt nodded. Lee nudged me. "What are you thinking?"

"I'm thinking about the cyber café and how Mac was drugged," I replied.

Sam chuckled, a deep throaty chuckle. "He's was pretty entertaining, Chicky Babe."

"Yep, he was, Mr. T!"

The chuckle became a belly laugh.

Kurt joined the conversation. "That was ketamine, yes?"

"Yes. In his coffee."

"And in your toothpaste, if I recall correctly?" Kurt added.

"Yes." So they told me. "Good memory."

"You made a lasting impression."

"Awesome."

When I grow up, I'll make less embarrassing lasting impressions.

"Having had some experience with ketamine, Conway … do you think that was the drug used here?"

That was a hard question. I gave it some thought. No. It didn't feel like ketamine. They weren't capable of anything once the drug took hold. Whatever was used dropped their level of consciousness lower than ketamine. They didn't not remember, there was nothing there at all.

I shook my head. "No. Not ketamine. Something else. Could sleeping pills be delivered via coffee?"

Kurt nodded.

"Would they make the coffee too disgusting to drink?"

"Probably not. You wouldn't need a lot and the bitterness of coffee would mask the flavor."

That sounds plausible. Don't think I want to try sleeping pills in coffee, though.

"I'll take your word for the taste."

"I'll look into the coffee-pill thing, but I think I remember something similar a few years ago."

I plunged my hand into my jeans pocket and pulled out a pen, leaving my glove behind. Fishing out the glove, I tossed it at Kurt. "We should be carrying small."

He caught the glove and smiled. "Thought you had small black Nitrile gloves?"

"I did. Don't know where the box went, I've been using the latex gloves on scene," I replied, dragging my notebook from my shirt pocket and losing the second glove.

Kurt chuckled as I threw it at him. "I'll grab a new box for you from stores when we get back."

"Thanks, that'd be helpful."

Troy was waiting outside for me. I stopped to talk to her. Kurt, Sam, and Lee carried on to the cars.

"O'Hare Security will provide scene guards. Can you handle security for our techs until O'Hare's men arrive?"

"Of course. I just had an update from the surveillance on Sarah Ng's home. A male approached the residence and knocked on the front door. Officers said he was carrying a clipboard and wearing a power company ID. They intercepted him down the street."

"Description?"

"Dark hair, six feet tall, translucent skin. Said he looked like a vampire."

Don't think we're looking for anyone with fangs. There weren't any characteristic teeth marks on the victims.

"Unfortunate. I'm interested in anyone with dark hair. Did they get details?"

"Yes." She passed me her notebook. I copied the particulars into my notebook.

"I'll do some background on him ... tell them thanks."

"We'll keep surveillance on Ms. Ng."

"Thanks, Troy."

I'd almost reached the car when my phone rang. "Hey, Sandra, got something?" I signaled to Kurt waiting in the car that I was coming.

"Have you seen The Washington Post today?"

I stopped walking. "No."

"You might want to get a copy and look at the In Memoriam page. I just saw it," Sandra said.

"That's a helluva way to capture my attention."

"You'll love this then. Someone posted a memorial with names under it. The names are Jane, Serena, and Terri."

"I'll get a copy and get back to you. Meanwhile ... see if you can find out who placed the memorial?"

"I'm on it, O Genie of the Fourth Estate."

I laughed, hung up, and tugged the car door open.

"Has there been a development?" Kurt asked.

"We need a copy of today's Post. Sounds like our Unsub posted a memorial."

Kurt located the nearest Seven Eleven and procured a copy. We sat in the car and flipped to the Obits. I scanned the page until I found the memorial Sandra had mentioned.

"Listen to this, Kurt." I paused for a moment as my brain and tongue wrapped around the words. "'Don't take it personally. It wasn't easy. Just listen. I broke when you looked at me. Life cracked wide open. Everything that came before. Spilled over the screen. Seeped into the keyboard. Shattered across the desk. Laughter replaced it all.'"

Kurt took the paper and read the piece for himself. "I recognize some of that from the crime scenes over the last few days."

"Me too."

He handed me back the folded pages pointing out the names at the end. "Jane, Serena and Terri,"

"I'm not liking that."

"We need to know when that ad was placed," Kurt said.

"The newspaper came out this morning. Terri was killed this morning."

Now we knew for sure she was chosen ahead of time. There wasn't anything opportunistic about these deaths. I was certain the killer selected the women for a reason and he knew enough about them to know he could kill them without being disturbed.

It was time to give proper consideration to the crime scene notes. Nothing about the short notes pleased me. Why leave lines from a poem at the crime scenes? For a second it all seemed so obvious and personal. It wasn't a secret that I once wrote poetry.

Maybe the question should be, why didn't more killers leave poetry at crime scenes?

"The notes ..." The words hung above the dash for a

few seconds before collapsing.

"You going somewhere with that or just thinking aloud?"

"Do you think they are for our benefit?"

"It would seem that way."

"Why?"

"Showing off? Making sure we're engaged?"

His words hit home. Perhaps it was a ploy to make sure Delta A led the investigation. Serial crime is our thing. We'd get the case regardless of any poetry at the scenes. No matter how I tried to explain the notes to myself, it felt personal.

Chapter Twelve
Just Older

"I need to check someone out," I said to Kurt.

"You could've done that while I was driving," he replied as I reached for my laptop.

No, I really couldn't.

"Better if we're stationary," I replied. "Corners are disruptive to my typing."

"Sorry but taking corners is better than trying to drive through buildings."

"Smart ass."

I flipped open my notebook and typed the name of the mysterious pale visitor to Sarah Ng's into the Sentinel search engine. A list of names and photos filled the screen. I narrowed the list by state and then county. That gave me six prospects. Six people named Kristopher Lette. Only one worked for a power company. That was encouraging. Even better that he lived locally. As I checked the other profiles, the surname wriggled about in my gut and poked me a few times.

"Kurt, we know someone with the surname Lette?"

He turned toward me, shifted his sunglasses to the top of his head and watched my screen.

"Does sound familiar."

It should. "The journalist, Rosanne. She's Rosanne Lette." I'd emailed her earlier.

Crap, media briefing. Damn!

I was running out of day to get that organized. I recognized a certain amount of reluctance on my part when it came to briefing the media and opening parts of this case to the public. People needed to know, but, panic wasn't helpful. Having the media breathing down our necks made our job harder. It was a balancing act and so far doing nothing was winning.

"Is she related to that Kristopher Lette?" Kurt asked, cocking his head as he squinted at the screen.

Sun rays bounced off the screen at odd angles. I tipped the screen forward slightly to combat the glare.

"None of the six Kristopher Lette's have rap sheets so I haven't got a lot to go on. One moment ..."

I input Rosanne Lette's details. Up popped her driver's license. I compared her address to each Kristopher. None matched. So if she was related they probably weren't living together.

"Bit hard to tell," Kurt said, sliding his sunglasses back over his eyes. "We'll run the names through a few more databases later."

"We need to look at employment records for the Lette who works for the power company," I said.

"Police spoke to him?"

"Yes, but I want to do our own investigating." Something felt off. "Doesn't hurt to double-check."

"Something bothering you, Conway?"

"You haven't heard from Noel Gerrard, have you?"

"No, not since the Navy Yard incident. Problem?"

"His mom called me. She's worried, she hasn't heard

from him in six weeks."

"Tried calling him yourself?"

"Not yet, but I will." I shut down the laptop. "I'm sure it's nothing. Gerrard is capable of taking care of himself."

And everyone else in his immediate vicinity.

Late afternoon had run into early evening. My eyes drifted to my watch before I climbed out of the car.

"Somewhere you'd rather be?" He shut his door and joined me on the pavement outside another house flying crime scene tape.

I nodded. Police cars were parked both sides of the street. Officers milled around the front of one house. Too many people on scene. Time to weed out the unnecessary people.

"What's wrong with this picture?" I said to Kurt as we walked side-by-side up the path to the house.

"I'm on it," he replied and changed trajectory. I carried on and spoke to a group of police officers about twenty feet from the door.

"I'm Agent Conway. Who is controlling this scene?"

They looked at each other. One pointed to a uniformed police officer near Kurt, who was writing in a notebook. "Officer Mendez."

"And you four are here why?"

"We were told to wait, ma'am," the youngest of the quartet said.

"Wait's over, officers. Let Mendez know you're leaving the scene. How many cops are inside?"

"One. She's just inside the door." He pointed at the

house. "It's Mendez's partner, Christy Reid."

"Medical personnel?"

He shook his head. "No, ma'am."

"Anything you need to tell me? Y'all traipse through the crime scene?" I passed my notebook and pen to the cop nearest me. "Write your details and pass it on."

The young cop answered my question, "No, ma'am. We've been out here the whole time."

Good.

Kurt appeared on my right. "We're good. Mendez and his partner will stay."

"This group is on their way," I replied, shooing the police officers toward Mendez.

"Back to our previous topic," Kurt said, guiding me up the path with a hand in the small of my back. "You need to be at that dinner tonight."

"I should be but it's not a need exactly."

Pre-wedding. Whole family. Last minute details. Time for us all to touch base before the big event. My fingers massaged the back of my neck for a moment, working some of the tightness from my muscles.

"Go, we'll take this."

I checked the time again. We stopped walking.

"It's early yet. Let's just see what this crime scene is like first?"

"Conway ..."

"I've got a crime scene to investigate, a press conference to organize and bodies piling up. Now's not a good time."

"It's never going to be a good time. You can go, we'll handle it from here." Kurt winked at me, his voice remained good-natured, bordering on amused. "Slacken those reins a bit, Conway. As much as we love having you with us, we are capable."

"I can't just go, this case is ramping up and we need to get in front of it before the Unsub kills anyone else."

"We can handle it, Conway."

"I know you can. I can't. I can't walk out on these women."

Kurt regarded me for a moment before accepting my response. Could I go eat, drink, and socialize knowing more women would die? Not without guilt. Mitch wasn't marrying someone who had a nine-to-five and he knew I couldn't walk away.

Sam appeared next to me. "Chicky Babe."

A smile flashed in his direction. "Come on, boys," I said with a hint of Mae West. "Let's go see what we have."

We filed up the path to the house. Kurt swung open the door and was greeted by a police officer who asked for ID.

"SSA Conway!" A female voice called from the street. I turned to see who it was. A reporter yelling for me and trying to dodge several police officers. Rosanne.

Great, just what I need.

Already I felt the Fourth Estate hounding me. Seeing her didn't make me want to set up the media conference in a hurry. A voice in my head reminded me I liked Rosanne. I grumbled back at the voice, Let's not get too giggly too quick. Like's an awful strong word.

Her appearance struck me as spooky. I fought the temptation to ask her what the fuck she was doing at my crime scene. Instead, I called out in a pleasant tone, "I'll talk to you soon. Need to get in here first. Wait for me?" It didn't kill me to be nice.

Imagine that?

"Sure. Which car is yours?"

I pointed to the first black Suburban. "Wait by the car."

Sam, Kurt, and Lee and I donned gloves and booties then entered the house, following the Fairfax PD officer to the bathroom. Once again the victim was in the shower.

I turned to the police officer. "You're Officer Reid? Mendez's partner?"

She nodded. "Yes, ma'am."

"Officer Reid, tell me what you know?" I said.

"This is Karen Frederick. She is twenty-seven and a teacher."

"Who called it in?"

"The victim's friend. She came by to pick her up for yoga."

"And?"

She consulted her notebook and a witness statement. "Jessica Shannon knocked at forty-thirty, there was no answer. She texted the victim. No response. She rang the victim's landline. No response ..."

Why didn't the friend assume she was out?

" ...Her car was in the driveway. Jessica walked around the house and heard the shower running. She waited twenty minutes. The shower kept running. After half an hour she called the police, fearing her friend had fallen and injured herself."

"First on the scene?"

"Me and Mendez, ma'am."

"And you found?"

"Karen Frederick dead in the shower."

She consulted the notebook again. "Access through a rear window. An upturned garbage can was under the window."

"Was the window forced?"

"No. I think it was already open."

"Anything else?"

"Karen didn't go to work today. She was home, sick."

"Thank you." I passed her my card. "Email your report directly to me, please."

She nodded and moved away.

I rested on the doorjamb and spoke to Kurt. "Guesstimate on the time of death?"

"Maybe this morning. Reason?"

"So far all the deaths have been morning and discovered in the morning. One a day. If Karen was killed this morning, then the Unsub has escalated the hell out of his killing. Two in one morning?"

"The victimology is intriguing me," Kurt said.

Something niggled in my brain. Karen was in the shower. Karen was unwell. Or was she unwell? What if she was killed while getting ready for work and the killer called in? If she was sick, wouldn't she tell her friend and cancel yoga?

"I'll be right back." I hurried after Reid. "Hey, wait up. Got a question for you."

She spun on her heels and stepped toward me as I ran down the hallway.

"Yes, ma'am."

"Who called her place of employment and said she was ill?"

She flipped open her notebook again, read something, and then looked up at me.

"She texted her team leader."

"Thanks." I turned to go back to Kurt.

"You don't think she did?" Reid asked.

"I don't know if she did or didn't. I think it's unwise to assume she did until we know for sure. Did you find her phone?"

She shook her head. "What makes you think she didn't send a text herself?"

"I don't know. I might be wrong."

Lee strode toward me and heard my comment. He grinned. "Might be wrong. Officer, if Agent Conway thinks something is amiss, it usually is." He touched my arm. "A word, Agent."

"Thanks, Officer Reid."

Lee and I went back to the bathroom. "Problem?" I asked.

"Kurt found the note," Lee said, passing me an evidence bag that I hadn't even noticed he was holding.

I read the words aloud through the plastic, "'I watched you fade away.'"

Sick bastard.

I passed it back and wrote the line in my notebook underneath the others. And underneath the memorial from the newspaper. The newspaper contained more lines, an entire stanza.

"Okay, so far we have," I said rocking my right heel, "'Everything that came before, lies fragmented on the floor. Don't take it personally. It wasn't easy. I broke when you looked at me.'" I paused for a second. "Those lines came from crime scenes. Then we have the rest of what I believe is that stanza, and we got that from The Washington Post today. It goes like this ... 'Life cracked wide open. Everything that came before. Spilled over the screen. Seeped into the keyboard. Shattered across the desk. Laughter replaced it all.'" I stopped and let the words sink in. "And now we have ... 'I watched you fade away.'"

No one said anything for what felt like an eternity.

"Sounds like the poem is going to get longer, Chicky Babe," Sam said.

His words rasped like a bastard file on my spine.

"I thought he was writing the poem as he killed, but he isn't," I said. "The newspaper had more and the memorial was in today's paper. Terri was killed today and her line featured in the stanza." The words contorted and finally lined up again. "I think the line we found here is part of a new stanza."

"Terri was killed this morning and her name was in the paper, why wasn't Karen's?" Sam asked.

"I don't know," I said. But it ramped up my curiosity. "And who was the anonymous tipster? We would've got a call anyway once police were on scene."

Images flashed before my eyes. I couldn't distinguish clear boundaries to say how many images there were. They blurred then sharpened. Faces. Dead women. Then the male I'd seen through Terri and Serena's eyes. Finally a glimpse of a different face.

I held my hand out to Lee; as if knowing my thoughts, he dropped the evidence bag into my outstretched hand. I looked at it again. Satisfied the handwriting matched the others, I gave it back.

"I need a few minutes with Karen," I said.

Lee and Sam moved out the door. Kurt stayed. "Do what you do, Conway, I'm just here to observe." He moved back to the doorway.

I dropped to one knee near Karen's head and said, "I'm Ellie. I'm here to help."

An exotic scent emanated from the body, its warmth filling me. I knew that scent. I breathed deeply letting the overall aroma reach deep into my nose, allowing my mind to associate the components with names. Neroli, citrus, tobacco, pepper, bergamot and lavender. Dolce & Gabbana Pour Femme? My eyes were drawn to the shower caddy. Shampoos, conditioners, body washes. Nothing appeared missing. Nothing matched the scent I could smell.

Maybe it didn't come from her but from the Unsub.

I breathed the scent again. Cedar. Dolce & Gabbana Pour Homme. It wasn't from her. And I hadn't smelled it at any other scene.

"Karen, show me who did this?" I said in her ear.

Her head turned to me. A spark ignited in her cloudy eyes as her hand reached up and pointed to the mirror. I clambered to my feet. From where I stood, I could see the doorway and Kurt's reflection in the mirror. Steam filled the room, edging across the mirrored surface, leaving a gap in the middle that framed a face. It wasn't Kurt. Brown eyes, shaved head, strong jaw. His slightly tanned face lined with age and wear. The mirror fogged over and he was gone. I sank down next to Karen, thanked her and promised to find the man responsible.

Kurt stepped forward when I finally stood up.

"From the outside there isn't a lot to see, but I have a feeling you have something to tell us ..."

"Different Unsub," I said. "This guy is older than the other one. Fifty to fifty-five. He has a shaved head, brown eyes, strong jaw and wears Dolce & Gabbana Pour Homme."

"We haven't released details to the media so it's a bit early for a copycat killing," Sam said from behind Kurt.

"It's not a copycat. There are two Unsubs. They're working together," I replied, surprised by my own confidence.

Pain behind my eye started up. It felt like a needle being pushed into my brain. The sudden onset of pain re-minded me I hadn't slept in two days or eaten since yes-terday. Things were on the way to getting pretty damn ugly unless I corrected one of those things.

"Good work, Conway. Scary but good," Kurt replied. "Now we just have to find him and prove the theory."

My phone rang showing Sandra's image on the screen. I touched the speaker icon. "You're on speaker. What do you have, Sandra?"

"The ad was placed right before the deadline last night. They won't divulge who placed the ad but say the person paid by credit card."

I liked those words. "Credit card. Get a warrant, San-dra. You've got the case number. I want that credit card information."

"I'm on it! Judge Hartwell is on standby."

"Good work."

Sandra hung up. I knew I was smiling. The use of a credit card might just be the break we needed.

"Haven't seen a smile like that in a few days," Lee said, nudging my arm.

"I'd like to get back to the office and start piecing to-gether what we know before something else happens," I said. "And Sandra might have information for us soon."

The three of them shook their heads at me.

"Seems you're supposed to be at a pretty important dinner tonight and we can do this," Lee said.

"Kurt?" I said, hoping he'd back me up.

Surely he knew there could be an answer in my head

just waiting to be discovered.

"Take a couple of hours, Conway. We'll keep the camp-fire burning."

A couple of hours? The pain behind my eye sharpened, requiring effort not to press my hand to my eye. I could do a couple of hours.

All night? No.

I checked my watch. I could make it to dinner. Under lights. Is roast lamb an emergency? It would be without mint sauce.

"If I say yes—"

"You'll make your fiancé a happy man."

"I'm out of here. I'll catch up with you all in about three hours. Have something for me?"

"Deal." He turned me around and pointed me to the door. "Go!"

I dragged my phone from my pocket calling Mitch as I ran to my car. "I'm on my way!"

"See you soon."

Rosanne stood by the car.

Damn.

"Hey, can we do this later?" I said, unlocking the car and clambering into the driver's seat.

She looked in the open door. "You in a hurry?"

"Yeah."

"Did I miss a briefing?"

"No, I haven't had time. It'll happen."

"You look exhausted. Long hours on this case?"

Choosing to ignore both her comment and question, I

said, "I promise I'll give you as much as I can later tonight."

She looked skeptical. Then conceded. "Okay."

Good, because I wasn't about to argue. Kristopher Lette slithered to the fore of my mind. I took advantage of the opportunity in front of me.

"Does your son work for a power company?" I asked, hoping it sounded casual.

Her face froze for a few seconds then her expression switched to neutral.

Odd.

"No," she replied.

My gut said yes. I've long since believed my gut over people. "I'll call you when I'm back at the office."

Rosanne waved, I pulled my door closed. It was half an hour to Mitch's folks' place in traffic. Twenty minutes tops under lights. I hit the switch on the dash and pulled out.

Screw it. Sometimes roast lamb is an emergency.

Chapter Thirteen
It's My Life

My dad and brother's cars were on the road, I pulled into the driveway behind Mitch's car.

With a quick check in the rearview mirror, I deemed myself passable. I took a moment and turned off the ringer on my phone before jumping out of the car. The front door opened. Mitch stepped onto the porch. Grinning. My heart thumped wildly.

"You're dressed," I said, allowing disappointment to coat my words. "Such a shame."

"Thought pants were a good thing for the office and dinner with the folks," Mitch replied as he waited for me to walk up the porch steps. "You made good time."

"Amazing what can be achieved under lights."

He laughed. "Seriously?"

Mitch hugged me.

"Uh huh. I've got a few hours off, then I'm going back to work."

"Tonight?" A twinge of disappointment stuck in his voice.

"Yes, sorry."

"Tell me you're not going back to work next Saturday evening."

"I'm not going back to work next Saturday evening. If this case isn't done by then, the boys are on their own."

With one last squeeze, he let me go. We walked into

the house hand-in-hand. My phone vibrated audibly in my pocket before we made it to the dining room. I ignored it.

The whole family had waited for me so we could eat together. I said hello to everyone and slid into the chair Joan pointed to. Mitch would sit next to me. Nice.

Aidan and Holly were at the other end of the table with baby Lucy. She chortled happily in the highchair next to Holly. Dad, Alan, and Mitch's brother, Chris, were talking. Mac's Dad, Bob, and Chris's wife, Susan, were deep in conversation. I watched and listened. Family noises. Happy sounds. Joan floated in and out of the kitchen placing dishes on the table. She refused assistance. Mitch helped anyway. They chatted and laughed. Mitch filled my glass with white wine and set a glass of water next to it.

"Thank you," I whispered, not wanting to break the spell.

"You okay?" Mitch spoke softly in my ear.

"Yes. Just enjoying this." I smiled and stole a quick kiss.

Dad caught my eye and smiled.

Before long everyone was seated and passing bowls and platters around the table. Filling plates. Talking. Baby Lucy squawked indignantly a few times as things were passed around her. Her little hands opened and closed trying to grab everything that came into view. Guess she didn't want to be left out. Holly reached down. A plush chicken toy appeared in her hand. She plopped it on the highchair tray. The baby considered the toy for a moment before throwing it to the floor. Even I knew the toy chicken wasn't what she wanted.

My phone vibrated again. I sipped my wine and ignored the insistent buzzing in my pocket.

Mitch heard it. "Do you need to check that?"

"Nope. It can wait. Dinner. Family. Us. Not work."

Lucy wailed. Holly lifted her from the highchair and rocked her. A few minutes later Aidan took the wailing bundle and let Holly eat.

Mitch nudged me. "Noisy but very cute."

"Yes." I chewed the tender roast lamb and watched Aidan with his daughter. He looked at me, an eyebrow raised.

"Will you take her for a few minutes, Ellie?"

Yay, we were playing pass the parcel with the baby.

Mitch intervened before I said something inappropriate. "Give her here, let Ellie eat."

Aidan dropped Lucy into Mitch's outstretched arms.

"What's all the fuss, little lady," he said, adjusting his hold on her and sitting her down on his lap.

Lucy looked up at him, blue eyes wide. A gummy smile spread across her face.

I laughed. "Uncle Mitch's magic lap."

"Works on Special Agents too," he replied with a wicked smile.

I moved my head closer to his and said. "We sit in your lap for completely different reasons."

Mitch laughed.

My phone buzzed like a trapped blowfly.

I carried on eating.

The conversation around the table flowed with ease. Everyone had comments regarding the upcoming wedding. By the time dessert appeared, all the plans were sorted. Everyone knew what they were doing on the big day. Joan produced a satin horseshoe with ribbons and lace and gave it to Holly. I pretended not to see. It was good luck to give the bride a horseshoe after the ceremony. Lucy would give it to me.

They'd need good luck. I'd seen the child in action. There was no getting them out of her vice-like grip once she had a good hold.

The doorbell rang. Alan rose from his chair but Dad was quicker. He pressed Alan's shoulder.

"I'll get it, Alan."

Alan didn't argue. He sat down and carried on his conversation with Aidan. Curious. I watched Dad leave the room. The hum of conversation started up again. I found myself with one ear on the table conversation and the other listening for Dad in the hallway.

Lucy snatched Mitch's fork. He couldn't get it out of her chubby little fingers and was in danger of losing an eye.

Joan swooped in and switched the fork for a cookie and hurried out of sight with it before Lucy realized what happened. Clever.

Voices in the hallway paused by the dining room door. I listened. Dad and a woman continued talking in hushed tones outside the closed door.

A woman? I wasn't sure if her voice sounded familiar or not.

"What's the matter?" Mitch asked, touching my elbow with his.

"Visitor ..." I replied.

"Are you aware you have your hand on your weapon," he said, his voice low and barely audible.

I glanced at him and then at my right hand. Yep. It was on my weapon. I picked up my glass of water instead. "Better?"

"Yes," Mitch replied. "Why are you jumpy?"

I moved my head a fraction from side to side. "Work. That's all."

My eyes focused on the door as I heard the handle move. The door opened and I knew the voice that drifted on the sudden breeze.

"Rosanne," I whispered. "What the hell ...?"

Mitch nudged me. "Who?"

"A journalist I know."

Dad ushered her into the room, his hand protectively in the small of her back.

"Looks like your dad knows her too," Mitch replied.

The cold dread was back. Was she the reason for the spring in his step, secret dinners and the strange smile that had resided on his lips in recent weeks? My mind scrolled back. It wasn't weeks. It was months.

Holy crap. Dad had a secret life.

Really?

I stood up. "Rosanne, you know I was going to call once I was back at the office," I said, hoping there was lightness in my voice.

Dad intervened. "Rosanne isn't here to talk work, Ellie. She's my guest."

I sank into my chair, wrapped my hands around the glass of wine and took a big sip. Regret was instantaneous. I switched to water.

So it was her. The mystery lady. She was a minimum of fifteen years younger than dad. Aidan hadn't moved but was leaning forward on his elbows, watching.

My phone rang and this time, I knew I had to answer it.

"Conway," I said into the phone.

"Are you done?"

"Yeah."

"I'm picking you up," Kurt replied.

"Something happened?"

"Easier if we talk in person. Wait for me out front?" I pressed the end call icon and sat my phone on the table.

Mitch slipped his arm around my shoulders. "Work?"

"Yep. Kurt is picking me up. Can we have a few moments?"

He nodded. "Come on."

Mitch passed Lucy to his mom then took my hand. We excused ourselves. Mitch led the way to the conservatory.

"You're going to be gone a while aren't you?" he said, pulling me into his arms.

"Could be. This case is not going well ... we need to get

a profile and some solid leads."

"Roz?"

"See what you can find out?" A thought surfaced. "Find out if she has a son and what his name is and if he has a job."

"That's a pretty specific list, El."

Yeah, it was. "See what you can find out during the rest of the evening, please?"

He kissed the top of my head. "I'll take notes." Mitch's voice ruffled my hair. "You think it's a coincidence that he's seeing her?"

"No. But I hope it is. I really do."

I stood wrapped in Mitch's arms for a few minutes, enjoying the scent of his skin and his beating heart.

Chapter Fourteen
Bed of Roses

I moved my car out onto the road so I wasn't blocking Mitch and noticed a piece of paper under the wiper blade. I took the paper and unfolded it as I pressed the button on my keychain and locked my car. Expecting a flyer of some sort, the handwritten contents gave me pause.

I read and re-read the note in my hand in the vague light from the street lamp overhead. Bone-chilling cold trickled into my being. Leaning on my car, I read the joke again.

An old blind guy wanders into an all-girl biker bar by mistake. He finds his way to a bar stool and orders a shot of Jack Daniels.

After sitting there for a while, he yells to the bartender, "Hey, you wanna hear a blonde joke?"

The whole bar immediately falls absolutely silent. In a very deep, husky voice, the woman next to him says,

"Before you tell that joke, Cowboy, I think it is only fair, given that you are blind, that you should know five things.

1. The bartender is a blonde girl with a baseball bat.

2. The bouncer is a blonde girl with a 'Billy Club'.

3. I'm a six-foot tall, 175-pound blonde woman with a black belt in karate.

4. The woman sitting next to me is blonde and a pro-

fessional weightlifter.

5. The lady to your right is blonde and a professional wrestler.

Now, think about it seriously, Cowboy ... Do you still wanna tell that blonde joke?"

The old guy thinks for a second, shakes his head and mutters, "No, not if I'm gonna have to explain it five times."

Five blonde women. I really don't believe in coincidence. We had five blonde victims. I pulled up a picture of one of the crime scene notes on my phone. A sigh of relief escaped when I realized the handwriting didn't match. The relief was short-lived.

If one of the Unsubs didn't place the note on my windscreen, then who did? And why? Who came into the house after me?

I stuffed the piece of paper into my bag.

Rosanne Lette.

Who knew where I was?

Delta A and apparently Rosanne Lette.

Shutting down that thought process, I walked past Aidan's car in the rapidly dimming light and saw his my family stickers in the back window. I muttered unflattering comments to myself. Those stickers were stupid, right up there with having your kids' school on a bumper sticker or stickers on the car that indicated where you parked or worked. People make it too easy for stalkers. What did Aidan's car tell me? I checked it out while I waited for Kurt.

Adding up all the stickers I came up with a profile. He was married to a woman who liked to read, they had a female baby and a cat. No guard dog to worry about there. He worked in the insurance industry and parked at Vienna Metro. He liked to visit one particular bookstore or maybe his wife worked there and they were affiliated with The Butterfly Foundation. All that from a few stickers.

Stickers.

Why not announce everything about ourselves on our vehicles and let criminals come knock on the door?

I felt an urge to add an NRA sticker to his bumper. Maybe that would tip the odds in his favor.

Stickers. My mind circled the word several times. Our victims had to have something in common, something we hadn't found yet. The Unsub wasn't killing them randomly.

Make that Unsubs. There was something else behind this. What?

Kurt pulled up and wound down the window. "You want to take your car?"

"Nah. I moved it out of everyone's way. I'll pick it up when I get back." I climbed into Kurt's car and fastened my seatbelt. I should've taken my car so I could escape as required but something a bit out of whack told me driving wasn't smart. "You decided to pick me up why?"

"Good dinner?"

"Yep."

Small talk?

"Kurt, what's up?"

"The notes. There's a chance they're placed to engage Delta."

"Yeah?" There had to be more to it than that, surely. "I've already gone there."

"They could also be directed at you."

"Is this a team collaborative thought?"

"Yes."

Great.

"I can take care of myself. Notes at crime scenes aren't entirely foreign to me."

"Just be a bit careful, Conway. This could escalate."

I thought about mentioning Rosanne and changed my mind.

"What?" Kurt asked.

"What, what?" I replied settling in for the drive.

"You're thinking about something. Share, Conway. Many minds lighten the load and all that ..."

"I don't think that's a saying," I replied, feeling a frown form and trying to turn it into a smile.

"You know what I mean ... spill it." Kurt's hands gripped the steering wheel a little tighter.

"Stickers," I said.

That wasn't what he expected at all. I smiled as Kurt tried to wrap his head around my answer. He certainly didn't relax his grip. That was when I heard Mitch in my head telling me to stop playing with Kurt. My laughter hit the windshield and slid down to melt on the dash.

"Something funny, Conway?" Kurt glanced at me, his

hands still tight.

"Yeah," I replied and didn't elaborate. Mitch told me off again. More laughter hit the windshield then pooled on the dash.

"Stickers are amusing?"

"No stickers are dangerous."

Without anything else being said he pulled over and stopped. Kurt twisted in his seat and looked at me. Mitch was in my head telling me to stop before Kurt sent me for another MRI.

"What's with the stickers?" To his credit, he managed to contain himself and use his reserved-for-patients voice.

He's a doctor, shouldn't be hard. I knew I often made it hard.

Yeah, I can stop anytime.

"I was looking at the back of Aidan's car. He has those ridiculous family stickers ... and some other stickers. From the stickers, I could create a profile and use that to find him, Holly and baby Lucy."

"Okay. People depicted as stick figures are dangerous?"

"Precisely."

"Where's this going?"

"To our victims." Questions rattled off my tongue. "Have we seen their cars? Do they have stickers? Are any of the sticker's things they do or have in common?"

"Got it. I think. We'll revisit every scene in the morning and check out their cars."

"Now, Kurt."

"Morning, Conway."

"Mornings tend to bring fresh crime scenes ..."

He couldn't argue with that. Made sense to check cars now before the pressure of the morning hit.

"Office first?"

"No need."

Happy, I smiled. Kurt drove. Mitch growled a little in my head but he was pretty happy too. Silence enveloped the car shutting out the world.

Kurt glanced in the rearview mirror a few more times than usual. Twice he adjusted the angle of the mirror and complained about the car behind trying to blind him with high beams.

"This person is either a total jerk or he's oblivious to the fact he's driving with his headlights on full," Kurt said, pulling over and letting the idiot pass.

I wrote the tag number down because that's what I do. Kurt pulled back into the stream of traffic while I made a call. "Comms. QV. Virginia plates. YHD six five four seven. Yankee Hotel Delta six five four seven."

"Wait one, Agent."

Headlights filled the car. Kurt adjusted the rearview mirror again.

"Another one. What is it with people tonight?" he said.

Comms came back to me. "Yankee Hotel Delta six five four seven, black Ford Taurus, reported stolen by the owner, Todd Black, two weeks ago from Richmond."

"Thank you." I hung up. "The first car, Kurt. Wasn't a

black Taurus, was it?"

"Nope. It was an SUV of some sort."

Headlights lit the interior again.

"Fucking idiot," Kurt said. "Get off my ass."

Whoa. Uncharacteristic use of foul language from Kurt.

He took the next left. The car stayed with us. Another left. Followed by a sharp right. My hand grasped the radio from the cradle on the dash ready to call comms. Our car lurched around another left corner. Headlights followed.

"What is the idiot's problem?"

"No idea but he's playing with fire."

I would've been tempted to slam on the brakes and let the little jerk freak out. Kurt wasn't so reckless.

"Can you see the license plate?"

"No, they're too close. All I can see is lights."

"I think they know we're feds and the driver wants to be stopped." Wouldn't be the first time. Could be someone needing help. "Our black Suburbans and federal plates aren't exactly incognito."

"Just in case ..." I depressed the button on the side of the radio in my hand. "Comms, this is SSA Conway. Request intercept. We are ..." I searched the dark for something that told me where we were. Nothing.

"About to be westbound on Arlington Boulevard from Sleepy Hollow." Kurt paused. "Beechwood Lane."

I relayed the information to comms and they told me they'd tap into our GPS and send local police to intercept the car following us.

We hit Arlington Boulevard with the car still up our tailpipe. Half a mile later, sirens wailed and flashing lights pulled over the car behind us. We pulled off the road ahead of them and waited. Time ticked by. We waited. A cop approached our car. Kurt zapped his window down and showed his badge.

"Did the driver say why he was following us?"

"No, sir, but he's driving a stolen car."

"I believe there was another car involved," I said, giving the officer the information on the other car.

"That puts a dark spin on things, Agent," the officer said, writing the information down. "We've arrested the driver ... he's calling himself Danny Wills."

"Calling himself Danny Wills or he is Danny Wills?" Kurt asked.

"We got a white male in his early twenties saying he's Danny Wills and the only Danny Wills I've found in the system is an elderly black male."

"Fascinating," I said. "I think I want to have a chat with Danny." I flung my door open and joined the police officer. "Lead the way."

Kurt stepped up beside me. Didn't think he'd want to sit this out.

Another police officer swung open the back passenger door to the squad car, revealing a young man in handcuffs.

"Hi, you are?" I said as he looked up at me.

"Danny Wills."

"Do you know who I am?"

He averted his eyes. I took that as a maybe.

"No."

"Try again, Mr. Wills, we're not growing mushrooms so don't require manure."

He fixed his gaze on the back of the seat in front of him. Tiresome.

"Your buddy, who passed us earlier, will be picked up. Maybe he'll be chatty."

"I was going home, on my own," Wills replied.

"In a stolen car," I said. "Pretty unfortunate that two stolen cars drew our attention and that you tailgated a federal car, wouldn't you say?"

There was an almost imperceptible lift at the corner of his mouth.

A radio crackled. The police officer who'd been standing nearby turned to us. "We have the first car, the driver is in custody."

"Awesome."

Sudden movement across the roof of the squad car diverted my attention. Christopher Chance leaned over the car from the other side.

"Fancy meeting you out here," he said with a lopsided grin.

"Chance ... what do you know?"

"Don't let this guy go. He's part of something and he wants out of it. You were right, El, he knows you're feds."

"Is he involved in the case I'm working on?"

"Yes and no. He knows something but he doesn't know

he knows."

I rolled my eyes. "Never easy, Chance, is it?"

Chance laughed and shrugged. "He saw something, Ellie, something that will help you. Don't let him go."

"Thanks, Chance," I said.

He winked and walked away.

Kurt motioned me to follow him out of earshot. "What do you see?"

"What makes you think I saw something?"

Kurt sighed. "If you didn't see something then we're going to talk about what the hell that was back there ..."

This wasn't the first time I wondered what happened outwardly when I had my little chats with Chance. "What'd it look like?"

"It looked like it always does. Like you've zoned out. And that's not what happened, is it?"

I shook my head. "Chance happened. He said Wills knows something about our case but he doesn't know he knows. He said not to let him go."

Kurt's head shook. "We can hold him – stolen cars."

"I know." I just didn't know what questions to ask to get the information we needed from him, yet.

"I'll talk to the cop, let's have both drivers escorted to our office. They can wait for us there," Kurt said.

Chapter Fifteen

Everybody's broken

Sandra had left a file on my desk. I opened it to find everything the newspaper had on the person who placed the memorial. Credit card details included.

I read all the papers in the file twice. Including the warrant.

The credit card belonged to Serena Sorenson. That was a nice touch. The ad was phoned in ten minutes before the cut-off time on Tuesday evening. Serena was already dead when the ad was placed.

I was pretty sure it was still Wednesday. I checked the clock on the wall. So the ad was placed last night. The person who took the call said the caller was female. I guessed a male using Serena's card would've raised some suspicion.

That spun my brain out a bit. Confirmation that a woman was involved in one aspect of this case did not thrill me. No good muttering at Kurt about keeping an open mind if mine is closed to the possibility.

The night felt long. The two car thieves were in interview rooms and I wasn't in a hurry to talk to either of them. I needed something. An idea of how to proceed with the interviews. Direction. Nothing surfaced. The best thing for me to do was to collate all the information I'd taken from the stickers on the victims' cars and worry about the car thieves later. They'd keep, for a bit.

I reached for the phone and called Kurt. "How long can we hold those guys from tonight?" I said without bothering to announce myself.

"Twenty-four hours then we have to charge them with something."

Grand larceny was a no brainer. Motor vehicle theft laws in Virginia meant we could charge them both with grand larceny. There was a chance they were stealing to order; could be bigger fish to fry there.

"Okay. We hold them as long as we can and then charge them with grand larceny, might be worth getting police to investigate. Might be a car theft ring – if it turns out it crosses state lines then we'll pass it on to another team here."

"Good idea. I'll get hold of Fairfax Police Department."

"Thanks. I'll be in touch."

"You need to go home, Conway. This can wait until morning. Lee, Sam, and I can handle the car theft."

I was pretty sure they could, except Chance told me Wills knew something about our case. That meant I needed to ask the questions.

"Hey, did you see the information from Sandra?"

"Yeah. The person who took the call thought it was a female placing the ad."

"Sounds like wriggly things falling out of a can ..."

"Maybe we should bait a hook with those worms and go fishing."

"Not a bad idea."

"Conway, go home. This can all wait until morning."

I imagined Kurt's mouth set into a grim line. Yeah ... I really don't think it can.

"You should be home too." Two can play at that game.

"Don't be late," Kurt replied, resignation heavy in his voice. "You have a fiancé waiting for you."

"And you have a partner and child at home ..."

He hung up.

It was already late. I had a feeling it would be early morning before I saw Mitch.

The cars had netted an array of stickers and much information. I sat at my desk and sorted everything into lists. It didn't help. I got up and walked to the far wall. Time to use my whiteboard wall. What a brilliant invention. Magnets and pens at the ready, I positioned photos of the victims in a timeline. Under each picture, I added the information from each car. Why was I so sure there was a link?

Because social media didn't provide enough overlap.

Because my gut said they weren't chosen at random and confirmed by the memorial notice. The Unsub had already planned to kill Terri before placing the notice.

With everything on the board, I started drawing lines.

What did I know? Not enough. I moved Violet Cramer to the side. Yes, I believed she was the first but she wasn't in Fairfax County. My concentration centered on the four Fairfax women, there had to be something to connect them to the Unsub or Unsubs.

They were all government employees of some sort. They were all blonde, blue-eyed, and athletic. They didn't participate in at-risk behaviors. They all had gym memberships but none went to the same gym. Two were linked to Matthew Collins. Three were registered as Republicans with the Virginia Department of Elections.

I flicked to the notes about Violet. No mention of any political affiliations and her voter registration was nonpartisan. My eyes hit the clocks on the wall above the door.

Screw it.

Midnight had disappeared into the wee small hours.

I reached for the phone and a piece of paper with the cell phone number of the cop I'd spoken to in Winchester. My mind mulled over the Republican thing as I waited. Three were Republicans.

That might be something.

A sleepy voice resounded in my ear. "Johnno Gliddon."

"It's Ellie Conway. I have a question about Violet Cramer."

"You have any idea what time it is, Agent?" He sounded wide awake now.

"Yep." I attempted to raise sympathy for the wake-up call. "Sorry, this case is getting out of hand. We're not going anywhere fast."

He sighed. "What's your question?"

"Was she affiliated with any political party?"

Silence.

"Johnno?"

"Yeah, she was. I saw her at a Republican event."

"Thank you."

"Why?"

"I'm looking for links between the victims and politics could be one."

"How many victims so far?"

"Counting Violet Kramer, five."

"Good luck with it," Johnno said and hung up.

I needed luck. Four victims were Republican or leaning that way. So what about Terri Kane? She was another non-partisan registered voter as far as the electoral roll was concerned. I scrolled through recent contacts and until I found Sam's name. He answered quickly.

"Chicky Babe, how can I help?"

"You don't sleep?"

"Light sleeper."

"Terri Kane – did we get her day planner or laptop or anything?"

"Yes. Her day planner is on my desk inside an evidence box. The iPad and laptop are with the computer forensic team."

"Thanks."

"Anything I can help with?"

"Nope, not at the moment. I'll let you know when I have something."

At Sam's desk, I sat in his chair, opened the day planner, and scanned every page looking for something that suggested she'd been to a political rally, even for a doodle of an elephant or a donkey. Anything would do.

By the time I got to the last entry I knew her menstrual cycle, how often she had met certain friends for coffee and where, how many times she'd eaten out with colleagues, training courses she'd attended, and how many times she'd been to the doctor and dentist over the last few months. No mention of anything political.

"Okay, Terri Kane, where do your loyalties lie?"

Friends and coffee.

Her friends would know. I scrawled initials and first names on a sticky note from a pad on Sam's desk. At the back of the day planner, I found corresponding phone numbers for the names. Calling friends would have to wait until morning. I put the day planner back where I found it, gathered up the sticky notes and went to my office.

I stuck the notes under Terri's name and rested on the edge of my desk. Letting all the images conjured by the words on the board settle into a pattern.

Government jobs and political affiliations. Similar physical descriptions.

What more did I need? Was I making it harder than it should be?

I had links but they didn't feel substantial enough. The Unsub must've been stalking the women to be able to kill them in the shower and be in their homes ahead of time. I believed they were drugged. If it was with the missing sleeping pills from Jane's home, then they had to be administered in such a way that the women were unaware. No one would take sleeping pills voluntarily before work.

Toxicology.

I picked up the phone and called the lab. "SSA Ellie

Conway. Any chance you have tox results for me?"

"Case number?" grumbled a male voice down the line.

"Three-zero-six dash HQ dash six-five-zero-nine."

"How many names am I looking for, Agent?"

"Four. Coded with the following two letters per toxicology report; JD – Juliet Delta; SS – Sierra Sierra; TK – Tango Kilo; KF – Kilo Foxtrot."

"Checking for you now."

My fingers rapped on the edge of my desk. Waiting for the cranky voice to return.

"Agent. JD samples contained four milligrams of lorazepam."

Lorazepam was the prescription in her medicine cabinet. Four milligrams. I flipped through the file looking for the reference to the missing pills. The prescription was for thirty, two-milligram tablets.

"Two pills," I said, thinking aloud.

"That would depend on the dosage prescribed, Agent. There was also coffee in her stomach."

"Her prescription was for two two-milligram tablets," I replied. "Is that enough to render a slim five-feet-four-inch woman unconscious?"

"She would be drowsy and fall asleep. We're looking at a toxic but not lethal dose."

"Any other reports back?"

"SS. There was a higher amount present. Six milligrams of lorazepam and also coffee."

That made sense; Serena was taller and about twenty pounds heavier than Jane. "The rest?"

"Still running those screens. The only reason you have any so far is the three-zero-six classification," he said with a moan in his voice. "We'll let you know as soon as the results are in."

Guess he didn't like queue jumpers. Well, I don't like serial killers.

"Thanks." I hung up.

It was too early to say that the Unsub took the lorazepam from Jane's home and used them on both Jane and Serena. Then again I don't believe in coincidence. My gut writhed and that told me he did and that the toxicology screens from the next two victims would show more lorazepam. So how did he get the women to take the pills? Did he add crushed tablets to their coffee? If he took those pills, then there could be thirteen unaccounted for after drugging Jane and Serena. That's if Jane had taken them when prescribed. Otherwise, there could be fifteen outstanding.

Confirmation that they were drugged tallied with what I'd seen. It also told me something about the Unsub. For reasons as yet unknown, he wanted or needed compliant victims. I'd seen a man, so who was the woman who placed the notice? I set that aside for the time being and considered the drug aspect again.

Jane was lightweight. Two twenty-milligram tablets seemed like a high dose especially if she'd never had sleeping pills before. I made a note to ask Kurt if he found anything in her medical records and also why they were prescribed by a different doctor.

I stood up and stretched my arms over my head then let them drop and relaxed my shoulders. I still had no idea what I was going to ask the car thieves in the interview rooms. Mitch swam into view. Sleepy. He rolled over in bed, his arm reached across the expanse next him. His eyes flicked open and I heard him sigh.

I'd long since given up trying to understand how I could see him as I did. It was just part of us and our connection. My cell phone was in my hand before Mitch's image faded.

"I'm coming home," I said when I heard his voice.

"I'm at mine," he replied. "See you soon, babe."

Halfway down the stairs, I realized I didn't have my car.

Jeez.

I ran back up to our floor and grabbed keys for one of the unassigned Delta vehicles from Sandra's drawer.

Chapter Sixteen
Walking in Memphis

My phone rang at five in the morning. Mitch's arm snaked around my waist as I tried to extract myself from his bed.

"Not so fast," he said, kissing my neck.

"I have to go ..."

He wasn't fooled by my feigned resistance as my body responded to his touch.

Fifteen minutes later my phone rang again. Mitch rolled with me as I picked up the phone from the nightstand. Kurt.

"Crime scene, Conway. You want me to pick you up?"

"Nope, I got a fleet car. I'm at Mitch's, send me the address."

"Okay, meet you there in forty-five minutes."

I hung up and curled back into Mitch. A map arrived on my phone. Looking at the address, I knew I had half an hour before I had to leave.

"I'm gonna take a shower," I said, breathing in his scent.

Mitch nuzzled my neck. "I'll be there in a minute."

Refreshing water poured over me, energizing my tired body and mind. I reached for the shampoo and washed my hair. With my eyes closed, I rinsed the last of the foamy bubbles away just as hands slipped around my waist.

My heart rate climbed. The heat from Mitch's body radiated against my back. Leaning against him, my skin tingled as his hands glided over my stomach. My back arched; warm kisses on my neck moved toward my shoulder. Reaching around, my fingers ran through his hair as I tipped my head back and pulled his mouth to mine. My body burned. His heart pounded strongly on my back. Turning to face him, he pressed me against the cool tile wall. Our staggered breathing synched perfectly as the intensity of the moment and our hearts drowned out the sound of the running water.

Mitch caught my hand at the front door. I turned to him. His kiss igniting a fire I knew would never go out.

"Go easy out there today, El," Mitch said, looking deep into my eyes. "You sure you're okay?"

I'm not at all sure and that isn't something I want to get into just yet.

"It's a shitty case, Mitch. I'll be glad when it's over."

"There's nothing more to it? This isn't something about the wedding?"

"God, no. I'm looking forward to our wedding, to us, to our life."

His head nodded just a little as kissed me again. Stoking the fire inside.

"Take it easy. We've got a honeymoon coming up ..."

Take it easy. Mitch's code for "don't get shot. A ripple

of amusement coursed through me: I hardly ever get shot. "I'll see you later. Have a good day." I ran across the yard and climbed into the black Suburban.

Twenty minutes later I pulled in behind another black Suburban and unclicked my seatbelt. "You're sure this is the same?" I said to Kurt, who waited on the curb as I opened my door.

"Yes," he replied. "Welcome to the fifth Fairfax crime scene."

"We got ourselves a couple of busy little Unsubs." I looked around. "Where are Sam and Lee?"

"Back at the office."

"Whose car?" I waved a finger at a government car I noticed in front of Kurt's car.

"Medical Examiner, I think," he said. "Let's go. Come on."

Impatient.

I bristled. "Don't rush me. It's not like the victim is going anywhere."

Kurt stopped, his right eyebrow rose. "What was that?"

"Don't rush me." I adjusted my tone; less snappy, more explanatory. "Let me get a feel for the area, please."

He held up his hands and took a step back. "In your own time, Conway." He barely disguised the patronizing edge to his voice. "You just let me know when you're ready to proceed."

"Yeah yeah."

Standing for a few minutes in the fresh morning air, I absorbed the energy from the street. It felt like a nice place to live. The neighbors would probably change their minds about that once they heard about the murder.

We gloved up, covered our shoes with disposable booties and entered the apartment. Kurt led the way to the bathroom. I was beginning to dislike bathrooms. The dislike caused a series of conflicting emotions. My love of showers and the disturbing images from shower deaths fought a determined battle in my head, the imagery conjured by the duel impossible to ignore. Mitch's smile as water flowed down his torso overlaid mutilated bodies slumped in showers. It felt like death might win. I breathed out hard and dislodged the images.

"Michelle Andrews, thirty years old," Kurt said.

My attention turned to the sight before me. Another sliced-up victim. The Unsub wasn't doing anything to alleviate my loathing of blades.

"Kurt—"

He leaped in before I could finish verbalizing my thought. "Something wrong?"

"Besides the obvious?" I waved a hand at Michelle's naked body.

"Yeah. Besides that."

"The wounds. There are a lot of stab wounds but how many on each body so far have been a potentially fatal wound?"

"There only needs to be one fatal wound, Conway."

"I know but how many were there that could've killed our victims?"

"My medical opinion without benefit of autopsy ...

one."

"And they were situated where?"

"Main arteries or main veins."

Messy. Very messy.

I let that percolate in my mind with everything else. I meandered through thoughts of torture and the order of the wounds. It didn't get me anywhere. The sooner I heard from the Medical Examiner, the better. Meanwhile, there was a body in front of me and she didn't deserve to be a crumpled shell at the bottom of her shower.

Michelle looked like all the others. Our killer definitely had a type. I knelt next to the shower door and Michelle's head. "You're not looking so good, Michelle." I paused. "I'm really sorry but I need you to help me out here. Who did this?"

Michelle's dead eyes stared at me. For a split second, I imagined her reanimating. I scrambled to my feet. Didn't pay to make it too easy for zombies.

"She not talking?" Kurt asked with a hint of humor.

"Something like that." I followed her eyes. Where was my little piece of paper? "Come on Michelle, where is it?"

I looked back at Michelle; her arm rose, index finger pointed. I followed the ghostly direction and spotted something poking out from a potted plant in the corner of the room. Reaching into the foliage, I extracted a small white piece of paper and unfolded it. I showed Kurt.

"'Seeped into the keyboard,'" he read, reading from the paper. "That's creepy."

"Yep." I bagged the paper. "Creepier because now we

know it's part of the first stanza of a poem."

"You sure that notice in the newspaper was the first stanza and not the entire poem, Conway?"

"I'm sure."

"And you'd know. You are the resident poet after all."

Yeah. Once upon a time that was me. There was a positive: the notes weren't addressed to me. I refocused on the crime scene.

"What's missing?"

Zombie reanimation or not, I needed to talk to Michelle. I sank down next to her, closed my eyes and let her show me her last moments of life. Standing under the hot running water, she reached for shampoo and washed her hair. She turned. With her back to the water, the last of the foamy bubbles swirled down the drain. Her eyes blurred. Red frothed around her feet. Her shrouded vision allowed one last impression to cement. A male hand clutching a knife. The blade stabbing into her torso. I jerked sideways, my eyes pinged open. Michelle's ghostly body dropped to the shower floor.

The non-fatal wounds came first.

"Conway?" Kurt touched my arm. "What happened?"

The hand and knife stayed with me. I moved the blade in my head, adjusting my field of vision, trying to build an image I could use to search our weapons database. What was I looking at? A hunting knife. I wished I could take a snapshot of the pictures in my head and just download them straight into Sentinel.

Mitch's voice filled all available space in my mind.

"Breathe, El. Just breathe."

The strength of my voice surprised me as I formed an internal reply and pressed send. "Don't worry, M. I got this."

"Conway?"

Kurt's hand rested on my forearm.

"I'm good. Two things … I saw the knife that did this to Michelle and shampoo."

"The knife?"

Kurt let go my arm, took his phone from his pocket and touched the screen. I heard an app open. He typed as I spoke.

"A fixed-blade hunting knife with a blood groove."

"Blade length?"

"Six inches maybe a bit more."

"Did you see any of the handle?"

"No, the Unsub's hand covered it. But the guard shone in the light."

Moments later he showed me some images on his phone. I scrolled through them, stopping at a Buck 119 Special fixed-blade hunting knife. I flipped back to the previous knife then settled on the 119.

"That one," I said handing his phone back.

"Good to know," Kurt replied. "I'll follow up on that knife when we get into the office. Now, what about shampoo?"

A sigh of relief tumbled from my lips. Every time I confessed to seeing or hearing something, there was the potential for Kurt to go all Doctor Henderson on me and start throwing letters around like MRI or CT. Every time he didn't, it felt like I'd dodged a bullet.

With my face close to her head I inhaled a faint scent from Michelle's wet hair. Not much smell left but enough. Better still I knew I'd recognize it if I smelled it again. "Her shampoo is missing."

Kurt stepped over the body and took a look in the shower caddy. "There is shampoo here."

"Pass it."

He handed it over. I flipped the lid and inhaled the aroma. "Not this one. How many conditioners are there?"

"Two. One that matches the shampoo you are holding and another one."

I held out my hand. Kurt took the shampoo from me and handed me the conditioner. I opened the lid and took a whiff. "This is it." I smelled it again. "Yep, this is it. There was shampoo that matched this. That's the one she used." She didn't have time to condition before he stabbed her. I wondered if he would've taken the conditioner if she'd lived longer.

Kurt put the conditioner back in the caddy. "Add that to the list."

Trophies, but not from every scene?

"Five murder scenes but only two trophies?"

"Only two we know of," Kurt replied. "We don't know yet what else could be missing."

True. I gave that some thought as I left the room. Why not every scene?

Casting my mind back to Jane Daughtry, I conjured

the smell I'd noted on her body. Faint. Still recognizable. Similar to the shampoo smell on Michelle. Similar but not the same. The base notes were deep and rich. Had I smelled that anywhere else?

"Kurt?"

He looked at me. "Conway?"

"There is something significant about the smells of the body wash or gel at scene one and the shampoo at scene five."

"To?"

"The Unsub. I need to talk to someone about the base notes of the products. Also, check the other scenes."

He was still watching me and it spelled trouble for me.

"You okay, Conway?"

"Yeah, why?"

"Little paler than usual. Getting enough sleep?"

The question amused me but it shouldn't have. I shrugged. "Been a few late nights, I'm tired, shitty case, impending wedding. Enough?" I threw one more thing in for the hell of it. "There haven't been a lot of opportunities to run so far this week. Lack of fresh air?"

For a minute it looked like Kurt was moving on.

Then he wasn't.

"Not buying. I'm going to schedule a checkup for you."

"After we sort this, I'm all yours."

Well, right after I get back from my honeymoon. Let's not get too carried away.

"That in itself worries the hell out of me."

"Some vitamins and fresh air and I'll be all good. You'll

see."

I shoved my hands in my jacket pockets before my fingers crossed. My mind rolled over the smell of the shampoo and the body wash. There was something familiar about the base notes.

"What are you thinking?" Kurt asked.

"I need to see the earlier victims' bodies again." Not so much see, as smell. I needed to smell their skin. Not something I wanted to say aloud even in the context of the case. Too much honesty happening for my liking. Sooner or later the mountain of odd occurrences would trip Kurt's doctor reflex and I'd end up in the donut of doom having my brain scanned yet again.

"Trip to the morgue then. Now or later?"

"Later."

Kurt nodded. "We need to talk to the car thieves and I want to research that knife."

"Office then."

Chapter Seventeen

Flowers on the wall.

My contact list contained two phone numbers in for Noel Gerrard. I called the first number. Disconnected signal. Six rings into the second, it went to voicemail. I left a message telling Gerrard to call his mom and me, in that order, A-SAP. My next call was to Sean O'Hare.

"Hey, it's Ellie Conway, you heard anything from Noel Gerrard?"

"No, not for maybe two months."

"How was he when you heard from him last? His mental state?"

"He was fine. Usual Gerrard."

"Was he working on anything in particular?"

"He retired. Last I heard he was working on catching fish and drinking scotch."

"Did he say he was going anywhere?"

"What's this about, Ellie?"

"He's UA. No one, not even his mom, has heard from him in weeks."

"All I can tell you is that he was fine when I last heard from him. You called Gerrard?"

"Yeah, landline is disconnected and cell went to voicemail."

"I'll see what I can turn up."

"Thanks, Sean. I appreciate it. I'm kinda swamped with this case."

I replaced the receiver. If Gerrard didn't want to be found, it would be almost impossible to find him; that wasn't something I wanted to tell his mom. I pulled the top drawer of my desk open and rummaged through it, searching for what used to be in there. Cigarettes. Old habits die hard. Shoving the drawer closed I popped a mint from the container on my desk, stood up, and stretched. Time to gather the troops and get back to work on the case in front of me.

The bullpen hummed with conversations. A low drone rippled down the walls and undulated across the floor when I stepped into the busy room. Sam and Lee sat at their desks. Both looked over. I raised my eyebrows, held up two fingers then tapped my left wrist.

My office, two minutes.

The rippling low hum became a head-pounding pulse. I turned on my heels and left the area. Stepping into the quiet of my office calmed me. I grabbed a bottle of water from the fridge and sat at my desk.

Sticky notes with the names and phone numbers of Terri Kane's friends stared at me from the surface of my desk. No time like the present.

I called the first name, introduced myself and asked about political leanings. She didn't know. Not that close then. The second name did know. She and Terri attended a Republican rally last week. I thanked her and hung up.

Maybe there was something in the Republican thing. Did the Unsubs not like Republicans, or were rallies the hunting ground of choice? Something to look into. That didn't answer the question regarding the two-month gap between the first and second deaths, though.

Lifting the lid on my laptop woke the machine from its slumber. Words flew from the screen, winding around my head and forcing their way to my eardrums. The Statler Brothers? I'd last heard "Flowers on the Wall" during the Hawk case. A shudder ran the full length of my body, leaving bitter cold in its wake. I let the lyrics take shape.

Mental illness. Solitude. Someone happy in their own world, unwilling or not wanting to join society. Maybe someone unable to join society? I found the song on YouTube and hit play.

Sam and Lee arrived just as the song started. I motioned them to sit down and we all listened to the song. I played it again.

"This is something," I said.

Sam nodded.

"You think the Unsub has been institutionalized?" Lee asked.

Wasn't just me hearing that aspect to the song then? Good to know.

"It's a possibility."

"Maybe between Winchester and here ..." I said. "And maybe not the first time."

"I'll look into recent releases from psych facilities and drug treatment centers," Lee replied. "See if we get a hit to the description you came up with."

I nodded. "Use the identikit image."

"Will do," Lee said.

"Being in a facility for mental illness or addiction could explain the two months between the Winchester death and the first Fairfax death," Sam said.

Lee and I agreed.

"I still think there are two Unsubs," I said, leaning into the back of my chair and stretching my legs under my desk.

Two Unsubs. And a woman.

"You saw two different men, yes?" Sam asked.

"I believe so. Also ..." I took a swig of water. "Things are missing from two crime scenes. I think body wash and shampoo."

"But not all," Sam said. "That could be why it's not all the scenes. One Unsub likes whatever scent it is."

"Yeah." That's where I was headed too. "I want one of you with me, I need to interview the car thieves before we turn them over to police." I stood and picked up a manila folder from my desk - a quick look told me it contained all the information Sandra had dug up on Danny Wills.

Sam rose to his feet, his muscular frame towering over my desk. A grin slid across his face. "I'm with you, Chicky Babe. Lee here is all over the hospital situation."

"There's a street map of Fairfax County in the bullpen, grab it for me, please."

His eyes held questions that never made it to his tongue. Good, because I couldn't explain why I wanted a map.

Sam met me at my office door. He opened his jacket and exposed the map in his inside pocket. Together we walked down the corridor and through several heavy doors into a more secure area on the right of our floor. Armed guards stood either side of two interview rooms.

I showed my ID and entered the first room. "Good morning, Mr. Wills. Hope you enjoyed your accommodation last night."

He shrugged and glanced at the door. Sam waved.

"Your real name is?" I asked, sitting across from the young man and placing the closed folder between us on the table.

"Danny Wills," he replied with a hint of a smirk.

"Date of birth? Social security number?" I took a pen from my shirt pocket as if prepared to note his answers.

"You have that information. I gave it to that cop." His smirk settled.

"I do have that information but from a different source. Your prints, Carmine, netted a plethora of information."

He swallowed the smirk.

"Does your mother know what you get up to at night while she's working?"

A vicious stare met my gaze. I took that as a big fat no.

"How this goes, Carmine, is entirely up to you. You can have a reasonable conversation with me now or you can talk to Fairfax PD and your mom. What scares you the most?"

He shrugged, swallowed hard, and tried to recover some of his cool.

Yeah, that's not happening.

"I suggest you think about the attitude you want to channel while you're in my company." I let that sink in for a moment. "You drew attention to yourself last night by deliberately tailgating a federal car?"

His head moved; the smallest nod ever.

"Maybe I did but you can't prove that." His eyes met mine. A hint of defiance swam in their brown depths.

I arched an eyebrow. "What did I say before about attitude?"

He lowered his gaze.

"Should this be about the cars?"

He shrugged again. I let it go: I could see his conflict. He was in over his head and last night wanted out of whatever he was involved in but now, wasn't so sure.

"Where did you come from last night?"

"Around."

"Specifically, Carmine, where were you?" Chance said he knew something about the killings; they happened in the mornings. I let my mind go blank for a moment. Chance appeared holding a calendar. His finger circled Monday. "Back up. Where were you at six on Monday morning?"

He frowned. "Taking coffee to my mom. I do it most mornings."

"At home?"

"No. She was at work. I took her coffee."

"She works where?"

"PSTO center."

"Public Safety and Transportation Operations Center?"

"Yeah." He nodded.

"Alliance Drive?"

"Yeah."

"What does your mom do there?"

"Nine-one-one operator."

Now we're getting somewhere.

"Where'd you get the coffee?"

"Fair Lakes," Carmine replied.

"Did you take West Ox Road to Alliance?"

"Yes."

I was so close to something that could help us I could feel it in my bones.

"I want you to close your eyes for a moment."

Skepticism settled on his features. "Why?"

"Because I need you to visualize the route you drove Monday morning."

He closed his eyes then opened them again.

I waited.

He shut both eyes.

"Listen to my voice …" I walked him through a mental exercise to help his mind focus on details. Then I started asking about Monday morning and getting him to describe the day.

All of a sudden his eyes pinged open. "A man crossed Ox road in front of me. He was carrying a bag that looked like it had blood on it."

Pay dirt.

"Can you show me where?"

Sam stepped forward with the map. He unfolded it on

the table. Carmine traced his route and pointed out exactly where he saw the man.

"Here."

It was maybe fifty yards from Jane Daughtry's front door.

"Did you get a good look at him?"

He described the first Unsub I saw, the swarthy Greek-looking guy. Sam reached around Carmine and showed him the identikit image on his phone.

"Yeah, he looked like that."

"How about the bag? What'd it look like?"

"A messenger bag. Maybe for a laptop or something. I remember thinking it looked cool. Pale colored with bloody streaks on it. Gruesome. Awesome. Ya know?"

No. I had no idea.

His face brightened. He really did like the bag he'd seen.

Not a fan of blood. Seen too much of it to ever find it awesome.

"Did it look as if there was something dripping through it at all?"

"No, just streaks of dark red. Looked like something from CSI. Ya know that show?" Carmine said.

Yeah, I know the show. I kept my opinion to myself.

"Yep, I know it."

"Not like something in it was bleeding. What's it called when it's a pattern of blood?"

"Spatter."

"Thanks," he said.

"You ever see anything like that before?" I asked.

"No, never. I wish. I'd buy one. Man, it was cool."

"Thanks for your help, Carmine. PD will want a word about the stolen cars. I'm prepared to go bat for you but I want you to be honest with PD, okay?"

"I'll do time ..."

"It's possible. I won't lie to you." I opened the file in front of me and scanned the information I had about Carmine Mendez. No arrest record. Surprisingly, no traffic violations either. Apprentice mechanic. Lives with his mom and two younger sisters. The father died in Iraq. Carmine would lose his job if he got a Grand Larceny conviction. His sisters needed him at home, not in prison. I sighed and closed the file. Mendez. Where'd I heard that name recently? Crime scenes stacked up like playing cards. One by one the cards turned over.

"Carmine, are you related to an Officer Mendez at Fairfax PD?"

"No."

Sam stepped up.

"Carmine, Supervisory Special Agent Conway will do what she can for you. We need assurance that you won't associate with losers anymore and that you'll tell Fairfax PD everything you know."

Carmine looked up at Sam and nodded. "If they come after me, my sisters, and mom?"

"Not on our watch, boy. The FBI has some skill when it comes to protection. Talk to PD. Tell them everything." Sam pressed his business card into Carmine's hand.

"Anything you need, you call me. Day or night."

"Why do you care?"

I managed half a smile. Sam did a better job, his lips curled upward and revealed teeth. I flicked my eyes at Sam, he nodded.

"Because, Carmine, we've been doing this a lot of years and we're not too shabby at judging people. You aren't a bad kid. You did a stupid thing but you're not bad." Sam's large hand dropped onto the young man's shoulder. "You want out, we can help."

I leaned across the table. "My opinion ... you deserve a second chance and I will try to make that happen. Don't fuck it up."

Sam and I left the room. Outside the door, I stopped. "Carmine's case will be kicked back to FBI. He wouldn't be worried about his family unless he's got himself into something big and very messy."

"Organized car theft, stealing to order, shipping out of State or even the country," Sam said.

We were on the same page.

I spoke to the uniformed agent near the door and told him to contact Fairfax PD, tell them the car thieves were ready and that PD could use our interview rooms if it made things easier. Made sense, especially as Sam and I thought the case would become an FBI one.

"Do you want to talk to Carmine's buddy?" Sam asked.

"No need," I replied.

Chance high-fived me as he passed by.

Chapter Eighteen

Follow me.

"Welcome to our Friday," Kurt said as the morning sun just tipped the trees. He leaned into the car. "You coming?"

"Anything familiar about this address?" I looked at the house hoping it would throw a memory at me.

"Not to me."

"Maybe I saw it written somewhere."

"Coming?"

"Sure."

The driver's door closed. Climbing out of the car and shielding my eyes from the brightness, I followed him up the driveway, through the house and into another bathroom.

Eight days away from the big day and making zero progress in the case. A fresh victim felt like a massive fail.

My breath caught in my throat as I saw the face of the latest victim.

God, no!

I spun around and ran from the house. Breakfast splattered violently into the garden outside the front door. I gathered my hair into one hand and held it out of the way as the retching continued. Eventually the spasms stopped and I straightened up. Too fast. A murky fog rolled across my vision, the deepening clouds revolved, gathering speed as they twisted and turned. I felt myself falling forward. Hands grabbed my shoulders and pulled me back.

"That was nearly," Kurt said. "You with me?"

"Yep," I said, my hand closed around cold plastic. I looked down and saw it was a bottle of water. Kurt crouched next to me. Guess he gave me the water.

"Didn't like your breakfast?"

"Apparently not," I replied then took a long drink.

"Go easy," Kurt warned.

Too late. I turned my head, water bubbled up from my stomach and sprayed across the grass.

Great. This is going well.

I wiped the back of my hand across my mouth and tried to smile at Kurt. "All good," I said.

"Can't wait for great if this is good," he said with a frown. "Think that checkup should be moved forward, Conway."

"Not necessary, Kurt. That was a reaction to the victim." I swallowed the steadily rising bile. "It's Phoebe Childs. I know her."

She moved recently. That's why the address seemed familiar. It was written on an invitation to a house warming.

Kurt stood up, reached out for my hand and helped me to my feet. He didn't let go straight away, probably smart. I felt like death having a bad day. I could only imagine how great I looked.

"Can you do this?" He flicked his hand toward the house.

"Yep. I can do this." I sounded more confident than I felt. No one ever expects to recognize a murder victim.

"The minute you want out, let me know," he said.

"I'll be okay. Let's go see what Phoebe has to say." I moved toward the door. "You can let go. I'm okay."

Kurt let go my hand but stayed close as we walked back into the house and to the bathroom.

"Phoebe Childs, age thirty-one," Kurt said. "When did you last see her, Conway?"

"We went out for coffee a month or so ago. She needed an off the record chat, well, more to vent really. A parent she was dealing with was causing issues."

"A parent?" Kurt questioned.

I bent down and said, "Phoebe, I'm so sorry. Say hello to Cassie for me." A slight coffee aroma rose from Phoebe. My gut twisted.

Kurt spoke from near my shoulder.

"Conway?"

"Yes, a parent. She's a social worker with Child Protective Services."

"Was, Conway," Kurt said gently.

"Was," I corrected. "She worked with a friend of mine. After her death, we stayed in touch."

"Cassandra Smith, right?"

"Yep."

It didn't pay to dwell on Cassie's death. I found her. Kurt tried to save her life. Enough said. I stood up and glanced around the room. A piece of paper stuck out of a closed drawer in the vanity unit. I pulled open the drawer and removed the paper. It revealed a sentence, just like the other crime scenes.

"Maybe he liked Phoebe," I said, passing Kurt the paper. "'Laughter replaced it all.'"

"That's not as dark as the other notes."

The drawer caught my eye again. I pulled it open properly. Perfume. Expensive perfume and lots of it. Perfume boxes four deep and three across, except in one row. The sixth box was missing. I photographed the drawer contents with my phone.

"There's a gap."

"A gap?"

"Yeah, look. He might've taken the sixth box."

"Any way to figure out what box number six contained?"

"I dunno."

What perfumes did she like? All of them by the look of the drawer.

I needed a perfumer. It's possible a perfumer could fill in the gap based on the selection still in the drawer.

The perfume thing bugged me. The body wash and shampoo thing bugged me too. So did the words and the poetry at the first scene, and the lack of mess. The Republican thing bugged the hell out of me. Didn't need to ask anyone about Phoebe's political inclinations. She was a card-carrying Republican. We'd enjoyed many animated discussions about politics because we didn't share the same political outlook. I stopped thinking about our lively debates. It was hard to believe someone so engaging and funny was lying drained of vitality in her shower. The bloodied messenger bag swam into view. The bag-carrying Unsub bugged the hell out of me. I was bugged.

We waited for the scene guards and crime techs to arrive. Lunchtime came and went. I drank water and ignored the hunger pangs in my stomach.

The medical examiner arrived as the Crime Scene techs finished up.

"Caroline," I said, walking toward her with my hand out.

She shook my hand. "Another one?"

"Yes." I put my hand on her arm. "It's Phoebe Childs."

"Oh, God," she exclaimed on a rush of exhalation. "Will you catch this prick, please?"

"I'm trying, Caroline. I'm trying."

She nodded. "I don't have enough hands on deck. I'm calling in another medical examiner. I've still got three autopsies to do."

"Let me know as soon as you have anything that'll help us."

"You know I will."

"I hate to ask, but will you prioritize her toxicology screen and stomach contents?"

"Yes."

Caroline removed the sadness from her expression; in its place, she wore a bland work face. She disappeared inside.

"I need to sit down with all the crime scene photos," I said to Kurt.

Sitting down seemed like an excellent idea.

"They're in the system. Office?"

"Yeah." I stifled a yawn.

"Keeping you up?"

"Let's just do this thing."

Any hope of going home early vanished with the thoughts rolling in my head. The day was disappearing. I settled the thoughts; they wouldn't do me or the investigation any good. Six victims and I doubted our Unsub had finished. Something triggered this daily killing of women. I had a feeling the double up was a coordination error. Someone got carried away and killed too soon.

My phone rang. Lobo's "I'd love you to want me" signaled the call was from Mitch. The music made me smile. I slid my finger across the screen. "Hey. How's your day?"

"Going okay. You all right, El?" Mitch said.

"Not really," I replied. "I'm at Phoebe's new house."

"Thought you were working a crime scene ..." There was an almost audible rumble as his thoughts slotted into place. "Oh, crap, El. Really?"

"Yes."

"You okay?" He paused then said, "No, you're not. Wish I could hug you."

"Hold that thought. I'll need that hug when I get home tonight."

"Where are you now?"

"Outside at Phoebe's. Do you remember when she moved, Mitch?"

"A few weeks ago, I think. Hang on." I heard his fingers tapping on keys. "She sent an invitation to her house-warming party, this coming weekend. She moved two and a half weeks ago."

Finally a time frame.

"Yeah, that party won't be happening now."

"There's something else going on. I can feel a disruption in the force, what is it?" His voice lightened a little. A smile crept in. "What's going on with you, El? You sure it's not cold feet?"

Dammit. I couldn't lie to him but I didn't want to get into anything yet.

"You know it isn't. Eight days and we're officially husband and wife," I said with a smile. "It's nothing. I got sick at the crime scene, that'll be what you're sensing."

"Not surprised. You okay now?"

"Yep." Changing the subject but not too much. "I need to find someone in the perfume industry to talk to."

"This case related?"

"Yes, I think the Unsub has a thing for a particular scent or maybe one Unsub does."

Mitch's breathing changed; I heard a sharp intake of air. "One of them?"

"Yeah. I think there are two," I replied. The theme song for "Three's Company" soared through the phone and whacked me hard on the ear. I reeled from the opening bars of the late seventies-early eighties TV show. Three? The TV reference was screwy but made sense to me. I'd seen two males. I knew a woman had placed the memorial notice. Two men and a woman, instead of the two women and one man in the television show.

"El? You there?" Worry creased Mitch's voice, sharpening the edges and sending arrows into my heart.

"I think I'm tired," I replied. Before I could halt my stream of consciousness, truth started dripping from my mouth. "I'm used to seeing Chance and hearing songs ... now my mind has gone old school and brought back old TV shows." The crazy flowing freely.

"Chance? You need to explain that one, babe ..."

"Christopher Chance. Ever read the Human Target comics?"

"Yeah, once or twice. So you see a comic book character?"

"Yeah. Nah, I see him as a real person from the Human Target TV show ... you know, Mark Valley."

Mitch's laughter softened the crazy. "Your mind is a fascinating place, El."

"Isn't it, though?" I replied, hoping there weren't any more questions. "I'll see you when I see you. Hopefully not late."

"Babe ..."

"Three things."

"Three things." The smile sprang back into his voice. "Don't be too late."

With a smile, I hung up, pocketed my phone and joined Kurt in the car.

"Office?" he said, turning the key. The engine fired.

"Yes. What time do you think it is in France?"

"Planning a trip, Conway?"

"Needing a perfumer to talk to and France popped into my head as a place where I might find one or two."

My mind quietened as the journey continued. Where had we come across a perfumer before? I didn't speak until I walked into my office and saw Lee sitting in a spare chair in front of my desk.

I threw questions into the air hoping he'd catch them. "Who was the perfumer? What company was it?"

Lee sat back in the chair and watched me sit at my desk. "You're talking about the Hawk case, yeah?"

"Yeah, remember the perfume and pendants? What was the company called?"

"It was cologne," Lee said turning my laptop to face him. "Men don't wear perfume."

"Whatever helps you sleep at night, Lee." I picked up a manila folder from my desk.

A memo from Sandra fluttered to the polished desk surface. I turned it over and read it. Just a note saying she'd printed the photos and had heard about Phoebe. A niggle forced its way to the front: if I didn't get this case closed quickly, I'd miss the funeral because I'd be on my honeymoon. Not that I thought Phoebe would mind, but I minded.

With the folder in my hand, I stood and crossed the room to the far wall where the magnetic white board waited with victims' photos in a timeline. Left to right. I added things we'd learned in the last twenty-four hours. Under that, I attached photos from the crime scenes of the notes found. Lastly, I added my own comments, initial impressions, what I considered were missing objects from the scenes and which scenes I thought were different, as in a different Unsub.

Resting against the edge of my desk, close to Lee, I surveyed the board. I'd considered our timeline wasn't correct early on, discovery isn't always the order in which things happen. We were waiting on the ME's reports, those reports would include time of death. I walked to the board and rearranged the photos, sliding them into various new positions on the board, hoping to get a new perspective.

It felt as though he spent more time with Jane or in Jane's home. Did he want her death to look like a suicide? Was he experimenting with death, finding his comfort zone? That was possible.

After messing with the photos and the order of deaths, I put them all back in the order of discovery. What I knew felt right. The pieces were forming a cohesive picture.

Flicking my hair over my shoulders, I surveyed the images and words in front of me. This time, I took the memos left at each scene and stacked them in the order they were found. The newspaper with the memorial notice sat on the coffee table by the couch. I cut out the notice and added it to the whiteboard then drew lines from the relevant victims to the clipping.

"The poem bothers me," I said to the wall.

"Did you say something, Chicky?" Lee asked.

"I'm not thrilled by this stanza."

If the second is as long as the first, we are likely to see

a lot more victims. Not a comforting thought.

"You think the Unsubs are just warming up?" Lee's words sent cold spikes through my brain.

"I hope not. But yes, that's what I'm thinking." There was something hinky about the double-up in deaths. "It could be because there are two Unsubs, communication might be slipping a bit. Two deaths in one day seem like a communication error." Or the second Unsub got tired of playing second fiddle and wanted to be in on the kill.

"Chicky, we could find more double-ups."

"Yeah."

Not something I wanted to think about for too long. Bodies were piling up but leads were thin on the ground and I still needed to hold a media conference.

Screw it.

What I needed to know was how they chose their victims and how much planning went into the deaths. From what I could tell, there had to be prior contact or the victims were followed home ahead of the deaths. Sleeping pills in the morning coffee: that was a level of planning that scared me. How was the Unsub getting the pills into the coffee? The victims had coffee in their stomachs or on their breath and so far two had sleeping pills in their systems. It made sense that coffee was the delivery method for the pills.

But when? Could the Unsub have been in the houses the night before the murders? What if he stayed the night, waiting for the morning?

That thought stopped me in my tracks.

There was no evidence to suggest anyone else but the victims stayed in the houses. Was there? I didn't recall anything in the reports. Didn't mean I hadn't missed something, though.

"Lee, anything to suggest anyone else stayed in any of the houses?"

"Looking." The quiet clicking of the keys on his laptop stopped. "Thorough searches of the homes in question turned up nothing of note. Victims didn't appear to have shared their beds with anyone recently. Spare bedrooms were home offices and craft rooms, the ones that had spare beds showed no sign they'd been occupied recently."

"Thanks."

The number of victims had the potential to work in our favor. The more people who were killed, the riskier it was for the Unsubs. The more victims, the more we'd learn. I couldn't shake the feeling that something else was going on here. Something I couldn't see.

Where was the music when I needed it?

I sighed and slid back into my chair.

My cell phone chimed with a text message from Sean saying he'd driven by Gerrard's home. It was empty with a sold sign in the front yard. I typed a quick thank you and asked Sean to check into Gerrard's financials.

Dammit. It wasn't great news about the house. Sold his house and went where?

With another sigh, I shook Gerrard from my thoughts. Phoebe and her house were front and center, Gerrard would have to wait a bit longer.

"Phoebe moved to her new house two and a half weeks ago, so the Unsub met her sometime in the last two and a half weeks or stalked her within that time."

Lee looked up. "We have a time frame?"

"Well, the beginning of one, maybe. Unless, she knew the Unsub before moving." Chucking the cat among the pigeons is what I do best. "I need to look at Phoebe's life over the last few months."

"I'll carry on with this search while you start on Phoebe."

I pulled up Phoebe's Facebook and Twitter accounts, running back over her timelines looking for new people, comments, anything that said someone new was on the scene. Or someone was paying more attention than they used to. About fourteen days back on her Twitter feed, I found a name I recognized. Kristopher Lette. He added one of her tweets to his favorites.

"Lee, Kristopher Lette follows ..." I stopped and corrected myself. "Followed Phoebe on Twitter. As far as I can tell, there was no direct interaction and she didn't follow him back."

"I know that name. Refresh my memory?"

"He was spoken to by police after approaching Sarah Ng's home. They described him as thin, pale, and almost translucent."

"The vampire," Lee said with a grin.

Vampire and an Unsub with a blood-spattered bag. A connection?

"It's possible he's related to the journalist Rosanne Lette." I looked at Lee as he continued searching through files on his laptop. "The vampire thing is sending up flares in my brain."

Lee chuckled. "I can only imagine what's going in your head. Did he do anything beyond watching?"

"Favorited a tweet about her new house."

"She didn't have location turned on did she?"

I scanned her tweets looking to see if the GPS sign appeared anywhere.

"Not then, she didn't, but a few months earlier she did … her old address showed up when I typed a tweet."

"Jeez."

"Yeah."

Lette could've used the old address to find her new location. Public tax records of house sales and purchases. Time-consuming searches if you don't know where to start, but he had an address.

Lette wasn't either of the Unsubs I'd seen through the eyes of the dead women. So why was his name popping up? Vampires like blood. I needed more information on Lette.

"You all good there?" I said to Lee, standing up.

"Yep, you going somewhere?"

"Not far, need to make a call. Be back in a few." I picked up my cell phone and wandered into the hallway.

"What's the likelihood of you being home soon?"

The warmth in Mitch's voice flooded through me. "I'm not sure. Hey, Mitch … did you find out anything about

Rosanne and her possible son, Kristopher?"

"Not a great deal. She didn't talk much and wouldn't be drawn. Even mom couldn't get her yapping about any kids she may have."

Sometimes it's what people don't say that tells me the most.

"Did she mention a son at all?"

"She said she had a boy in his twenties and that was as far as the conversation went."

"Did she refer to him by name?"

"No."

"Thanks."

"Sorry I wasn't much help, El."

My smile bounced over the airwaves. "But you were M, you were. I'll see you when I see you."

"I'll be here."

We hung up. So Rosanne didn't like talking about her son. That fascinated me. It was at odds with the parents I knew. They all talked about their kids' achievements or lack of; you didn't always get detail but the sense of pride or disappointment was evident as they spoke.

Ideas about why a mother wouldn't talk about a son sparked an inner debate. He could be some kind of freak. He could have a criminal record. He could be estranged for a variety of reasons, not all of them bad. I paused; in my experience, someone cropping up in a case of mine was usually bad. I saw no reason why Kristopher Lette's appearance would be an exception.

I walked back into my office stepping over Lee's outstretched legs to get to my desk.

He was still reading old case files. Lee glanced at me as I sat and scooted my chair into position.

"You good?"

"I'm good," I replied. "How you doing?"

He grinned. "Got it, Chicky. The company is KS."

"Based?"

"Milan and New York."

"Got a contact?"

"I have, Chicky."

"I need to talk to whoever that is first thing." My eyes settled on the row of clocks above my door. It was nearly eight, too late to make a business call.

"Our files say a man by the name of Sasha Petrovovich is the person we want. He's head perfumer and jewelry designer. His wife is Kendra Masters. They own the company."

"And Mr. Petrovovich is based where?"

"He's based at the New York head office."

"Great."

The Rolling Stones "Hand of Fate" bounced from the direction of the closed window. As I listened to the lyrics, I saw an image of a vampire shoot a man, grab a girl and run.

Well, fuck, that was something.

"Chicky?"

"The vampire … I think he killed someone to save a girl from a violent relationship," I said.

Lee's right eyebrow shot up. "That's quite the quantum

leap, we were talking about a perfumer a few moments ago ..."

I shrugged. "'Hand of Fate' ..." Was all I had by way of explanation.

"Rolling Stones. Gimme a minute, let's pull up a You-Tube clip."

We listened in silence.

"I'd be surprised if he did work for a power company. Not hard to falsify an ID. And saying you're from the power company is a good way to get someone to open the door. Or maybe he really does work for a power company and is using that to get inside houses."

"Does he look anything like the Unsubs you saw?" Lee said.

"No, that's the problem." I thought about the situation with Lette some more. "I also think the girl he saved is someone Phoebe knew."

"Why?"

"Because I can't find a reason for Kristopher Lette to follow Phoebe on Twitter. I found no evidence of interaction between them and yet I get the feeling there was a connection."

"Maybe her tweets were interesting?"

"Only if you like knowing what she ate for breakfast, lunch, and dinner." Or how many miles she ran in a week.

"Does he follow a lot of people who talk about food? Could be his thing."

"Don't imagine vampires care about food." I rechecked

his Twitter feed. His tweets were all about art and how tough it was to get gallery space. I skimmed a few feeds from some of the people he followed. Mostly artists and musicians.

"You really think this guy killed someone to save a girl from a bad relationship and that Phoebe knows the person?"

Did I think that? It sounded a bit more nuts than usual. "I don't know what I think, but something's eating at me and it's to do with Phoebe and Lette."

"All right. I'll play. Do you think Phoebe knew about it?"

I shook my head. "She would've said something to someone. We'd know by now." The thought that Lette found a way to legitimately knock on doors and possibly gain access to houses fermented as Lee's fingers clunked on the keyboard in front of him. I called Sam on my cell.

"Hey. Did anyone you spoke to during this investigation mention someone from a power company being in the area?" I waited, listening to the rustle of turning pages.

"No, Chicky Babe. No one mentioned door knockers of any sort."

"Okay, thanks." I hung up.

"You sure Phoebe would've talked if there was something going on?" Lee ventured.

A frown formed. "What did you find?"

"Ever meet Phoebe's sister?"

"No."

"Check this out." Lee spun the laptop to face me.

On the screen were photographs of a woman, depicting facial injuries, massive amounts of torso bruising, a broken arm, and a gash on the back of the head.

"When?"

"The most recent is the image of the gash at the back of her head and that's three weeks ago."

"And the woman is Phoebe's sister?"

"Yep." He sighed. "The day after that photograph was taken at the hospital, her husband disappeared."

"Disappeared?"

"Yeah, he went away on business and no one has seen him since."

"What kind of business?" I asked.

"The lawyer kind," Lee said with a grimace.

"He's a lawyer?"

"Yeah, the scumbag is a lawyer. He was bailed out within three hours of his arrest for male assaults female and left on a business trip the next day. Failed to appear in court. There's a warrant out for his arrest."

"I don't think anyone is going to find him ..." I said.

"It doesn't sound like it."

"What's the feeling on this, from a police perspective?"

"That he took off and has a new identity, new life." He read for a few seconds. "Warrants are active but the case is on hold. No one is turning over any stones to find this guy."

"Why is no one actively looking for him?"

"I'm looking, Chicky, but nothing is mentioned here."

"We could do the whole new-identity-new-life thing within a few days. But we have access to experts at setting up backstopped new identities. Who else has that capability?"

Lee's eyes met mine. "You think he's in Witness Protection?"

Did I? "Don't think we can rule it out."

"Let's keep that in mind."

"I want to know where Lette was when the lawyer disappeared," I said. "And the wife?"

"Christine Locke, she's still in the family home. There is a protection order to prevent him coming near her should he resurface."

Yeah, because they work.

I wanted to talk to Christine Locke. "I'm going to take a run at Phoebe's sister ... see if she knows anything that might shine some light on this case."

"What about her husband?"

"Locke ..."

"Yes."

"I came across that name during this investigation." I sat back in my chair. "Is the lawyer Charles Locke?"

Lee nodded.

"Well, fuck."

Charles Locke was someone else I wanted to know more about and preferably find.

Chapter Nineteen

Come a little bit closer.

I waited on the porch of a two-story colonial in one of the older suburbs of Fairfax County. The door opened about four inches. A woman with red-rimmed eyes peered at me through the gap.

"Yes?"

I held my badge up for her to see. "Christine Locke?"

"Yes."

"FBI, ma'am. SSA Conway. I'd like to talk to you."

"Is this about my sister?"

"Yes."

She opened the door and ushered me over the doorstep. "Come in, Agent." Christine led the way down a hallway and into a large kitchen at the back of the house. "Hope you don't mind being in the kitchen. I'm in the middle of baking a cake." She checked the oven temperature then wiped the counter.

"I don't mind at all." I sat on a chair at the kitchen table.

"Can I get you a hot beverage?"

"No thanks, but I wouldn't say no to a glass of water."

She placed a coaster on the table then set a glass of water on it. Condensation formed immediately in the warm kitchen air.

"Christine, do you know Kristopher Lette?"

Faint lines appeared on her brow, consternation in her

eyes. "Yes."

I silently thanked the universe for giving me the song and leading me to Christine. "Where did you meet him?"

"At the doctor's office."

"When?"

She sat across from me. "I don't understand, Agent. What has this got to do with my sister?"

"That's what I'm trying to find out. Bear with me, please."

Warm baking smells permeated the air. I couldn't quite tell what flavor the cake was from the smell but it made me want cake with lemon cream cheese frosting. Any cake would do.

"We met about four months ago."

"Would you say you were friends?"

"Yes. We meet a few times a week for coffee and go to galleries if there's an interesting exhibit on."

"Did you tell him about your husband?"

Christine pulled the fruit bowl closer and rearranged apples. "He saw bruises and asked."

"His reaction?"

"Anger. He wanted me to leave him or kick him out."

Reasonable reaction.

"When you met Kristopher ... what were you doing at the doctor's office?"

"Blood tests. We were both getting blood tests." A smile lit her eyes but faded fast. "We have the same blood type. AB negative. It's rare and that's how our conversation started and I guess, our friendship."

"Did Phoebe have the same blood type as you?"

She nodded.

And now she has no blood at all.

A phone chirped somewhere in the kitchen. Christine stood up. She lifted a dish towel on the counter and revealed a cell phone. I watched her check her messages; when she was done, she put the phone on the counter and sat back down.

"Do you tweet?"

"Yes."

I didn't see anyone called Christine on Lette's friends' list.

"Do you use another name when you tweet?"

She half-smiled and nodded. "SummerBreeze."

"Why?"

"Because my husband was jealous or insecure or ..." her voice dropped. " ... an a-hole."

I smiled. "All of the above?"

She smiled back.

"Did Kris know Phoebe?"

Christine shook her head. "Pretty sure they never met."

"Do you know where your husband is?"

Her eyes met mine. "No."

"When did you last hear from him?"

"I haven't heard from him. My lawyer said he was arrested and released on bail and we got a protection order so he can't get near me or contact me."

"And he hasn't?"

"No, not at all."

"Has Kris said anything about your husband?"

"He hoped he'd get beaten up in prison but other than that, Chuck isn't part of our usual conversation."

I'd like to think he got a few beatings in jail too but sometimes karma is slow and needs help.

"How angry was Kris when Chuck put you in hospital last time?"

Why does the name Charles so often end up as Chuck? Hardly flattering.

Christine rearranged a bunch of bananas and moved a few apples to the other side of the fruit bowl. A mix of hot dark chocolate and vanilla filled the air. She rose and headed to the oven just as the timer buzzed. I sipped my water and let her take the cake from the oven and rest the pan on a cooling rack before reminding her of my question.

"What are you asking, Agent?"

"I'm trying to ascertain how Kris was feeling when he saw you in hospital. He did see you, didn't he?"

She nodded. "I called him to tell him Chuck and I were finished."

"Did he come and see you right away?"

"No, he was working on a piece for an exhibition. He came the next day."

"Did Kris mention seeing your husband?"

She shook her head. A frown settled. "Why would you ask that? Someone murdered my sister and you're asking about my friend and my soon-to-be ex-husband."

"Just trying to get a few things clear in my mind, Christine. I will find the person responsible for Phoebe's death. I will."

"She'd only just moved to her new house, it's all so unfair." Tears trickled from her brown eyes. I spotted a tissue box on the counter near me and passed it to her. She pulled a few tissues from the box and dabbed at her eyes.

Her eyes were definitely brown. Phoebe's were blue.

"I'm sorry to be asking so many questions and upsetting you. I just wanted to get a clearer picture of things. Was Phoebe seeing anyone?"

Christine shrugged. "I don't know. We'd really been bad at keeping in touch. My husband was very ... he was ... controlling."

I bet.

"Have you seen any of Kris's artwork?"

She shook her head. "Not really. He showed me a painting ..." her mouth turned up at the edges into a brief smile. "I'm afraid I didn't understand it."

"What was it?"

"Multi-colored lengths of wool stuck to a back canvas. He called it 'Perfect Storm.'"

"There's art and there's art." I sipped my water. "I'm more into pastoral landscapes or secret gardens."

Her smile returned. "Recognizable art? Me too."

I rose from the chair. "Thank you for seeing me. I'm very sorry about Phoebe." I extended my hand and took myself by surprise when the handshake became a hug.

On the drive back to the office I was sure I'd learned

something vital but knew I didn't have enough pieces to make the puzzle fit together.

Chapter Twenty

Time in a Bottle.

Tick, tick, tick. The clocks on the wall grew louder and louder. Mitch popped into my head sending a smile across my lips. The thought of going home was elusive and I knew the smile wouldn't last.

I couldn't put off talking to the media any longer. Six victims and I knew they weren't done yet. The public needed to be aware. Containment wasn't working for us. Spinning my chair I faced the windows and night, trying to see beyond the reflection of the room and into the shadow world. There were monsters in the dark.

My phone rang. Assistant Director Owen's name flashed on the screen.

There were monsters in the building.

My jaw clenched and unclenched. Calls from the Evil Queen were never good.

"AD Owen, how can I help?" The fingers of my free hand tightened into a fist.

"Have you briefed the media regarding case number three zero six dash HQ dash six five zero nine?"

She knows damn well I haven't.

"Not yet, ma'am."

"Are you planning on waiting until more women die, Agent?"

No, you evil troll Queen.

"No, ma'am. I'm trying to catch a killer without causing panic."

"Are you closing in on the perpetrator?"

"We're doing our best."

How about you try? You couldn't find your way out of a paper bag, but by all means, tell me how to do my job.

"This is not a straightforward case."

"I believe one of our own was killed. I would've thought that would be incentive enough to fire Delta's engines and have an arrest by now."

One of our own. Jane Daughtry. That's why Owen is poking her manicured fingernails in my direction.

"I'd like to arrest the right person, not just a person."

"Keep me informed," she snapped.

Curl up and die.

I hung up. My jaw ached and my hand was reluctant to unfurl. I gave myself a few minutes to get over Owen's interference. Unsuccessfully.

What's her problem anyway? Like she knows anything about investigative work. She's still under supervision as far as I know. Supervision. Someone must've crawled up her ass and lit a fire. Wouldn't have been Director O'Hare. She'd come to me.

Enough.

My fingers rubbed my temples. Before Owen interrupted me, I was about to organize the press conference. I picked up my phone and called Sandra. "I need you to set up a media conference for tonight. Use the media room downstairs. Let Troy Fallon know. I want her in front of the bloodsuckers with me and make sure

Rosanne Lette gets an invitation."

"On it, O Esteemed Leader." Sandra's fingers tapped at lightning speed at her keyboard. "Fairfax PD has named the case—"

"I know. Steer clear of using that Hitchcock referencing label, please. There will be enough panic out in the world after this briefing … let's not add to it." I wasn't naïve enough to think they wouldn't come up with something similar themselves but we didn't need to plant any seeds. The media will latch onto a label and run with it. It was only a matter of time before they grasped the Hitchcockian aspect of this case and splashed it all over the newspapers and television.

"Understood, O Genie of Horror Movies."

"Also, get as many agencies in on this as possible. Our Unsubs are hunting federal, state, and city employees." Everything I knew about the victims collided, sending a shiver down my spine. My reflection stared at me from the dark window. They weren't that different from me.

"Sick bastards," Sandra said as she typed.

"Set up a 1-800 anonymous tip line. Uniform can monitor it." As much as I hated the thought of every crackpot in the District calling up with their crazed notions, amongst the shite gems might be uncovered and we were desperate.

"I'll let you know the details of the media briefing within the hour," Sandra said and disconnected the call.

Meanwhile, I spun back to face my desk and settled into some background checking. I wanted to know why

Rosanne Lette didn't talk about her son. Was it because she knew what he'd done? Making assumptions based on very little, annoyed me. Never assume. If I had a son who'd killed someone, I wouldn't be keen on chatting about him to the family of an FBI agent. There was another way to find out more about Lette's son: Dad.

I pressed Lette aside and started searching for Charles Locke. And bam, found a Charles Locke on two of the victims' friends lists. Facebook said he was a maintenance man. It couldn't be the same man. This one was active on Facebook four hours ago. Two minutes more and I had an address – in D.C. He was a building super at an inner city apartment building and had a basement apartment there.

Time to see if he was home. The clocks ticked. I stood, took my holster from my drawer and slid it into my waistband, checking my weapon was snug before pulling on a jacket.

"We going somewhere?" Lee asked.

"Yeah. Nah. You stay, I won't be long. Sandra will have that media briefing set up soon. If I'm not back, start without me."

"Chicky?" A flash of panic crossed his face.

"I'll be back in about an hour. Hold the fort until then." I winked and left.

The shadowy edge of the dark city required me to be alert as I walked down the street. It was Friday night and it felt like the city was going supernatural on my ass. No sign of demons lurking in alleyways but I knew they were there.

Their red eyes burned into me and I wished the Winchester boys were with me as I hurried past another deep alleyway. Could've sworn eyes were watching as I crossed the street.

Outside the building where Charles Locke lived, I pushed the supernatural crap away and opened the door.

People. I deal with people. Flesh and blood. If it bleeds, I can kill it.

I felt my eyes roll as soon as the thought manifested.

I knocked on his apartment door. Shuffling noises approached the door then stopped. I stepped to the hinge side of the door and knocked again. The movement sounded again. Locks released. The handle turned. The door opened fully, revealing a man in his late sixties.

"Charles Locke?"

"Yes. How can I help you?"

I produced my badge. "I'm Agent Conway. Are you related to Charles Locke Junior, last known address Reston, Virginia?" He nodded, almost imperceptibly.

Not keen on the association perhaps.

Locke's voice shook as he spoke, "He's a disgrace."

"I take it you knew he hurt Christine?"

"The things he did to the beautiful girl he married. I hope you catch him, Agent."

"That's the plan."

"I'll never forgive myself for not working it out earlier and stopping him." His head shook. "Hot-headed idiot."

"A lawyer?"

"Yes. You'd think he'd know better but all he knew was how to hide evidence and silence people." Locke paused, looked me right in the eye and said, "He wasn't raised like that, Agent."

I knew enough to know he was probably telling the truth; some men are just idiots no matter how much love they're raised with.

"You don't know where he is?"

"No."

"Haven't heard from him?"

He shook his head. "I'd be the last person he would contact. His lawyer pals would hear well before me."

I wrestled one of my cards from the back of my credential wallet and handed it to him. "Just in case. Or if you think of something."

Locke rocked his weight from foot to foot. "Why are the FBI keen on finding him? Isn't it a police matter?"

"It is a police matter," I replied with a shrug. "I just found out what he did. Christine's sister is a friend of mine." I didn't want to say was a friend. Hard to think of her in the past tense.

"So it's personal ..."

Yeah and nah. I don't like assholes.

"I don't like people who think they're above the law."

"Good luck with your investigation, Agent."

I'm not done with you yet.

"You know a couple of people I have come across recently, Mr. Locke. Do you mind if I ask a few questions?"

"Come on in, no sense standing in the hallway when

there is a perfectly good table we could be sitting at."

I nodded and followed him through the door into a tidy, clean, modern apartment.

Locke pulled a chair out from the dining room table and invited me to sit. Nice to come across good manners. A twinge started up in my gut. The man who walked freely across the apartment ahead of me was at odds with the shuffling noises I'd heard approach the door when I arrived.

Curious.

"Do you live here alone?"

A frown creased his already heavily lined forehead.

"I do. My wife passed away three years ago."

"I'm sorry for your loss." The twinge continued. Odd. Ignoring it, I carried on. "Mr. Locke, your name came up on two Facebook friend lists. I just want to clarify your relationship with the women who own those accounts." I flipped my notebook open. "Serena Sorensen, how do you know her?"

He rested on his elbows, his fingers steepled, just touching his lips. A knot formed in my stomach.

He moved his fingers forward as he spoke, "I met Serena at a writing workshop."

"Whereabouts?"

"George Mason University. About six months ago now."

"You became friends?"

He smiled. "No, not really. She sent me a few short stories to have a look at, there was nothing more to it than that."

"How about Michelle Andrews?"

Locked nodded. "Same workshop. Nice girl, Michelle. She wanted me to read some of her writing."

"And did you?"

"I did. It was very dark. Disturbingly so."

I made a note. Might be worth finding her stories and having a look.

"Did you see either of the women outside of the Workshop environment?"

The steepled fingers returned. The knot in my stomach tightened.

"I thought I saw Michelle from a distance about three weeks ago. She was coming out of a store here in D.C."

"Apart from that instance?"

"No. Haven't heard from either of them."

I stood up, put my notebook in my pocket and shook Locke's hand.

"Thank you for your help. If you think of anything, let me know."

"I will, Agent."

Locke showed me out. Standing on the street in the glow of the building's security lighting, a creeping sensation moved through my body. Eyes. I glanced up and noted two security cameras.

Definitely being watched. Maybe the monsters weren't just in the dark city alleyways.

It was hard to shake the sense of eyes watching as I walked back through town to our building. Something was off with Charles Locke. My gut said he was withholding and it was about Serena and Michelle more than his son. There would be another visit to Mr. Locke, of that I was sure.

Chapter Twenty One
Hand of Fate

Lee was still in my office, waiting for me.

"How'd you get on?" he said as I sauntered through the door and dumped my stuff on my desk.

"Charles Locke senior is withholding. Doesn't think much of his son – pretty sure he's telling the truth in that regard. I'm not convinced he hasn't heard from him. Also, I have the feeling he's holding back when it comes to Serena and Michelle."

"I'll take a look into their backgrounds. Fresh eyes."

"Thanks, I appreciate it."

My desk phone rang. I hooked the receiver into my hand and listened.

"We're all set down here for the media circus," Sandra said. "Your friend Rosanne Lette hasn't shown or replied to the invitation."

I wondered why. Calling her my friend was an over-statement. Rosanne Lette irked me.

"I'll give her a call," I said. "See you down there in five."

The receiver slipped from my grasp and crashed into the shiny desk surface. A little bit of the broken plastic shot across the room, narrowly missing Lee.

"What happened there?" Lee reached for the receiver and inspected the damage.

"Dropped the phone," I replied with an apologetic

smile. "Sorry."

"Just the case, nothing important. Not like you to be clumsy."

I shrugged. "Let's hope I don't have to draw my weapon ... could get messy."

Lee didn't laugh. The expression on his face told me he was adding things up and not liking the answer.

"There's something going on with you," he said with care. "Is there something Delta need to know?"

My head shook without my bidding. "You're adding two and two and trying to make six, it's not going to work. Just tired."

Lee leveled a stare at me. "I don't think so."

Time to change the subject.

"I need to call Rosanne Lette then we'll go down and deliver this brief." I looked at the broken phone receiver and opted to use my cell.

She answered on the fourth ring. Traffic noise flowed past her voice making it hard to hear her words. Bluetooth can be a real pain in the butt sometimes.

"It's Ellie Conway. You coming to the media brief?"

"I'm on my way," she replied. "Almost there."

"Good. See you soon." I disconnected the call and pocketed my phone.

"Ready?" Lee asked from the doorway, holding the door for me.

"Yep."

An hour later I was back in my office. The briefing went as well as could be expected considering the topic.

Journalists were warned not to sensationalize the murders, though I wasn't green enough to believe they'd listen to instructions. The next news broadcast would send waves of panic through the beltway and there wasn't a lot I could do about it. People had to know. Owen was on the warpath and wanted the public informed. It might make it harder for the Unsubs to hunt out victims or maybe give the next victim a fighting chance. I wanted to tell women to prepare their coffee with fresh ground beans and not leave their coffee sitting anywhere before drinking it because I believed the victims ingested sedatives with their morning coffee. That thought implied someone was in their homes before they made their coffee in the morning. Instilling panic was less than helpful. Throwing a spanner in the works regarding the coffee and sedatives might cause more victim suffering but not fewer deaths.

Catch-22.

"Conway?"

My eyes flicked to the doorway and Kurt. "Henderson?"

"Did you get time to talk to Rosanne privately?"

"Nope. You?" A spark of something flitted across his eyes and I knew he had. "What did she say?"

He stepped into my office and shut the door.

That good.

"Your dad is seeing her?"

"Yes."

"Serious?"

"I dunno." He'd never brought anyone to a family occasion before, so, serious had crossed my mind. "Maybe."

"What has your dad told you about her?"

A sigh escaped. Just tell me already. "Fishing expedition? Really?"

"Conway ..." He lowered himself into the chair in front of my desk. "Answer the question."

"He's told me nothing. He's been walking around with a grin on his face for months and out a lot. But he's told me nothing. I had no idea he was dating Rosanne until she turned up at Mitch's folks' place."

"They've been seeing each other for nearly six months."

Jesus! How did I not notice?

A phone screen popped into my head, Mitch's name glowed. Yep, sidetracked. Caught up in my own world as usual.

"Okay, what else?"

"There's something not right about her."

"Tell me something I haven't figured out ..." Secrets. Everyone has them but hers felt dark and brooding.

"I watched her during the briefing and before I had a chat. She's sick, Conway."

Hang on. Back up the bus.

"She's what now?"

"She's sick."

"What sort of sick? She got a cold, Ebola, plague?"

Kurt arched an eyebrow. "Love how you jump from a cold to Ebola and the plague. It's not that kind of sick. She's not contagious."

"You're sure?"

"Yes. Do you want to know?"

I nodded. "Yes."

"She has a brain tumor."

"How did you know?"

"Something seemed off. So I paid more attention and noticed she was having trouble with balance, she's also displaying weakness to the left side of her body."

I gave him a long look. "Could've been a migraine ..."

"Yeah, but it wasn't, Conway. I spoke to her. I asked."

I could imagine that conversation. Bet it was uncomfortable.

"Fatal?"

"That's often how it goes with cancer."

"Well, fuck."

I wondered if Dad knew.

Probably. She wasn't exactly going to be around long term. Not about to be my new mommy then.

It occurred to me that I didn't have any feelings regarding that. Nothing.

"I'm sure she probably said something similar when she was given the diagnosis two weeks ago."

My eyes met Kurt's.

"Two weeks ago ..." This was bad. "That changes things. She's only just found out. She and Dad have been seeing each other for almost six months. He's invested."

"You didn't know about her?"

"That doesn't mean much." I shrugged. Work-life balance has never been easy for me. I tended toward eighty-five percent work and that didn't leave much time for life. What time for life I had was spent with Mitch.

"We really need to work harder on injecting some balance into your life, Conway."

That would happen all by itself soon enough but I didn't feel the need to share my thoughts.

At a quiet knock, my eyes flicked to the closed door.

"Come in," I called.

The door opened, Lee stepped inside. "You want it shut?"

I shook my head. "Nope, Kurt and I are done."

Kurt's right eyebrow rose. "You sure?"

"Unless you have some more information regarding Rosanne Lette and her son?"

He shook his head.

"Chicky, I finished looking into Charles Locke and his relationships with Serena and Michelle," Lee said, placing a manila folder on my desk. "Found something else too."

I flipped the cover of the folder open and skimmed the pages inside. Locke and the girls met at a writing workshop as he said. At the last page, I stopped and looked at Lee.

"Wow," I said. "Just wow."

"How do you want to proceed?" Lee watched as Kurt reached for the file and spun it around to read.

Familiar feelings crashed into each other as an order I'd given on another occasion hit me with full force.

"Sweep all the crime scenes for cameras and audio surveillance equipment."

"Have we released any for clean-up?" Lee didn't look at me as he scrolled through a screen on his phone.

"No."

Kurt placed the file back on the desk in front of me. "He was a surveillance system expert. Ex-military."

"And now he's a maintenance man …" Lee said, tapping his phone screen. "And we have seven victims and the only way the Unsubs could've killed as they have, is with the benefit of surveillance and pre-planning."

We heard his phone dialing then ringing. The conversation was brief. Moments later, Lee pocketed his phone and turned to face me.

"And?" I inquired.

"A team will go scene to scene with RF detectors and conduct a hands-on thorough search."

"Good." I stood up and surprised myself with my own words. "Come on, we'll check Phoebe's place ourselves."

Kurt rose to his feet. "You don't need to, Conway. Go home. Get some sleep."

"You're wrong, Kurt. I do. There's something we've missed. I've missed." I scooped my stuff up. "You coming or not?"

Something to do with Lette and Locke. I was sure there were answers in that house.

He hooked my keys from the objects in my hands with one finger. They jangled in midair as he tossed them up and caught them in his palm. "I'm driving."

Suited me.

"Where's Sam?" I said as I joined Lee outside my office.

"Coming. He was in the bullpen looking for anything else to connect the victims."

I heard heavy footsteps behind me, followed by Sam's deep, "Chicky Babe. Lee said we're going to Phoebe's?"

"Yep."

Lee excused himself to get his bag. His bag contained a state of the art zillion dollar RF detector. His favorite accessory.

Forty minutes later we stood in the hallway of Phoebe's house.

"Phones off," Lee said, taking his toy from his bag. "I'll go room by room."

"Okay. Sam, go with Lee," I said. We all switched off our phones and put them away.

Kurt waited silently beside me. Lee and Sam disappeared into the first room off the hallway. I closed my eyes and let the memories created in Phoebe's new home filter through me. When I opened my eyes, the hallway flattened. Lines blurred. Black outlines appeared. Colors changed. Muted reds, browns, and yellows over creamy white. Familiar. My life became a comic strip. Or maybe it was a graphic novel. A page at the end of the hallway turned, revealing a new scene. Christopher Chance stepped through a doorway. He waved. We met in the middle of the hall.

"Chance."

"Ellie," he said with a dimpled grin. "You figured the camera thing."

"Yeah. I missed something here, didn't I, Chance?"

"Come with me." He held out his arm, encouraging me to walk with him. We entered Phoebe's bedroom. The black lines surrounding the floor rug melted into the carpet, photo-perfect order restored. Chance stood next to me and said, "What don't you see?"

My eyes roamed the room, taking everything in. The gray and pale pink décor, the jewelry box on her bureau, the clock on her nightstand. I looked closer at the clock. No alarm set. The room was tidy. Bed made. I turned down a corner of the quilt. No blankets, no sheets.

What don't I see? Life. There is no life in here.

"Life," I said. "She didn't use this room." I wondered if she had used it at all since moving in. The room felt devoid of all human occupation.

So where did she sleep?

I left the room, followed by Chance. The next bedroom felt the same. There was no life here. I checked the last bedroom, it was set up as a home office. Again, no leftover personal impressions.

How was she killed in the shower of a house she wasn't living in?

I followed Chance into the bathroom. Thick black lines outlined the faded comic-strip coloring as the room flattened on creamy pages. Chance opened the drawer containing the perfumes.

"That drawer doesn't make sense," I said. "It made sense before when I thought this was a house she lived in, but it doesn't now."

"No, it doesn't," he replied, closing the drawer again and running his fingers down folded pink towels on a shelf. "You need to look harder at Phoebe, Ellie."

"Kitchen," I said heading for the door. The house changed as I moved through it, each step took me further into the graphic novel that was Phoebe's life. I opened the refrigerator door. A carton of milk. A container of yogurt.

Chance opened the pantry. I peered inside. Empty bar a few cans of fruit and a loaf of bread.

The dishwasher was empty and completely dry, not a drop of water to be seen. Probably not used. The cutlery drawer contained a knife, fork, dessert spoon and teaspoon. The coffee maker on the counter. It was used. I could still smell the coffee grinds. I spun around and opened all the cabinets. No coffee.

"No coffee."

Chance nodded. "Yet the coffee maker was used. That's how the drugs got into her right?"

"We don't know for sure but that's a possibility. Ground sedatives in the coffee sounds plausible but I haven't checked if that's possible, yet."

Garbage. I opened the back door, a garbage bin stood a few feet away. Empty.

A voice broke in. The pages disintegrated. Ink ran, pooling on the carpet and soaking through the remnants of paper. The same voice spoke again. Louder this time.

"Conway!" My head jerked around, eyes settling on Kurt's face. "Welcome back."

"Back?"

I turned my head again as Chance made a call sign with his right hand then walked away from me. I wanted to call out or run after him but the look in Kurt's eyes stopped me cold.

"Back, Conway. You've been frozen on the spot for about five minutes."

I gave a dismissive shrug. Chance wanted me to call him? That's not what he meant. Phoebe's phone.

"Did anyone find Phoebe's cell phone?"

Kurt shook his head. "Not yet. Lee and Sam are still searching the house."

I jumped as a car door slammed.

Thoughts tumbled around. One finally broke free and stopped moving. Phoebe's phone is in her car. Her car is in the garage.

"Garage," I said. Chance poked his head round the door at the end of the hall and winked. "Garage. Let's go."

"Why?"

"Because her phone is in her car and her car is in the garage," I replied, pulling the door to the garage open and running my hand down the wall inside the door looking for a light switch. My fingers connected with hard plastic and light flooded the spacious garage, illuminating the red Ford Focus I knew to be Phoebe's mode of transportation. I walked around the car and checked it for stickers. There were none apart from a Government parking sticker on the windshield. It was coded but it wouldn't be hard to Google it and find out where she parked during work hours. I peered through the driver's window and saw her pocketbook lying in the passenger footwell.

Who goes inside without their purse? Someone who isn't intending to stay long? So what was she even doing in a house she clearly wasn't living in and why have a shower?

"Conway?" Kurt stood in the doorway watching me. "Talk to me."

"Phoebe wasn't living here," I said, opening the car door and taking her handbag. I opened it and found her phone. "Mitch and I were invited to her house-warming party this weekend but she wasn't living here."

"What?"

"Follow me, I'll show you. I just want to look at recent messages on her phone first." I woke up her phone. Plenty of charge left. "Her last conversations were with a woman." I scrolled through the message thread. "She met her here."

"Name?"

"Mallory Stevens."

Lee called out from within the house. "Yo, got something!"

"Us too," I hollered back.

We joined Lee and Sam in the living room. Sam held a smoke detector in his hand. He handed it to me.

"Audio," I said, inspecting the tiny chip that shouldn't be inside.

"Yep. Audio in every smoke detector," Lee replied. "Found cameras too. One in the bathroom and one in the kitchen."

"Jeez."

"What'd you find?" Lee asked.

"Follow me." I led the way to Phoebe's bedroom and turned back the quilt. I then opened the empty drawers. "She wasn't living here."

Kurt cleared his throat. "You and I went into the garage, we never came in here. How did you know?"

"Chance." Silence dropped like a fire blanket over the room. You'd think they'd be used to my special ways by now. "Phoebe met a woman named Mallory Stevens here before she died."

"What do you know about the Stevens woman?" Sam asked.

"From the conversations on Phoebe's phone, I'd say they were lovers," I replied.

Sam summarized, "She wasn't living here, this Stevens woman was the last person to see her alive, and there is surveillance equipment strategically placed throughout the house."

Kurt's phone rang. He walked away to answer it.

I closed the drawer and fixed the bed.

Why wasn't she living here? Was she ever going to? Where was she living? But the party was planned for here.

"You all right?" Lee said as I sat on the edge of the bed.

"Yes. Just thinking. This is the house she purchased … why wasn't she living here? Why did she want people to think she was living here?"

Phoebe had secrets.

Everyone has secrets.

I needed to unravel hers to understand how she died in the shower of a house she wasn't living in. Her phone was still in my hand. Photos seemed like a good place to start. I opened her photo stream. At the bottom of the screen I saw the shared folder icon. It bore a little number one. I opened the folder. A photo of Phoebe. Naked. In the shower. Mallory Stevens name was next to the caption: You're stunning. Don't ever forget it.

And everything twisted into a ball of threads so tight, I couldn't find the end.

I glanced at the watch on my wrist. Saturday morning was fast approaching.

"Can we trace the signal of those bugs?" I asked. "Would a better question be – are they still sending information?"

Lee grinned and made a phone call. A minute later he handed me his phone. "Cyber want a word."

I gave my authorization code and asked that they attempt to get receiver location information from any signal originating from Phoebe's address. The possibility of the bugs still being active was slim but it was worth a shot.

We were done for the moment. Our phones were all back on. My screen lit up with messages from the team running RF detection on the other crime scenes.

Every scene contained audio and video surveillance. All the audio was found in smoke detectors, the cameras were found in each kitchen and bathroom. Made sense.

Someone monitored the feeds and knew exactly when to enter the houses.

One part of the puzzle: I still needed to know how the victims were chosen and who installed the equipment. I'd found nothing to suggest they all used the same security company or fire security company or that Charles Locke had anything to do with all the women.

Fire. The word flamed in my head.

*

We trailed through the corridors of the Hoover Building. Tiredness and our own thoughts made for a quiet group.

"Go home," I said, looking over my shoulder at the team as I wrapped my hand around my office door handle.

"You too," Kurt replied.

"Yeah, I will."

Sam, Kurt, and Lee chorused goodbyes moments after I settled into my chair. I wanted to make a few notes in the case file before I left.

I tipped back in my chair, put my feet on my desk and closed my eyes. Five minutes shut-eye wouldn't hurt.

Chapter Twenty Two

Lay your hands on me.

The smell of freshly brewed coffee woke me before Mitch bent down and kissed me.

"You sleep in your chair?" He placed a take-out coffee cup on my desk along with a glass of water.

"For a little bit," I replied, checking the time. Six-thirty. "Thank you."

His smile reflected back at me. "Eight days," Mitch said.

Which meant it was Saturday and I was running out of time.

From his pocket he produced a tube of Berocca and dropped one of the effervescent tablets into the water. I watched it fizz as it dissolved.

"That was really thoughtful," I said, picking up the glass and downing the still fizzing liquid.

"Figured you'd need a bit of a pick-me-up."

"You're pretty awesome, you know that?"

Mitch laughed. "Yep."

"Walk with me?"

"Sure, where we going?"

I picked up my cup and stood up. "Just need to stretch my legs – round the block?"

"Sounds good."

We walked down the corridor, I gave Mitch my coffee and disappeared into the bathroom before we continued.

Halfway down the stairs, my mouth started to water in an unfortunate way. Black spots danced in front of my eyes. My hand grabbed the rail as everything swam out of focus. Before I could react, a less than delicious combination of Berocca and coffee splashed freely across the concrete steps.

"Wow," Mitch said, holding my hair out of the way as the retching continued. "That's a lot of orange. Berocca not a good choice then?"

"It would seem not." I wiped my hands across my mouth and straightened up.

Mitch let my hair go. "You okay?"

I nodded. "I think so." I looked at the steps, thankful it was only liquid.

Yuck.

My jeans and boots were untouched, a miracle and a blessing. I looked at Mitch. He was both concerned and amused. Good combination. "Sorry."

"You want to keep walking?"

"Yes." Fresh air. I had to call the janitor too. The steps. Just yuck. I fished out my phone and called the janitorial number for the building. However tempted I was to say 'Clean up in aisle five,' I didn't. Amazing.

Once out of the building, fresh air hit like a freight train. Cold, clean, exactly what I needed. I sat on a bollard for a moment. Needed to make sure it was just what I needed.

Mitch sat next to me. "Do you absolutely have to be here today?" His fingers closed around mine.

We both laughed. He knew the answer.

"You know I do."

He nodded. "Are you feeling better?"

Not really.

"Sure."

"Going to finish your coffee?"

Nope.

I shook my head. "I'm good, thanks."

"You should eat."

The thought of food stumbled around until it settled on a single word later.

"Later. Let's walk."

Much later. Not feeling great was inconvenient. I spent most of the walk convincing myself I was fine.

Say it enough and it'll be true?

Mitch didn't speak for almost ten minutes. It might've been a new record. "I'll be in my office all day. I have a few late meetings. I'll have my phone with me. Call if you need me."

"Thank you. I'm calling a perfumer soon. Found someone who might help."

"Great." He stopped walking and turned to face me. "What aren't you telling me?"

Now is not the time to go there.

"Not that I'm not telling you." I paused, the right wording was important. "It's that I don't want you to carry this case around."

His eyes searched mine. "Unblock me. This isn't good. I can cope, El."

"It's horrible, Mitch."

"I've seen a lot through your eyes."

"It doesn't make it right."

"Is this that bad, really?"

As crime scenes go, no, they're not. They're clean, tidy, all the mess was flushed down the drains.

Why was I blocking him? Because there was a conversation I didn't want to have until we'd closed the case and we could talk properly. Mitch had a lot on. I was busy. The conversation we needed to have required us both to be present and focused on each other. That the conversation might have to wait until our honeymoon didn't please me much.

"El? All right?"

"Uh huh."

Consciously I opened a door in my mind. Light flooded out. Mitch blinked. I knew he felt it. Exhaling I relaxed my shoulders. Mitch wrapped his arms around me and hugged me close.

"And we're back," he said in my ear. "This is how it should be."

He was right. More right than he knew. A thought popped into my head. Saltines.

"Saltines?" Mitch said aloud. "You're really not feeling well, are you?"

"Just a bit of an upset tummy. Could just be lack of food and the Berocca fizziness."

"And you're first food thought is Saltines?"

"Can't think of anything else I want to eat right now."

"Fair enough." He looked up the street. "I think there is a convenience store up the street. Let's get you some crackers, water, toothpaste, toothbrush, and hand sanitizer."

Contagion sprang to mind. Good choice of scary movies. I shuddered. Mitch's arms tightened around me.

"I'm okay, M."

"I really don't think you are."

I wasn't exactly convinced myself but I had to be okay. Lives depended on me stopping these Unsubs. Funny that I didn't consider he was finished. Six victims is a lot but it felt as if he was just warming up.

"Maybe not. But I have a case. There's nothing to worry about."

My phone alert chimed. A text from Sean with more bad news regarding Noel Gerrard. He hadn't touched his bank accounts in six weeks and prior to that he pulled five thousand dollars out of his daily account.

I replied: Can you view the bank CCTV footage of Gerrard withdrawing money?

Sean: I can as long this doesn't interfere with a case.

Me: It's not a case. It's friendly curiosity. Unless you find something.

Sean: I'll get back to you.

Chapter Twenty Three

Lifestyle of bleeding

I kicked my office door shut and checked the time. Seven-thirty and no call about a fresh crime scene. That didn't mean much except that maybe no one had found the next body yet. Pushing those thoughts aside I concentrated on things I could do.

There were calls to make. The first of which was to Sasha Petrovovich. The only way to tell if Sasha Petrovovich was at work on a Saturday morning and taking calls was to make the call.

I punched his phone number into my desk phone instead of my cell phone. My desk phone routed through the FBI phone system and would show up on caller ID as FBI.

He answered on the sixth ring just as I was getting ready to hang up.

"Sasha Petrovovich."

"Good morning, Mr. Petrovovich. I am FBI Special Agent Ellie Conway."

"Yes?"

"We have a case that requires a knowledge of perfumes. I was hoping you could help."

"I'm a busy man." His voice sharpened. "How much help do you require, Agent?"

"Do you think you could determine which perfume is missing from a collection by looking at photographs of the remaining perfumes?"

He sighed. This was not going as well as I'd hoped.

"Send them to me. I'll have a look." Reluctance reverberated. "Do you have my email address?"

I'm FBI. I have everything even when I pretend I don't.

"Yes, I do. Thank you." I paused. "There's something else."

"Go ahead."

I couldn't place his accent. It was an unusual accent and also unusual that I couldn't place it.

"Some items may be missing from some of the crime scenes." Maybe. I couldn't prove they were missing or even existed.

"Like?"

I heard papers being moved, his attention elsewhere.

"Possibly body wash, shampoo, perfume … so far."

"And you want?"

"To know if they're related in any way."

"I would need to know more about the connections between the missing items, and maybe the victim's preferences when it comes to scents. I am presuming there are victims of whatever crime this is?"

"Yes, there are victims. Can we bring you in to consult on this case?"

"Are you sure there is a link to scent or perfume?"

"Yes. I am."

Can I prove it? No.

But I hoped Petrovovich could help me do just that or give me something more substantial than a gut feeling.

The Unsub likes a certain scent or combination of scents and that has something to do with some of the murders. Or maybe it didn't. It wasn't every scene, as far as we knew. More than one trigger? My attention snapped back to the phone call.

"I can make myself available." He paused. Pages turned. "Tomorrow, Agent. I can spare six hours on Sunday."

"Could we make it today and could you extend that time frame? I'm in D.C. We need to fly you in." I was pushing it, I knew. But the sooner we got some idea of what we were looking for, the better.

Silence.

Pages turned, paper shuffled, computer keys clicked. An intercom buzzed and a muffled unintelligible voice followed. Moments seemed like hours. I took note of the time and used the silence to check the availability of the Delta jet.

"I can rearrange my schedule somewhat."

"Thank you. I'll send our jet." I typed a quick memo to the pilot. "We will fly you out of JFK at nine this morning. Do you have a helipad on the KS building?"

"Yes."

"I can have you helicoptered to the waiting jet at JKF."

"Thank you."

"No problem."

He gave me his cell phone number. I scrawled it on my notepad and finished up the required details.

"I've booked pilots and flights. An FBI helicopter will

pick you up from your helipad in two hours. The Delta jet will be standing by at JFK."

"And you will return me to KS?"

"Yes, sir, we will. Your flights are booked. You will be back at KS at approximately nine pm."

"That's more than six hours, Agent Conway."

"We're flying you to D.C. There are six crime scenes. Crime scenes take time." Silence. "I really appreciate your help."

"I have a family. We have an engagement this evening." His voice hardened as resistance crept in. "My wife will not appreciate my absence."

I felt my expert slipping away. Instinct told me to let him come to me.

"Six crimes scenes?" Petrovovich asked with reluctance.

And he was back. "Yes, sir. Six crime scenes."

"When you say crime scenes, Agent Conway, do you mean murders?"

"In this instance, yes, I do."

"The bodies?"

"Will not be in the scenes."

They're in the morgue. Where all good freshly dead folk belong. Safe, cold, waiting for a Y-shaped incision that had the potential to provide a few answers.

"They are all women?"

"Yes."

"Two hours on my helipad?"

"Please. I will meet the jet at Washington National

Airport."

"I look forward to meeting you."

He hung up leaving me staring at my phone. He was coming and it didn't kill my budget. I just hoped he could make sense out of what my gut thought and give me something tangible we could work with.

The next call was to Mallory Stevens. I rang the number I'd copied from Phoebe's cell phone.

"Good morning Ms. Stevens," I said as a husky female voice answered the phone.

"Good morning. You are?"

"Special Agent Conway with the FBI. I'd like to talk to you about Phoebe Childs."

"I ... I don't ..." she faltered, "... I haven't seen Phoebe in a while."

Really? Why can't people just tell the truth?

"How about you accept that I know about your relationship and we move on from there?"

"I really don't think I have anything to say to you, Agent."

"But I think you do." Something told me she didn't know about Phoebe. "Would you like to come into my office or shall I come to you?"

"Um, ah, can we meet somewhere?"

"Sure, where do you suggest?" I crossed my fingers, hoping it wasn't a café. Coffee and I were about to end our long-standing friendship. Water was my new best friend.

"The Firehook in forty minutes?"

Dammit!

"If you're not there I will issue a warrant."

She mumbled something unintelligible and hung up. I rocked back in my chair and thought about her response.

A knock on my door snapped me out of my thinking zone. "Come," I called.

The door swung open and my team walked in, one by one. The last one through was Sam, he shut the door. They pulled up chairs and sat in front of my desk. A room full of large men. All of a sudden there was no air. Heat curled around me, closing my airways. The fingers of my left hand pulled at the fabric of my shirt lifting it away from my neck.

"You all right?" Kurt asked, leaning an elbow on my desk.

"Just seems close in here," I replied with a shrug, letting my shirt go.

Sam opened the door. Lee opened a window. Cross breeze. That felt better.

"Let's get this case closed, shall we?" I said, swinging my chair and bringing up the case file on the laptop that sat on the left of my desk.

"Update time," Lee drawled. "We're not having any luck finding an overlap with the women and any security companies."

That was less than good news.

"A perfumer is flying into Washington National this morning. Kurt and I will meet him. The plan is to take him to the crime scenes. He will hopefully be able to tell us something about the scents missing from the scenes and maybe enlighten us as to the motive for taking them."

Sam and Lee nodded.

"I've been talking to the medical examiner," Sam said. "None of the bodies bore defensive wounds. Still waiting on the rest of the toxicology reports."

That's significant.

"Anything under the fingernails of Serena Sorensen?" I scrolled through the crime-scene photos.

"They were recently broken and possibly during some struggle with the Unsub but nothing was found under her nails. The ME thinks they were cleaned," Sam said.

"Okay, that's something. Our Unsub may have obvious scratches. And is more thorough than we knew when it comes to cleaning."

Everyone made a note.

"How long for the rest of the toxicology reports?"

"Could be days."

Yeah, it could.

We'd just hit the lab with six victims on top of their already crushing workload. Caroline called in another ME to help her with the autopsies but the lab work would still take time. I made a mental note to keep an eye on it. If necessary, I could speak to Sean O'Hare and see if we could use his lab. Outsourcing might be the best way to go. My budget could handle it.

"Theory time ... why are the Unsubs killing in the shower?" Lee said.

I rocked in my chair and offered my opinion, "They like to kill clean women ..."

"That could be something to do with it," Lee said. "But why?"

"Because they had shower gel, body wash, or shampoo residue." I looked at Lee. "By residue, I mean I could smell it on their skin or hair. They were showering when the Unsub surprised them. They weren't killed as soon they stepped into the shower. There was time for them to clean themselves or maybe just time for the sedatives to work?" I paused. "I'm pretty sure the toxicology reports will confirm the presence of sedatives in all the blood samples."

Sam nodded in agreement. "Only Serena possibly fought back," Sam said.

"That could be why the Unsubs waited until they'd been in the shower a few minutes," I said. "Let those sedatives work. Compliant victims are easier to deal with."

"That means ..." Lee said, "... that there is something about the Unsubs that requires them to render the women unconscious or near to it before the stabbing?"

"The man I saw was about six foot tall. He wasn't small. He didn't seem incapacitated by any kind of physical disability. Could be that they like unconscious women," I replied.

"Do we know if there was any sexual component at all?" Lee said to Sam.

"Not at this point," Sam said. "Apart from them all being naked … which could be part of it."

"Most people shower naked. Makes it easier to get clean," I said. Rocking back in my chair and swigging water from the bottle in my hand, I surveyed the men in front of me waiting for the next observation.

"You don't think the nakedness is a factor?" Lee addressed me.

"That's not what I said. I just don't believe it's a sexual thing. I don't know what the hell is going on here, but it's not sexual."

I was pretty sure the Unsub wasn't getting off on the killing but there was another reason for the killings.

Chance's voice sounded so clear I thought he was in the room not in my head, "I think you're right. Your mission is to prove it."

The Mission Impossible theme blared from the walls of my office. Chance's laughter filled my head.

"You're not as funny as you think you are," I said. Wishing he'd chosen a better theme song to taunt me with; that one smacked of short men and I wasn't a fan.

"Who isn't?" Kurt asked, rejoining the discussion at the worst possible moment for me.

Typical.

I shook my head. Chance slipped, skidding across the surface of my brain until he dangled precariously off the edge. I shook my head again. He tumbled out of sight leaving his laughter behind.

"No one," I replied smiling sweetly at Kurt.

His brow furrowed. "That was Chance, wasn't it?"

"Don't be silly," I replied. "Just a random thought that popped out of my mouth. That's all."

"So what is it?" Sam said.

I turned my attention to Sam. "What is what?"

"What is it that's going on, why the deaths?"

"Fucked if I know," I replied with a thin smile. "There is something deeply disturbing happening, We just don't know what, yet."

The cleanliness of the crime scenes weaseled into the forefront of my thoughts. Clean and bloodless. There was something to that. If the Unsub didn't like mess, then why stab? Stabbing isn't exactly the tidiest way to kill someone. He got them halfway there with sedatives, why not just increase the dose to a fatal amount, very little mess then. They could still die in the shower if that's what he wanted.

Lee's voice spilled over my thoughts bringing me back to the conversation around me.

"Women are hardly likely to shower with a stranger in their home. If he broke in while they were in the shower – then he wouldn't have been able to sedate them – they would've fought back. There would at least be a few defensive wounds or bruises as they struggled."

Kurt's phone rang. He answered and looked at me, holding up an index finger for us to wait until he finished the call.

"He could've been to all the homes earlier and set his sedative in motion," Lee said. "Kurt, is that possible?"

He nodded. "About a month ago I was called to look at

the evidence from an attempted murder. Wife tried to kill her husband. She crushed up some of her husband's Lorazepam prescription and added it to freshly ground coffee beans. She then brewed the coffee and took him a cup."

"So it's still effective even after being brewed in a coffee maker?" Now that interested me. "Two victims so far had coffee in their stomachs and sedatives in their blood."

"Yes, it's effective even after being brewed and yes they did." Kurt rubbed the side of his face. "That was the lab, confirming the presence of sedatives and coffee in two more victims."

"What about the prescription we found in Jane Daughtry's medicine cabinet? Could that be used the same way, in coffee grinds?" A Post-it note appeared in my mind with the word 'prescription' written on it. "Stick a pin in the coffee thing for a second," I said. The Post-it note scrunched into a ball and flew into the trash basket in the corner of my mind. "The prescription, Kurt, why was it from a different doctor?"

"You'll love this ..." Kurt flipped over a few pages in his notebook. "I spoke with the doctor. He told me she had difficulty sleeping and couldn't get in to see her regular doctor."

"How did she find that doctor?"

"Referred by a friend. A Mr. Emilio Herrera."

"Our Emilio Herrera?"

"Yes."

"You spoke with him?"

"I did and he informed me he suggested Jane tried his doctor but didn't know that she had."

"And we're good with that?"

Kurt nodded.

"Are we back on the sedatives in the coffee yet?" Lee rocked back in his chair.

"Yes," I said.

Lee let the chair drop back onto all its legs. "How much would you need to knock an adult out or make them happily compliant?"

"Four to eight milligrams of Lorazepam would be enough to knock an adult out for about six hours," Kurt said.

"How fast does it work?" Sam asked.

"The victim would become sleepy after about fifteen to thirty minutes. So not long." Kurt looked at me. "Conway suspected the coffee was a delivery system for drugs."

"Yes, I did. That's why I suspect he was in their homes the night before which is when he would have doctored the coffee." I took another sip of water and continued, "He may or may not leave. We could have a freak who is spending the night in the homes with the clueless victims." I set the water bottle on my desk.

I checked my watch, gave it a minute for my stomach to settle, and then stood up.

"Conway?" Kurt questioned.

"Going to meet Mallory Stevens at the Firehook for a chat," I said.

Kurt rose to his feet. "Could do with a coffee."

I don't recall asking for company.

"It's not necessary. I can bring coffee back," I said, sliding my holster inside my waistband.

"I'll come for the drive," Kurt replied.

I knew I wasn't getting out of the building without him. I sighed. "Okay, let's go." At the office door, I paused. "You two let me know if you find anything we can use."

"Will do," Sam replied. "You bringing back coffee?"

"Yep."

Because that's the nice thing to do.

Chapter Twenty Four
Foxtrot Uniform Charlie Kilo

Kurt and I ordered. He wanted coffee and I decided on hot chocolate. I checked the DMV image of Mallory Stevens on my phone to refresh my memory. Mallory Stevens was ten minutes late. I saw a woman who fitted the image walk in and waved her over.

"Ms. Stevens?" I said as the woman stood awkwardly at the end of the table.

She nodded. "Agent Conway?"

"Yes. Have a seat."

Kurt introduced himself. "I'm SSA Henderson."

She didn't say anything to him.

"Why do you want to talk to me?"

"Have you heard from Phoebe since you met her at her house on Thursday night?"

She shook her head. "No. I didn't expect to. We had an argument. She needs time to cool off."

She's pretty fucking cold now.

I smothered the smirk that tweaked the edges of my mouth and reminded myself that Phoebe, cold or not, was a friend.

"You argued about what?"

Mallory frowned and adjusted her jacket. "We just argued. It's personal."

My phone rang. Lee's name flashed across the screen. I excused myself from the table and walked outside before answering the call. "What's up?"

"Charles Locke junior. What'd you like him for?"

"Beating the crap out of Phoebe's sister, Christine."

"That's right. His name just surfaced while I was digging around looking at the Mallory Stevens chick's background," Lee said.

"Now that's something we should look into."

"I thought so."

"You're sure it's junior not the old man?"

"Junior."

"Anything recent?"

"Yeah. Thursday night. They had a Facebook messenger conversation."

Not dead then. So Lette didn't kill Locke. Would've been a public service if he had.

"Before or after Stevens met Phoebe?"

"The conversation was early in the evening and over by five-thirty."

Good to know.

"Anything I need to know?"

"Yeah, she told Locke she was meeting Phoebe at seven at her place. He replied that he'd see her afterward."

A cold foaming waterfall crashed over me, pooling at my feet.

"Anything about Phoebe's sister?"

Part of me hoped that this was what it was about. That he wanted information about Christine and was using his friendship with Mallory to that end.

"No. No mention of her at all. He mentioned his father. Said he hadn't seen him or spoken to him since the incident."

"Incident?"

"Not sure, could be referring to his arrest for domestic violence."

Could be.

"Great work, Lee. I'll see what I can find from this end."

I hung up and rejoined the table.

Mallory Stevens knowing Charles Locke felt all kinds of hinky. That Lette didn't kill him felt wrong on a few levels too. If he wasn't dead, why did no one seem to know where he was? No more being nice. I wanted answers.

"Ms. Stevens what time did you meet Phoebe on Thursday night?"

"It was after dinner. Seven, I think."

"Who knew you were meeting her?"

She clasped her hands together while resting her elbows on the table. "No one. We weren't public about our relationship."

Mental note to bring the conversation back to the relationship as soon as I'd dropped Charles Locke's name and watched the reaction. Kurt caught my eye. I smiled with all the sweetness I could muster. It wasn't much.

"And you met with Charles Locke when?"

Stevens froze.

She actually froze.

"Breathe," I said.

Her body shuddered.

Kurt spoke softly, "What time did you meet Locke?"

"I didn't meet him," she said, her voice wavering. "I didn't meet him ..."

Kurt's eyes flashed at me. I raised an eyebrow.

He tried again. "What time did he meet you?"

"After ten ..."

"Where?" I asked as Kurt shifted back into his seat again.

"On the street."

"What street?" I asked.

She fidgeted with a napkin. Folding the corners then unfolding them again. I reached my hand out and removed the napkin. Balling it up in my hand, I watched her. The fingers of her right hand covered her mouth for a split second.

"I don't remember."

"Ah, but you do," I said. "I think we'll take this conversation back to our office. I've got a plane to meet and I'm not a fan of liars." I looked at Kurt. "Sam and Lee can continue with Stevens, yeah?"

He nodded. "Yeah, they'll enjoy it."

"I don't know the name of the street ..."

Incredulity filled the space between us as I said, "You know Phoebe's address."

Her eyes widened.

Kurt and I stood up. I let him do the honors.

"Mallory Stevens, you are accompanying us for further questioning regarding the death of Phoebe Childs."

Bam! Just like that all the air left her body and she fell forward; with a sickening thud, her face hit the table.

Kurt placed two fingers on her neck. "Alive," he said.

I saw a moving red line spread from under her face and called for paramedics. We had a plane to meet; I didn't want Kurt doing his doctor thing this time.

"Broken nose, maybe," Kurt said, watching the blood pool grow.

"Face planting on a table will do that," I replied, pushing my phone back into my pocket. The smell of the fresh blood tweaked a few barf strings and had me looking for an escape. "I'll order take-out coffee for Sam and Lee then wait outside for the paramedics. Can you pick up the coffee when it's ready?"

Kurt nodded as he looked at me. I saw him jump into doctor mode.

"Fresh air, Conway, go."

The paramedics arrived a few minutes later; I pointed them in the right direction and waited for Kurt to join me.

He emerged with a smile on his face carrying two coffees on a tray. "Didn't expect that reaction from Stevens. How long have we got before we meet the plane?"

"Two hours," I said. "Just enough time for me to do something."

"You want company?"

I glanced at the coffees Kurt carried. They would get cold.

"Yeah, sure."

"Where are we going?" Kurt asked as we walked back to the car.

"Navy Yard."

"This is to do with Gerrard?"

"Yep." That and I needed to get away from the crazy case for a bit. Noel Gerrard disappearing bothered the hell out of me. He'd taken being a private person to a whole new level. Fifteen minutes later we were at the Navy Yard.

My phone rang. Owen.

Damn.

"How can I help?" I said, trying to maintain some civility in my voice.

"Have you made any headway with the case, Conway?"

"Progress is being made."

"Have you made any arrests?"

"Not yet. We have someone helping us with our inquiries."

"The woman in the hospital?"

"Yes."

I drummed my fingers on the console.

"The case files mentioned male Unsubs. What about Charles Locke?"

"Is there something you want?" The temptation to hang up was high.

"What are you doing in the Navy Yard?"

Someone must've told her how to access the car GPS tracking maps. Idiots.

Instead of drumming my fingers, I fiddled with a pen

I'd found. "Conducting an avenue of inquiry."

"Your time would be better spent talking to Matthew Collins and Charles Locke Snr."

Holy shitballs, Batman, she's stabbing my last nerve with her stilettos.

"With all due respect, ma'am, I don't think you're in a position to tell me how to do my job."

I hung up. Backlash would be forthcoming. The Evil Troll Queen would make sure of it.

Kurt never said a word.

We headed into the NCIS building.

"What are you two doing up here?" Jules' good-natured voice flowed as I walked across the floor toward her desk while clipping a visitor's pass to my pocket.

"In the neighborhood. Thought we'd check out the rebuild," Kurt replied.

"Fancy up here now," she said with an easy smile directed at Kurt.

If it weren't for an understated memorial plaque and hunks of a bomb called Big Boy embedded in the concrete, you'd never know what'd happened here.

Last time I stood in the NCIS bullpen, the world rocked, cars crashed from the sky, and terror gripped Washington. Pushing screams and carnage aside I dragged myself back to the present and Jules.

"It's an impressive workspace," I said, looking around. High tech, open, but comfortable feeling.

Jules nodded in agreement. "Now, what are you really doing up here in the Navy Yard?"

I perched on her desk. "Have you heard from Noel Gerrard?"

He was her boss until he retired eighteen months earlier.

"Not since the explosion," she replied.

"Do you know where he is?"

"No. Guess he's fishing or playing golf somewhere."

Fishing maybe, golf no.

"So nothing since the explosion. Really? Nothing?"

"Not a dickey bird," Jules regarded me with interest, or that's what I thought it was. "I take it you haven't heard from him either?"

"No. Had a phone call after the Hoover building explosion. Nothing since."

"Tried calling?" She grinned at me.

"Disconnected."

"Been over to his house?"

"A mutual friend paid him a visit. The house is empty and sold."

"How about his parents?"

"Only his Mom, she hasn't seen him or heard from him in six weeks."

Hence, I'm here. I'm picking she didn't know he'd sold his house either.

"He's probably somewhere hot enjoying a vacation."

"She didn't think so."

"Okay, what's this about?" She looked up at me then glanced at Kurt. "Do we need coffee?"

There were still two coffees in the car.

"You might, I'll settle for water thanks."

I knew that was a red flag statement but I just left it there and ignored her interrogative eyebrow and the heavy silence from Kurt. Jules stood up and motioned for us to follow her.

"Let's go for a walk," she said, heading for the door.

We walked along the waterfront past the USS Barry.

"Why the sudden interest in Gerrard?" Jules asked, stopping at a coffee stand.

"People don't generally disappear the way he has."

"It's Gerrard. He's a reserved person."

That's true.

"His mom asked me to look into his disappearance."

"What do you have so far?"

"Not much. He doesn't have a credit card. His bank accounts haven't been touched in six weeks. Before that, he withdrew five thousand dollars in cash."

"You sure it was him?"

"No, not confirmed. I've got someone working on that," I said.

"State of mind?"

"I spoke to a friend of his and he said he sounded okay a few months ago." I had nothing to go on but Sean's word. Last time I heard from Gerrard, he was angry. "He was pretty angry when he arrested the Director of NCIS, so much so he resigned. Think that shook his faith in people a bit." Understandably. Shook mine too. "How was he when you last spoke to him?"

"He seemed a bit preoccupied. Hard to tell. It was

chaos. We lost a lot of people and he knew all of them." She sipped her coffee. Even the smell of it made me feel ill. "How was he when he called you?"

"Concerned. Was a short phone call. He established I was all right and Delta was intact and that was it."

Jules considered what I'd said for a few moments. Kurt listened to our conversation but added nothing. I could see the cogs in his brain turning.

"I saw him at funerals. But he didn't join us. He hovered in the background."

"Unusual. Didn't think anything would keep him away from you and Liz," Kurt said.

Kurt was right: that was unusual. Gerrard was all about his team. They were family.

"You know him as well as I do, Ellie. He felt guilty. You could see it."

"Yeah, he would've. He left. Bad shit happened. He would've felt that he should've been there to protect his team." I get it. I know exactly how it would've affected him. "I better get back to work."

"Keep me posted."

"Of course." I turned away then turned back to Jules. "If you think of anything, or hear anything, let me or Kurt know."

She nodded.

We took a shortcut back to the car. Something in the distance glinted. I tried to see behind the glint and followed it to a window on the far side of the parking lot. The angle changed, causing the glint to disappear then came back.

Binoculars? A rifle scope?

"Kurt, what do you think that is?" I asked, trying not to be too obvious with my pointing.

"A reason not to be here," he replied. "At worst a rifle scope, at best binoculars."

I lost sight of it once we were in the car.

Someone was watching.

Instant paranoia rolled over me and mingled with the smell of coffee. One or maybe both made me feel ill all over again.

Someone was watching me and Kurt or me, Jules, and Kurt. Who would be interested in two FBI agents meeting with an NCIS agent? Something to do with our case or something to do with Gerrard. Could Gerrard be involved in our case somehow?

Being watched gave me the willies. Just lately it felt like I was being watched a lot. I called Jules as Kurt drove.

"We were being watched from the third floor of a building across from the parking lot. Facing NCIS from the Barry, the building on our left."

"You leaving?"

"No, parking out of sight."

Kurt's mouth turned up as I spoke. He pulled the car into a parking space behind the nearest building.

"Coming?" Kurt said, opening his door.

"Nah, you do it," I replied, checking my weapon and laughing.

"Third floor?" Kurt asked, pointing to a building nearby. "It was that building?"

"Think so." I climbed out of the car and shut my door.

Kurt opened the trunk and passed me a bulletproof vest. Once upon a time, I would've felt weird about wearing a vest in the Navy Yard. Times change. Nothing will ever be the same again.

Jules opened the door to the front entrance of the building as we got there.

"Anyone leave?" I asked.

She shook her head. "I called and had the building put on silent lockdown before we got here."

"Good thinking." No alarms. No scrambling around creating a scene. Just quiet locking of doors and arming of front-desk personnel. I looked toward the front desk. Two men in navy uniforms stood on either side of the civilians manning the desk.

"Access to the upper floors is via two elevators and two stairwells," she said. "I've got three agents and a couple of marines inside."

Liz waved from across the lobby where she stood talking to two marines and a couple of people in civilian clothes. I guessed they were the other two agents.

After brief introductions, Kurt and I took one stairwell, the marines the other, and the NCIS agents took the elevators. Halfway up the stairs, I questioned the wisdom of being in another stairwell. Distracting myself with potential scenarios once we reached our destination helped.

Kurt paused by the door to the third floor. "Okay?"

"Yes," I replied with more confidence than I felt. "Let's go."

My phone beeped. I glanced at the screen as Kurt swung the fire door open. It was a map of the floor with a circle around the room Jules thought the glint came from. We took the left stairs. I counted rooms.

"Kurt, go right, it's the tenth room on the left of the corridor."

"Got it," he said. We stepped into the well-lit corridor. At the other end of the hall, I heard an elevator ping followed by the sound of a heavy door closing. Seconds later I caught sight of marine uniforms walking toward our position.

Every room had large glass windows into the corridor. That would make a stealth approach tricky and potentially impossible.

Brazen it out then. We had one option, stroll on in and announce our presence.

NCIS, Marines, and us, converged on the room at the same time. I stepped back with Kurt to let Jules and Liz handle the entrance. Their jurisdiction, not ours. I could see through the large glass window. A male wearing civilian clothing ducked behind a partition near a workstation.

"He look familiar?" Kurt asked.

"I don't know. Didn't get a good enough look."

The door opened. Marines and NCIS swept the room. Jules held up a rifle with a scope for me to see. A marine lifted a long black case off the floor and opened it. I could just make out the foam inside it. There was a short scuffle. Moments later a handcuffed male was lead toward the door with a smirk on his face.

"How about now?" Kurt asked, holding his hand up for the procession to halt.

He did look familiar. My brain darted through memory drawers and files.

"Remember me, Conway?" he drawled, the smirk grew into a sinister smile.

Everything fell into place. My right hand closed into a fist and I punched him so hard his head snapped back.

Guess he didn't expect that.

Pain shot up my hand into my arm. I shook my hand. Sharp stabbing pain zapped from my knuckles into my wrist and up my arm. Worth it.

Kurt grabbed my right arm before I could strike again. My left fist connected with the other side of the idiot's face. His smile disappeared. He spat blood and a bit of tooth onto the floor.

"Yeah, I know you, asshole," I said as Kurt pulled me away and a marine stepped in front of me.

"Conway?" Kurt said, pushing me against a wall as NCIS marched the bleeding man away.

Jules looked back at me. "We'll talk."

I said nothing.

"Let's go," Kurt said, taking my arm.

Blood trickled from the knuckles on my right hand. I looked at it closely. Grazed not cut. That was good. My hand was already swelling. That wasn't so good. And it hurt like a sonofabitch.

Damn.

I inspected my left hand. Bit grazed across the knuckles but otherwise unscathed. Kurt opened the fire door and ushered me down the stairs and out to the car. He opened the passenger door. I climbed in. Kurt went into the back and came out with his backpack. He dropped two cooling packs in my lap then nestled the backpack in the footwell by my legs.

My door closed. The driver's door opened. Kurt settled into the seat then reached out and bent one of the cooling packs; it cracked and ice spread throughout the pack. He placed it on my right hand.

"Hold it there," he said, reaching around me for the seatbelt. He clicked it into place. "We're running out of time before we meet the plane. You need X-rays."

"Let's just go to the airport."

"Conway, you've probably got a boxer's fracture."

My right eyebrow rose all by itself. More like a bar room fracture. My own stupid fault. I shouldn't have hit him or I should've hit him with my elbow, not my fist.

"I'll live. Airport."

An awkward silence filled with unasked questions draped its arms around the car. The need to tell Kurt why I did what I did fought with my desire to block out the past and ignore what just happened.

He shouldn't have been there anyway. Why was he there? Why was he watching? How the hell did he get a rifle into the building? Who was the target? Jules? Kurt?

Me? Someone else?

Someone else.

My mind hummed.

I saw him by accident. That was his nest. He would've been set up to stay there as long as it took. He should've been more careful.

If one of us were his target, we'd already be dead. He was one helluva marksman. I fumbled my phone trying to get it out of my pocket. My right hand didn't want to move and my left was too awkward. The vest wasn't helping. I took Kurt's phone from the console without asking and called a number I knew by heart at the CIA.

"Tierney," I said as soon as the ringing stopped. "Did you know John Miller was in town?"

"No."

"You're sure?"

"Where did you see him?"

"Navy Yard. Any clue who his target is?"

"No."

"Why don't I believe you?"

"Because you are not very trusting, Ellie."

True.

"He's one of yours and you didn't know he was in town?"

There was a loud rumble and screech of metal as thoughts jammed together and created a picture.

"Stay safe, Ellie, I have a meeting," Tierney's tone sounded dismissive.

"Call him off, Tierney. Or I'll finish him."

"I got notification that he was arrested by NCIS. Not your call, Ellie."

"You'll have him out within the hour. You forget, Tierney, I know how it works."

"You'll never see him again."

"Call him off."

"He's got a job to do. Just like you. I advise you to do yours and leave him to do his."

"He should've been more careful. Now he's on my radar."

I can't let him do his job now. Taking someone out on US soil. That's not how the game is played.

My mind swung back to my last brush with a CIA operative. He went off the reservation big time and tried to take out Tierney.

"Tell me this isn't anything like the last time I came across one of your operatives in D.C."

"John Miller is on a sanctioned assignment."

I looked at my watch. Fifteen minutes had passed since I smashed my fist into Miller's face.

"He's already free, isn't he?" And I just bet he planted audio or GPS trackers on Jules or Liz. Whoever he wanted had to be tied to NCIS. My thoughts stampeded through my mouth. "The target. Miller's only just picked up the scent. God. It's not a coincidence that I've just started looking into Noel Gerrard's disappearance and Miller turns up."

"How's your hand?" Tierney asked.

Yep, confirmation that Miller was free and had

checked in.

"Better than his face," I said. "Call him off."

"He has a job to do."

I hung up.

Kurt's hands gripped the steering wheel until his knuckles were white but he remained focused on the road and traffic. I didn't want to talk. He'd heard enough to worry him and make him think and there wasn't much I could do about that. My thoughts radiated in many directions but each avenue pulled me back to Gerrard. Something was very wrong. He hadn't disappeared. He'd gone to ground. The only trail Miller caught was mine as I tried to find Gerrard; he must've had Gerrard's mother's phone bugged. I wasn't going to lead a killer to Gerrard. I called Sean.

"Hey, about Gerrard ... pull back. He'll find us if he needs to."

"El?"

"Trust me. Don't look for him."

"Explain."

I couldn't. I had a gut feeling and a bit of circumstantial nonsense that said Gerrard was Miller's target. Half a smile floated across my lips. I'd had less and done more with it. This time, I was treading on CIA toes with steel-capped boots and the potential for ugly backlash was extreme.

"Not on the phone. Trust me. Shut down any avenues you have open."

"We need a face-to-face."

"Yeah, we do. As soon as I get a minute."

Chapter Twenty Five
Take this job and shove it

I zipped my jacket against the freshening breeze. Kurt and I waited on the tarmac close to the FBI hangar.

"Keep your hand up by your shoulder," Kurt instructed. "It'll help reduce the swelling and the pain."

I held my hand across my body and rested it on my collarbone. I could see the jet making its final approach. Mallory Stevens was under guard in hospital, waiting to be released into our custody. Lee and Sam were on standby to grab her the minute the hospital gave them the green light. Sean had closed down all investigation into Gerrard's disappearance. My hand ached like a bitch. Today was going well. I checked my phone. No messages.

"You want to tell me why you hit whatshisname?" Kurt said, watching the plane.

"I owed him."

"I gathered you two had history."

Not pretty history. He was part of the team I was seconded to.

Words spilled from me before I could check them. "Once upon a time in the sandbox, Miller was to be on the other end of a rifle. My backup. My eyes. Everything turned to custard. I was on the verge of proving that Dion was working both sides. All of a sudden, I had nothing. It looked like he was dead. Miller couldn't confirm because he wasn't in place. Jump forward to New Zealand eight months later and an explosion that took out some good people and then just eighteen months ago to a spate of deaths in Virginia of Conway women."

"Miller?"

"Not directly, but because he wasn't in place when I needed him, people died and people kept dying." I looked at Kurt. "I owed him."

Kurt nodded.

My phone rang. Unknown number. Something told me I needed to answer it. I planted my injured hand back on my collar bone and used the phone with my left, which was less awkward than it felt.

"Conway," I said, watching the aircraft taxi toward us.

"I don't have long," said a familiar quiet voice. He shouldn't have called but I listened in silence. "I screwed the pooch. When this is over you'll get a package. It will explain everything. Sanitize it before sharing with my mother."

"Stay frosty, Oscar Mike."

The phone beeped in my hand as Gerrard disconnected the call.

The aircraft taxied to the hangar.

Kurt coughed lightly attracting my attention. "Do I want to know who that was?"

I moved in and whispered, "No."

But he knew anyway. "He okay?"

My head shook. "I don't know what's going on and I can't pull resources to find out." I scrolled through a flurry of emails that arrived on my phone while the crew opened the door and let our guest alight. Kurt nudged me. I looked up in time to see Sasha Petrovovich walking toward us.

"He looks like Misha," I said, turning to Kurt.

"Uncanny, isn't it?" Kurt replied.

I let lightness wash over me and the concerns about Noel Gerrard float away. "Do all Russian men look like they've escaped from a romance novel?"

Kurt chuckled. "Maybe."

I stepped into a small patch of sunlight and extended my busted hand to the tall man wearing a long leather coat. I pulled it back as soon as I realized what I'd done. His brow furrowed then smoothed as he smiled. Swooping in, he kissed both my cheeks. Charming.

"Agent Conway," he said. "I am Sasha Petrovovich."

"Thank you for coming," I replied. "This is SSA Kurt Henderson."

"Agent Henderson," Petrovovich said with warmth as they shook.

"Kurt will do fine."

Introductions over, we escorted our charge to the waiting car. Kurt explained where we were going first and gave him a bit of background regarding the case. I dragged on the seat belt with an uncooperative hand, not quite making it to the clip before it snapped back.

Jeez.

I reached across and used my good hand. Hoping to keep my silliness to myself.

Kurt's mouth turned up at the edges. I ignored him.

"I saw something about the case on the news this morning, right before I left New York," Petrovovich said. "It seems challenging."

"That's one way of putting it," I replied, clicking the belt in place.

Forty minutes later we were back at the Hoover Building and I handed him a folder of photos to look at. No bodies included. They were photos of the contents of the bathrooms.

Sasha Petrovovich sat at my desk and pored over the photos and notes I'd made regarding scent. Kurt insisted I sit on the couch and let him play doctor. Not as much fun as it sounds. After a close inspection of my hand and rather more pain than I appreciated, he declared the possibility of fractured knuckles on the fourth and fifth metacarpal. The bruises and grazes weren't very attractive either. On the plus side, there was no displacement.

"I'm taping your fingers. But this needs X-raying." Kurt took strapping tape, scissors, iodine, and gauze squares, from his backpack and set it all on the table in front of him. He cleaned my hand with iodine. It stung but I've had worse. He strapped my pinky and ring finger together then taped them to my middle finger. No birds would be flying from my right hand anytime soon.

"That'll do until we can get that checked," Kurt said. "Try not to use that hand. Keep it elevated as much as possible and let me know if you lose feeling in those fingers."

"Feels a bit better," I said with a small smile. "Thanks."

"Just doing my job," Kurt said. "Don't hit anyone else."

"No promises."

Owen sprang to mind. If the thought of Owen ramped up my blood pressure, no telling what would happen if the Evil Troll Queen appeared before me.

Kurt packed away his medical stuff and picked up his laptop. I wandered into the corridor outside my office in search of coffee or water. Four paces down the hall I knew it was water I was looking for.

Footsteps ran toward me; I spun around. Sandra running in the halls of the FBI. Really? We don't run.

"Ellie!" she called, waving a manila folder.

"Problem?"

Stopping abruptly and puffing, Sandra thrust the file at me. "New victim."

"You could've called me," I replied, taking the folder.

"Check your cell. I've been calling. Where were you?"

I tucked the folder under my right arm and hooked my phone from my pocket. Six missed calls. All from Sandra.

"Sorry."

"I was worried," Sandra said, her breathing returning to normal. She focused on my right hand. "Looks like I had reason to worry."

"I tripped," I replied, brushing off her inquisitive look.

A cloud of disbelief crossed her face but she let it go. "Kurt wasn't answering either. Sam and Lee are following up a lead."

And somehow this week Sandra had become camp leader?

"Kurt was with me. He was driving. We picked up a perfumer from the airport. Kurt is with him in my office."

I opened the file. A DMV photo and crime scene report from local police. Ashley Stewart, twenty-six years old, slim, blonde, attractive. A Middle school teacher in Fairfax. The next fifteen photos weren't so pretty.

"You all right?" Sandra asked.

"Sure. Kurt and I will head over to the crime scene as soon as we can. Have police secure the scene and wait for us."

Sandra nodded. "You're worrying me. Never have I seen you look so pale." Her gaze hardened, becoming scrutinizing. I wanted to hide or leave. "And now the broken fingers?"

"Possible fractured knuckles. It's nothing. I'm tired is all."

"Heard you've been ill. Some sort of stomach flu?"

"Probably. I'm okay now."

"Funny no one else has had it. Maybe it was food poisoning."

She was pushing.

"Maybe."

"You're still very pale. Take it easy, Ellie. Let the team pick up any slack." She paused and smiled. "Wedding soon, what is it, eight days?"

"Yep."

"Mitch will want you to be able to enjoy your honeymoon."

So much concern for my well-being. I felt like a fish

caught on a hook. Didn't matter how much I squirmed and pulled, I wasn't breaking free.

"I'd better go," I said.

"Before I forget, Emilio Herrera from HR has called a few times wanting to know how the case is progressing."

"Emilio ... ah, Jane Daughtry's carpool pal," I replied. Why did I get the feeling Herrera was buddies with the Evil Troll Queen Owen? I shrugged it off. Just because she breathed her rank stench down my neck doesn't mean she's pals with Herrera.

"Do you want to talk to him yourself?"

"No. Just give him the standard line about us doing everything we can to find the person or persons responsible and to bring closure to the families."

"I'll let him know. You sure you're feeling all right?"

"Thanks, Sandra, and yeah, I'm okay." I turned and tried for a casual stroll back to my office but suspect it came off like panicked escape and I knew Sandra was watching.

I scooped my laptop up from my desk with one hand and sat in one of the large armchairs opposite Kurt. Setting the laptop on the coffee table between us, I checked the alerts on my phone. Texts from Holly, my sister-in-law, and two from Mitch's mom. Voicemail. Two Voxer messages from my brother. Several dozen emails. I answered the texts as best I could. Holly and Joan wanted to catch up for coffee. That wasn't going to happen until the case was closed. Aidan wanted to know if he was looking after my cat while we were on honeymoon; his next

Voxer message suggested he should just keep the cat. I answered him and told him he should. Shrek liked him more than he liked me anyway.

Voicemail was next. Dad. He said it wasn't important and was touching base. The last thing he said was, 'Stay frosty.' I knew he'd spoken to Gerrard. Dad trained Gerrard so maybe he'd decided to confide in someone he could trust. I hoped that's what happened and moved on. I put my phone down and checked the emails on my laptop.

Mostly the emails were requests from other divisions or police for information regarding various operations Delta teams were involved in. I forwarded a lot of them to agents who could better answer the queries. The last email wasn't from law enforcement.

The subject line read 'Psycho.'

I opened it. As I read the contents, my blood cooled. Slowly at first then faster and colder. My bones ached as the cold took over. I read the contents four times.

A partial poem, signed Kristopher Lette.

I was right about the crime scene memos. But the email contained another line, one we hadn't seen.

"Kurt ..." My eyes stayed fixed on the screen in front of me.

"Conway? Whatcha got there?"

"Part of a poem."

"Yours?"

"No."

He crouched next to my chair and read the email.

"God," he said. "You think it's Lette?"

"He'd have to be pretty stupid to sign it and send it from his email address." It was signed and the email address appeared to be his. I copied the source information into a little program we liked to use that gave us the ISP emails were sent from and then the physical address of the sender. Our cyber division kept us up to date with the latest developments.

Don't take it personally
It wasn't easy
Just listen
I broke when you looked at me
Life cracked wide open

I reached forward and picked up my phone. Kurt went back to the couch. Dad answered on the sixth ring.

"It's me. Have you met Rosanne's son yet?"

"No. I was supposed to meet him the other day. Rosanne invited him to lunch with us but he didn't show."

"You've been seeing Rosanne for a while and have never met the son?"

"That's right. He's a strange lad by all accounts."

No kidding.

"He's an artist?"

"Yes, I believe so. Is there a problem, El?"

Ignoring Dad's question I continued, "What sort of artist?"

"Fiber, whatever that means. I've never seen anything he created. Rosanne hasn't talked about exhibitions or anything. Maybe his artistic endeavors are fledging."

"Does he write as well?"

"I don't know, love. What's going on?"

"Just need some background information is all. What do you suppose a fiber artist does?"

"Something with fabric or yarn ... I really don't know."

"A knitter?" Knitting might have started with fishermen back in the day but it wasn't what I expected in this instance. A knitting vampire. Large diameter wooden needles became stakes and rammed into his soulless heart.

"I don't know if he knits, Ellie, but fiber art could be anything. He might weave, or sew, or throw paint at fabric."

"Does Rosanne talk about him much?"

I wanted to ask if he knew she had a brain tumor and what the hell he thought he was doing. Dating the nearly-dead didn't seem like a good life choice. Instead, I stuck to questions about Kristopher. Safer ground.

"We've only been seeing each other about six months, El, and she's a private person."

Private or secretive? There is a difference. Six months and he hadn't met the son. A little light went on in my head. She hadn't met me, officially, either. And by Aidan's reaction at the family dinner, he hadn't met her either. Dad could be pretty secretive himself.

My silence filled the airways. I could hear Dad thinking. I knew what was coming.

His voice changed, his wording quiet and deliberate, "What has this got to do with the case you're working on?"

To lie or spill the beans?

Maybe partial truth; I was getting good at that. Before I had time to form my partial truth Dad said, "Just tell me, Ellie. I know your silence and don't need sugar coatings or partial truths. Just tell me."

A sigh escaped. I looked over my shoulder at Petrovovich sitting at my desk. Not here. Standing, I left the room.

"Just got an email containing part of a poem. It's comprised of memos we found at the crime scenes but not entirely. The email is signed Kristopher Lette, it came from his email address, it tracked back to a fixed ISP belonging to Kristopher Lette."

Having had someone send emails from my ISP not so long ago, I knew it was possible that Lette didn't send the email but it really wasn't looking good.

"I see."

"Dad, I never mentioned the memos in the media briefing. Only people directly involved with the case know about the poetry."

"Rosanne doesn't know?"

"No one outside the investigation knows."

"And this is my heads-up that all isn't right?"

"Not exactly, Dad, I needed information ... but ..."

"I'll let you know if I hear anything."

"Thanks, Dad."

I hung up and went back into the office. The email still sat on my screen. My gut said Lette didn't send it because why would he send it to me unless he wanted to be caught? Wouldn't be that unusual for a killer to almost cry out to be stopped. We needed to find him and bring him in.

Knitting? I didn't think so. I called Sandra and asked for in-depth background on Lette. It was a simple request: get me everything.

Sasha Petrovovich coughed lightly from my desk attracting my attention. I moved chairs to sit in front of my own desk, facing Petrovovich.

"The person responsible for these crimes is layering fragrance. He's collecting components from the crime scenes. When you layer, you start at the base. Body wash or soap, shampoo and conditioner, body lotions and finally perfume."

"Do you know what the fragrance is that he's drawn to?"

"I think you know, Agent. You're looking for confirmation."

Maybe I do. "Tell me, please."

"Base notes of bergamot, pepper, neroli, tobacco, citrus and cedar."

I nodded. I'd smelled all those at various crime scenes.

"And that matches?"

"Dolce & Gabbana pour Homme."

"I think the Unsub wears that cologne," I said. "I

smelled it at one of the crime scenes. Residual scent in the air."

Petrovovich smiled at me. "You have a sensitive nose."

"I'm pretty good at identifying scents on people if I've smelled them before." Even diluted by the wind in a tunnel at a concert. Scents change, they become individual as they warm on the skin, making identification easier for me.

"Can I see the bodies? This will sound bizarre but I'd like to see if I can detect perfume on their skin?"

"Yes. I want to see them again myself. We can do that. If you're sure?"

"By the look of the products you say are missing, he's building layers by taking particular items containing base notes he's drawn to from the scenes. Therefore, the women should have that scent on them. If so, I can probably narrow down the brand of lotion or body wash. Would that be helpful?"

"Yes, it would."

"When can we leave?"

Eager.

"We have a new crime scene, which I need to get to. Do you mind tagging along?"

"Not at all."

"I will ask you to stay in the car unless I require your help within the crime scene." A civilian traipsing about a crime scene potentially contaminating evidence? Not on my watch.

"That will be acceptable."

Chapter Twenty Six
Painting Pictures of You

I stood next to Kurt looking at Ashley Stewart in the shower. Obvious stab wounds. No blood. At first glance, her crumpled body told the same story as the previous victims. It wasn't getting any easier. Blonde, pretty, slim, dead.

"You want to do your thing before I start?" Kurt asked.

"Please ..."

Kurt walked to the door. I didn't need to look to know he was standing in the doorway watching me.

I knelt on one knee next to Ashley. She was twenty-six and a teacher. We'd have to get counselors into the school to help her students cope.

"I'm Ellie. I'm really sorry this happened to you."

Talking to the dead again. It's a skill. Or insane and I'm talking to myself. Jury's still out.

Her head moved. I blinked and looked again. Nope, her head still rested on the bottom of the shower. I observed her head move again.

This isn't at all insane.

Slowly, Ashley sat up and rubbed her eyes. I swallowed hard and forced myself to remain calm. I glanced at Kurt. He wasn't reacting. Pretty sure he'd react to reanimation. So whatever was happening was for me and not real. Ashley was not a zombie. I felt for the weapon on my hip. Just in case.

Ashley looked right at me. Her hand reached out and grabbed mine. Iciness spread from her touch, freezing my hand. She pulled me into the shower and thrust a cake of soap into my hand. Water poured over me. Struggling to breathe I choked on the volume of water. Ashley spun me around until I faced the shower door. Steam fogged the glass. I shivered as cold shot through my body. Ashley stepped inside me. She didn't pass through. She stayed. My eyes became hers. Her cold clammy hands grabbed my head and forced me to look toward the door.

A shadowy figure loomed. I wanted to look away but she wouldn't let me. The pounding in my chest escalated as the figure moved closer. Holding my wrist with her ghostly hand, she guided my palm across the wet glass. As the fog cleared, a dark-haired, dark-eyed, olive-skinned male stared back at me. A smile stretched across his thin lips, exposing uneven and yellowed teeth. My stomach twisted. I'd seen him before: Unsub number one. Abruptly, he turned, as if he'd heard a noise. Another male appeared at the shower door. Unsub number two. My vision blurred. A draft blew over me as the door opened. Ashley sank to the floor of the shower. Her hand trailed down my arm as she folded into a heap, leaving me shaking from the cold.

"Conway?"

"Yeah," I said, but not convinced I was speaking.

"You all right?"

Sure. Let's say I am.

"Both Unsubs were here. It's the first time they've both

been at one scene," I said, ignoring his question, my eyes scouring the room looking for the piece of paper I knew would be there. It peeked out from behind the mirror just above the basin. I pulled it out of its hiding place and unfolded the paper. "'Close the windows. Draw a line in the sand.'"

"Two lines?"

"Yep." I knew I'd seen two before. My mind flicked to my whiteboard. Yes. I'd seen two before. "Winchester had two lines as well."

Kurt took the note from me and bagged it. "You said two Unsubs were here and we have two lines ..."

"Yeah, I know, perhaps they started doing this together in Winchester and then went solo."

"That's something we should consider." He made a call to Sam and asked him if we'd heard from the Winchester cop regarding the identikit. I couldn't hear Sam.

"Put him on speaker ... Sam," I said.

"Yo, Chicky Babe. How can I help?"

"Send the cop the second image. You'll find it on my laptop. I worked it up the other night." While I was supposed to be home sleeping. "Tell him to imagine both men with facial hair. Or if you have time add mustaches to the images. Fairly full and partially concealing their mouths."

"You saw facial hair?" Sam enquired.

"No. Just a thought. Could be why he hasn't recognized Unsub One ... he's changed his appearance somehow. I think he's Greek – mustache seems to work?"

"Sure. Okay. I'll tweak copies of the images and send them out."

"Ciao."

Kurt hung up.

"Conway, you're scary."

"So you say."

Time and time again.

It wasn't the most helpful thing to hear. I made my thoughts center on Ashley. Young, pretty, dead. Did she drink coffee? I went back to her body and asked her.

She smiled. "I had coffee this morning."

I tried to ask her if she prepared the coffee maker the night before but she couldn't answer any more questions. A bright light opened above her and the essence of Ashley left her body in a thin stream of dusty light.

Ashley has left the building.

"She had coffee," I said.

"I'll have the techs do a toxicology screen on the coffee grinds as well as her."

"How did the Unsubs gain entry?" I asked.

"Backdoor has tool marks on the lock. Police think that was the point of entry," Kurt said, writing something in his notebook.

I turned slowly, taking in the clean, tidy bathroom and the corporeal shell of Ashley Stewart all at once. "There's something else we haven't figured into the victimology ... look around, Kurt. What do you see?"

Kurt stood next to me and turned full circle. "The Unsubs' aren't cleaning the bathrooms, they're already very clean," he said.

"Like every room in every house we've visited thus far. These women are super clean and house-proud." I looked at Kurt. "This is beyond what you'd expect in homes that are lived in."

Kurt nodded. "Where would our Unsubs meet women like that?"

"Not all at the same place." If some support group for over-cleaners anonymous were missing seven people, we'd have heard about it. "I think there is something to one Unsub being in a psychiatric facility or something similar which will account for the gap and geographical difference between Violet and Jane and the rest of the victims."

Kurt called Lee. "How far did you get on the recent releases from hospitals or rehab units?" Kurt touched the screen of his phone. "You're on speaker."

"I have lists of seventeen people from Frederick County, five from Clarke, eighty-one from Loudoun, six each in Warren and Fauquier, forty in Prince William, ninety-seven in Fairfax. All released two weeks before Jane's death."

Two weeks. That should allow for stalking and so forth.

"Crap!" I said. Doing the math in my head. "Two hundred and fifty-two people."

"Tell me about it. I'm fifty-five in. How far south do you want me to go?"

"Just work on those for now," I said. "I want you to go

back over anyone you've already spoken to and find people who joined support groups for anything after their release. Get Sandra to help." I paused. "I need that list A-SAP, Lee."

"On it, Chicky." The call disconnected from Lee's end.

So they came in the back door, but when?

"Did they sweep for cameras and audio?" I asked Kurt. "Yes. Same as the other scenes. Surveillance in place."

"What's the range on the equipment found?" I talked as I left the room and walked down the hallway looking at the ceiling. Kurt followed me. "What if I were right, Kurt? What if one or both of the Unsubs came in while the victims were at work and stayed until morning?" At the end of the hall I saw what I was looking for; a recessed trap door into the ceiling crawlspace. "What if they were using the crawl space or attic?" I pointed up.

"And they got up there how?"

"If I were them I'd come prepared. I'd have a ladder, supplies, and a way of monitoring the goings-on in the house."

"We're going up there, aren't we?"

Been a little while since we'd been in anyone's roof space.

"Yep."

I walked back to the front door and the cop standing guard.

I handed him my keys and asked him to fetch a ladder from the back of the Suburban.

"You FBI have everything," he said with a grin. "Anything else, while I'm there, ma'am?"

Actually, yes.

"There is a man in my car waiting for us. Tell him we're sorry and will be with him as soon as we can. Also, there's a black case about so big ..." I held my hands apart about eighteen inches, "... in the back with the ladder. Bring that too, please. Can you manage?"

"Yes, ma'am."

I spun on my heels and rejoined Kurt. "That nice young cop is checking on Petrovovich and fetching our ladder and the black case."

"Good. Take off your jacket," Kurt said with half a smile and sparkle in his eye.

"Really?" My right eyebrow arched all by itself.

"Really," he replied. His smile settled. "I said jacket ..." he let his voice fade, "... not clothes."

"Kurt ... something you want to say?"

"Timing," he said, almost under his breath.

"It's always sucked," I said, matching his tone.

His voice strengthened again. Kurt was back. "It'll be hot up there and you're still looking pale."

I did as he suggested.

The cop and ladder arrived. Behind him, I saw a dark leather-coated figure carrying the case and shook my head. Petrovovich.

"Do you need a hand?" the cop asked, propping the ladder against the wall.

"We're good, thanks," Kurt replied, his eyes landing on Petrovovich. "You can escort Mr. Petrovovich back to the car."

"I needed to stretch my legs and the young man looked like he needed help," Petrovovich explained.

"You can't be in here, it's a new crime scene," I said. "You could contaminate it." I looked down; he was wearing protective booties. His hands were gloved. The cop wasn't stupid, easily swayed but not stupid.

"I won't get in the way."

A sigh escaped before I could check it. I couldn't believe what came out of my mouth next. "Okay, stay, but don't move from that spot." I pointed to where he stood. "No wandering off. You stay put."

"Of course, Agent Conway."

Why didn't I believe him?

The cop went back to his post. Kurt extended the ladder and opened it to create a stable A-frame. "I'm going up first."

I wasn't arguing. Kurt took the case from Petrovovich and climbed the ladder; resting the case on a rung, he pushed the trapdoor inward. He called down to me from inside the attic, "I think you're right. Get up here, Conway."

I put one foot on the first rung and turned to Petrovovich. "Don't move!" I said then carried on climbing.

Kurt peered out at me as I neared the top. "You okay to climb in here unaided?"

"Of course."

I climbed into heat that must've been ten degrees higher than the house below. The area was surprisingly roomy; Kurt and I could stand, with about a foot of clear space above Kurt's head at the lowest point of the roof. If it were my house, I'd add folding stairs, bigger windows that opened, and use it as a room.

Sun streamed in through small windows at both ends. The closest window to us illuminated dust, reminding me of Ashley's essence leaving her body. There was a hardwood floor, not just joists and insulation, with boxes stacked in neat piles along one area of the outer wall. Ignoring the heat was difficult. It sucked the moisture from me. I knew I couldn't stay up there long. Murky spots danced in front of my eyes. I blinked them away and tried to concentrate on the task at hand. Unsuccessfully.

"Someone dragged something in through the trap door," Kurt said, pointing to freshly chipped paint and drag marks across the floor. "It's the width of a ladder."

"Yeah, I can see that." I followed the drag marks to an area by an outer wall. "It was left here." Disturbed dust and low marks on the wall. "Looks like something was against this wall."

"Come over here," Kurt said from the back corner.

I joined him. He pointed out a dust-free area and a piece of a shiny wrapper.

About two feet away from the cleared area was an impression in dust. "Look at this," I said. "Someone sat there."

Kurt had the case open. He got busy with dusting powder looking for fingerprints. I picked up the small piece of shiny wrapper and bagged it. Shiny, not paper but foil. We could print it. Save the lab and get a quick result.

I handed him the baggie. "See what you can find on the wrapper, both sides."

Kurt nodded. He prepared a clean work surface then dusted the foil. I carried on looking around. The top few stacked boxes contained Christmas decorations. Kurt called to me. "I got a partial."

"Yes!"

He photographed it with his phone and dropped it into the app we used. Smartphones are smart and ours connect to our databases.

"Cross something, Conway," Kurt said, wiping his gloved hands with wet wipes before packing up the stuff he'd used.

Things were starting to fall into place.

Petrovovich's voice resounded through the opening in the floor under my feet. "Agent Conway, soap is missing from this scene."

Yes, the soap. I saw Ashley holding soap but it wasn't there. And how did he know?

I shook my head and indicated to Kurt that I was going down the ladder. "I'm taking him outside."

Placing my feet and left hand firmly on the ladder, I climbed down as quickly as I could.

Petrovovich waited, leaning on the wall. Dark, mysterious, and way too like Misha Praskovya for it to be a coincidence. Every time Misha appeared in my life, shit got messy and complicated. I've yet to decide if that's because

Misha is a magnet for trouble or because he's our friendly Russian FSB counterpart and breezes in when trouble heads our way. I hoped the physical resemblance was all they had in common.

"I told you not to move," I snarled.

"I thought I could help."

To his credit, he didn't look as though he enjoyed the experience.

"You did, but, I'd prefer to have been with you when you viewed Ashley," I said, hoping I kept the annoyance from my voice.

"Ashley," he said. "That's her name?"

"Yes."

"Death does horrible things to a person."

I almost felt sorry for him. Almost. People need to do as I say; it stops them seeing things they're unprepared for.

"You learn to see past the death mask and find the person that once was," I replied, taking his arm and leading him outside. "It's not a job for everyone."

Understatement of the day.

Chapter Twenty Seven

Remember

Petrovovich and I sat in the car and waited for Kurt. I swigged warm water from the bottle I'd left in the foot well in an attempt to rehydrate after the drying heat of the attic. Warm was better than nothing.

"Now what?"

"Now, the morgue. I need to see the other bodies," I replied.

"May I?"

"Yes."

"Then?"

"We found something at this crime scene that we didn't know before. The other scenes have to be searched again."

"Do you do that yourself?"

"Sometimes."

Not this time. I turned the ignition key and pain shot up my arm.

"Jeez!" I zapped my window down. I needed air. Two seconds later I flung open the door and vomited violently into the gutter. My timing, as usual, impeccable. A shadow fell over me before I straightened up. My heart sank and stomach twisted. I didn't want to have a conversation about what just happened.

"Getting to be a habit, Conway," Kurt said. He placed a hand on my shoulder as he reached past me for my water bottle. "Here, drink."

"Thanks."

Kurt straightened up and rested one arm on the top of the door and one on the roof of the car. I sat in his shadow. His blue eyes watched me with all the scrutinizing power that came with years of medical training and practical application.

"You were right about the heat." I'd told him he was right and it hadn't killed me. Who knew? I hoped it was enough to thwart the questions I saw in his eyes.

No questions, yet. There's no time to get into it. Killers to catch. Wedding to make. Escape in the form of a honeymoon.

"Where to?" Kurt asked, motioning for me to get out of the driver's seat. "I'm not buying the line about the heat, Conway. I'll drive."

"Drama queen. I'm all good." I climbed out of the car anyway. "Morgue."

Kurt grinned as he slid in behind the wheel. As I walked around the back of the car I heard him say, "We should get coffee on the way."

Make mine a hot chocolate.

He reached across and opened the door for me.

"Thanks," I said.

"We're leaving the ladder. Techs can use it when they arrive. I'll pick it up later."

Kurt's phone buzzed. He checked it as I fastened my seat belt.

"We got something, Conway, the partial fingerprint

came back with a possible match. Let's get to the morgue and get that over with."

"Sure."

He dropped his phone into my lap. I looked at the screen.

Fuckadoodledo.

Troy Fallon was in the roof?

I stared at the image on the screen. "She wasn't either of the Unsubs I saw."

For starters she's a she and secondly she's a cop.

"I know, Conway, I know."

I moved back into the seat and closed my eyes. Petrovovich started to say something. Kurt silenced him.

Eyes closed. Thoughts in progress. Do not interrupt. I considered that I should have a speech bubble above my head warning people.

Fallon. What the hell was she doing in the roof space? She wasn't even at this scene. Was she?

"Kurt, whose scene was it?"

He knew exactly what I was asking. "Not hers. She was never here from what I can tell. That young cop we met was first on the scene and said no detectives showed up. Word went out to all officers that anything like this, we were to be called directly."

I sank back into my thoughts. Fallon's presence didn't make sense. To be fair, crime rarely made sense. But a detective's fingerprint in the roof space of a crime scene? I thought about the shiny foil. Familiar. Candy bar familiar. Baby Ruth. So someone who likes candy bars was in the roof. One fingerprint on something that was easily transportable wasn't conclusive proof of a person's involvement. Someone could have put it there on purpose.

I stretched out my left leg and jammed my hand into my pocket to fish out my phone. "Sandra—"

"At your service, Warrior Princess."

Petrovovich's presence in the car meant I needed to be careful and not use Fallon's name. I hoped Sandra would make the connection.

"Background check on that new helpful friend at Metro, I want everything and I want it fast."

"I am your servant ... and the new friend, is that Detective Troy Fallon?"

"Yes, indeed it is. Sandra, if there's dirt, I want it. I want to know what she had for breakfast and what toothpaste she uses."

"Got it."

The sound of fingers tapping at lightning speed on a keyboard filled the airways.

"Let me know A-SAP."

I hung up and let my head meet the headrest. My eyes closed without bidding. Tired and frustrated pushed each other around until fatigue became the clear winner. Dusk descended on my mind bringing shadows from the recesses. A shadow I recognized as Chance crossed my vision.

He paused, turned, and came back. "What are you doing in here?" he said with a lopsided grin.

"It's my head. I live here," I snapped. That grin of his

wasn't going to work this time. "Why are you here?"

"I like the dark, you have plenty of it," he quipped. His dimples deepened as his smile increased.

"You're trespassing."

He tipped his head back and Chance's laughter bounced across the gray and slammed into the darker shadows at the edges of my mind. "You know you really love me."

I shrugged. I wouldn't go that far. "You can be an infuriating sonofabitch. But I like having you around, sometimes." I decided I needed a qualifier in there. No need to stroke his ego unnecessarily.

He grinned. "How do you like me so far?"

The wiseass was mixing up his series.

"If you call me Moneypenny, I'll evict you."

His infectious laughter flowed over me. "While I'm here ... you want a hand?"

I nodded. "I do. What's with Fallon?"

He froze for a second. His eyes met mine. When he looked down, I followed his gaze. In his hand was a can opener. That didn't bode well.

"You sure you want to go there?"

"She went there. She was deep inside a crime scene."

"You need to look at Stevens too. They know each other."

"What do they have to do with the deaths?"

"Think about it, Ellie ... you have two male Unsubs. How did they gain access to women's homes?"

"Broke in, mostly. Apart from one scene, where there

was no forced entry."

Chance rocked on his heels, dropped the can opener, and shoved his hands in his pockets. "Would single young females open the door for strange males?"

No. Or I'd like to think not.

"Are you telling me I have four Unsubs and two of them are women?"

"I'm telling you to keep an open mind and work all the leads."

"Fallon is a detective ..."

He nodded. "Stings when it's close to home, doesn't it?"

Yeah. It does.

"Locke senior?" I still thought he had something to do with the surveillance. And his son knew Stevens.

"Does Fallon have the expertise to rig surveillance equipment?"

"Probably, or if not, she'd know who to ask."

"Take it easy, El, you look like crap." Chance winked and disappeared. Magic.

My eyes pinged open.

Houston, we have a problem. We have a potentially dirty cop.

I needed her surgically removed from the investigation and all information we gathered to stay within Sentinel.

"Are we there yet?"

"Nearly." He glanced at me. "Were you sleeping?"

I shook my head. "Not sleeping, thinking."

"About?"

"Tell you later. Let's do this scent thing first."

My eyes closed again. I was back in the roof space. I walked around the room. By the farthest window from the trap door, I smelled something.

White musk? Sandalwood? No, a combination of the two.

It wasn't a perfume as much as the heavier aroma of an essential oil. Cloying in large amounts but this was dilute and diffused.

Why didn't I notice it when I was in the house? Preoccupied with death and the discovery of the shiny piece of wrapper.

I twisted in my seat and looked at our guest in the back. "Mr. Petrovovich?"

"Yes, Agent Conway. Please call me Sasha."

Sasha and Misha were too close for comfort.

"Did you smell any other scents near the body, other than the missing soap?"

His brow creased. I could see thoughts processing in his dark eyes. "I thought as I walked to the trapdoor area of the hallway that I smelled sandalwood."

"Do you think it was a perfume base note or an essential oil?"

He nodded with approval. "Your nose is very good."

"Thanks, which is it?"

"You tell me."

"I smelled white musk and sandalwood in the attic. It was dilute but heavier than a perfume. I don't even know if that makes sense."

"To me it does. I think, Agent, it was oil."

I nodded.

It wasn't either Unsub. Neither of them wore essential oil.

"Where do you get something like that?"

"Fairly good quality essential oils that can be worn on the skin are mixed with a carrier oil. They're available from new age stores all over the country and also online. We use oils in the production of perfume but they're pure and very expensive."

Kurt pulled into a car park.

"Rachel goes to a New Age store for incense, you want me to give her a call and find out where it is?" Kurt asked me.

"That might be helpful, thanks."

The owner might just recognize Fallon or Stevens. Just because we didn't find Stevens' prints doesn't mean she wasn't there.

Kurt called home and I zoned out. One partial print that came back as possibly Fallon's wasn't a whole helluva lot. The sandalwood/white musk scent wafted past me again. I'd smelled it before.

Where?

"Coming in, Conway?" Kurt asked, opening my door for me. I hadn't noticed him get out of the car.

"Yeah."

"What's on your mind?" His fingers lightly held my elbow as he escorted me off the road and onto the pavement outside a severe, cold looking building. County

Morgue.

"The white musk and sandalwood, I've smelled it before."

The can opener Chance had in his hand fell from nowhere along with a can. The can rolled, stopping at my foot. As I watched, the can opener attached itself to the top of the can and gave a few turns. A worm wriggled through the tiny opening and plopped onto my boot.

Yuck.

"When we're done here, you're going home," Kurt said. "I have no idea what you can see down there, but I don't like it."

I dragged my eyes away from the worm on my boot and looked at Kurt. "A worm fell out of a can." After a couple of slow beats, I knew where I'd smelled the fragrance before. I whispered in Kurt's ear. "Jane Daughtry. The scent came from her home, maybe even from her."

"We're whispering why?"

"I want to see if he ..." I inclined my head to the Russian, "... can detect it on Jane's skin. I couldn't but he might be able to." I stopped.

Cloak and dagger, much? Conway, Ellie Conway. Had a nice ring to it.

The thought made me chuckle; thankfully the laughter was contained in my own head.

An hour later we were back outside the morgue. Sasha smelled as many scents as I did but unlike me, he could name the products they came from. One was even from his own line. Most of the missing items from the crime scenes were high-end products. All but one of the products came from perfume counters or duty-free stores. The odd one out was one he thought was Black Amethyst. The cheapness of that fragrance didn't sit right compared to the others. We debated the possibility it was Black Orchid by Tom Ford rather than the mass produced Black Amethyst.

"I did not smell the depth of fragrance I would expect from Tom Ford. The composition is different and sillage stronger."

In my mind I was again in Jane Daughtry's home, walking through the room until I reached her bedroom. "When I sat on her bed there was a light shroud of scent."

Why didn't I notice it at the time?

In my mind's eye, I looked around the room. I didn't notice it because the existence of the poetry threw me back to another case. "I don't think that scent was Black Amethyst."

"Nor do I. You're talking about the sillage, for the scent to remain in the room like that the sillage would be medium and above."

"The shower gel was Black Amethyst but she wore another perfume, something darker with strong sillage."

He smiled. "You can work for me when you grow tired of the FBI."

We took Sasha back to the office and let him use my desk. He wanted to build a scent profile for the Unsubs and victims alike. Kurt and I joined Delta in a meeting room.

"Time we laid out a few things," I said, closing the door firmly. "There is a likelihood we have a cop involved in the killings."

No one reacted. Not a raised eyebrow in the room. Silence.

I sat at the table.

Sam rocked his chair back, hooking his fingers under the table top to stop himself toppling backward.

"Who?" Sam asked.

"Detective Troy Fallon."

"The chick who worked the first few crimes scenes and came to the media briefing as your guest?" Lee said.

"Yep."

Sam shook his head. "What do we know?"

"That we have a partial print and it came back as hers," Kurt said. "The print was in the roof space of the latest crime scene on a piece of a candy wrapper."

"That's not good," Sam said. "You talked to her yet?"

I shook my head. "Sandra is trawling through her life as we speak. I'll talk to Fallon when I know everything there is to know about her."

She's a cop; I need to have done my homework to interview her. Is dotted, Ts crossed.

Interviewing cops had the potential to be challenging. I wasn't all that sure I was up to the task.

"Anything else we should know?" Lee's pen stayed poised over his open notebook.

Time to let the crazy out.

"I think Fallon knows Stevens, and I think both

women are involved. Maybe even at the crime scenes."

"You can back that up with some kind of evidence?" Lee asked.

"Yeah. Nah. Not so much. That's where good old fashioned investigating comes in. We need to prove Chance's theory."

As soon as I heard his name fall from my mouth I knew I was in trouble. Wishing the floor would open up and swallow me wasn't even close to how I felt.

"He's chatty lately. Any particular reason he's back? Chance have any ideas how to prove his whacked-out theory?" Kurt said.

"No, no reason, and proof is up to us." I inhaled and exhaled slowly. What I was about to say wouldn't make me sound any less like a fruit loop. "Fallon may have supplied and even installed the surveillance in the houses."

Lee flipped pages in his notebook.

"Neighbors at scene three, four, and five remember seeing a Fire Security Services van at those houses a week before the deaths."

"That's good to know," I said. "Maybe not Fallon?"

Or maybe she's clever.

Sam opened his notebook and read something before saying, "Charles Locke senior worked for Fire Security Services as a technician until six months ago when he left to become a building super."

"Great. And Mallory Stevens, who I believe was Phoebe Childs' lover, knows Charles Locke Junior, the man who nearly beat Phoebe's sister to death," I added. "There's a tangled web of bullshit going on here. Let's start pulling on threads and see what stinks as it unravels."

Kurt nodded and checked the time. "I've asked Delta C to work with us on searching the crime scenes for hiding places and evidence that the Unsub or Unsubs spent the night in the houses before killing the women. Sam and Lee, you're with Delta C, scene by scene, please."

I looked at Kurt. "I'd like to be in on that."

He shook his head. "You and I need to return Sasha Petrovovich to the airport for his flight home and then, Conway, you are going home. I don't want to see you until tomorrow morning."

So shut your eyes.

To be fair, my heart wasn't in it and I didn't complain. Two weeks ago I would've screamed bloody murder at being sent home. Now, I just wanted some quiet time to myself.

Chapter Twenty Eight

Something to believe in

"Hey," I said as soon as he answered and then touched the speaker icon.

"Hi. Where are you?"

"Home. Am I expecting you anytime this evening?" I moved from room to room closing curtains and turning on lights as I talked.

"Late. Sorry," Mitch replied.

"Long day," I said; a statement, not a question. My fingers locked on the lid of a bottle of water and twisted off the cap.

"You all right?"

"Of course," I replied taking a big swig of water.

"Wine?"

"Water."

"El, really?" Mitch sounded preoccupied, distracted even. Computer sounds and office noises accompanied him. I decided to leave him to it. "Still working the case?"

Because that's the only reason I'd drink water not wine after a long shitty day.

"Yeah. Not making a lot of progress but a few things have fallen into place."

"And you're okay?"

"Yep. I'm okay. Don't work too late. I finally have an evening home."

"Sure. I'll pick up a bottle of Pinot. There isn't any in

the wine rack," he replied, his smile evident in his words. "One glass wouldn't hurt."

I didn't know if I could stop at one glass. Best not to tempt fate.

"Don't be too late," I said with a small laugh. An envelope on the kitchen counter drew my attention. I touched it, dragging it closer to me with a finger. I picked it up and turned it over. "Hey, did you call in here today?"

"Nope." He paused. I heard him typing. "Why?"

"There's an envelope on the counter addressed to me."

"Not me, babe, maybe your dad came in?"

"Maybe."

It wasn't Dad's writing but that didn't mean he hadn't put it on the counter.

"Don't be all night, M."

"Wait up?"

"Think I can manage that."

He laughed. "See what you can do."

I hung up, set my phone on the counter and took a closer look at the mystery envelope. No postmark. There was a twinge of regret about handling it to start with. Rookie mistake. Investigators look with their eyes first not their ungloved hands.

Who knew that would be a thing in my own kitchen?

Me! I should've.

Definitely not Dad's handwriting, not Aidan's either. It didn't look like anyone's that I knew.

So how did it get on my counter?

Walk? Nope.

Envelopes don't have legs. Someone helped it.

My hand felt for the Glock on my hip. Unease crawled across the kitchen floor. A deep bone-chilling cold lapped at my boots. I opened the alarm company app on my phone and checked on code use. Dad's code was used.

Maybe it was Dad.

I didn't believe that for one second. Dad would've left me cupcakes or some other edible treat. It's what he did.

"Just this once, I'm glad you're late, M," I said to no one. With a sigh, I made another call. I had to check. As soon as I heard Dad's voice I spoke. "Did you come by today?"

"No. Why?"

"You didn't put an envelope on the kitchen counter?"

"No."

A bang shuddered in the distance as a door closed.

What the hell?

Listening, I held my breath.

"You okay? Where's Mitch?"

"I'm good. M's at work. Nothing to worry about, Dad."

Another door closed.

That wasn't good.

"I hope not."

Footsteps above me. Someone was in my house.

That shouldn't even be possible.

"Gotta go, Dad. Talk soon."

"Honey, call Delta or push the panic button."

"It's nothing, Dad. It's just an envelope."

"Ellie!"

"Okay, okay. I'm calling."

Later. Once I know who is in my house.

I hung up. I slid my Glock from the holster on my right hip using only my index finger and thumb. Awkward. Switching the weapon to my left hand, I adjusted my grip as best I could. I'm not the best with my left hand. Quietly, I walked down the hallway to the laundry and shut down the power to the house. The silent house alarm would trigger as the alarm system switched to auxiliary power.

Plunging the house into darkness worked in my favor. My home. I didn't need light to find my way. I did take a small flashlight from a drawer under the laundry sink. I switched it on to check it was red light. Safety first. Might be my house but I have no desire to fall while climbing stairs in the dark. Red light doesn't travel as far as white light. It wouldn't alert anyone to my presence until it was too late. My right hand ached. Standing in the dark hallway near the back stairs I listened. A door opened upstairs followed by a vibration as someone bumped into a wall.

I stood for a moment at the bottom of the staircase. Above the sound of my pounding heart, I heard tentative footfalls moving toward the stairs. There was definitely someone in my super secure house. Weird. Should also be impossible.

Footsteps moved downward. I flicked off the flashlight and waited.

The steps paused then continued. Every few feet the

footfalls stopped. Tentative? Someone who didn't know my house and had no idea how long the staircase was?

I supported myself on the wall at the foot of the stairs and waited. My eyes had adjusted to the darkness. I did a slow blink. As I opened my eyes, a dark shape appeared then stumbled over the last stair. Instinctively my hand shot out and connected with a soft body. A hard shove caused the black shape to fall with a resounding thud. Pain surged up my arm. Air rushed from the person in an undignified squawk. I flicked the red light on and illuminated the face of the intruder. Holding the flashlight in my mouth I wrestled my phone out of my pocket, pain no longer registering. The flashlight on the phone shone brilliant white light on the person's face. I spat my small flashlight onto the floor and shoved my Glock into my waistband.

Rosanne.

What the hell? Made sense though; someone used Dad's code. Who else could get it?

She shielded her eyes from the light.

I reached out and helped her up, turned off the flashlight on my phone. Then holstered my weapon and said, "Stay put."

Returning to the laundry, I flipped the switch flooding the house with light again.

Back in front of Rosanne, I demanded an answer. "Explain!"

"I came by to see you ..."

My head shook. "Try again." I watched her pulling together her thoughts. "Did you put an envelope on the counter?"

"I came by to see you." She paused. "There was an envelope addressed to you in the mailbox."

"My mail is usually in the mailbox courtesy of the mail carriers who, you know, put it there."

"Thought I'd bring it in for you."

"Uh huh. And you got through the gate and into the house how?" I knew how but wanted confirmation.

"I used a code."

Good that she wasn't lying. "You don't have a code. So what you mean is … you stole a code."

A sheepish look crossed her face.

I continued. "It's breaking and entering."

"More creative entering than breaking and entering," Rosanne replied.

"No one likes a wiseass." I felt the solid wall against my back. "And you creatively entered why?"

"Because I need to know what you know about your current case. That media briefing wasn't the whole story."

"You couldn't have asked me?" I motioned for her to follow me to the living room. "Take a seat. Cutting the power triggered my silent alarm." I checked my watch. "We'll have company soon."

Men in tactical gear carrying automatic weapons. No need for anyone to get shot unnecessarily.

Her eyes flicked from my banged-up hand to my face. "What'd you do to your hand? Looks painful."

"Broke it on the last person who pissed me off," I

replied, letting the chill in my voice speak louder than my words. I gave Dad a call.

Yeah. Nah, I wasn't keeping his lady friend's antics to myself.

"Can you come over, please?"

"You okay, kid?"

"Yes. But you need to be here." I hung up.

"Who was that?" Rosanne asked. She appeared to have lost some of her composure.

"My dad."

Her face fell, mouth drooped and head shook. "Why?"

"Really?" Maybe the brain tumor prevented her putting two and two together. Because it wasn't rocket science. "You stole his code and used it to access my home. You could've gotten shot." Not even an exaggeration. "You used my father to get close to me and you were spying." I looked at her for a beat. "Any of those things seem bad?"

Who was I kidding – she's a journalist?

I was wrong about her. I'd thought she was an okay person. The only journalist I'd liked. She even helped me out once. Once a journalist always a journalist. It's all about the story.

"That's not how it happened," she replied.

Headlights streamed through a gap in the curtains.

"Hold that thought and do not move!"

I hurried to the front door and flashed the exterior light three times before opening the door.

Three armed men stood bathed in my security lighting.

"Ellie?" said the tallest man, standing in the middle.

"Sean. I had a situation, it's contained. My father will be arriving in a few minutes. Have someone escort him to the living room."

"Sure." He turned to the man on his right. "Stand the team down. Escort Simon Conway in when he arrives."

"Sir. Yes. Sir."

"Sean, with me," I said and lead the way into the house. Sean shut the door behind him then fell into step with me.

Rosanne was shaken not stirred.

"Is this the breach?" Sean asked. Dressed in black, carrying an assault rifle, wearing body armor and several obvious weapons, Sean's six-foot-seven-inch frame imposed upon the room.

"Yes. Rosanne here stole Dad's code and let herself in."

"That wasn't very smart." He addressed Rosanne, "Do you have a death wish?"

"I'm seeing that my decision wasn't very clever." She mustered fragments of intelligence and rammed them back inside her skull. "There are extenuating circumstances."

"Save it for the judge," Sean said and turned his head toward the door a little.

I heard the voice too. We looked at each other.

"Simon is on deck," Sean said.

"I can hear," I replied. "He's going to be all kinds of upset."

Sean nodded.

"Give me the word and I'll remove Rosanne and have Delta pick her up from my custody. When you're ready. No rush."

I nodded. "Thanks." My eyes focused on the doorway.

Waiting for my father.

Chapter Twenty Nine

Need you now.

Dad's stern expression, knitted brows, and sharp tone announced he was unimpressed with Rosanne's behavior. Second biggest understatement of the week, right there.

It took a bit to settle him down. Understandably. Sean removed Rosanne. I called Kurt. When he arrived, Dad went home.

Kurt and I stood in the kitchen. Neither of us spoke for a beat.

"Hand okay?" Kurt did not take his eyes off the envelope on the counter.

"No. Hurts like a bitch," I replied, willing the envelope to give up its contents.

Kurt opened the freezer and took out an ice-pack. He handed it to me.

"Put that on your hand."

I did. The cold hurt, I couldn't tell if it was worse with the ice or without.

The envelope just lay there upon my counter daring one of us to open it. Could be that the envelope was the innocent victim of my inherent mistrust of people. That the lack of a postmark was because someone I knew dropped it off in person rather than mailing it. That it was an invitation to an event and not at all sinister. Also, pigs fly and unicorns poop rainbows and no one has ever tried to kill me or broken into my home before.

My laughter took me by surprise.

"Share?" he said.

"It's an envelope ... let's just open the freaking thing." I tilted my head toward him. "What's the worst that could happen?"

"I don't know ... perhaps fiery death, viral death, zombie apocalypse? Or all of the above." He grinned at me and lifted the ice-pack to check my hand. "It's you, Conway, you attract some peculiar people and most of them want to shorten your life."

"It's a gift."

"Sure is."

Kurt picked up the envelope and felt it. He stood for a second with the envelope resting across the palm of one hand. I knew what he was doing. Judging the weight.

"And?"

"Feels okay. But then C4 feels okay when it's rolled real thin."

"Cheerful thought."

I passed him a flashlight from under the sink. He switched it on and held it under the envelope.

"Paper? What do you think?"

"Looks like it. Nothing weird looking in there. Tip it."

Kurt tipped the envelope. Nothing loose moved. No powder rushed to the lowest corner. Probably not anthrax or heroin or cocaine. Love that I thought anthrax before schedule I and II drugs. Could be paper laced with the Ebola virus. For all I knew, that could be a thing now. I felt as though we should be wearing Level A Hazmat suits – the ones with self-contained breathing apparatus.

Kurt walked around the counter and opened a drawer. He removed a steak knife and slipped it under the seal of the envelope.

"Now's a good time to pray, Conway," he said with a grin as he slit the paper open and carefully extracted a folded piece of paper. He unfolded the paper.

I could see his eyes over the sheet of paper as he read. It didn't look good. "What is it?"

"Fan mail."

"What now?"

He looked over the paper at me. "Confusing little words are they, Conway? "

"I thought you said fan mail?"

"I did, do you prefer love letter?"

"I'm not going to like this, am I?"

His head shook a little.

My heart sank. Another lunatic surfacing was the very last thing I needed. Kurt handed me the letter. I scanned it not really wanting to read it at all. By the time I got to the end of the page, I knew I didn't want to read it and it was too late to stop my brain processing the words.

"He ..." I looked at the name at the bottom of the page, checking that it was a male. Hank. Probably a male. "Hank seems like a nice fellow."

Warning bells boomed in my head. The contents and the name on the letter meant something but it wasn't ce-menting into anything I could narrow in on.

Kurt laughed. "Probably a real sweetheart. You really

should stop sending subliminal messages to four-hundred-pound gorillas, Conway."

"I should. Can't promise though. As this fellow says, I speak to him on a visceral level. Not sure how to turn that off."

"Animal magnetism, Conway?"

"Yeah, shut up!" I thrust the paper back at him. "You can deal with Hank. I do believe his return address is a federal prison."

"And how did your new pal Hank get this missive of love and adoration delivered to you?"

I didn't want to think about how an inmate got my address or how he got a letter to me out of the prison. His name wriggled about in my head then jumped in and out of old case files until a neon flashing warning sign lit the dark in my brain.

Holy fuck, Batman. I could be in trouble.

"Kurt ..."

Hank liked puzzles. He liked to make puzzles out of people. It was a Delta case. When we arrested him, he told me he'd like to make a puzzle out of me. Every image associated with Hank and his fascination with jigsaw puzzles and scroll saws flooded back. Everything blurred and swayed as the horror took over. He liked to use a reciprocating saw first up then move to a scroll saw for the more intricate patterns. Two of his victims were sliced up using a band saw in welder's workshop. I'd never seen a mess like it and hoped I never would again.

"Yes," he said looking up from the letter. "Whoa, sit

down."

Drab confetti danced in front of my eyes and encroaching blackness threatened. I felt his hand close around my arm but couldn't see it.

My next thought came in sharp pointy shards, it pierced the dark, creating rips big enough for me to see through. Mitch.

"El, you awake?"

Mitch.

A groan escaped as thoughts of Hank returned. I tried to push the thoughts away. He made a big mess and it was hard to scrub that from my conscious mind.

"Groaning isn't indicative of wakeful speech, El. You need to say words."

"Mitch ... thought you were going to be late?"

"Babe, I am late. Kurt called me but I was almost home." His fingers brushed my bangs away from my eyes. "You in there?"

"Yep."

An inventory happened without my bidding. My mind ran through its checks. Yep. I was okay. No harm done. I looked around. I was on the sofa in the living room. My last memory was being in the kitchen and Kurt grabbing my arm.

God. I passed out. That wouldn't go down well.

"You need sleep," Mitch said. His tone suggested arguing was futile.

Legs wearing dark blue suit pants appeared in front of me. I followed them up to a dark blue jacket, white shirt, and striped blue-on-blue tie. Kurt.

"Sleep. I'll pick you up in the morning."

What no questions? Color me stunned.

"Thanks for not letting me hit my head," I said.

"You're welcome. See you in the morning." He frowned at me for a second. "I've ordered armed security for here and Mitch's home effective immediately and until I say otherwise. While you were out, I did a search on Hank." He didn't need to carry on; I knew only too well what he found.

The sofa cushions moved as Mitch stood. I heard him and Kurt talking on the way to the front door, then the door opened and closed. Mitch's footsteps paused at the living room door.

I sat up slowly. Everything felt okay. Nothing spun out of control, no murky gray or darkness lurking.

"All right?" he said, walking toward me.

"Yes. I'm going to go get something to eat."

The black bear rumbling in my stomach reminded me how very hungry I was.

"Tell me what you want and I'll get it for you."

And there was the problem. Starving, but no clue what I wanted to eat.

"I'm not sure, I'll go see what there is."

"Can you manage?"

Can I manage?

For a second there I didn't understand. Pain flooded back as I ran my hand through my hair, in an attempt to sweep my bangs out of my eyes. Sharp tugs as hair caught on the tape didn't help.

"I got this."

"I don't doubt that, just thought I could help."

I smiled. "No, you read the paper and unwind. I'll be back."

Mitch liked to sit for a bit and read the paper to unwind. His was a long day and I figured I'd let him do his thing in peace. Also, fewer bothersome questions if I was in a different room.

Chapter Thirty

Shattered

"Hey, I'm going up to bed," I said from the living room door.

Mitch looked up from the newspaper, then glanced at his watch.

"Good idea." He folded the paper and placed it on the floor by his chair. "If you can't sleep we could watch a movie?"

"Or you could while I fall asleep," I replied. Although, with Hank skulking in my mind at the boundary between reasonable thought and insanity, sleep might not be such an easy thing to come by.

Mitch smiled and stood up. I held out my hand, he reached it in three strides. "You're cold," he said. His free hand touched my face. "Really cold."

"Yeah."

I couldn't get warm. Cold both inside and out.

Hand in hand we climbed the stairs. Our room was dark. I wanted dark and cozy. Mitch knew, he just knew; instead of turning on the main lights he flicked on a lamp on my dresser and another on the nightstand.

Mitch stepped in front of me and looked into my eyes.

"What's up?"

"I'm tired."

"It's like something extinguished your flame. This isn't just tired." His blue eyes searched mine. "El? What happened?"

I shook my head. I'm not sharing the Hank stuff and I didn't want to get into Rosanne being in the house.

"My body aches. I'm tired and I can't get warm," I replied. It was truthful, just not the whole truth.

"Hot shower and bed," Mitch said.

"That sounds good." It did and I was grateful the questions had ceased. I sat down on the bed. It would be so easy to fall back and sleep but I'd bet good money on nightmares not being far away. Mitch was talking. I heard the shower running.

Talking. Time to pay attention.

"El?"

"Yep?"

"Shower?"

I stood and walked into the bathroom.

"Jump in. I'll find you some pajamas."

"Pajamas? Top drawer of my dresser."

"Pajamas until you warm up," Mitch replied with a smile.

I peeled off my jeans and dropped them in the laundry hamper. The rest of my clothes followed as quick as the constant thrum of pain in my hand would allow.

A thought surfaced: the laundry hampers at the crime scenes were empty. Where were their worn clothes or pajamas or whatever? I needed to hang on to that thought until I could do something with it. The hot water stung my cold skin, gradually warming me.

"Okay?" Mitch asked.

"You coming in?"

He laughed. "Yep."

The shower door opened and closed. Warmth radiated from Mitch's body. I turned to face him. Mitch plunged his hands into my hair, pulled my face to his and kissed me until I forgot everything except that very moment.

His arms wrapped around me as I melted into him. Mitch said, "Don't shut me out."

Dry and in warm pajamas I snuggled in bed next to Mitch. My head rested on his chest as he flipped channels looking for a movie to watch.

He settled on The Time Traveler's Wife. His left arm wrapped around me, fingers gently caressing my upper arm. The movie played. My eyes closed.

Time travel was one helluva superpower. I wanted to go back to the minutes before the first woman was killed and stop it. Bits of the movie filtered into my thoughts then became part of my internal viewing.

What if the cameras were still active when we arrived at the crime scenes? What if the Unsubs were listening to us?

I opened my eyes. "Mitch, you're a techy kinda guy ..."

"Uh huh."

"Do you think the cameras and audio surveillance gear at the crime scenes enabled the Unsubs to ..."

His arm tightened around my shoulders. "You think they were watching you?"

"I don't know."

"It's possible. If they had cameras at every scene, they

could've been used for surveillance prior to the murders and then disabled via software afterward. Rinse and repeat."

"Could've, might've, perhaps, maybe." Not what I wanted to hear.

"This is your case. From what you know so far, what do you think?"

"I hoped they abandoned the spy gear and moved to the next place."

Mitch played with my hair. "Go to sleep, El."

Hank weaseled his way into my thoughts. My mind ran through a weapon inventory then our route from the bedroom to the panic room. Once satisfied I'd covered everything and knowing armed security guards were stationed outside the locked front gates, sleep hit like a sledgehammer.

Chapter Thirty One
One Wild Night

Sunday started with a new crime scene and more shit than I knew how to process. It felt as though I was failing on all fronts but I'd managed a few hours' sleep and felt physically okay. All police were asked to leave the scene before we arrived. The scene turned over to uniformed FBI. It was a strange situation and I didn't much like shutting out local police or using uniformed agents when we usually used Sean O'Hare's security company. I truly disliked the idea of a cop being inside this case but until we knew for sure, police involvement needed to be limited.

We waited outside for the bug experts to clear the scene. The last thing I wanted was our investigation broadcasted. After the all clear, two techs showed us four evidence bags containing cameras and audio devices.

"All good?" I asked. Paid to double check.

"Yes. We did a thorough sweep of the entire building. Nothing else is present," said a female agent.

The thought of being overheard and watched still gnawed at me.

"Any way to tell if the Unsub was monitoring police presence in the houses after the deaths?"

"No, ma'am."

"Thanks."

"You're welcome," she smiled. "Happy to come out

whenever Delta need us."

"Log those items with Delta A and use this case number, please. Three zero six dash HQ dash six five zero nine."

"Yes, ma'am."

Ma'am. Seemed like maybe I should just go with it. She was twelve. One day some twelve-year-old fresh-faced agent would be calling her ma'am. They took the devices with them and left the scene.

I struggled with my nitrile gloves. There was no way I was getting my taped-up fingers in one hole.

"Here," Kurt said handing me one of his gloves. "Wear this one on the broken hand. It's a large."

"Thanks." I looked at him for second as I tried to decide if I should mention the possibility of aspects of our investigation being overheard.

"Something on your mind, Conway?"

"The surveillance at the crime scenes. If we were listened to, the Unsubs will know about my newfound ability." I eased the glove over my fingers. "It bothers me."

"I've given that some thought as well."

"And?"

"I think if they'd heard anything, they would've used it by now, somehow. We didn't do a lot of talking in the camera areas."

Good point.

"Maybe."

Once I was gloved up, Kurt tapped my shoulder. "Let's get in there."

I steeled myself for what I was about to see and followed Kurt into the house. A uniformed FBI agent directed us to the bathroom.

"She's a husk," I said, staring at another young woman's drained body, in another spotless bathroom, in another immaculate house.

"Good description," Kurt replied.

"Sidney Churchill, age twenty-nine. Worked in the paleontology department of the Smithsonian," I said, reading from the notes given to me by the first agent on scene. I looked down at the once-animated face of a slim blonde blue-eyed young woman. Frosty tentacles slithered into my bones. "She's also a Republican." Another Republican bites the dust. Political motivation didn't feel right. Perhaps it was opportunity? "Hey, did we find out if any of these women attended support groups of any kind?"

"As far as I know Sam and Lee are working on that. Places like AA don't keep records of people attending. Anonymous still means something in a few circles."

"I suppose it does." I stiffened and sucked in air as another raging, cold torrent raced up my spine.

A light frown creased Kurt's forehead as he looked up at me. "I get why the strong reaction to that letter last night. Before I picked you up today, I had a look at some of the crime-scene photos from the 'Hank "Saw" Creole' case."

I nodded. "We are not having a conversation about that."

"Fair enough."

Kurt would add my reaction to his mental folder labeled PTSD. I knew that and didn't care. One day it'd be a thing that I couldn't ignore but not yet. My mind was already busy with thoughts of our current case, no room for jailbirds like Hank Creole and his warped love letters.

"Eight victims."

I knew as soon as I said it that was wrong.

"Nine," Kurt said, letting the shower curtain fall back into place. "Violet Cramer in Winchester, remember. There are nine."

Yeah, nine. Nine victims, two Unsubs or four, depending on whether or not Stevens and Fallon were involved.

With the body hidden by the shower curtain, it was just a bathroom. A very clean bathroom.

White tile walls and a canary yellow splashback behind the sink. I crouched down and scanned the room. Where was Sidney's note? A small white triangle peeked out from under the vanity unit. Pleased to have found it, I wiggled out the paper with my gloved fingers. Unfolding it with care.

"What's it say?" Kurt asked.

"I think the better question is 'why hide the notes?'"

"And your theory is?"

"It's some kind of game. They're not hidden well enough to make it too hard."

"Why bother at all?"

"Because it amuses them for whatever sick reason. If it didn't, then surely the notes would be left in the open."

"Or, it reminds us that they did not feel hurried and

had time to conceal something."

"I think you have something there, Kurt."

He smiled. "What does that note say?"

"'Taking the light with you,'" I replied, handing it to him then standing up and moving back to the door. My head swam. I waited. A few deep breaths and it subsided.

"Conway, is there something you want to share?" Kurt asked, placing the piece of paper in an evidence bag.

"Someone or something has to be common to all of the women." I watched Kurt from the doorway. "These murders, these women, they're not a coincidence."

I was back thinking about self-help groups, surveillance equipment, political rallies and stickers on cars. Still too many variables. They didn't all use the same security company. They didn't all have their life story in stickers on the backs of their cars. They attended different political events. I needed to widen my view and see the whole pattern.

Kurt interrupted my thoughts. "That's not what was happening a few seconds ago, but good subject change."

I shrugged.

He was thinking but I knew it was about the case and not me which was good. His brow creased as the thoughts gathered momentum. While he was thinking and before steam came out his ears, I decided I needed time with Sidney.

"Gimme a few minutes with Sidney?"

Kurt nodded. "I'm not leaving. I'll be over there," he said, pointing to the doorway.

Whatever.

I pulled back the shower curtain, revealing Sidney's naked damp bloodless frame. Crumpled, alone, cold. I felt for her. Her day had just started and now her life was over.

Sidney didn't react as I crouched next to her. Probably a good thing. I got closer to her head, and said, "Sidney, I'm Ellie. Can we talk for a minute?"

An incorporeal arm moved. I watched with fascination as her ghostly being stirred and extended toward my hand. A chill encompassed me when Sidney made contact. She tugged hard. It took me a moment to realize she was pulling herself into me, not me into her. Stone-cold death took over my body. Her eyes looked out from mine, showing me all she saw before a drugged haze took her vision and someone took her life.

Unable to look away, I watched the shower curtain open. I clearly saw Unsub number two and a knife jab at me. The first cut a precursor to a gruesome and terrifying death. Noise alerted me to someone else in the room. Using Sidney's ears, I forced myself to focus on it. The sound led me to red boots. Sidney's vision was fast blurring. Someone stood behind the Unsub. All I could see was red boots through Unsub two's legs. I committed what I saw of the boots to memory and Sidney was no more.

Sidney's ectoplasm extracted itself from my body, leaving rivers of cold running through my veins. I'd discovered the reason I felt so cold so often during this case:

death. Makes a person cold from the inside out.

"Someone else was here," I said, as I stood up and looked at Kurt.

"Who, Conway?"

"A woman. I saw red boots and they weren't men's boots." I eased past him in the doorway and propped myself against the wall in the hall to sketch the boots in my notebook. I looked at the picture I'd drawn. Not the best drawing I'd ever done but I knew those red boots.

Using my phone, I Googled women's boots. Not steel capped cowboy boots like mine, I was looking for Doc Martin's. As soon as I found them I knew I was right. They were Fallon's boots. Sometimes being right sucks.

I showed Kurt the image. He nodded and said, "I've seen boots like that before."

"You met Detective Fallon, right?"

"Yes, at the media briefing." He looked at me. I watched a whole roll of quarters drop - this was too big for a single penny. "Her red boots are very similar."

"Distinctive, aren't they?"

"Very."

"How do we prove what I saw?" I was really thinking aloud. No answer required. Kurt knew that.

He smiled and leaned his back on the wall across from me. "I have faith, Conway."

"We need to turn this place inside out. I want a print and there is bound to be one somewhere. I don't care how careful she thinks she's being. There has to be something irrefutable linking that woman to this crime scene."

That was a topsy-turvy way of thinking. A little voice in my head warned me to look at the big picture and step back from Fallon. Another voice argued that this was the second strike for Fallon and I was right. It felt messy. Everything was muddied up and I struggled to get a clear direction.

"Let's start," Kurt said. "First, we should find out where they were hiding or if they were hiding."

Yep. My eyes roamed the ceiling in the hallway looking for a trapdoor. I pointed at a recessed area.

"Trapdoor?"

"Could be."

Kurt and I stood under it and looked up. We needed the ladder, again.

"Did you pick it up?"

"The ladder? Yeah, on the way home last night."

Five minutes later we were hunched and uncomfortable in the hot stuffy ceiling space. Not a lot of headroom, no floor, just joists and insulation.

"More a crawl space this one," Kurt said, picking his way carefully across joists to the other side of the ceiling. "Someone was up here … can't have been comfortable but someone was up here."

The heat overwhelmed me before I was halfway to Kurt. Continuing smacked of falling through a ceiling and horrendous embarrassment. Self-preservation kicked in.

"I've gotta get out of here," I said. The walls were closing in as I turned around and made my way across joists to the ladder. As I descended, I saw the marks on the paintwork. Someone had dragged something over the rim of the trapdoor. The marks fitted with the width of our ladder. Kurt was right, someone had been up there.

"Conway?"

"Yep," I called back from the safety of the floor below. "Just wanted to check something." My fingers crossed all by themselves.

An hour later we were back at the office. There was no point us waiting around at the scene for the crime scene techs to do their thing.

I shifted back in the chair. Sunlight streamed through the windows, filling the room with warmth and yellow. Any other day the yellowness of the room would've made me smile. Today it felt close and claustrophobic.

I went back to checking followers and friends of the latest victim on Facebook and Twitter accounts. A name jumped off the screen. Charles Locke.

Again. Damn!

I did a quick control-f on every page I had open and typed his name into the box created. Yep, he was on her Twitter friends list, and her Instagram, as well as Facebook. But which Locke was it? I opened his Facebook profile. Not much was public but it was Locke Junior.

Damn.

Junior. Three times now I'd come across him.

Time to bring Mallory Stevens back in and find out where Charles Locke Junior was hiding out. The private Facebook account was annoying. I needed to get in and see what he talked about and who his friends were. A workaround popped into my mind. I hooked up my desk phone and punched in three numbers.

"It's Ellie Conway," I said when the voice answered.

"What can Cyber do for you, Conway?"

"Hack a Facebook account for me." No point dancing in circles.

"Got a warrant?"

Nope.

"Not exactly."

"You do or you don't, Conway, there's no gray ground here."

He was right.

"Say I do?"

"Then send me a link to the Facebook account and before you can say battery-operated boy, you'll have all the access you need and no one will know."

"I'll get back to you in fifteen minutes." I hung up.

Will I? Hell yes. Warrant. No problem.

I flipped through the list of judges available for warrants. The answer to my prayers was third down the list. Filling out the paperwork took five minutes. I printed it and headed out the door to catch Judge Hartwell. We had history. Good solid foundations of trust. Also, it didn't hurt that I rescued her one Christmas from a lunatic. Especially when my asking for a warrant might be a tad premature. I hoped there were brownie points for asking and not letting Sandra sneak into Facebook and hack the shit out of it. If I didn't get my warrant, I'd turn it over to Sandra. That had inadmissible evidence written all over it so wasn't the best way forward.

Ten minutes was all it took. Well, ten minutes and a promise that Judge Hartwell would be invited to Murphy's for the customary end of case drinks. I like helping people out, and it all comes back when you need it most.

As soon as I was back in my office I called Cyber and let them know an electronic copy of the warrant was on its way. I heard the email ping as I was talking to them. To save time I'd included the Facebook link before forwarding the warrant.

"We'll give you access as soon as we have it, Agent Conway. Check your email. Cheers."

Disconnecting the call I thought about Charles Locke junior and how likely or unlikely it was that his father hadn't heard from him. Locke senior seemed genuinely disgusted by his son's actions yet I felt he was holding back in other ways.

Sean popped into my head. Locke senior apparently worked for O'Hare Security at one point and I still hadn't spoken to Sean about him.

I wasn't entirely happy with the chat I'd had with Locke senior. He needed revisiting. Maybe Sam could do that. He was a pretty persuasive sort of guy.

I wandered to my office door and whistled. Keeping it classy.

Sam appeared with a laugh. "You whistled, Chicky Babe?"

"Got a job for you, Sam. Charles Locke senior. Can you take a run at him? Bring him in and do it here. Just have a feeling he's holding out on us."

"I'll go pick him up now."

"Thanks."

Happier, I returned to my desk and gave Sean a call.

"Just me. Two things … One, do you still have Rosanne? And two, did you ever have a Charles Locke on your payroll as a surveillance technician or anything that would involve installing surveillance gear, alarm systems, or smoke detectors?"

"I still have Rosanne. Someone should come get her. Not you!" He stopped. "I'll do a database search, I don't recall the name but then again, I have a manager who handles that side of the business."

Sean was more hands on in the responding to alarms and scene guard areas. Or that was my experience. His company provided scene guards for law enforcement agencies, mainly us, Homeland, and DEA. He had some hefty government contracts.

"I'll send Lee for Rosanne."

"Sooner rather than later, we've had her since last night."

"I know, sorry, we had another crime scene this morning. The case takes priority, especially a fresh scene."

"Cutting it close, Ellie … she starts screaming for a lawyer and you'll get toasted."

I typed on my keyboard, opened a chat window and messaged Lee to please go get Rosanne from Sean. He replied and said he'd leave immediately.

"Lee is on his way to you."

"I'll have John contact you with any employment records for Charles Locke," Sean said. "Good luck with the case, yell if you need anything else."

"Thanks."

I hung up, rocked back in my chair for a few minutes while taking stock of the current situation. As I tried to wrap my thoughts around the two people who needed interviewing, my email program dinged like a maniac and insisted I take notice. Emails flooded into my inbox. Two hundred unread emails. Maybe there'd been an email blockage that suddenly cleared?

I scrolled through, looking for any flagged as urgent. There were twenty of those.

About fifty emails were ignorable. I hit the delete key on those. Clearly I never received them.

The rest could wait a while. A quick scan of the senders and subjects told me I didn't really want to open any of them.

With a sigh, I reached forward and instead of hitting close, hit refresh. Two more emails jumped into my inbox.

Damn.

My mood plummeted faster than a frozen turkey falling from the monument.

Didn't want to open those either.

A shadow passed my open office door. I pushed my chair from my desk, stood up, crossed the floor and closed the door. Considering my mood, an open door was an invitation and that invitation could get someone hurt.

Not an ideal situation.

My cell rang. Mitch.

I let it go to voicemail.

The desk phone rang.

I let it go to voicemail.

An email arrived.

It took all my willpower to leave it unopened.

The need to talk to Mitch was growing exponentially and I didn't have the time to start and finish the conversation.

An email arrived from Cyber. That I opened. It was my freshly hacked backdoor to Locke junior's Facebook page telling me where he was and what he was doing. Messages to and from Mallory Stevens told me he was doing Mallory Stevens. She was dating Phoebe Childs. Mallory batted for both teams. Can't say I was surprised. Not surprised but not overjoyed with the news.

If I could find Locke so easily, why hadn't the police?

That was hinky as hell.

I picked up my phone and called Sandra. "Get me someone ..."

"Who shall it be, O Champion of the Under Dog?"

There was a light rap on my door and Iain Campbell walked into my office. Just the person. "Never mind he just walked in."

As I hung up, I heard Sandra say, "Iain just walked past me."

"How's it going?" Iain pulled up a chair.

"Ever swum in mud?"

"Can't be that bad ... my spider sense hasn't twinged lately."

"It must've twinged, you're here. I was about to call you." I just didn't know it was him I wanted to talk to.

"Needed to get out of the office. Going a bit stir crazy, thought I'd drop in and say hi."

"Feel like you're missing out?"

He stretched his legs then crossed one over the other. "A bit."

"Hypothetically ..."

Iain's eyebrows rose. "Ominous start."

I ignored his comment. "If there was a warrant-to-arrest out for lawyer A, and I found him easily, which to me indicates police should have found him without any real effort – why wouldn't they?"

"How easily did you find him?"

"He's here in D.C. and all it took was a quick hack of his Facebook account."

His brow creased as he thought. A moment passed then he looked at me. "He could've paid the police off or he's going to give evidence and that's worth more than his arrest."

Didn't feel like he was finished but he'd stopped talking. "Or?"

"Or someone told the police to back off."

"The warrant is current, it's not been pulled or amended."

"Doesn't have to be an official request. Who is he buddies with?"

"He's a criminal lawyer." Boy, was he ever. I scrolled through his Facebook friends. "His friends list is peppered with influential people." My mouse pointer hovered over someone who stood out. "Rusty Cookson."

"Chief of Police," Iain said. "Know each other well?"

I scrolled through photographs: Locke, and two other men, one of whom I recognized as Peter Bradley the Deputy Mayor of D.C., playing golf and tennis. There were other photos of Locke and Cookson with their respective partners at Christmas and what appeared to be Cookson family events.

"Yep. Looks like they've known each other a fair while and are close."

"Could be your answer right there."

"I get the feeling he's waiting for his new life to kick in then he'll be gone."

"Explain that ..."

"Police can't be held at bay forever. If I were him, I'd be organizing myself a new identity and a new life. For us that's pretty easy, we often have several lives we can step into but he probably doesn't. Creating a new identity so he can leave and never look back will take time."

"You think his friendship with the Chief of Police has bought him that time?"

"Yeah."

I also think I'm going to upset Rusty Cookson by messing with his pal Locke.

"Hate to pick your brain then run." I stood up. "Nice to see you, Iain. Don't be a stranger."

Iain rose, dragged the chair back where he's got it from and said, "I think I'll go say hello to whoever is in the bullpen before heading back to work." He left with a backward wave.

From my desk drawer I took my gun and holster. On the way to the door, I took a jacket from the coat rack in the corner of my office and pulled it on, making sure my injured hand went in first.

A cacophony of noise flowed down the corridor from the bullpen. Electronic alerts, ringing phones, low murmurs, and then deeper voices greeting Iain, all mingled together. I walked in the other direction. If Facebook and my gut were correct, finding and arresting Locke would not be difficult. I paused at the arresting thought. That might not be super simple.

"Where are you going?" Kurt called from behind me.

Turning slightly I replied, "To see a man about his life choices."

"Does this relate to our Hitchcockian case?" He caught up and walked beside me.

Glad it wasn't just me who saw the old horror movie aspect.

"Yes."

"And you were going alone?" Kurt held the stairwell door open for me. I stepped through and started down the first of the eight flights of stairs that led to the ground floor.

"Guess so."

The stairwell smelled weird. Not like Berocca vomit

but unpleasant and difficult to pinpoint. I grabbed for an image that evoked happiness and fresh air. A meadow full of flowers wrapped around my mind.

"Conway, you all right?"

"Yeah." I kept about four steps ahead of him and moved quickly. Tempted to go through the next fire door and take the elevator. As I walked, I decided to stick with the stinky stairs. The more my mouth watered, the more flowers I imagined. Kurt was talking and I had no idea what about. His voice faded in and out, lost in the heat and my concentration.

I stayed ahead of Kurt and forced myself to stop thinking about anything except the case. Nothing else mattered. I opened the last door and stepped out into the airy foyer. Relieved to be out of the closeness of the stairwell I let the image of the field of flowers dissolve.

"Where are we going?" Kurt asked.

"12th Street. Thought I'd walk."

"Who are we seeing?"

"Charles Locke."

"You spoke to him already?"

"Not this Charles Locke, I found the son. Meanwhile, Sam is taking a run at Mr. Locke senior and Sean is getting one of his managers to get me any employment records his company has for senior."

We walked up Pennsylvania, side by side. The fresh air helped clear my head.

"Grab a drink on the way?"

"Sure," I replied. Hot chocolate sounded pretty good.

"You're very quiet this afternoon," Kurt said. "You sleep last night?"

A smile tweaked the corners of my mouth. "Yeah."

"Charles Locke, what's the connection to the case?"

"Mallory Stevens met with him after she saw Phoebe Childs," I said.

"Interesting."

"It gets better, he's screwing Mallory Stevens."

"Thought she was in a relationship with Phoebe."

"Cheating," I replied, watching traffic for a moment. "At first glance, his Facebook page contains a few of our victims as either friends or friends of friends who have commented on status updates he's posted."

Kurt nodded. "He's married to Phoebe Childs' sister?"

"Yes. He's the wife-beating asshole who put her in hospital several times. Lawyers are right up there with journalists in my book." Keeping contempt from my voice was impossible.

"What do you know about Locke?"

"Metro have a warrant out for his arrest. Has a criminal record. And he's a slimy scumbag lawyer with a big firm which has been protecting him."

"Violent?"

"There were three charges of male assaults female in his past and a slew of domestic violence charges relating to the last six months. So I'm going with yes."

"And you were going alone."

Yeah, shoot me. Or let me shoot him. Can't see how that wouldn't be a winning move on my part.

We dodged shoppers and sightseers who seemed to take the entire sidewalk with no regard for anyone else. I felt a bark brewing.

Keep right, for fuck's sake and let us get through. Bet they were all over the place on escalators too. I hoped to never find out.

"What's the plan?" Kurt body-checked someone who tried to force their way between us. He apologized with half an ounce of sincerity, "Sorry, bud, didn't see you there."

My smile radiated and I stopped it before it became all-out laughter. Seeing Kurt body-check someone floated my boat.

"I'm going to talk to Locke, probably not shoot him." Might arrest him, though. Or I might just call Metro and let them deal with him.

"Probably not?" Kurt's tone suggested probably was the wrong word.

"Can't make any promises."

His voice filled with a smile. "Conway, how many days until your wedding?"

Subtle.

"Not enough to go through an internal inquiry because I shot Locke, if that's what you're asking."

"I was merely asking how many days."

Not believing that for a second.

"Seven. Seven days."

"Yeah, you're right, if you shoot Locke now, the inquiry could mess up your honeymoon plans."

Hence, I probably won't shoot him. Unless I'm forced, in which case, it'd be a righteous shooting. With a bit of luck, they'd find a weapon on him. Have I really become someone who thinks that's an okay thing?

I hoped not. I hoped it was stress causing fucky thinking.

A woman barged past me, knocking her shopping bags into me. I stepped sideways and controlled the urge to ankle-tap her.

What the hell is wrong with people?

A scowl formed, as tension mounted.

"Conway?" Kurt's hand touched my forearm. "Relax your hand."

My what?

I looked down. My left-hand was a fist. I uncurled my fingers and shook my hand. Kurt wasn't done yet, I could tell by the pressure on my forearm.

"What?" I asked.

"Take your right hand off your weapon."

I didn't even know I had my hand wrapped around the grip of my Glock. A warning bell sounded in my head. Might be the right time to consider a career change before I become someone who shoots first and covers it up afterward or worse.

I lifted my hand and dropped it to my side. My knuckles complained. I wanted to open and close my hand a few times to release the tension but the reward would be more pain and I wasn't going there.

"Bit tense," I offered as an explanation.

"Shake it off, Conway, we don't want any accidents."

I nodded. "I'm good."

His sideways look said he doubted the sincerity of my words. He might know me better than I care to admit. Or he might think he does. It seemed smart to say nothing and not push him to a place where it'd go badly for me.

I looked around, taking stock of the buildings and numbers on doors. We were half a block away. I looked back down the street and found it hard to believe that Locke senior didn't know where his son was. They were situated within three blocks of each other.

"How far?" Kurt asked as I turned back to the view ahead.

"Half a block."

I filled Kurt in on my thoughts regarding Locke and how I considered his good friend Chief Cookson could be protecting him to a certain extent. Always a good idea to have as much information as possible.

Chapter Thirty Two

Carry on Wayward Son.

"Let me do the talking," I said to Kurt as we stood in the foyer of the building. "We're taking the stairs."

"What floor?"

"Two."

We climbed in silence. This stairwell smelled as bad as every other stairwell I'd been in recently.

Kurt opened the door to the second floor. There is nothing wrong with men opening doors for women. It should be encouraged.

I walked down the off-white hallway until I found apartment ten. I knocked with my left hand and stood aside so I couldn't be seen through the peephole.

Listening.

Nothing.

He might've gone out but I doubted it. After all, there was a warrant out for his arrest. Here he was, hiding in plain sight in an apartment rented under his company's name. I bet he was still working too. I knocked again.

Kurt said, "He might be out?"

"He's there," I said as the door swung open.

Face to face with Charles Locke Junior, I smiled. "Mr. Locke. I'm Ellie Conway. I'd like to have a word."

"I'm a busy man." His eyes darted around the hallway. He took a step back when he saw Kurt.

Nervous?

"We won't take up much of your time, sir." Being polite to an ass like him wasn't easy. Down the hall, a door opened a crack: someone interested in our presence. "Might pay to invite us in, unless you want your neighbors involved."

His door moved. I stuck my foot in the way preventing him from closing it.

"That's not very friendly," Kurt said, shoving the door hard and taking Locke by surprise. He staggered backward.

We entered the apartment and closed the door behind us.

"Who are you?" Locke said, recovering enough to regain his footing.

"FBI," I replied, moving my jacket so he could see my weapon and my badge. "Any more questions?"

He shook his head.

"Have a seat, Charles, or do they call you Chuck?" Kurt said, pointing to a chair in the living room.

"No one calls me Chuck," he said and sat.

"This is where you tell us about Mallory Stevens and your relationship with her," I said, sitting opposite him.

His eyes darted around the room. "Why would I do that?" A smarmy smile settled on his face.

"Because you're a lawyer and you know we wouldn't be here if we didn't have evidence of a relationship."

"What has my relationship with Mallory got to do with you?"

"We're interested and right now we're talking about

Ms. Stevens but if you don't play nice, we might start talking about the whereabouts of your wife." His smile faded. "Remember her? You beat the crap out of her then disappeared." His smile disappeared. "Something about that feel familiar?" I turned to Kurt.

He held up his phone. "Want me to call Metro?"

"Yeah, I think so."

"What did you want to know about Mallory?"

"Hold that thought," I said to Kurt and then focused on Locke. "How long have you been seeing each other?"

"A few months."

"How many months?"

I watched him trying to come up with a number.

"Four, I think."

"You sure about that?"

He nodded. "As far as I can remember."

"You beat your wife three weeks ago and promptly disappeared. So, you were having an affair?"

"Looks that way," he replied; the smarm had crept back in.

"Where's your wife?"

He looked directly into my eyes. "At home. She got the house. I got a restraining order. I haven't contacted her in three weeks."

"Okay." I let it go. My interest in Locke pertained to his relationship with Mallory Stevens and the death of Phoebe Childs and possibly the other women. "When did you last see your sister-in-law?"

"I don't know."

"Try again, Charles. This time, aim for the truth."

"A few weeks ago, maybe."

"Can we skip the bullshit and just get on with it?" I said, trying to keep the irritation from my voice.

"I don't know what you mean, Agent."

"I'd like to know if I'm going to find your fingerprints in Phoebe's house."

"Probably, she is my sister-in-law, we visited."

"Where was she living?"

He frowned. "She sold her house recently and moved in with her girlfriend."

"Did she?"

"Yes."

"Got an address?"

He pointed to a sideboard and a notebook. "I need that book."

Kurt walked across the room and picked it up. He passed it to Locke. He flipped pages until he found an address and read out the address where we found Phoebe dead. But we knew she wasn't living there. We also knew she'd recently bought that house and had intended to live there or have a house-warming party there. Something changed in the weeks after the purchase. She wanted people to think she was living there. Why?

"Who was she living with?"

"I don't know. She never mentioned a name."

"And you didn't ask?" I found that hard to believe.

"Why so much interest in Phoebe?" Locke asked. "Does she need a lawyer? I know a few."

"I'm investigating her murder. She doesn't need a lawyer ... but you might."

He leaped to his feet. "Sit down," Kurt said, taking a step toward him.

Locke sat.

"Now Mr. Locke, how about you engage your brain and tell me where Phoebe was living," I said with as much calm as I could muster.

"I told you."

"That's right you did. You know what? I forgot you'd called around there the other night, Thursday night."

He paled and shook his head. "I haven't seen her in weeks."

"You said that. So you didn't call in to see Phoebe ... what were you doing there so late in the evening?"

"I don't know what you're talking about."

"Want to lawyer up?" I asked with all the pleasantness of a rattlesnake. "Because I can have Metro here within minutes and they'll be happy to take you into custody and provide you with the names of some mediocre public defenders if you can't afford one yourself."

He shook his head. All the smarm vanished. "I didn't kill Phoebe," he said with quiet resolve.

"Good to know."

I waited to see if he'd elaborate on his reason for being outside Phoebe's home the night before she died. He said nothing. I willed myself to maintain control.

Kurt pulled up a chair next to me. I smiled at him, time for Kurt to ask a few questions. All I wanted to do was get out of the apartment and into some fresh air.

"Talk to us, Locke. Tell us about Mallory Stevens and why you met her outside Phoebe's home," Kurt said.

"I've been seeing her. We're lovers."

"And she is a friend of your sister-in-law?"

"Yeah, looks that way."

"You didn't know?"

He shook his head.

"She asked you to meet her at Phoebe's address and you never asked why?"

That wasn't what happened according to the messenger conversation I read. I waited to see if Locke would correct the story. He didn't.

"Yeah, that's right."

I touched my watch; Kurt nodded. He pulled his notebook from his pocket and pretended to find the appropriate page. A bit of subterfuge in order to get to the truth.

With a charming smile, Kurt said, "Our information must be wrong. Because I could've sworn that Mallory Stevens told you she was meeting Phoebe at her place at seven on Thursday night and that you knew she was talking about your sister-in-law and arranged to meet her outside the house at ten."

Locke grimaced. "What do you want me to tell you?"

"The truth," Kurt replied. "That's all we want. Then we'll carry on our merry way."

"All right. I knew she was visiting Phoebe. They were friends. It didn't concern me. They'd been friends a long time."

"Did Phoebe know you were screwing Mallory Stevens?" Kurt asked.

He shook his head. "I don't think so. If she did, she never said anything to me."

"Do you know the nature of Mallory Steven's relationship with Phoebe Childs?"

"Friends," he said. "They were friends."

Kurt shook his head slowly. "Try again."

Confusion crowded Locke's features. "Friends?"

"They were more than that. Phoebe and Mallory were lovers."

"What? No. Phoebe had a girlfriend. A chick called Thelma, I remember thinking it was an old-fashioned name."

I looked at Kurt. He frowned. Mallory told us she and Phoebe weren't public about their relationship. She never mentioned a Thelma. My head started to pound.

"Did Mallory mention an argument with Phoebe that night or since?"

"No. We didn't talk much. I picked her up and we came back here."

I held up my hand. "Hang on. You picked her up. You didn't just meet her?"

"Yes. I picked her up. Drove her here."

"And her car was where?"

Lines formed on his forehead as he gave my question due consideration.

"I didn't see her car. Never occurred to me to ask." He shrugged. "I was more interested in taking her to bed than asking questions."

"How long did Ms. Stevens spend in your company?"

"She left just after five-thirty in the morning. Her alarm went at five."

"And is that usual?"

"She usually stays until eight."

"Sit tight," I said to Locke and motioned for Kurt to follow me out of earshot. "Could the car have been in the garage?"

"It's possible."

"If Stevens went back for the car after leaving Locke ..."

Kurt wrote in his notebook. "I'll get Sandra to check cab companies and see if she took a cab back to Phoebe's."

We rejoined Locke.

"Thank you for your help," I said. "We'll be in touch."

Kurt and I left Locke to his musings. Outside the door, I called Metro and gave them the address. Be much easier for us to stay in touch if Metro had him in custody.

We waited outside the door for Metro to arrive and followed them down to the street with their prisoner.

"Wonder if his pal Chief Cookson will help him out this time," I said, watching Locke encouraged into the back of a police cruiser.

"The smug look on his face tells me he thinks Cookson will help." Something in Kurt's tone made me look at him.

"What do you know?"

The police cruiser pulled away from the curb. I waved.

Locke glared.

"I sent a text to a friend in the District Attorney's office that mentioned Locke and Chief Cookson had a relationship and that Cookson might be helping his buddies out."

We walked back to the office, it was a pleasant evening in D.C. I said goodnight to Kurt at the entrance to the Hoover building.

Home was where I was headed.

Chapter Thirty Three
Wild Horses

Monday morning I arrived at the office early and got stuck into trying to locate the elusive Thelma.

"You okay?" Kurt stood in my doorway.

I looked over my laptop screen and nodded. "Working."

"Anything you care to share?"

"Not yet." I typed another search parameter and willed the glass of water I'd been sipping for the last hour to stay down.

"Intense," Kurt said with a grin and sat in a chair in front of my desk.

"I found mention of a Thelma in relation to Mallory Stevens."

"Tell."

"There's something happening here. Something ..." I sighed. Mallory Stevens had more in common with our victims than I first realized. She used two aliases that I'd uncovered. "Mallory Stevens was also Sharron Stevens and Thelma Gardner."

I'd found her on all the victims' Facebook pages and other social media. When I delved further, large cash deposits were made into her bank account the day of each murder, then disappeared from her account the next morning. The day we found two bodies, there were two payments. She'd notified the bank on each occasion saying there must've been a bank error.

Fair enough once, maybe twice. But continual bank errors? Doubtful. Someone was putting money in there on purpose. But why? And why was she reporting it as an error? It didn't look like she kept any of the money. Remorse?

Nah.

I looked at it from a different point of view. What if she were being set up? Two aliases made me think otherwise.

"Intense expression followed by a loud sigh," Kurt said. "Want help?"

"Yeah, maybe."

Maybe Kurt could see what I couldn't.

"Brief me."

"Let's walk." I picked up my tablet and shoved it into my shoulder bag, closed my laptop and left it on my desk.

"Where are we going?" he said, falling into step beside me.

"Woodrow Plaza."

"That's not random."

No, it's far enough away that maybe the fresh air will help me feel better. Plus, it was somewhere I liked to be, even though it was yet another place I'd been shot at in the city.

"It's a nice day. I like the plaza," I replied. On such days, it bustled with life. I wanted to see happy people going about their day. Death was overshadowing the good and I didn't like it much.

At the stairwell door, he placed a hand firmly on my

arm. "What's up?"

"There's something fishy going on with this damn case."

"Conway?" His tone suggested there was more. He was right, there was but it wasn't case related.

"That's it."

We started down the stairs. A smell hit me. I couldn't describe it but it was almost like musty feet mixed with public bathroom. The stairwell shouldn't smell like that. Although, I conceded that closed fire doors on every floor, no windows, or ventilation to speak of, had to have some effect on the air quality.

Before the next floor, Kurt stepped in front of me and blocked my way. Mitch's face danced across my internal screen. He called my name.

"I know you. This isn't about a case."

I tried ducking around him. He caught my arm.

"Conway, stop."

"Kurt, it's the case. I can't figure out why or who repeatedly put money into Stevens' account, even though she reported it every time as a bank error." When I put it into words, it did sound pretty odd.

"You're right. It doesn't make sense. Let's have a chat with the bank manager?"

"Yeah, good thinking."

"Let's get a coffee," he offered. "The bank will still be there in twenty minutes."

Let's not.

My mouth watered. So much saliva. I swallowed. My

hand closed over the railing and I vomited. Mostly water and froth.

Kurt was beside me tying my hair back. When the retching finally stopped, he guided me down to a step. "Just sit for a minute or two, then I'll call the cleaners and take you home."

"I'll be fine in a minute. Just need some air. It's so stuffy in here." I wiped my mouth on my sleeve.

Kurt's fingers were on my other wrist. He was looking at his watch. "You're going home."

"Just let me get some air."

"Did you eat today?" Kurt asked looking at the foamy puddle on the steps below us.

Food.

Another bout of retching overwhelmed me. I managed to mumble, "Not really."

"Drink?"

"Water."

My phone rang in my pocket. I dragged it out and saw Mitch's icon. Mitch smiling from a snow-covered mountain. "Hey."

"Hey, yourself. Lunch?"

Food. God. No.

I moved the phone just in time. A fresh bout of retching erupted. Kurt's hand covered mine and he took the phone and glanced at the screen. "Hey, Mitch, Kurt Henderson here. Conway is unwell."

"How unwell?"

"Possible stomach flu. I'm taking her home."

I knew by the way Kurt said stomach flu, that he didn't believe that for a second.

"I'm okay," I said, trying to take the phone back. "I'm okay."

He wouldn't give me the phone. Instead he spoke to Mitch again, "She's going home." Kurt listened. "Really? When was that?" He listened again.

Dammit.

He hung up, handed me the phone, which I pushed back into my pocket. Five minutes sailed by before I felt like moving.

"This is not the first time, Conway. You've had a bad week when it comes to losing your breakfast, lunch, and dinner. Home," Kurt said, taking my arm and helping me to my feet. "Take it easy. We'll get to the elevator through the next landing door."

I shook my arm to dislodge his grip. Didn't work. "I'm all right," I said. "This is unnecessary."

"You're not."

I missed a step through inattention and stumbled. Kurt grabbed me, then slipped an arm around my waist.

"Stop," I said. "Just stop. I can do this."

He held his hands up in surrender. "Okay. But one more misstep and I'm calling for an ambulance." He paused. "This, Conway..." his arm waved at me. "...is not okay. You're sick. It's kinda my field. Let me help."

Words stumbled over my tongue. "It'll pass."

That was some kind of red flag. Kurt stopped in front of me. I could see the glowing green exit sign beyond his shoulder. So close.

"Conway, how long have you been sick? Because Mitch said you've been off-color for a week or so." He stopped. "You've been sick a few times that I know of."

"It's been three or four days."

"That's all?"

Nah, Mitch was right. About a week.

"The exit. Can we go?" I pointed past him.

"Yeah. I think we better."

In the parking garage, I threw him my keys. "You're driving."

"Yes, I am."

Forty minutes later Kurt pulled the car into my driveway and waited. The magic gate opened. He drove up the long driveway; as we neared the garage, the magic door opened. I sat in the car for a few minutes. I felt better. I hoped.

My phone rang.

Mitch.

"I'm home, right behind you."

Kurt opened my door. I dropped my phone into my jacket pocket.

"Mitch is here," I said.

Kurt nodded. "Does he need to be let in?" He keyed the code into the panel on the garage wall.

"Really?"

Idiot!

"Sarcasm?"

"Stupid question?"

"You're mean when you're sick, Conway."

Whatever.

I heard the buttons beep as I walked through the door and into the short hallway that leads to the main hallway. The whole house opened off the main hall.

Tires crunched on the gravel by the front door. I didn't wait. Instead, I hurried upstairs to my room and into the bathroom.

Cleaning my teeth started the whole retching process again. There wasn't any fluid left in my body to vomit up, not even bile. I wiped the foamy toothpaste from my face.

Voices on the stairs came ever closer. The mirror told me the color was returning to my face.

"Ellie?" Mitch called.

"Be right there," I replied, washing my face with cold water.

"I got you some ginger ale and more Saltines."

Considerate.

"Thanks."

I emerged from the bathroom to find Kurt, Mitch and a tall glass of flat brown liquid waiting. I could smell ginger. Dad used to give us flat ginger ale when we were sick as kids. Kurt's bag sat on my bed.

"You don't need that," I said, pointing to it.

"Not even to give you an anti-nausea shot?"

"I'm okay. I'm sure the ginger ale will help. Don't need a shot."

Kurt's lips twitched in the corner, a smile tweaked. "You look better, now. Drink the ginger ale. I'm going to make some calls downstairs."

"Okay, we'll be down soon."

"I'll be back. You ..." He pointed at me. "Rest."

"Yeah, yeah."

Kurt left. Mitch passed me the glass. I took a few sips and hoped it stayed down.

"How'd you know to bring ginger ale?"

"Mom. She swears by flat ginger ale. That and lemon ginger tea."

"Clever woman."

"You should rest. Kurt said. He might know what he's talking about." Mitch grinned and indicated the bed. "Lie down."

I wanted to but the ginger ale wanted out. Heat rose. Saliva rushed into my mouth. Before I could move toward the bathroom, I was puking in my hands.

Lovely.

Ginger ale ran through my fingers and onto the carpet. A towel appeared. Mitch cleaned my hands and sat me on the edge of the bed. "Maybe that shot would be a good idea."

"No." I watched him mop up the frothy mess from the carpet.

He put the towel in the laundry basket in the bathroom and came back with a cold wet face cloth.

"Here," he said wiping my brow and face. "How's that?"

"Nice. Thank you. I think I might lie down for a little bit."

"Good idea. Maybe try slower sips of ginger ale in a few minutes. I'll fetch a bucket. Just in case."

"Thanks again."

Mitch grinned. "Don't mention it. Be right back."

I knew he was going to tell Kurt I'd vomited. I also knew I needed to drink but I couldn't face it.

I reached over the side of the bed and picked up the phone. Remembering Lee's number took me a few minutes but I got it right eventually. He answered on the first ring.

"It's me. I'm home, sick. There's something hinky about the case. Can you have another look at the financials of Mallory Stevens? She's using two aliases. Sharron Stevens and Thelma Gardner. Phoebe was supposedly living with someone called Thelma. Find out where she was living. Also, get Sandra to set up a meeting with her bank manager for me ... tomorrow's good."

"Everything okay?" Lee asked.

"Sure. See what you can find out."

"You were looking into her, yeah?"

"Yeah, I was. Something doesn't make sense. Need fresh eyes. You're it. What'd you do with Rosanne?"

"Interviewed her. My opinion is she was trying to get the scoop on this story. Not liking the secretiveness regarding her son."

"And?"

"Turned her loose. I'd hate to be her and have to face your father after what she did."

"That could be punishment enough," I replied. "Not."

"Take it easy, Chicky."

Renewed vomiting pre-empted my next call; luckily I still had the washcloth. I cleaned up the mess and threw the cloth at the bathroom door. This was going so well.

I tried again and got Sam on the phone. I let him know I wasn't coming back in and asked him to re-interview Mallory Stevens and find out where she left her car on Thursday night and to keep me informed. He filled me in on Charles Locke senior and told me a manager from O'Hare Security had dropped off an employment file. Locke was employed as a surveillance technician and also installed some of the equipment on occasion. I asked Sam to get records of work carried out by O'Hare Security on any of our victim's homes.

Phone calls made. Work sorted.

I put the phone back into its cradle and lay down. I don't know what I expected. Maybe that lying down would be an instant cure. It wasn't. Nor was ginger ale.

Mitch came in with a blue bucket. He placed it next to the bed. Within arm's reach.

"Can I get you anything?" he asked, sitting by me.

"No. Thank you." I leaned back on the pillows and tried not to think. Mitch entwined his fingers with mine. "Mitch?"

"Yep."

"I'm not sick."

"Honey, you really are," he smiled.

"Nah-uh. I'm not."

His eyes sought mine. "Ellie?"

I swallowed saliva but couldn't swallow fast enough. I let Mitch's hand go and grabbed the bucket.

Bye-bye ginger ale.

"I'm not sick."

"This from the woman who can't stop throwing up," Mitch said. "You want to rethink that?"

"Nope. Bathroom cupboard, go see."

He frowned and went into the bathroom. I heard the cupboard open and close. He came back holding a white stick by the very tip of one end.

"You peed on this, right?"

"Not on the outside. It's got a cap on it. You're quite safe," I replied.

"It's also got two blue lines."

Kurt's voice came from the doorway where he was leaning on the frame, "That's a positive result."

He straightened up and walked into the room. "You couldn't have told me?"

"Not before I told Mitch," I replied.

Mitch stood in the middle of the room staring at the two blue lines.

"How?" Mitch said as a smile settled on his lips. "And wow. Not what I expected from today."

"Maybe Holly's grandma was right, nature cunning," I said and that was all I had, nothing else made sense.

Kurt chuckled. "She is right. Trust me. I learned a long time ago that somethings are meant to be regardless of our interventions."

"Meanwhile, let me give you something so you don't feel ill all the time," Kurt said.

"Something safe," I replied.

"Of course. Undo your jeans and pull them down a bit."

Mitch hadn't moved. Kurt walked around him.

"Why?" I asked, unzipping.

"Humor me." He moved a little closer and rubbed his hands together. "Sorry, might be cold. I want to feel your tummy." He pressed quite hard on my lower abdomen. "Okay?"

"Yeah." I tried not to wince. "Uncomfortable."

"When was your last period?"

"Seven and a half weeks ago."

He pressed again, felt like his fingers were pressing right through to my spine. He stopped.

"You're sure?"

"Yes. Very sure. Why?"

"I'll tell you in a minute." From his bag, he took a vial and a syringe. "Roll onto your left hip."

I did. There was cold, a stinging sensation, then cold again.

"That should help, it might also make you sleepy."

"Thanks." I rolled back and pulled my jeans up properly. "Tell me why you questioned my dates?"

"Because I can feel your uterus above your pelvic bone by about two inches."

"And?"

"An ultrasound would be a good idea. Have you seen

an OBGYN yet?"

I stared at him. "Not yet. Should I be worried?"

"No. You might be further along than you think. I'll get an ultrasound scheduled soon. I know a guy. He's the head of the Obstetric Department at Inova Fairfax. I can get you an appointment with him."

"That would be good, thanks."

Mitch sat down next to me on the bed. "We're pregnant?"

"Technically just me, but yeah, we are."

He smiled. I don't know what I expected but I don't think it was a smile.

"What now?"

"I don't know."

Kurt packed up his bag. "I'll leave you two to talk. Yell if you need me."

"Thanks," I replied.

Mitch nodded. "I'm going to need a bit of time to catch up ..."

I waited to see if he was mad or going to mention the fact I hadn't said anything and had blocked this from his radar. I'd done nothing but think about this for the last two weeks ... well, this and the wedding.

"This wasn't something on either of our life plans, so, we need to think and talk and figure this out together," I said, surprised at how grown up I sounded.

Mitch chewed his lip and looked at me. His hand found mine. "No wonder you've been so distracted for the last few weeks. I knew it wasn't all work and the wedding.

Hasn't been easy for you, has it?"

"No, it hasn't."

"I wish you'd confided in me from the start." He kissed my forehead.

Safe. I sighed. "Me too. I just needed time to get my head around this, you know?"

"That's understandable."

"And because there could've been a natural resolution." That was still a possibility.

"And to be able to support you, if that were the case, I'd need knowledge." His fingers squeezed mine. "El, I'm not going anywhere. This is about us."

He had me there.

"I should have told you."

"This is your first and last warning, almost-Mrs. Iverson ... there better not be a next time."

I laughed at his attempt at sternness. "Fair enough."

"And I should've noticed." His smile faded a little. "That's why you blocked me."

I swallowed hard. Hate being caught out and not pleased at all about blocking him. Would've been easier and less stressful to tell him outright in the beginning.

"Partly."

"Now we know ... how do you feel? Up to a chat about the changing future?"

"Not really."

"Me neither. Shuffle over. Let me get in there." Mitch crawled up beside me and pulled me into his arms. My head rested comfortably on his shoulder. "Don't throw up on me," he said, kissing the top of my head.

"We're okay?" I asked as I curled into him.

"Of course," Mitch said. "We're great."

"You are more than I deserve, Mitchell Iverson."

I knew he was smiling when he said, "We're having a baby." And held me close. "Still feel sick?"

"Not so much. Kurt's magic shot worked." My eyes closed. The absence of nausea and the relief that Mitch knew, left me feeling both relieved and tired all at once.

Chapter Thirty Four
Demons

I watched from the car as Mitch ran across the parking lot and disappeared through the door to Safeway. My smile reflected from the car window as I waited. It was Tuesday. Five days before our wedding and I was feeling okay.

A phone call distracted me from my vigil. Kurt.

"Conway?"

"Yep."

"Everything all right?"

"Yeah. I'm on my way to work."

Pretty sure the silence on his end was filled by a hamster running on a wheel.

"We have another death."

"I'm twenty minutes away."

"About that ... you've got an appointment this morning with my pal Jeremy Johansen."

"And he is?"

"The doctor I mentioned yesterday. The appointment is at ten."

My watch said it was half-eight.

"Where's his office?"

Mitch opened the car door and angled in behind the wheel. He reached over and dropped a box of crystallized ginger in my lap. I smiled at him and mouthed 'thank you.'

"Kurt? Where do I need to be?" I hoped it was D.C.

"Falls Church."

Damn.

"Where's the latest crime scene?"

"Reston."

That wasn't going to work. "Are you in the office now?"

"Yes."

"Wait for me. I'm coming to you." I hung up.

Mitch's hand was on the ignition. "Problem?"

"Scheduling conflict," I replied. "How flexible are you this morning?"

He took his hand off the ignition and turned to face me. "Kurt got you an appointment with the specialist?"

"Uh huh, at ten in Falls Church."

Mitch took his phone from the cradle on the dash and made a call. I tuned out, my mind flipping between another death and thoughts of the specialist appointment. When the hum of Mitch's voice stopped, I glanced at him. He placed the phone back in the cradle and said, "I'll need to work late tonight but I've cleared my morning."

"Thank you."

I hadn't expected him to come with me, and that he wanted to, meant everything. We'd both be working late and that was okay.

"I need to go to the office before we go to Falls Church."

He nodded and turned the key.

I zoned out almost as soon as the engine started. Words danced around me. A few took form and dropped into my lap. A poem?

Before I could consciously stop it, the rest of the poem manifested. My brain whirred. The odds of it being a random poem about a scent were nil. For a few seconds, I was inhabited by every victim all at once.

Someone spoke. I had no idea who; apart from Phoebe, I didn't know any of their voices. But I did know it was one of the victims.

"A simple scent dragged me back to hell. Lighting incense brought a tale to tell. A flash went off in my disturbed brain. Throwing me back into turmoil again." Her voice faded into the vortex of faces that inhabited my mind.

Lines of another poem appeared on a whiteboard written by an ethereal hand. Chance swing through the door drew my attention away from the emerging words. He grinned and stood next to me, facing the whiteboard.

His arm draped around my shoulders. "What are we doing?"

"Reading. One of the victims, I think, wrote a poem."

"How many of them were poets, El?"

"Just one as far as I know, but two wrote fiction. Jane Daughtry was the poet."

"Jane was FBI?"

I nodded. "This might be something then," I said. The ethereal hand vanished taking the white board marker with it. Revealing a poem.

Patchouli

I smelled the scent before
Long ago and far away
When you knocked upon my door
Your cologne wafted through my home
Lingered on my clothes
Every room in which you went
Lay heavy with that earthy-musky scent

I never knew what the base note was
Until I smelled it again today
Back came the total horror of you
I'd so carefully hidden away
You unlocked the door to immeasurable pain
Never will I be trapped here again.

Patchouli lingers in the air
Its drifting tendrils everywhere.

Chance and I read. He stepped back and I read it twice more.

"Chance, she knew the killer ..."

"Looks that way."

"We were looking at self-help groups or therapy groups because their houses were almost OCD clean."

"And now?"

"I think it's more than Obsessive Compulsive Disorder. I think it's a symptom of abuse. Control. They clean to regain control over their lives or part of their lives." I couldn't prove that either, but it felt right. Deep in my bones it just felt like it.

"And Jane?"

"She was the intended victim all along. She knew one of the Unsubs. What if one of them was someone who had abused her in the past ..." Thoughts collided and re-formed as new ideas. "She could also be an anomaly. A neat freak with no history of psychological damage." I needed to look into that. Whatever it was that drew me back to Jane was important.

"Is that unusual, killing the intended victim early and then carrying on killing?"

"Every nutjob is different."

"I thought that was snowflakes," he said with a chuckle.

Chance was so close I could feel his presence. Comfortable. Warm. Weird. My mind knew he wasn't there and I wasn't in my office standing in front of my white-board, so why could I feel Chance?

Best not to dwell.

"We were looking at the wrong kind of groups."

"Not necessarily, El. Just not looking deep enough."

That made sense.

"Jane knew her killer. If he abused her, if he was an ex-boyfriend, who would know that?" Then the other thought forced its way to the front of the queue. "What if Jane knew her killer but there was no abuse. Who would know people she'd met recently?"

"A current boyfriend would know her friends and she may have confided in him if there was historical abuse."

"A paramedic ..."

Matthew Collins.

Time I had another chat with Matthew Collins. Don't think he shared everything he knew about Jane. Benefit of the doubt might be necessary, though I didn't specifically ask if she had an ex-boyfriend who was an abusive fucktard.

I straightened up as Chance stepped in front of me, obscuring most of the poem. "How you feeling?"

"Okay." Suspicion mounted as he stayed in front of me. "Why?"

"You haven't been well. Thought you were looking pale."

"I'm pregnant, Chance. Nothing to worry about."

He smiled, not the warmest smile I've ever seen from Chance.

"Be careful El, you fit the profile and the killing isn't done yet."

"You worry too much, Chance."

"I saw the letter from Hank. I don't think I worry enough." He turned and walked away. He paused and looked over his shoulder. "You've got more to lose, you need to be careful."

I watched as Chance melted into a puddle of denim-colored paint in the doorway.

The scenery beyond the window drew my attention. We were approaching the office and the entrance to the underground parking garage.

"Hey. You're back," Mitch said, glancing sideways at me.

"Yeah."

"Okay?"

"Yep."

The guard on the gate pressed the button releasing the barrier arm and waved Mitch through.

"Anywhere in particular?" Mitch asked, driving down the ramp into the dark below.

"Delta teams park on the far side by the elevators."

Several minutes later we were in the elevator and I found myself questioning the cleverness of steel boxes that moved at speed. It was still better than the stairwell. Maybe.

Sandra greeted us with her usual enthusiasm as we approached her desk.

"The happy couple!" she crooned. "How long now?"

"Five days," Mitch replied, beating me to it.

"Sandra, I need Matthew Collins in here. There are some more things I think he can help me with."

"I'll give him a call, O Genie of the White Veil."

"Ask him nicely and let him know I would like his help."

"If he refuses?"

"Send a car, I need his help," I replied. "Get someone from Delta C to pick him up if necessary." A phone rang, reminding me we had a 1-800 number set up. "Anything on the tip line?"

"Every lunatic in D.C. is on the tip line," Sandra said, scrolling through comments on her screen. "Uniform are coping with the calls. There were a few I kicked back to them to investigate but so far nothing useful." The scrolling continued. She paused. "Hang on a minute. Did someone mention a bloody bag?"

"Yeah, the car thief mentioned seeing someone with a bloody bag."

"I got something here. A gentleman called in saying that an art gallery near him had bloody bags, cushions, and aprons."

"His reason for calling?"

"Lonely?"

"Send someone, if our Unsub purchased the bag from a gallery, they might have a credit card receipt."

"Worth a shot, O Genie of the Underworld."

"Thanks, Sandra. We'll be in my office. Kurt said we have a new crime scene."

She nodded, stuck a pencil in her hair and typed at a frantic pace. "New scene, Jodie Norris. I have an appointment for you with Mallory Steven's bank manager at half-one this afternoon."

"Send me a reminder and thank you." As I was about to walk away, I stopped. "Did Sasha Petrovovich send a report through yet?"

"Just checking ... bear with." I waited while Sandra checked email. "Not yet."

"Okay, thanks. Better go see Kurt."

Keys clicked under her fingers. Sandra smiled at me

over her screens. "He's in your office."

Figures. No one's ever in their own offices these days.

Kurt looked up from behind my desk.

"Vacate," I said motioning to him. "That's my chair."

"I'm done. Was printing crime scene photos for your board." He pointed to a pile of paper sitting in the out tray of the printer in the corner.

"Thanks."

Kurt passed me and sat in one of the two chairs in front of my desk. Mitch sat on the couch and picked up a book from the coffee table. He didn't want to be part of the conversation. Not his job. I sat in the warm chair. That never feels right.

"You look like you know something ..." Kurt said. "You sharing?"

I nodded.

"There was something I couldn't grab on to at Jane Daughtry's home. The poetry, it felt like something but no one else seems to write poetry and her having my book actually looked like a coincidence."

Kurt laughed. "Trying to imagine you even considering coincidence as a possibility."

"I know ... not easy." I sighed and rested my elbows on the desk. "I saw a poem on our way here."

"I almost don't want to ask ... but the curiosity might kill me ... how?"

Letting the crazy out. Never easy.

"I saw a ghostly hand write it on my whiteboard." My eyes flashed to the board. No poem. Disappointing.

"How, really isn't that big a deal. It's what it said that's important and who wrote it."

"Carry on."

I stood up and walked over to the board. Could I replicate it? Hope sprang eternal. Pollyanna was alive and well and living in me. Unicorns do exist and shit doesn't stink.

The whiteboard marker in my left hand drew a line down the board and then wrote. The entire poem emerged. It was messy but legible.

By the time I'd finished Kurt was standing next to me. "Impressive for your left hand," he said.

"Surprised myself."

Kurt read the poem aloud. "What do you want to do?" He turned his head to face me. "Never mind, I know. We're going back to Jane's place to find that poem."

"Yep, and because I missed something. I missed a scent."

I didn't really miss it, I just didn't comprehend the relevance. That faint smell of musky wet dirt in the bathroom clothes hamper: now I knew it was relevant.

"Not like you."

"Nope, but it happens."

I Googled patchouli. It definitely fitted with the wet dirt smell in the clothes hamper. What surprised me was discovering the plant was related to mint.

"Find what you need?"

"Think so, but to be sure I need to talk to Petrovovich."

"Do it now, we've got a crime scene to get to and if you

want to revisit Jane's place, we might have to make that after your appointment."

Fair enough. Maybe not the best day to have an appointment with a specialist. Timing. Sucking. Again.

I sat back at my desk and called Petrovovich.

"It's Ellie Conway." I didn't wait for him to speak. "There's a scent I couldn't place. It didn't register. A musky wet earth smell, really faint, inside a clothes hamper."

"Patchouli," he said without hesitation. "I smelled it too. It's in my report."

"Thank you. I needed you to confirm what I thought."

"You're welcome. My report will be with you within the hour."

"Thank you for your help." I hung up. Kurt was waiting. "He said patchouli."

"Then we should get there as soon as we can and see if we can find the poem."

"Yep. Also, Sandra is asking Matthew Collins to come back in. If Jane was in an abusive relationship in the past, he might know about it."

"What about her parents? Or the guy who carpooled with her?" Kurt asked.

I didn't feel her parents were holding anything back when they talked about Jane. Possibly she hid it from them.

"I'll talk to her parents again when I get a chance, if I need to. I'm not keen on telling them something that'll hurt them more now. She'd dead, that's bad enough."

Kurt stood by my desk. "Support groups. We need to revisit that list and look for support groups for victims of violent crime including rape, and groups for people with post-traumatic stress disorder."

"Yes, we do. I think we'll find they all have some kind of abuse in their pasts ... the houses are so very clean. It's a control thing, isn't it?"

"Can be."

"In this case?"

"It's possible, Conway. Even though none of the background checks turned up police reports regarding violence, it doesn't mean it didn't happen. Rape is still way under-reported."

Something horrible jumped into my mind. Yes, rape is an under-reported crime. Could a cop be running a support group and if so, how would women hear about it, if they weren't reporting the crimes?

Because they did report the rape but it never went any further.

Why? The complaint would still be in the system.

Troy Fallon.

"Fallon is homicide now, but what did she do before?" I wasn't really asking, just thinking aloud while I checked out her service record. I went back seven years and found a brief stint with the Special Victims Unit at Fairfax PD. "Kurt, Fallon was seconded to special victims for six months early in her detective career. The appointment was to cover maternity leave and she requested to go back to homicide once the six months were up."

"Another nail in her coffin."

Yep.

"I want her case files. I want to know exactly what she did over there."

"I'll get Sandra to get everything for you. You get ready, we have to go."

Crime scene time.

Chapter Thirty Five
Save a Prayer

Another bathroom.

Another clean house.

Another drained blonde.

Another reason not to shower.

Jodie Norris, twenty-eight, administrator at the Crime Museum.

"Let me do this," I said to Kurt. "Jodie and I need to have a talk."

"Yeah, sure, that's probably the creepiest thing you've ever said. I'll be right here." He stepped into the open doorway. "In case she reanimates and has a sudden craving for fresh brains."

A smile crossed my lips. Good thinking. Trust no one, not even the dead. I looked around the room before crouching down next to the shower and Jodie.

"Okay Jodie, this is the thing ... you're dead and I need you to show me what happened, right before you died."

Nothing happened. I waited. Jodie remained inert. No incorporeal arms moved. Nothing.

Not helpful. From my position I easily saw a small square of white paper tucked behind a large potted fern on the floor. I retrieved it and read aloud, "'Trapped behind the line.'"

Kurt came forward with an evidence bag for the note.

"Jodie's not talking," I said with a sigh.

Felt like a fail on my part. Maybe she didn't like me. Perhaps she had already left the building. A sudden rise in my body temperature took me by surprise. Bile swirled in my gut, saliva pooled. I swallowed hard.

"Conway?" Kurt's tone expressed concern. "Looking a bit flushed. All right?"

I wanted to nod but my head shook.

Traitor.

My vision clouded. A female voice grew stronger as it came closer. From the corner of my eye I saw shadowy movement. Jodie? The voice told me it was. I could feel her. Cold fingers dug into my back and pulled my flesh apart. The cold climbed inside filling every crevice and organ with trepidation. All I could hear was Jodie. She walked me through her morning. She got up early, didn't make coffee because coffee makes her ill.

God.

Images of Jodie throwing up filled my mind.

That was too much for me. Dizziness hit like a sledge-hammer.

Nothing.

No Jodie. No bathroom. No noise.

The next thing I saw were Mitch's blue eyes hovering above me. That was pretty clever. How'd he do that?

"You in there, El?"

"What if I say no?" I replied, with a groan. Pain radiated from the left side of my head. "Jodie ..."

Someone touched my wrist. I couldn't turn my head, it hurt. My eyes wouldn't focus.

"What about Jodie?"

I knew that voice. Kurt.

"She was pregnant," I said, letting the pain in my head take over and push me back into the dark.

I thought I heard Kurt say, "So were you."

Chapter Thirty Six
Was I wrong?

Background noises grew louder and more insistent as the black lifted, revealing soft light and deep gray shadows. I didn't want to move. There seemed little point trying. I didn't need to open my eyes to know where I was. The familiar smells associated with a hospital assailed me. A deep sadness rolled over me like a fleecy blanket.

The nothingness seemed preferable to reality but I couldn't get back there. I emptied my mind and waited.

A screen appeared. Mitch's name and his picture sat above the green call button. I pressed the button. His voice filled my ears. Not my head. It took me a minute to figure it out.

"Open your eyes, babe."

I don't want to.

I don't want to.

"Sleepy," I replied, unsure if my words were audible.

"I know. For me, okay? Open your eyes. I need to know you're okay." Mitch was close. I felt pressure on my hand. Warmth spread as fingers closed around mine. "Please, El."

I don't want to.

Drifting into the dark felt better than moving closer to the light. It wasn't fair of me. Life didn't feel very fair. I could justify the hell out of anything in the dark. The noises softened, fading until the nothing swallowed them all.

I breathed. The dark lightened to cream. Heavy black outlines drawn in Sharpie emerged on the cream. A paint box sat on an outlined desk. Watching a brush move and color the scene fascinated me. I knew where I was. I recognized the glass partitions and the leather chairs before I saw Chance sitting at his desk. He looked up. His lips set in a straight line. Uncharacteristic. He always smiled when he saw me. That wasn't right.

"You should sit down, Ellie," he said, motioning to a chair. "I'll be right with you."

The chair was comfortable. The leather soft. "Why am I here?" I asked, taking note of the spacious office and the lack of noise. A silent office. Strange.

"You don't know?" Chance said, putting down the papers he was reading.

"No."

"They can't get through to you."

"Who can't?"

Chance moved the screen on his desk so I could see what he'd been watching. Mitch sitting next to a hospital bed. Kurt pacing the room.

"Mitch and Kurt, Ellie. They can't get through to you. You're not responding."

"Am I dead?"

He shook his head. "No. You just don't want to wake up."

"Then why am I here?" I sighed.

"Because you have to wake up. Delta can't close the

case … you still hold information in your head that they don't know. Without it and you, no one will make the connection between Fallon and Stevens or Fallon and the victims."

"Of course they will."

Chances eyes hardened. "They won't. You hold the key. Get your shit together and wake up."

"I don't know who Unsub One is … I don't know why Jodie's vision was cloudy when she wasn't drugged."

"She was drugged, just not with lorazepam. Think outside the square. That second Unsub isn't Greek like the first one, Ellie, he's an Eastern European."

I felt my forehead tense. I ran through countries I thought were Eastern European. Croatia, Serbia, Bulgaria, Romania, Belarus, Poland, Czech Republic, Russian Federation, Moldavia, Latvia. I'm sure I missed some and none felt like it fitted.

"That doesn't help me. I don't know anything."

Chance's hands flattened on the desk, he pushed himself to his feet and moved toward me.

"Unsub One, Ellie. You know who he is. Think about it. Think about Hank. You know this."

I wanted the dark back.

Thinking about Hank was not something I wanted to do, it was way up there with waking up. Hank had been in prison too long for this to be coming from him. He didn't kill these women. All I could see was a band saw dripping with blood and meat.

"This isn't helping me, Chance."

"It will. Think, Ellie. Think about Hank and his visitors. Find out who is hanging out with him."

No! There is no obvious link between Hank and this case. The women were not turned into human jigsaw puzzles: they were drained of most of their blood.

No amount of thinking gave me a connection between the crimes I was investigating and Hank.

"There's no link ..."

Chance shook his head. "Think, Ellie."

"I am thinking."

When did Chance become such a nag?

I slumped in the chair and let the case notes scroll through my mind, comparing the new investigation with Hank's messy pastimes. The one similarity was unconscious victims. Hank favored fentanyl.

"Fentanyl spray. Hank used Fentanyl spray to knock out his victims." I gave it a minute to let that thought work through to a conclusion. A light went on. "Fentanyl spray is a Russian invention."

Chance winked. "I think you're starting to see ..."

"But we never found the source of the fentanyl."

"Check the prison logs. You'll find it and when you do, you'll find Unsub Two."

"Two?" No, he said I'd know who Unsub One was if I thought about Hank. "What about One?"

"Keep thinking, Ellie. It's right there ..."

How did Hank get a letter delivered to my house? How did he get a letter out of a prison and to my house? Someone smuggled it out? Who could get close enough to a maximum security prisoner to do that? A lawyer or a family member. I doubted a lawyer would risk losing their job doing something that stupid.

"Crap! Hank is related to someone within this case ..." The thought meandered around in my head looking for something to latch onto.

"Got it yet?" Chance asked leaning closer to me.

I shook my head. The thought sloshed from side to side and spilled over the edges of my brain. Thoughts dripped like clocks in a Salvador Dali painting. Clocks. Time. Melting. I looked closer at the faces of the melting clocks. I didn't get it. Felt like everything hinged on time. Time. A headline oozed over two of the clocks. Not time but The Times. As I watched, the headline morphed into a letter posted in a mailbox. Times. Post. Journalist.

Rosanne Lette.

A door crashed into its frame, shaking the images around me. Walls ran. Colors merged. Puddles formed. Clocks slid to the floor taking all the images of Hank's destruction with them. A pool of frothy red formed at my feet.

Crap! No wonder she doesn't talk much about her son. Her son's father is Hank. Kristopher delivered the letter. He was the reason Rosanne broke into my home. She wanted to know if I knew about Hank. Oh, man!

"Ellie?"

"Uh huh."

"You got it?"

"Kristopher Lette is Hank's son."

Which is great an' all but he's not the guy I saw. He's not one of the Unsubs.

"Yes."

"Doesn't help me narrow down the Unsub any, Chance."

"Come on, Ellie, use that brain of yours … it's not rocket science."

Wiseass.

Maybe it is rocket science. What did I know? Unsub One was directly linked to Jane Daughtry. Possibly an abusive ex. According to Chance, Unsub Two was a Russian with a link to Hank.

I'd missed something.

What happened at the last crime scene?

What didn't I want to see?

"Chance?"

"You're going to have to look, Ellie. I know you don't want to. You have to." His voice was soft, firm but soft. Whatever it was that I didn't want to see was bad. He only ever used that tone when shit was bad.

I sank further into the chair and let myself be transported back to the crime scene and Jodie Norris. This time, I walked in the door and focused on Jodie. I saw her blonde hair hanging over the side of the bathtub. I moved the shower curtain back so I could see the rest of Jodie, aware that I'd only seen her face before. Her torso displayed stab wounds. Her arms and legs bore a few slashes. A long incision across her lower abdomen.

Was pregnant.

The fetus was in the bath near her. No blood anywhere.

Both mother and baby drained.

"How old was it?" I asked looking into Chance's eyes then back at the baby. "She, how old was she?"

"Seventeen point four weeks. Look closer at the baby."

I zoomed in on the image. The cord was torn.

"Baby bled out just like Jodie." Chance nodded. "Ripping a fetus from a uterus is different from stabbing women and taking perfume or body wash."

"Yeah," Chance replied. "Ya gotta wonder about someone who could do that sort of damage to two human beings."

"This is the Russian's handiwork?"

"Yes."

"He's escalated." Those words sat there for a second before they were followed by my next question. "How would he have known about the pregnancy?"

Chance smiled a knowing smile and said nothing. Not helping. I had to admit he'd been pretty helpful so far.

He looked at me and grinned. "How do you like me so far?"

I shook my head. "Really? You're still going there with mixing television series?"

"Could be worse."

True.

"Thanks for choosing a series I liked." Chance morphed into Keen Eddie then back to Chance. "Was that fun for you?"

356

His dimples deepened as he grinned. "Yeah."

"Not helping."

"Ah, but I am."

Yeah, he actually was.

His tone changed, less playful, more serious. "You have to go back, Ellie. You need to get this case closed, they need you."

"They—"

"Delta and Mitch. They. Need. You."

"But—"

"It's not what you think, Ellie. It's okay to go back."

The room shimmered like an oasis in the desert. Sparkling like sand on a hot day. Chance blurred. Now what?

Someone picked up my world and shook it. Life became a snow globe full of glitter. A voice broke through the sparkles. As the clouds of silver glitter cleared Mitch came into focus.

He looked upset. My doing, I supposed. Didn't make me feel good at all. Another tick in the box marked fail. I couldn't quite get why he wanted to marry me. That wasn't helpful thinking either. I had enough clues not to say that aloud.

I hoped.

"You're back." The relieved timbre in Mitch's voice tugged at my heart. "Can you open your eyes?"

I did as he asked. Light bounced from all angles. Firing spiky lightning bolts into my eyes. I winced.

"The light," Mitch said and the brightness dimmed to a

much more manageable level.

"Thank you," I murmured.

"Don't mention it," he replied. "You've been out awhile, El. We were getting jumpy."

We?

"We who?"

Dad. Of course. That made sense. Where else would he be? Home with his crazy lady friend and the potential serial killer of a son.

That could be awkward if she didn't die and they got married. A serial-killing stepbrother would not make me a favorite in the hallowed halls of the FBI. Bad enough that my cases were used at the academy and not always as shining examples of how clever we were!

"You okay there, kid?" Dad said, stooping down and kissing my forehead.

"I'm good, Dad, don't know what the fuss is all about."

Not even being facetious, I really didn't know.

Dad chuckled. "Never known you to be anything other than good. One day perhaps you'll acknowledge things could be better."

Mitch laughed softly. "Then I'll really worry," he said, squeezing my fingers under his.

"Where's Kurt?" I asked, sitting up a bit and regretting the movement. My head swam.

"I'm here," he said from the other side of my bed.

He didn't sound happy. I didn't want to ask what had happened. I launched into a list of things I needed him to check on regarding the case. Everything Chance told me or I remembered. Kurt wrote without comment until I stopped talking.

"We're looking for a Russian, yes?"

"Yes," I confirmed. "A Russian who has a connection to Hank."

"And Rosanne Lette's son is Hank's son too?"

"Yes."

"And you can prove all of this?"

"No."

He rolled his eyes.

Come on, he should be used to this.

Dad interjected, "I might be able to help ..."

"You can?" I said, turning my head to face him.

"After that incident at your home, Rosanne and I had a big talk. She told me about Hank. I can confirm he is her son's father." Dad paused to regroup. "For obvious reasons, she doesn't tell people."

"Okay. How did she meet him and how long ago were they together?"

"She met him at college. He was campus security. She was doing her masters. We're talking twenty-five years ago."

"And?"

"They dated briefly, the result was Kristopher."

"Hank knows?"

"Yes."

"Does the offspring know?"

"Yes."

I turned my head and said to Kurt, "I want a list of

everyone who has ever visited Hank in prison and I want it now."

Kurt pulled his phone from his pocket and walked out the door. I could hear him talking outside the room. That was the moment I realized I wasn't in the Emergency Department. I was on a ward in my own room.

That didn't seem like a good thing. That seemed like they expected me to stay for a while.

I couldn't see it as something I'd be doing.

Kurt poked his head around the glass door. "Anything else I can do for you while I have Sam on the line?"

"Yes, find out where Jane Daughtry met Unsub One. My money is on college. She went to George Mason. I want to know if she was ever seen by the campus medical staff for unexplained bruising, breaks, or anything that might have been abuse. Find her school records. If she ever reported a rape or sexual assault, I want to know about it."

Kurt nodded and relayed the information to Sam.

"Anything else?"

Oh boy, yes!

"Yeah, but not for Sam." I waited while Kurt said goodbye. As soon as he was back in my room I started up again. "Where's Matthew Collins?"

"Sandra called him in, he couldn't get off shift but said he'd swing by when his shift ends."

"Good. He might know the name of whoever it was that used to like patchouli and who hurt Jane."

"There's nothing in her recent past."

"I think whatever it was, happened when she was at college, so it's not recent."

"So why did the Unsub wait until now to kill her?"

"That I don't know. Could be one of several things. He may not have been able to get to her. He may have been quietly planning this the whole time. Something may have triggered this killing spree."

Kurt nodded. "You think he knows the Russian who knows Hank?"

"Yep, they're working together."

"When did they meet?"

"Could be on campus. I think the Russian is older than the other Unsub. I didn't get a good enough look at him to know for sure. But if he were a rent-a-cop on campus he would've had a bit of perceived power, which might have made him an attractive friend to Unsub One."

Kurt nodded in agreement. Always nice when people agree with me.

Mitch squeezed my hand to get my attention. "I know you need to spit out everything you've got in your head regarding this case, El ..."

Dammit.

He wanted to talk. I was pretty sure I didn't want to know. I felt okay and it was the first time I'd felt really okay in weeks. Seemed like a bad thing. Pollyanna assured me it didn't need to be bad, that maybe I was just used to feeling like crap and didn't notice anymore. I looked at Mitch. Trying to gauge his thoughts. I couldn't hear them in my head. No clues.

Suck it up, Princess, the conversation is going to happen whether you like it or not.

"Okay, let's do this," I said, with more resignation than I intended. "Tell me."

He let my hand go and fished something out of his pocket. A piece of paper. Carefully he unfolded it and handed it to me.

Black and white.

Not the easiest picture to see.

After carefully studying the image, I was none the wiser.

"What am I looking at?"

He moved closer and pointed to part of the image. "This here is baby one."

My brain stopped. Rewound and froze again. There was a jolt and it lurched forward.

"Sorry, say that again, because I thought you said baby one?"

Mitch smiled and nodded. "Look ..." He pointed to the shape again. "Baby one."

Crap! He did say baby one.

"Uh huh." Words failed me.

"And this, on the other side ... baby two."

Nope, nothing. I heard the words, I saw blurred darkish shapes on a small piece of paper, and it made no sense.

I felt a switch click in my brain. "I thought you just said there were two babies."

Mitch laughed. "I did."

I didn't sign up for that.

Two. I don't think so!

I was barely coping with the thought of one.

Two? Jeez. How is that a good idea?

Clearly it was a mistake and the second image was a shadow or some kind of anomaly.

"I don't think that will work for me," I muttered, staring at the image in my hand. Babies? Really? Looked more like nondescript blobby things. "Pretty sure this isn't going to work for me."

Mitch's hand found mine. He extracted the picture and handed it to Dad.

"Give it a minute, El. Let this sink in."

"I might need longer than a minute."

It took me over two weeks to almost get used to being pregnant to start with.

The universe was messing with me. I could hear it laughing. No, not the universe. I knew that laugh. Chance. Somewhere in the blurriness that was my mind, Chance was laughing. Great.

Chapter Thirty Seven

Fear

Despite Kurt's best effort at keeping me in hospital for some forced rest, I did what I always do and made him remove the drip from my arm and discharged myself. I felt great. Kurt informed me it was because of the intravenous fluids.

No sense lying around. Killers to catch. Wedding to attend. Honeymoon to go on. Anything that was going to happen after that could wait.

The sudden admittance to hospital meant I no longer had to go to the appointment Kurt had set up for me. It also gave Kurt time to scan my hand. Fractured fourth and fifth metacarpals. Not serious. Just inconvenient and painful. I checked my phone. Almost time to meet with Mallory Stevens' bank manager.

"Now what?" Mitch asked, pulling me into his arms and hugging me in the hospital parking lot. I melted into him for a few minutes. Enjoying the scent of his cologne and the warmth of his body.

"I'll head in with Kurt. We have an appointment at a bank and then I'm going to talk to Jane Daughtry's former boyfriend and a few other people. I want to narrow in on the suspects by tonight." I hadn't moved, relishing the closeness. "We're getting close, I can feel it."

"Good luck. I'll be late tonight, El." His words ruffled my hair.

"I'll be late too. I want this case over." I pulled back a bit in his arms and looked up at him. "Meet you at home."

"My place tonight?"

"Yep."

He smiled. His lips met mine. And everything was okay.

"Take it easy."

"I will."

The bank manager wasn't the most helpful person I'd ever met. She warmed to Kurt so in the interest of getting information, I left him to it and went in search of food.

Suddenly starving, I knew what I wanted. Cream cheese and smoked salmon on a bagel. Just had to find it.

My phone was pretty good at locating whatever I needed, and this time was no exception. I found a place with exactly what I needed to eat. I took my bagel and walked down the street as I ate. Felt good to eat and not feel sick. Window shopping wasn't an unpleasant way to kill time. Just as I finished the bagel and started on the ginger beer I'd purchased, a macabre window came into view.

Bloodied aprons on naked mannequins. What the hell?

My eyes searched above the window for the name of the store.

Valentine Gallery.

The name suggested romance; the displayed art reminded me of a crime scene.

Fragments of everything I'd seen or heard over the last week floated down from the sky. The pieces took shape as they grew closer. Jigsaw. Two corners dropped at my feet, one had part of an apron attached.

I swung open the gallery door and stepped into the air-conditioned interior. My eyes adjusted to the dim light, drawn to spotlights around the room, shining on various works. I thrust my hand into my pocket and pulled out my phone. Unlocking the screen, I pressed Sandra's name.

Moments later her voice filled my ear. "O Genie of the Emergency Department, how can I help?"

News travels fast.

"I'm in an art gallery, Valentine Gallery in Fairfax. Get me everything you can. I'm looking at bloody aprons, cushions, covered notebooks, and bags. The patterns I'm seeing are forensic. Someone knew what they were doing."

"Can you snap a few pics and send them to me?"

No one had appeared from the back. I noted several CCTV cameras. Using my phone, I snapped a few pictures and sent them to Sandra.

"Gruesome," I said taking a closer look at a cushion with a decent-looking directional blood spatter. "The color's good."

"The color is good," Sandra replied. "Backup?"

I almost said no then I remembered my morning. "Yes, Sam or Lee, or both if they're available. Kurt is at the bank a block over. I'll let him know where I am."

"Your GPS is active. I'll send the address to Sam and Lee."

I hung up.

From the end of the room, I heard a noise. A light cough.

"Hello!" I called.

"Hello," came a reply. The owner of the voice didn't emerge from the shadows.

"Who's the artist?" I asked. "These are astounding."

"A young upcoming artist. Kris Lette," the voice said. "He's someone to watch."

Yeah, he is.

I peered closer at an apron. The color was very realistic. Every piece. The variation of color was what I'd expect to see in dried blood. Clever. Maroon and deep reds with a smidgen of reddish brown.

I searched for a price tag. A bag hanging from another naked mannequin's shoulder had a small tag attached. I flipped it. Nearly five hundred dollars. Wow. Guess it was art and not just paint squirted on calico. "I'd like to purchase a piece ..."

"Of course."

I jumped. The voice was right behind me. Creepy. My hand rested on the top of my holster. Reassurance.

*

Whatever I was on felt hard and cold.

My hand touched water?

A puddle. A cold puddle. Fingers moved and wetness made a sound. It felt like water. Not sticky. Not thick or slippery. The viscosity said it was water or water-like. The lack of smell also suggested water. A deal of relief came from believing it wasn't anything sinister like blood. At the back of my mind, I heard the word plasma and stopped the thought. It wasn't comforting to know that plasma had a similar viscosity to water.

No smell.

Not blood.

My next thought was chilling. My eyes were reluctant to open or couldn't open, I wasn't sure which. I screwed up my nose: something was tied around my head. That explained why I couldn't see. Blindfolded. The fingers on my right hand moved but my hand wouldn't rise. I should've been able to feel pain when I tried to move my broken knuckles. My legs were immobile. Left hand. I thought about my left hand. Twisted. I turned my wrist and heard metal on metal. Something chaffed against my wrist.

Metal handcuffs. Mine?

I took a breath and tried to sense my surroundings. Apart from cold and wet, I had very little. No images. No sound. A light breeze brushed against me. From the breeze came a faint scent. Wet dirt. Musky wet earth.

Crapadoodledo.

Patchouli.

Being handcuffed and unable to see wasn't as big an issue as the smell of patchouli. I figured my weapon was gone.

A shiver started at my feet and vibrated throughout my body.

Time wasn't working for me. There no way to gauge its passage. Apart from my ever growing desire to pee.

I determined I wasn't hit. Whatever dropped me was not a blow to the head. Wet dirt. Russian. Fentanyl spray.

Everything was wrong.

Mom's voice soared ever louder in my head. "No, Gabrielle, it's right. You fit the profile. You should know that, victimology. You fit the profile of every victim."

And I'm not drinking coffee these days.

But I wasn't at home or in the shower.

The art gallery.

Think. GPS.

Sandra knew where I was. Wherever my phone was now, it would still be sending the signal. Even if they think they've turned it off or taken the battery out. Our little trackers were powered by tiny batteries independent of the phone's operating system and main battery. There was no display or LED o indicate the phone was sending a signal.

All I had to do was survive until the cavalry arrived.

The phone screen I often saw in my head popped up. The image was Mitch's. Under it a green call button. I pressed the button and waited.

It went to voicemail.

What the actual fuck?

Are you kidding me?

Voicemail?

I shrugged internally.

. Something fell, startling me. Metal clattered against the hard floor. It sounded about ten feet from me. Filling my mind with my favorite meadow scene, I let calm wash over me. The meadow faded. Calm remained. Time to employ the senses I did have to work for me and not bother about my inability to see. I could hear, smell, feel, and taste.

More clattering. Blades? Then the sound of things being put on a surface.

Don't think, just be.

I tried calling Mitch again.

Voicemail.

Fuck!

The noise stopped. Silence again.

I tried my internal Mitch call again. This time I heard ringing followed by his voice.

"What happened?"

"I've been taken."

Silence for a beat.

"El?"

"Tell Kurt I think the Russian has me or maybe even Kristopher Lette. I was in the art gallery. I don't know where I am now."

Could still be there. Another voice interjected. "Your call is being transferred."

Do what now?

Kurt's voice filled my head. "I'm in the Art Gallery. This art is pretty screwed up. Where are you?"

"I don't know."

He didn't seem concerned that he could talk to me like this.

It occurred to me, quite slowly, that he might not be talking to me at all. That this could all be a delusion.

"The last thing I remember, I was in the art gallery."

"Stay alive, El, I'm coming for you."

Heavy, almost labored, footsteps moved toward me.

"You might wanna hurry and bring SWAT."

Footsteps stopped in front of me. I breathed in. Patchouli. More lively footsteps hurried across the floor and joined the first. They moved with more freedom than the first set of steps. A younger person or a happy person. Not a good time to think about anyone's happiness or the cause of their happiness.

"You shouldn't be so nosy."

I tried to place the voice, in case I'd come across it before. American, gravely, ex-smoker? I couldn't smell smoke so ex-smoker felt right. Older male. Fifty something was my guess. It was the voice from the art gallery.

Another voice joined in, the younger male. "I'll get the fabric. There's a big order to fill."

Fabric?

"Bring the new bolt," the older voice said. "The heavyweight unbleached calico."

The younger footsteps hurried away.

Fabric? Where's Lette the vampire? Surely they wouldn't proceed without him?

The older voice addressed me, "I'm going to enjoy you."

"Hold that thought," I replied with a snarl.

He laughed, sending foul air in my direction. Bile rose

as I tried not to breathe in his stench. The man choked, then spluttered, coughing uncontrollably.

Sick? Could that be why the two-month gap?

I didn't really care. If he was sick, that gave me something I could use or take advantage of.

The coughing eased.

"You're going to be fun," he rasped. His throat sounded dry and added more menace to his voice. "The others weren't." He paused to catch his breath. "I've wanted a conscious one since we began this venture."

"Junior doesn't like them awake ..." I was thinking aloud rather than conversing. It's a business venture. Stevens and Fallon weren't dating these bozos; they were in business with them. The art business. Bile seethed in my throat.

"You going to vomit?" the male asked. "If you are, do it now. I don't want you throwing up on my fabric." That was when I heard a faint remnant of an accent. Russian or similar.

I swallowed hard.

And continued my thought about the art business. One of them was motivated to kill Jane but it wasn't the purpose of the killings; it was a convenient happenstance for the Unsub. That's why the killings continued. She was the target but not the target.

God!

He'd really dropped the ball this time, letting these freaks live. Time God started micro-managing. Clearly, things have gotten out of hand.

Mitch's voice interrupted my thoughts. He told me they were coming. That my GPS was active. I detected a little bit of panic. Not like him. Calm. Controlled. Planned action was like him. Panic? Not really a thing. Neither of us did much of that. Ever.

All I had to do was stay alive until the cavalry arrived.

Footsteps approached bringing with them a dragging sound. Must be a big bolt of fabric or the younger male isn't overly strong or both. What did I know about him? I dragged the image I saw once front and center so I could study it. Greek descent, I thought. I moved the image around a little trying to see more of him. Thin. I saw an arm. Didn't look like he worked out. Another image formed. They overlaid. How old was he? Not that young, just in better physical condition than the coughing guy. Thirty-something. Something told me he wasn't the person who abused Jane when she was at college. Not that I could prove that happened, yet.

So why kill Jane? Why was it about Jane for him?

Ask?

"Hey, Jane Daughtry ... what the hell was that about?"

Nothing. I smelled something. Fear. That wasn't there before. The older guy wasn't scared. So it was the younger one.

His voice cracked as he spoke, "None of your business."

So he wasn't going to confess all before my death. Some talk when they think they're safe, some don't. I like the talkers.

"What's your name?"

Low voices. I couldn't make out the words. The pounding of my heart overshadowed the talking and made it harder to hear.

"You don't need to know."

"I don't. But if you're going to kill me, I'd like to know who to haunt."

There was a lot of movement near me. I could hear fabric unrolled from the bolt.

"Don't you need the artist?" I said, straining to hear if anyone was present.

The Russian ignored me and carried on. "Lay half on the floor, then hang the rest on the clips."

Clips. I was handcuffed to something metal. A rail? If they were hanging fabric then maybe I was in the middle of a frame and the fabric would be hung around like a shower curtain.

Fuckadoodledo.

Surely they didn't drape the crime scenes with fabric and let the blood fly? It'd have to be treated to preserve it.

Oh jeez, that wasn't paint cleverly mixed to look like blood. It was blood.

I revisited the gallery in my mind. I looked at the tags on the pieces. One apron had a tag that contained the price and a blood type. O negative. A cushion had a price and the words AB positive. Didn't make me feel any better. What looked like cute labels were blood types of the victims? I scrambled through my notes in my mind. Blood types. Violet Cramer. O negative. The apron I saw could be Violet.

God, you really fucked up!

With more braveness than I felt, I asked another question, "How do you stop the blood clotting and breaking down when you're using it?"

The young one perked up at that question. "It's quite clever. I use a mix of potassium oxalate and sodium fluoride for some."

"And they do what?" Without Kurt to interpret I had no idea what those things did to blood.

"Potassium Oxalate is an anticoagulant and the fluoride is a preservative."

"That is clever."

He was still keen to impart information. "I got the idea from specimen collection tubes."

"You said for some, what about the rest?"

We're talking a lot of blood. A death a day. They weren't using it all at once, surely? Maybe there was quite a bit of waste in the process.

My mind flowed over the thought that they were draining as much of the victim's blood as possible, while they were alive, then stabbing to make it look like they bled out via stab wounds. There had to be a wide-bore needle involved. I thought about Jane.

Maybe the first cut to the wrist was to gain access to a main vein. No outward needle marks if they cut into her first and approached the vein that way. But that would require some skill. Cutting the vein would defeat the purpose. One of these bozos had medical training.

The young one spoke again, "Same as blood banks for larger quantities. Flexible collection bags containing sodium citrate, phosphate, and dextrose."

The older male hissed, "Shut up."

The younger one was too pleased with his own cleverness to heed the advice.

"You work in a medical field," I said, not a question. A statement. Then another piece of the jigsaw fell into place. George Mason University. He was a nurse or similar in the student medical facility. That could be where he met Jane. Or he knows a mutual friend of Jane's. I threw a name out to see what happened next.

"Matt Collins."

The younger male laughed. "You're not clever enough to work it out."

I doubted he knew Collins and moved on to thinking about Violet and Winchester. Because he was from there and went back for whatever reason.

"You're not from Fairfax but you worked at George Mason a few years ago."

I knew I was right by the second hissed warning to shut up from the older male. I heard clips being attached to something. Fabric probably.

Why Violet?

What was it about her?

Crap! It was unfortunate timing. She turned him down. Didn't want to know.

"Violet didn't want to go out with you." Again a statement. He could refute my observations at any point.

"You talk too much," the older male growled and kicked my feet.

I pulled up my feet and kicked out hard. My boots slammed into something solid. The solid object buckled and yelped. The yelp became uncontrollable coughing.

The younger male spoke quietly. The coughing drowned out the words. And there I had the connection between the young and the old.

They met through the older man's illness. Possibly a private nursing company or even in a hospital. So the older man needed constant care or just liked having someone on hand and the means to ensure that happened.

"Hank's a friend of yours?"

My words drifted into the coughing and mingled with the quiet voice of the nurse. I'd decided to call him The Nurse. So, I had The Russian and The Nurse.

A partnership made in heaven.

The Russian coughed more.

"And Kristopher Lette is Hank's son. Guess you knew that too. Made it easy to twist him around. Get the artist to help you ... he isn't killing, though. He hasn't evolved enough for that yet."

I spun back to Violet. It all started with Violet.

Spatter patterns filled my mind. Violet started the whole thing. It was unwitting. Patterns created by her blood squirting up the walls triggered something, not right away, but some time later Lette became involved and started dreaming up his forensic apron and bag idea.

"How did you get Lette fired up enough to create pieces of art?" I listened, trying to detect another presence in the area. "And shouldn't he be here for this?"

Violent coughing ensued. My mind darted over bits of information.

"Shut up!" the nurse said. "You don't know anything."

Touchy. Must've been a nerve. Ideas fitted together. Hank had a hand in his son's participation but how would he know Kristopher would be interested?

"Photographs. You showed Hank pictures of Violet and the blood pattern on the wall. He told you to get his kid involved. The struggling artist needed a break."

A break? More like a bucket and a mop. He wasn't destined for greatness in the art world.

So who sewed them?

That's what the freaking money was for!

Mallory Stevens.

Kurt needed to hurry up before all the puzzle pieces died with me.

"We have to move her," the nurse said.

"Why?" The Russian's coughing finally ceased.

"The order, the new gallery wants pooled blood and transfer patterns."

New gallery. They were branching out. Nice.

"Was that the duvet cover order?" His voice weakened with each bout of coughing.

"Yes."

"Where's the boy?"

"We were told to leave him alone today."

"Now we're artists and that little shit gets all the credit …"

Artists? I've seen monkeys with more talent.

"He sent instructions."

"He should be here. Splashing the red around is his job, not ours."

The whiff of dissension gave me something to exploit.

"He? Are you talking about Lette? He's the talent, right?" The lack of derision when I said talent impressed me. "He should definitely be here. Why should you do all the work? Must be hard, being so sick and having to do everything."

"Shut up!" the Russian said, the violence of the delivery threw him into another coughing fit.

It took several minutes to subside.

"I'd make Lette come down here and do his part."

"Shut up!" he said, giving my foot a kick. His wheezing worsened. He couldn't project his voice much beyond a hoarse whisper. "What did he say to do?"

"Treat the fabric once we have the pattern on it, he said it'll be more authentic if we let it pool naturally."

I was going to be a duvet cover.

Come on, Kurt, any minute now.

"Let's do the cast off first," the Russian said. "She's a little too feisty to move yet."

That didn't sound good.

The nurse complained about the state of me. I found that rude.

"This is why I like the coffee/shower thing," he said

with a sigh. "She's not compliant and one of us is going to have to remove those clothes."

"Good luck," I said with a smile.

"You'll have to spray her again," the nurse said.

Not keen on that idea.

"Then we'll have to wait until she wakes again," the Russian said, he didn't sound impressed with the idea. "We don't have time for that."

Good to know.

"You undress her then," the nurse replied. It sounded like a dare.

"Yeah, you do it," I agreed. "No drugs. How hard can it be?"

My free hand was now mobile, which meant I could sit up more. I wasn't sure how much movement the hand-cuffed arm allowed me.

If I could stand it'd be even better.

My feet being tied was annoying but I'd already proved it wasn't impossible for me to inflict damage. Ignoring the pain, I used my free hand and pushed myself to a sitting position, turning more toward my cuffed hand to relieve the strain. That allowed me to try lifting that arm. It moved upward. Standing may not be beyond my reach.

My movement didn't go unnoticed.

"Stop," the Russian cautioned.

"Make me," I retorted, moving some more. Nausea returned in a massive wave. It was going to get messy. I knew I was sitting up enough that I wouldn't choke on my own vomit. Wondering what a regurgitated salmon bagel would be like kept my mind occupied for a few seconds. The Russian was close. I could smell him. He coughed. Within arm's reach. I needed him closer. "I'm wearing a stab proof vest under my shirt," I told him. Being helpful.

I heard him move then felt the heat radiate from his body. Too much heat. He was sick. He'd bent down, his hands tugging at the buttons on my shirt.

He coughed in my face. The salmon bagel mixed with bile flew up my esophagus and spewed out my mouth. For once I didn't mind vomiting.

The squawk of disgust and horror made it all worthwhile.

"Fucking bitch," the Russian said, retching.

The sound caused more vomit to spray from my mouth.

A surprised yell morphed into a thud and a wet splash in front of me. Guess the Russian slipped and fell in my vomit. Nice.

Nice.

I remembered there was water near me when I woke up. Water. That would make my puke go further. Ignoring the pain of the broken bones, I scraped my sore hand along the floor, gathered vomit and liquid and flung it as far as I could. The nurse yelled.

"Stop that!"

I did it again.

Playing in my own vomit – what had I come to? I had to fight not to laugh like a lunatic.

More puke left my hand. I heard it splat onto something. The fabric I hoped. That'd ruin their little attempts at turning me into an art collection. Derision rose along with more bile. Pretty hard to make chunks of salmon bagel look like art. I was glad I'd eaten.

I grabbed the blindfold with my dripping vomit-covered hand and pulled it down.

What a mess!

Now I could see the Russian and the nurse.

Should've done that sooner.

There was a crash somewhere beyond the room and the mess. Followed by booted feet moving quickly. Years of training with SWAT flooded back. Only move as fast as you can shoot. No point running if you can't hit shit when you shoot.

Before I could refocus on the approaching noises, I saw a flash of metal from the corner of my eye. I pulled myself out of the way using my cuffed hand. Not far enough. I felt pressure on the top of my right arm. I pulled up my legs. The Russian slashed at me again; this time I could see him coming and kicked him. Both feet straight in the lower abdomen. He expelled foul air as he doubled over. The knife fell and landed in his own boot.

My fingers just reached it. I stretched as far as I could and grabbed the hilt. One sharp pull released the knife. The Russian wheezed and coughed.

I pulled back. As he straightened up. I threw the knife, slamming it into his chest. Wide-eyed, he stared at me.

A loud voice from the end of the room called, "Hands in the air. Turn around!"

I could just see past the Russian and make out five men in SWAT gear moving into the room.

The Russian turned. The nurse tried to run. A single shot rang out. With a sickening thud, the nurse hit the ground.

Booted feet ran across the floor to the Russian. Within seconds, he was handcuffed and sitting in the middle of the floor with two rifles trained on him. Andrews appeared in front of me.

"Hey, Conway, you good?"

"Yeah, I'm great. Sorry about the mess."

And the smell.

He chuckled. "We expect a certain amount of mess when you're involved." He undid the handcuffs and cut the tape from my ankles. "Can you stand?"

"I think so," I replied, letting him help me to my feet. "That bastard cut me."

I glanced at my arm. Blood soaked into my shirt sleeve.

Andrews pulled a dressing pack from his pocket, ripped it open with his teeth and pressed it against the wound. "Before or after you vomited on him?" He looked at the floor and the fabric hanging near me.

"After."

Andrews laughed. "And you threw puke?"

"Slowed the Russian down a bit."

And I ruined the fabric. That was a win.

Andrews shook his head and laughed. "Resourceful, Conway."

I stepped closer to the handcuffed Russian. His dark cold eyes looked up at me.

"What?"

"Why the notes and the poem?" I needed to know.

"Someone told me the FBI liked poems."

"Who?"

He shook his head and closed his mouth.

"Hey!" Kurt called, walking toward me. "Did you have to make this much mess?"

"I didn't have a lot at my disposal and I needed to buy some time, you took too long."

He wrapped his hand around the wound dressing on my arm and led me toward the door.

"You need a shower ..."

Pass.

Chapter Thirty Eight

Respectable

I don't know why Kurt let me in his car covered in vomit and reeking but he did. I felt a sense of relief once we were in the parking garage under our building. That much closer to cleanliness.

"Take off your boots, wipe them with this and put them over there ..." Kurt threw me a rag from the back of the car and pointed to the wall by the door. "Then come back and stand over the drain."

I did. He unrolled a hose from a reel on the wall and turned the nozzle. Water squirted across the concrete. We had several hoses on each level. Sometimes our cars needed to be cleaned before being valeted professionally. Sometimes we needed to decontaminate our trunks. Sometimes it's us that need decontaminating.

"This will be cold," Kurt said as I stood over the grating in the floor. "You ready?"

"Yep." I closed my eyes and braced myself.

I shuddered as the first blast of cold water hit me, sticking my clothes to my frame. After that, it didn't matter. It's not like I could walk through the building dripping biohazardous material from my person. By the time he turned off the water, I no longer smelled like puke. For that I was grateful. I did a quick look around the area. No one about.

"Give me a hand?" I asked Kurt.

"With?" he replied, placing the hose on the ground.

"I can't undo my jeans, need to take them off and wring out some of the water before we go upstairs."

He smiled, walked over and undid the button then the zip. "Hold onto my shoulders. You won't be able to get wet jeans down with that hand."

Wet jeans are difficult at the best of time.

I placed my hands on his shoulders. Kurt tugged my jeans down making sure my underwear stayed in place. I stepped out of the jeans steadying myself against the car. He picked them up and wrung them out a few times then handed them back.

I struggled to get them back on. If it weren't so frustrating, it'd be funny. Exasperation voiced as a hiss as I tugged one side up then the other.

"Conway ... let me."

Kurt pulled up my jeans and refastened the button and zip making me feel like a three-year-old.

"Thanks."

"Anytime," he said with a grin and rolled the hose back onto the reel.

My wet shirt and jeans stuck to me. Hands and feet were frozen. Water ran from my hair in icy streams down my back. I pulled as much of my hair to one side as I could and squeezed it with my good hand. Water dribbled down the front of my shirt and dripped onto the concrete.

"Okay?" Kurt asked rolling the hose back onto the reel.

"Sure."

Saturated clothing is not super comfortable. Shivering,

I picked up my boots and squelched my way up the stairs. On the plus side, I no longer felt ill breathing stairwell air. Not sure I ever wanted to get back in Kurt's car, though. I heard him on his phone as he followed my wet footprints.

"My car needs cleaning before it's used again. Tell the detailing company to wear gloves and protective clothing when they pick it up." He hung up.

"You're making me sound like I have the Croatoan virus," I said as I reached the landing for our floor.

"The what-now, Conway?"

"Croatoan … never mind. Supernatural thing."

Kurt opened the door for me. "Croatoan … I've heard of it."

"Tell me it's not real."

"Plenty of real viruses are horrific but that's not a real one," he said as we walked down the hallway. "I've watched Supernatural."

Who knew?

I took my go-bag from the closet in my office. Everything I needed to be human once again was in that bag.

"Won't be long," I said to Kurt.

"I'm going to locate Troy Fallon and check where Mallory Stevens is. We'll pick them up once you're ready."

I nodded and hurried down to the women's bathroom. It didn't matter how many women were drained in showers, hot water and soap held great appeal.

Fifteen minutes later I felt clean and warm. I shoved my saturated clothing into a plastic bag and then into the trash. The odds of the stains coming out were slim and I didn't need the reminders. Before putting on a fresh shirt, I blasted my hair with the wall-mounted hairdryer in the bathroom until it was almost dry. Red in the mirror caught my eye. The cut on my upper right arm was bleeding again and needed attention. It didn't look too bad. I took a clean dressing from my bag and stuck it to the wound with some paper tape. Kurt would do what needed doing. I pulled on a clean shirt and fastened the buttons. That'd be easier without broken knuckles.

Dry, and feeling as okay I could expect to feel, I headed back to my office.

Inside, I kicked the door shut and dropped the bag on my desk. It was time to take it home and restock it.

"How you feeling?" Kurt asked from the couch.

"Not too bad. Arm needs stitching, I think."

"Yeah, thought it would. Come over here and sit down." I spotted his medical pack by his feet. He lay it on the couch next to him and unzipped it. "Take your shirt off, please."

"Because you asked so nicely," I said, avoiding his eyes.

I removed my shirt and sat on the coffee table in front of him while he took off the dressing and had a closer look at the cut.

"I've seen worse," he said with a smile. "Definitely stitching ... local?"

Didn't usually give me a choice.

"Yeah, local."

While Kurt took out his gear and prepped the wound site, I had time to think. My mind skirted the perimeter of waking up on a cold floor and zeroed in on the men and the art.

Art.

God. Art from human blood. Spatter patterns. Maybe vampire wasn't too far off the mark. Some people are sick. They defy reason with the things they do. I imagined the media frenzy that would follow the breaking of this story. The pieces that were already sold would sky-rocket in value. That revolted me.

"All right?" Kurt asked, tying off the suture.

"Yep." No, I wasn't. "No."

"Conway … what?"

"Fentanyl. That's how they got me." I paused. Not liking voicing my concerns. "Fentanyl. Will that harm the space-invaders?"

"While you were in the shower I looked up the Federal Drug Administration guidelines for Fentanyl use in pregnancy."

Not just me that had concerns then.

"And?"

"It's an FDA category C drug. That means animal reproduction studies have shown adverse effects on fetuses and there are no adequate and well-controlled studies in humans."

"That doesn't sound reassuring."

"Category C also states that the benefits from the drug may outweigh the potential risk."

"I'm not encouraged, Kurt."

"I dug a bit further. I think the space-invaders will be just fine. I'll let your specialist know and he can monitor you as well. Trust me, Conway, I don't think you have anything to worry about from a single inhalation of fentanyl."

"Okay."

Maybe. Pressing thoughts of drugs to the back of my mind. "I need to check something. I can't see the connection between everything I think is connected."

"All right. Do what you need to do, just take it easy."

"I'm planning on using the computer not running a marathon."

All the things I'd come across regarding the case converged. Somewhere everyone involved met. I needed to find that place. It wasn't prison but Hank was the key.

I opened a search engine designed to work within the Darknet. Sure it was possible that they all met because of a Craig's List classified ad, but I doubted it was that open. I could feel Kurt's presence as he sat in my office, waiting.

My conversation with Christine surfaced. I thought about the expression on her face when I asked if she'd seen Lette's artwork. Unimpressed. I had a feeling she'd be horrified when she found out the truth. Perfect Storm. That was what she said he called it.

I typed Perfect Storm into the search engine. Up came a photo of a piece of art, colored wool on black canvas. It was exactly as Christine described it.

Winning.

I had a feeling the image wasn't just an image but a link to a web meeting place. I called Sandra and asked her to come to my office.

Seconds later she bounced into the room. "You summoned me, O Esteemed Leader."

"I need your skill and I need it now, I want you to hack into this site."

I beckoned her to my desk and showed her the screen. I moved so she could occupy my chair.

Sandra sat and moved my laptop to a better position for her. "Darknet. I hate it in here," she said. "It's murky and monsters hide in the depths."

"Yes, they do. As soon as you get in, call me, I need to know what you find straightaway."

"Yes, O Holder of the Flashlight."

It was hard not to smile. Sandra never ran out of unique ways to address me.

"We're all done. You ready to go pick up Fallon?" Kurt asked.

"Yeah." The sound of fingers typing followed me to the door.

"Where's Stevens?" I asked. "We have her, yes?"

"Oh yeah, we have her. She's in custody."

"She was sewing the pieces, she created those atrocities."

Kurt nodded. "Yes, she did. Sam and Lee found the studio where she was working. We think Lette designed and she sewed."

Who first? Lette or Fallon? I deemed Fallon more of a

flight risk simply because she was a cop.

"Let's go get Detective Fallon." Paused by my desk. My brain stopped.

"Conway?"

"Where's my weapon?"

"Hasn't been recovered yet as far as I know."

Annoying. With my left hand, I reached into the third drawer down and withdrew my backup weapon and holster.

"Badge?" I asked, looking at Kurt while I fastened the holster to my belt.

"That I do have," he replied, flipping a black object through the air at me.

I caught it with my left hand. My badge wallet.

"It's clean ... "

"Yeah, and your phone's okay too, they were in the younger male's pockets."

I shoved the wallet into the pocket of my jeans. Kurt passed me my phone. I looked at it for a moment as my mind rolled over the possible outcomes regarding Fallon. I didn't for one moment think it would go well.

"We good now?" he asked.

"Just about." I woke my phone and called SWAT.

Andrews answered his phone on the third ring. "Conway, how can we help?"

"We have an arrest to make and I'd like SWAT along for the ride."

"Send the address," he said. "You're clean now, right?"

"Yeah, I'm clean," I said with a laugh. "Thanks for

that."

Andrews' laughter stopped abruptly when I hung up. I looked at Kurt and waited, he knew what I wanted. He gave me the address for Fallon and I texted it to Andrews.

"Now?" Kurt asked.

I nodded.

"Yeah. Now."

Chapter Thirty Nine
Under my Thumb

It took forty minutes to get to Detective Fallon's home. As we entered her street, we passed a police car parked on the side of the road. There was another one about fifty yards up the street from Fallon's home. A black truck rolled in behind us. SWAT.

"Our doing?" I asked, nodding to the police cars.

"Yes."

"How badly will this go, do you think?"

"Not smooth," Kurt replied. "I've had her under surveillance since you disappeared. She's at home."

He pulled a wad of papers from his inside jacket pocket and handed them to me.

"A warrant to arrest and a search warrant," I said as I opened the paperwork and ran my eyes over the legalese. "Good work."

Kurt's right eyebrow rose. "Obtained mostly on your gut feeling, so I hope you find something to corroborate what you think you know."

We needed records for the support groups she ran. Attendance records or notations telling us who was at each meeting. Something solid that connected her to our victims and then to the whole mess. Better still the files and victim reports that I was sure existed but weren't in the system.

If I were in her position, I would've been busy shredding and burning.

But then I wouldn't be in her position because I'm not fucking stupid.

"Right, so we go knock on the door with SWAT and get this evil bitch off the streets."

Kurt swung his door open and got out.

I didn't move. I wanted to but I didn't. Kurt ducked his head and looked into the car. "You joining me?"

"Yeah." I reached across my body and opened the door with my left hand. Dread built so fast it almost swamped me. I pushed it down and climbed out of the car.

"Conway, something bothering you?" Kurt asked from the sidewalk.

"There's something wrong here," I replied, looking at the house. "We should've moved on her earlier."

That's what it was. Death.

Andrews appeared beside me. "Let's do this."

Jerry and Tom were next to Kurt. Every time those two teamed up, I ended up with a cartoon running in my head.

We approached with caution. Jerry and Tom first, then Kurt carrying the paperwork and me, with Andrews and two other men in the rear. The two men behind Andrews peeled off and went around the back.

Kurt knocked on the front door.

My heart pounded as the seconds ticked away.

He knocked again.

Tom and Jerry peered through windows near the door.

"You sure she's home?" Jerry asked over his shoulder.

He moved to another window, listening. His expression changed. "Talbot says the shower is running."

Guess he was one of the guys who'd gone round the back.

Shower. That can't be good. Hair on the back of my neck stood up.

Andrews touched my arm. I jumped. "What is it?"

"Something's wrong."

There's nothing good in that house. "Let's get in there," I said.

Tom and Jerry acknowledged me with a nod.

My gut said we were too late and Fallon was dead.

Tom tried the door. It opened. Not a good sign.

He and Jerry went in first. We followed behind with Andrews as they cleared rooms and located the bathroom. Tom banged on the bathroom door.

No answer.

He looked at me. My heart pounded in my chest as I nodded. He turned the handle and the door swung open. Running water. No steam. Clothes folded neatly in a pile on a chair by the vanity. Folded clothes, not missing clothes as at the crime scenes.

"Hello!" Tom called.

Nothing.

"Tom," I said looking past him. "The shower."

The black shower curtain was closed. A cloying metallic smell roiled my gut. Blood. That was different from every crime scene I'd been to lately. The smell told me this one hadn't been cleaned.

Tom flicked the edge and then ripped it back. Red streaked the white walls. I followed the blood spurts up the walls. Noting how it'd run back down. Looked like several of the pieces I'd seen in the gallery.

Arterial more than artistic.

Away from the water at the back of the tub lay the bloodied naked body of Troy Fallon. Kurt stepped around me and bent down, his gloved fingers checking her pulse. Habit. Her cloudy eyes said she was long gone. The shower head pointed downward with most of the water going straight down the drain. He reached up and turned the shower off. Instant silence.

"There's a knife in here," Kurt said. "Deep gashes severing arteries on both wrists."

"Suicide?" I asked, looking at the mess up the walls and all over her.

"It's possible," Kurt replied.

I looked at the shower head and at the position of Fallon's body. The way she lay, the water couldn't quite reach her. I could see where blood ran from her body and joined the stream of water and ran diluted down the drain.

I turned and left the room in search of fresh air. I called out before opening the back door. That wasn't locked either. She made it easy for us to get in and find her.

"Conway coming out."

Two SWAT geared men greeted me when I stepped through the doorway.

"What happened?" one asked.

"Possible suicide," I replied, dragging my phone from my pocket and sitting on the back step. "Stand down."

The men turned and walked away. Dead people don't fight. There was no need for SWAT to stay with me. Watching them walk away, I saw Andrews heading back to the truck. He probably had the same thought as me.

I made a call to Delta A. "Sandra, send the ME to my location, please."

"Trouble?"

"No. Troy Fallon was dead when we arrived."

I flicked a small stone off the step and watched it bounce across the path.

"Anything else?"

"No. We're good. Send the ME. Let Sam and Lee know that Fallon is dead."

"Consider it done, O Genie of the Arrest."

I hung up but stayed where I was. Going back into the house wasn't a good idea. I flicked another small stone off the step and watched it bounce as it hit the concrete. She killed herself. Made sense after what she'd done. My finger smacked another small stone, harder this time; it flew off at an angle into the side of the garbage bin near the back corner of the house before landing on the ground. There was something on the garbage bin. Dirt. A smudge. I jumped to my feet. Four strides and I was next to the bin. Definitely a dark smudge on the side of the bin. I looked at my legs in relation to the smudge. It was a high mark. Almost hip height. Transfer. I was sure I was looking at blood. Someone with blood on their clothing bumped into the bin.

Spinning around to face the house, I yelled, "Kurt. It's a crime scene!"

I ran out to the curb and signaled the closest police car. The car door opened and a cop ran toward me.

"Ma'am?"

"Did you note all traffic using this street since you were stationed here?"

He nodded and pulled his notebook from his top pocket, opened it, and showed me the page. I ran my finger down the list. Times, car description and tags. On the second pass, I paused on a red car. Why? I checked my watch. Two hours since the red Ford Taurus was seen.

We'd come across a lot of cars since the case began but only one red Ford Taurus leaped to the fore. Emilio Herrera's car.

"SSA Conway, have a QV for you." I rattled off the tag number to comms.

"Registered owner Emilio Herrera." Comms paused before giving me his address.

The sound of Emilio's name dragged spiky twigs up my spine.

Moments later I handed the notebook back to the cop in front of me.

Herrera lived two blocks away. Could be that he traveled that way regularly. Maybe this was nothing but a coincidence. The voices in my head laughed. Maybe's ass.

The cop waited. I smiled at him. "Good work."

"Need anything else, ma'am?"

"Set up a perimeter please."

"Yes, ma'am."

I headed for the SWAT truck. Andrews swung open the door and climbed down.

"Problem?"

"Yeah. You could say that. We need to go visit an FBI employee."

Kurt ran up. "We've got evidence of her involvement in creating and running support groups and found some police complaints matching our victims. We've also found shredded evidence," he said. "She was about as involved as she could get without actually killing anyone herself."

"That's good." Not for the victims but from our point of view. I thought about the destroyed evidence. "We can reassemble shredded paper."

Kurt smiled. "Yes."

Maybe she did kill herself. If someone killed her then why leave evidence behind?

"Any mention of Emilio Herrera in what you saw?"

"No." He took a step back and eyed me with interest. "Strange question to ask."

"It may be nothing," I said.

Yeah. I didn't believe that for one second.

"Conway, it's never nothing when it comes out of your mouth."

One day it will be.

"Herrera's car was seen two hours ago on this street but he lives nearby so could be his usual route."

"You think otherwise …"

"Hmm, I don't know what to think." Herrera being in the vicinity bugged me. "If someone was going to visit Fallon and saw the police cars, how else could they get into the house?"

Andrews had an idea. "All the properties on this side of the road back onto woods, those woods back onto properties on the next street over." He climbed into the truck and emerged with his iPad. "Take a look at this." Andrews showed us a satellite image of the area. "See that?" He pointed to what looked like an access way into the woods.

"There's one farther up Fallon's street too," I said, pointing to another access way. "The woods are public land?"

"Yes, they are. No back fences to speak of, either," Andrews said.

He was right. Fallon and her neighbors backed right onto the woods. No problem for someone to walk up the access way on the other street, through the five hundred yards of woods and into her property. I waved at the cop I'd spoken to and he came back.

"Ma'am?"

"I want you and your partner to take a walk through the woods behind Fallon's house and see what you can find. You're looking for evidence. Also, find the access way to the next street and see if anyone over there saw that red car on your list." Too narrow a field of inquiry. "See if they recognize any of the cars on your list."

"Right away, ma'am."

I heard the radio squawk as he called his partner while he walked away.

Kurt was waiting, I could tell.

"Okay, what?" I asked.

"You wanna go talk to Herrera?"

"Yeah, let's drop in because we're in the area to see how he is after losing his colleague and let him know we've made arrests in the case."

Kurt laughed. "Clever."

"Sandra said a few days ago that he'd made inquiries about the case. I told her to tell him we were doing all we could."

Kurt smiled. "Standard company line."

My phone rang. Sandra.

Uncanny.

"What can I do for you?" I asked, tapping the speaker icon on my phone. "And you're on speaker."

"Jane Daughtry's team leader dropped off a greeting card. They were packing up her office and found it. It's from someone called Emilio who professed his love for Jane and said he liked Black Amethyst and hoped she did too."

My heart rate slowed. I knew that wasn't a random thing to say. Cogs clicked as they turned. She did like black something but not Black Amethyst. Her taste was more expensive than that.

"I know what that is …"

"A range of products from Bath and Body Works?"

Conjuring images of the first Fairfax crime scene, I put myself back in the shower with Jane. What was missing? Shower gel.

"Yes. Check they do shower gel?"

"They do."

Petrovovich was right.

"Was the card from Emilio Herrera?"

"Cannot confirm but the team leader said it looked like Herrera's handwriting."

"Anything else about the card?"

"Sending you a photo of the handwriting now. It was at the bottom of a locked drawer." My phone buzzed in my hand as the image from Sandra arrived. I opened it as she talked. "They knew they carpooled together and apparently Jane was looking for someone else to either join the carpool or to carpool with her alone."

I read the words on the photograph. My mind compared the style of handwriting to the notes from the crime scenes. I couldn't be sure.

"Thanks, Sandra. We're on our way to Herrera's now," Kurt replied.

"Bag the card, Sandra, and send it for analysis. Have them compare the writing to all the crime scene notes," I said. "Anything from the Darknet?"

"I'm throwing everything I have at it, this is some impressive encryption. Stay safe," Sandra said. The screen went black as the call ended. Kurt and I looked at each other. His eyes mirrored my feelings with regard to Herrera.

Jilted wannabe lover.

"We'll wait here unless you need an escort," Andrews said.

"We should be good, if we rock up with SWAT he'll be suspicious. On our own, he's less likely to act up," I said. My words tumbled around the ground in front of me picking up dirt and leaves as they rolled to the curb.

The words that took the longest to fall into the gutter were 'less likely to act up'.

Chapter Forty

Nobody Takes me Seriously.

Herrera's red Ford was parked in the driveway of his home. We pulled up at the end of the driveway. Blocking him in. I checked my weapon. Wearing a holster on the left felt awkward. Part of me hoped that would serve as a warning or a reminder and that next time I was faced with an asshole I'd keep my emotions in check.

No guarantees.

My emotions were the closest they've ever been to the surface.

"Let's go say hello," Kurt said and climbed out of the car. He straightened his tie and adjusted his suit jacket. I joined him on the sidewalk.

"Smile and relax," I said in a half-whisper. "Friendly, friendly, friendly."

Kurt glanced at me as he walked up the driveway to the front door but said nothing.

I knocked.

Emilio Herrera's smile lit his face. "Agent Conway, what brings you out here?"

"We were in the area and wanted to see how you were doing." I returned his smile with less enthusiasm.

"The whole department misses Jane," he replied, swinging the door open wider. "Come in."

"Just for a minute or two, we're on our way back to the office," I said, stepping over the threshold and hoping there was something in plain sight that would give me cause to get a warrant and justify the sick feeling I had about his car being on Fallon's street.

Herrera showed us into the living room. "Please, sit," he said, gesturing at a large sofa.

"Not going to be here long," I replied. "Just making sure you're coping and thought you'd like to know that we've made some arrests."

"That's good," he said, still smiling. "Yes. Very good. Closure for the families is very important."

"Yes," Kurt said. "One of the arrests was only two blocks from here."

Cunning. Calling Fallon an arrest.

"Really?" Surprise registered on his face.

I watched Herrera as Kurt talked.

"Yes. She is a police detective," Kurt added. "Always upsetting when one of our colleagues is involved in violent crime."

Herrera's smile changed; it slipped becoming more of a smirk. Kurt talked. I listened and observed while I tried to think of a way to look through the house. Bathroom. The urge to pee grew stronger by the second.

"Sorry, Emilio, but could I use your bathroom?" I said, interrupting their conversation. When he didn't immediately say yes and point me in the right direction, a little red flag flew at half-mast in my mind. "Bathroom?"

"I'm sorry. It's, ah, not been cleaned this week. My cleaning lady is ... on vacation."

"I'm sure it'll be fine."

"No," he said. All trace of his smile disappeared.

Who stops people using their bathroom?

Kurt looked at me then at Herrera. He stepped closer to Herrera, dropped his voice to a conspiratorial tone and said, "Agent Conway is pregnant. If she needs the bathroom, she needs the bathroom."

Herrera faltered. I could see his thought process on his face. Caught between a rock and a hard place. If he said no again, he'd look like an asshole and raise too much suspicion but if he said yes, I could see whatever it was, he didn't want me near.

"Sorry, Agent Conway, how rude of me. Of course. Down the hall second door on the right."

"Thank you," I said and hurried away leaving Kurt to spend more time chatting with Herrera.

The hallway doors were all open. Handy. I glanced into the first room I came to. A bedroom. Master bedroom by the look of it. Nothing out of place or of interest in the open. Across the hall was a bedroom, possibly a guest room, nothing stood out. Next to that the bathroom. I knew immediately why he didn't want me in there. I could smell the blood from the doorway. I closed the door, used the toilet, washed up and then checked out the laundry hamper sitting next to the shower. The smell hit me hard when I opened the lid. Peering inside I saw bloody clothes. I touched nothing in the hamper. Dropping the lid didn't do a lot to contain the smell. Saliva built up and I swallowed hard in an effort to stem the churning in my stomach. Bloodied clothes were an amateurish mistake. I didn't know if he was stupid, or confident we wouldn't link him to the murders.

My curiosity insisted I check out the shower. There were three shelves on the far wall of the spacious shower. They contained assorted body washes, soaps, shampoos and conditioners. I checked the rest of the bathroom. Very male orientated. No makeup, nothing I'd associate with a girlfriend or wife. I took another look at the shower shelves; this time, I snapped a photo with my phone and sent it to our perfume expert. Without touching the bottles and opening them I couldn't tell if I'd recognize the scents, and again I didn't have any disposable gloves on me. One bottle stood out. Purple with a silvery lid. Black Amethyst. I was dying to know what the shower gel smelled like straight from the bottle and had a feeling there'd be base notes of patchouli among other things.

My phone beeped quicker than I expected. A text message congratulating me on finding all the missing items from the victims' showers. The only thing missing now was a bottle of perfume and I had a feeling we'd find that at Troy Fallon's place, somewhere.

I texted Kurt: Herrera is involved. Laundry hamper full of bloody clothing and all the missing items from our victims' showers on the shelves in his shower. Found the Black Amethyst.

Kurt's reply was fast and short: Bastard.

I left the bathroom door open and rejoined Kurt and Herrera. One of them didn't look happy and it wasn't Kurt.

"Emilio, thank you for the use of your bathroom. I feel much better," I said with a smile. "A little tip ... when you murder someone, wear coveralls and dispose of them before you get home. Nothing screams amateur like a laundry hamper full of bloody clothing."

Not to mention a shower full of trophies.

I guessed his team had instructions when it came to collecting things from crime scenes or they sent photos back to him and he chose what he wanted.

"Where's your phone?" I asked, all smiles and politeness while looking around the room. "Never mind." I picked it up off the dining table and flicked through his photo folders. Finding photos of shower caddies, I showed Kurt. "Familiar?"

"Yes," Kurt said. He took his cuffs off his belt and told Emilio to turn around.

On our way back to the office Sandra called.

"I'm having trouble getting through the encryption. I've got a couple of techs from Cyber coming in to help me. We're going to need more computer power."

"Whatever you need ..."

"Thank you, O Shiner of the Light."

Chapter Forty One
Homebound Train

At eight on Wednesday morning, Kurt thumped a newspaper onto my desk. I'd been finishing off the paperwork for the case since six. We had one more arrest to make and it was case closed.

"Something upset you?" I asked, leaning back in my chair.

"Read, you'll see."

"Do I have to guess the page or will you help me out?" The look on his face told me all I needed to know. Horror trickled through my veins as I turned to the obituary page. There was no missing what had upset Kurt. Right in the middle of the page was a poem.

The poem was dedicated to Violet Cramer, Jane Daughtry, Serena Sorenson, Terri Kane, Karen Fredericks, Michelle Andrews, Phoebe Childs, Ashley Stewart, Sidney Churchill, Jodie Norris.

And me.

Addiction.

Don't take it personally
It wasn't easy
Just listen
I broke when you looked at me
Life cracked wide open

Everything that came before
Spilled over your screen
Seeped into the keyboard
Shattered across the desk
Laughter replaced it all.

Don't take it personally
It's not easy
Just listen
I watched you fade away
Retreat behind your walls
Taking the light with you
Lock the doors
Close the windows
Draw a line in the sand
Laughter begins to wane

Don't take it personally
Life isn't easy
Just listen
Trapped behind the line
Powerless to breach the doors
With a broken heart
Fresh tears fall
Everything that came before
Lies fragmented on the floor
Laughter consumed by pain
Unable to walk away
Addicted to you.

"Nice and cheery, isn't it?" Kurt said as I looked up from the newspaper.

"Yeah, it's lovely."

"No signature," Kurt said. "But it seems to be the finished poem. You were right about it not being finished before."

That's comforting. Not.

"Do we know who placed this in the paper?"

He shook his head. "It was done over the internet via the newspaper's website and paid for using Jodi Norris's credit card, yesterday afternoon."

"Nice that they included me. Does that mean whoever placed this was involved in the art gallery?" I asked.

Who else would know I was there?

"I'd imagine so," Kurt replied. "I want to increase security just until you are safely married and off on honeymoon."

"I already have armed guards sitting outside my home and Mitch's house," I said.

"No, you did have armed guards. Once we closed the case they were removed."

"Okay, do it then. Use uniformed FBI. Make sure they have marked cars."

I didn't believe those words came from my mouth. Judging by Kurt's expression, he didn't either.

"Who are you?" he asked, leaning over the desk. "And what did you do with the real Ellie Conway?"

I smiled. "It's me. I might have a bit more to be cautious about at the moment. I'd kinda like to make my wedding and you know … do the whole family thing."

Just not sure about the twin thing. That needed more time.

Kurt nodded. "I think you'll make a great mom."

"I think you're talking shit, but I know Mitch will be a great dad." I folded the newspaper so the poem was visible. "We need to find out who did this."

"Did anyone pick up the Lette kid, Kristopher?"

"Not yet. But everyone is looking for him."

"He signed half the poem in an email, as far as we can tell it was actually him, yes?"

"Yes."

"Chances are …"

And just like that, I was transported to an office I recognized. Chance smiled at me from across his desk.

"Really?" I said, sitting in a chair and shaking my head.

"Fun, ain't it?"

"Not so much, Chance. Do you know where Lette is?"

"Find the mother, you'll find the son."

Find the mother.

"Of course. Thanks, Chance."

"Take care, Ellie."

Kurt was staring at me when I looked up.

"Problem?"

"Your eyes went black. You weren't here." His arm swept around the room. "Where were you?"

"Chance's office."

Too much truth is a bad thing but it was too late to take it back.

"Mentally hilarious. I stand by my diagnosis."

"Thanks."

That was all kinds of comforting.

"Did Chance have something to say pertaining to this case?"

"Yep. He said if we find the mother, we'll find the son."

I stood up.

"And she is where?"

"No idea, but I bet Dad knows." I reached down and pressed the speaker button on my desk phone then input Dad's number into the keypad.

He answered on the fifth ring as I was about to give up. "Ellie?"

"Dad. Where is Rosanne?"

"George Washington hospital."

My heart sank. "Serious?"

"She's not going to get any better, Ellie, if that's what you mean. She's as good as can be expected."

She seemed okay last time I saw her. I looked at Kurt. "We need to talk to her."

"You better make it today then."

Dad gave me the information necessary to find her room. I hung up.

"Kurt, she was okay the other day ..."

"Yes. Brain tumors can be unpredictable. It was only a matter of time. Let's go. Her son is probably with her."

My phone rang.

"Sandra, good news?"

" We're in. We have names, we have connections, we've got it all."

"Tell me ..."

"Perfect Storm is a forum where people looking for like-minded souls come together."

It almost sounded pleasant.

"And?"

"Delving into the depths and subforums off the main branches we found Hank Creole. Hank can't post on the forum himself, prison computers can't access the Deep Web or Darknet. Someone called Grekov and someone called Kristopher post on his behalf."

Grekov, the Russian. "Putting you on speaker, Sandra."

Sandra continued, "Herrera and Fallon found their way to the forum together. They caused quite a buzz and there was a lot of talk about whether they should be allowed to stay due to their occupations. Fallon offered her services, which went a long way to gaining the trust of Grekov and Lette. Together she and Herrera chose the victims. Grekov and his nurse did the killing. Lette painted fabric and created art."

"There's more?" I reached for my water and sipped it.

"This is a web of revolting threads. Stevens was brought into the group by Fallon when Lette said he needed someone to sew for him."

"How did Fallon know Stevens?"

"She didn't to start with. She advertised for a sewing

machinist in a local newspaper."

"They discussed that in the forum?"

"They did. This was the place where they all got together and discussed distribution, art galleries, sales, and the next victim."

"Was Stevens on the forum?"

"Yes, but not often, she was an employee."

"Any mention of Christine Locke?"

"Yes. Lette wanted AB negative blood. He suggested Phoebe Childs because he knew she had AB negative, he didn't offer up Christine because her eyes are brown and she didn't fit the criteria when it came to career."

"Excellent work, Sandra. Thank you."

"I'd say you're welcome but I feel I need to go scrub my eyeballs now."

On the drive to the hospital, questions circled in my head. Would I arrest him in front of his dying mother and remove him from her side? Maybe. Would I arrest him and let him stay until she passed? I had no clue.

We walked to the wall of elevators inside the hospital foyer. Kurt pressed the floor we wanted. A few minutes later we both walked into Rosanne Lette's room to find her son by her bedside.

"Kristopher Lette?" I said, showing him my badge.

He nodded. "What do you want?"

"To give you a medal, what do you think I want?"

He shrugged. "How would I know?"

Rosanne mumbled incoherently.

"Step outside," Kurt instructed.

"No. I'm staying here."

"All right then, we do this here," I said.

Kurt took cuffs from the case on his belt. "Stand up."

Lette stayed where he was. I smiled at Kurt. He stepped forward and snapped one cuff on Lette's left wrist, then attached the other cuff to the bed rail.

"You're under arrest."

"What for?" he snapped. "I've been here since last night. What did I do?"

"You're under arrest for your involvement in the murder of ten women," I said with a smile. I can be nice when I arrest people. "We already have your buddies."

"That's crap," he squawked, rattling the cuff against the bed.

"No. It's really not. Your exciting gallery display of blood-drenched and forensically designed articles and the things you sold to some boutiques here in D.C and Northern Virginia mean you are someone we very much want to talk to regarding the exsanguination of ten women."

He rattled the cuff against the bed rail again.

"Settle or we take you now," Kurt warned. "Just give me a reason ..."

Kurt and I left the room. We could see Kristopher Lette from the viewing window.

"What do you want to do?"

"Leave him for now. Let's get someone to babysit him. I don't want to stay."

Kurt made a call to Sam. He and Lee offered to sit with

Lette until we could set up a roster of uniformed agents to take over. As soon as his mother died, we would take him in and the games would begin.

Chapter Forty Two

Here without you.

The peppery scent of his cologne released from the fabric of the shirt as I slipped my arms into it and fastened a few buttons, successfully stopping it sliding off my shoulders. I glanced at the bed. He stirred, his eyes flickered under closed lids. With a smile I went to the kitchen and opened the windows, letting the fresh morning breeze flow over me. A shiver ran up my spine as the cool wind spiraled down my body, touching bare legs. Glad of his shirt, I made the coffee.

The aroma of the freshly ground beans filled the air. For a moment, I wondered how smart an idea morning coffee was.

What's the worst that could happen?

I made coffee and found some roasted pecans in the cupboard. Deciding to let Mitch sleep a bit longer, I took a cup of coffee and a bowl of pecans to the living room. Comfortable on the couch I ate pecans and laughed to myself as I read Dilbert cartoons online.

Engine noise from a boat outside drew my attention away from Dilbert. I watched the water ripple on the Sound in the wake of a large white launch. The sun reflected bright rays off the water's surface. I knew why Mitch bought this property in New Zealand years ago. He'd found paradise. Mahau Sound was peaceful and stunning all at once. Reaching for my coffee, I found it was lukewarm; the sea was quite a distraction. I abandoned all thought of coffee.

"Whatcha doing?" Mitch's voice made me jump. He laughed. He leaned on the doorframe, hands in his pockets, a smile on his face and a gleam in his eyes. I got the impression he'd been there a few minutes.

"Eating nuts, surfing, and watching boats," I replied, putting another salted pecan in my mouth. "You want some?" I chewed the nut. Pecans reminded me of brains, if brains were slightly salty, yet crunchy and tasty.

"We still talking about pecans?" Mitch said with what was possibly the most innocent expression I'd ever seen on his face.

It needed work.

"Not necessarily." A smile settled on my lips. "Thought you were tired?"

"That was then, this is now," he replied with a cheeky grin. "I'm rested now."

I don't need much encouragement. I closed the screen on my laptop, placed it on the couch, and stood up.

Mitch smiled as I covered the distance between us with three strides.

"Don't let me interrupt ..." he said as I neared him. "We've got another week of vacation here ... that's one hundred and sixty-eight hours ... so if now's not good for you ..."

"Shut up," I murmured kissing him while wrapping my arms around his neck.

"Morning, Mrs. Iverson," he said in my ear. "My shirt

looks good on you."

About the author:

Cat Connor is a prolific crime thriller author hailing from New Zealand. Her expertise in the genre is reflected in her engaging and suspenseful narratives, which have garnered a loyal following. Her work is known for its intricate plots, dynamic characters, and relentless pace, keeping readers on the edge of their seats until the very end. She has authored multiple books, including the popular "Byte" series, which follows the exploits of an FBI unit that investigates serial crime.

Cat's passion for crime and espionage is evident in her writing, as she strives to create a world that is both authentic and thrilling. Her meticulous attention to detail and extensive research have won her critical acclaim and accolades from readers and peers alike. In addition to writing, Cat enjoys speaking on topics related to writing and publishing. Her talks are known for their candidness, humour, and practical advice. With her unique blend of talent, expertise, and passion, Cat Connor has established herself as one of the most exciting and accomplished authors in the crime thriller genre.

Her other passions include music, reading, tequila, red wine, coffee, and chocolate. When she's not writing she can be found binge watching TV shows and spending time with her much adored animals; Diesel the mastador, Patrick the tuxedo cat, & Dallas the tortie Birman.

You can follow and contact Cat at the following places:

Website: www.catconnor.com
Twitter: @catconnor
Facebook: @cat.connor
Instagram: @catconnorauthor
Bluesky: @catconnor.bsky.social
Threads: @catconnorauthor

Also by Cat Connor:

The Kiwi set Veronica Tracey Spy/PI series:
[Nothing happens here] -2020
[Lure the lie] - 2021
[Leave a message] - 2022
[Whiskey Tango Foxtrot] - 2023
[Foxtrot Mike Lima] - 2024

The FBI based Byte Series:
Killerbyte - 2009
Terrorbyte - 2010
Exacerbyte - 2011
Flashbyte - 2012
Soundbyte - 2013
Snakebyte - 2013 (novella)
Databyte - 2014
Eraserbyte - 2015
Psychobyte - 2016
Metabyte - 2017
Qubyte - 2018
Cryptobyte - 2019
Vaporbyte - 2020 (red)
Vaporbyte -2020 (purple)
Raidbyte - 2021 (collection of short bytes)

Whispers in the water - the poetry of SSA Conway and SA Connelly
Torrent - a collection of short bytes